KU-024-868

ACKNOWLEDGEMENTS

Many thanks to Sean McMahon, Kathleen Gormley and Mavin Devlin for their help and support. My gratitude also to the staff at Marino, particularly Jo and Seán, for tidying up the loose ends.

Class No. F(ir)   Acc No. C102930

Author: Sheerin, C.   Loc: 6 JUL 2006

LEABHARLANN
CHONDAE AN CHABHAIN

1 3 FEB 2012

1. **This book may be ~~kept~~ for three weeks. It is to be returned on / b~~efore the~~ last date stamped below.**
2. **A fine of ~~~~ will be charged for every week or part ~~of a week overdue.~~**

C102930

The Arts Council
An Chomhairle Ealaíon

First published in 2001 by Marino Books
An imprint of Mercier Press
16 Hume Street Dublin 2
Tel: (01) 661 5299; Fax: (01) 661 8583
E-mail: books@marino.ie

Trade enquiries to CMD Distribution
55A Spruce Avenue
Stillorgan Industrial Park
Blackrock County Dublin
Tel: (01) 294 2556; Fax: (01) 294 2564
E.mail: cmd@columba.ie

© Chris Sheerin 2001

ISBN 1 86023 128 4

10 9 8 7 6 5 4 3 2 1

A CIP record for this title is available
from the British Library

Cover design by SPACE
Printed in Ireland by ColourBooks,
Baldoyle Industrial Estate, Dublin 13

This book is sold subject to the
condition that it shall not, by way of
trade or otherwise, be lent, resold,
hired out or otherwise circulated
without the publisher's prior consent
in any form of binding or cover other
than that in which it is published and
without a similar condition including
this condition being imposed on the
subsequent purchaser.

No part of this publication may be
reproduced or transmitted in any
form or by any means, electronic or
mechanical, including photocopying,
recording or any information or
retrieval system, without the prior
permission of the publisher in writing.

CHASING SHADOWS

CHRIS SHEERIN

CAVAN COUNTY LIBRARY
ACC No. C102930
CLASS NO. F(IR)
INVOICE NO 4557 Waterstones
PRICE £7.99

For Mavis, my mother. Thank you.

Prelude

Most people took Seamus Doherty for being simple. A simple bastard, they'd call him when he was older, as thick as two planks, a Blue-Card. But Seamus hadn't always been like that.

He'd been smart when he was younger, perhaps one of the smartest in his primary school, and everybody had said so. He'd been at the college up in Bishop Street for two years, even managed to curry favour with one or two of the teachers there – which others said was nearly impossible – who had perhaps recognised his potential. So when they said that he was simple, he alone knew they weren't talking about him being simple as in simple-stupid.

They were saying that he was more simple-mad-in-the-head, as it were, or simple-off-his-rocker. He wasn't simple-stupid. He never had been. There was a difference between those two definitions, a very big difference. One meant you had been born that way and no amount of education would ever change you. The other meant that maybe you'd been normal in the first place and you'd had to change due to circumstances: maybe you wanted to fit in and you thought that acting mad was the only way to go about doing it; or maybe because you didn't care what anyone thought about you and you merely wanted to stand out, to be seen as someone special. Or then it could simply have been that you were the sum product of your da's many mistakes in this world and you had no real choice.

Still, Seamus had never denied that he blamed his father for the way he had turned out, and he never would. Ever since he was eleven years old he'd never believed anything else. He blamed his father for everything. For neglecting him when he was younger and never giving him the things that other kids had. For never being there for his mother when she was always there for him. For making the biggest mistake of his pathetic life and letting the young boy go to France with the Holiday Projects crowd when he should have let him remain there in Creggan and maybe changed the course of both of their lives by doing so. Though perhaps most of all, he blamed his father for getting himself shot dead shortly before the Brits took over the no-go areas in that one fell swoop known thereafter as Operation Motorman, thereby leaving him and his mother all alone.

Well, he didn't exactly blame the man for getting himself shot dead, because things like that happened sometimes. Especially if you had yourself a war situation going on, with the Brits trying to retake the no-go areas of Creggan, the Bogside and the Brandywell every now and then, as they'd been trying to do for very nearly a year. And, what with his da lying in a back garden up in Creggan Heights with the rest of 'the Boys' firing their Armalites and grenades up in the direction of the back fields and the Brits firing back, someone was bound to get shot dead eventually. When that kind of thing goes on for nearly a year, then death – someone's death – was probably inevitable.

And it just so happened that Seamy's da was one of those who were unlucky enough to get themselves killed during the near year-long fight to keep the Brits out of his own particular housing estate. Which would have been all right, Seamy reflected wearily, if he had just gone and got himself killed heroically – and quite normally – as he was trying to push the bastards back over the fields, out past Haterick's farm and eventually into that shit-hole known as England. But his father hadn't done that. He couldn't have gone and done it so simply because, if anyone was ever a simple bastard, it had been him.

Seamy's da, the simple bastard. It was because of him that they'd had to watch a black-and-white television when nearly everyone else was watching colour, Seamy remembered bitterly. It was because of him that they'd had to eat sugar or dripping sandwiches two days after his father had drunk his brew money. It was because of him that Seamy's mother had finally found life too hard to bear and ended up the way she did for a time. And it was because of him that Seamy was now lying here bleeding to death in a mucked-up field in the middle of God only knew where with an impassive hooded figure standing there to his front and watching him die.

Seamy cursed his father and held a hand across his stomach to stem the flow of blood as it slowly mixed with the puddle of murky water beneath him, the dirty brown-red mixture saturating his new shirt. The air was growing colder now, and he couldn't understand why this was, as the mornings had been warmer of late, balmier, with the relentless approach of summer. He held his breath for a second, hoping to lessen the pain, and tried to concentrate instead on a spider that was moving across the roof of the small forest of docken leaves to his front, tracing a slow and methodical path into the secure ebony blackness of the hedgerow beyond. Trying to forget the nightmare scenes he had seen over the last twenty-four hours, the nightmares in which he himself had played a pivotal part.

He released that breath and winced as barbed flashes of pain surged like angry fire through his arms and across his legs. Like the spider, he thought wryly, the hooded figure standing there in front of him would soon lose himself in the temporary cavern of night, his work complete. Though Seamus wondered if the figure would walk away gloating or walk away pondering just why this act of barbarism had been ultimately so different from those he had most likely carried out many times before.

Seamy cursed his father again. The curse didn't hold the same strength or conviction this time, however. He was dying, lying here dying slowly and painfully in this obscene manner, after all he had been through – after all everyone had been through. Though it had been mostly his own fault – he had to admit that now. And maybe, just maybe, Seamus thought wearily, his father hadn't been the only simple bastard in the family after all.

ONE

Finding himself mentally abused by the wealth and grandeur the Lord God Almighty had chosen to impose upon Protestants throughout the entire North of Ireland – and the resulting poverty and unemployment that He had also, for some reason, contrarily decided to impose upon his equally devout Catholic worshippers – Seamus Doherty's father took up dealings with a demon. And like many others throughout the length and breadth of the world in general, he would soon grow to learn that this particular demon provided escapism for many when life fell short of providing answers and, too, that despite its darkly acidic taste and often mind-numbing bitterness, it offered all sorts of sweet solutions to every problem a man could ever know. Of which at that time, everyone – including the Doherty family – throughout the entire North of Ireland knew, to their regret, there were many.

A few years after that first innocent calling – when Seamus the younger was just beginning to be abruptly schooled by various cataclysmic political and social events into forgetting the innocence he had been guaranteed in the promise of childhood and forced to mature hurriedly into a young man – the demon decided that he liked things so much in the Doherty household of three that he might go on holidays for a spell now and then but he was never going to leave completely while Seamus the older was still alive. Never, that was, unless Seamus the older gave him a damned good reason for doing so.

Seamus Doherty senior had lived along with Mary, his wife, within this particular run-down enclave of post–Second World War houses known as the Creggan estate for most of his life. So now, most usually, he frequented the Telstar bar up on Central Drive because it was often more convenient and safer to visit – and didn't involve either a long walk down the town or the taking of a taxi back home again afterwards. And for a time, the solutions to his own particular problems lay there within the mouth of a bottle. But Seamus Doherty senior was to find a very good reason for cutting down on the drink during the last few months of 1968, with the advent of what were to become known as 'the Troubles'. Some two and a half years later he rarely came back to the Doherty household in a state of complete drunken inebriation, though, when such occasionally occurred, he did have his reasons for doing so. The demon had provided for that, of course, for it had a quaint way with words: a way of mixing up ever-varying percentages of the blatant truth along with downright lies and multiple shades of grey in a verbal palette so that they could never again be separated. And he had taken care to impart that knowledge rather quickly to the older Doherty, thus ensuring that life, in the main, was never overly boring for either his son or his wife, even when those two benefactors of the experience quite often wished it could be.

Aye, each journey to the Telstar was – and, of course, always had been – absolutely necessary, Seamus the older would reassure his young son and his wife. This explanation was usually given upon his less-than-stable return from that run-down establishment as he clanked four bottles – six or eight less than he'd once used to manage on – down at his side, fumbled off his coat and dropped rather heavily into the worn and patched brown armchair in front of the fire, a seat he'd succeeded in remoulding perfectly to fit his short, squat frame over the last number of years. Whether it was because 'the Boys', as he and everyone thereabouts called them, had been holding a meeting up in that shabeen-like pub or because they were just celebrating the completion of 'some sort of a thing' they'd been working on – and that same 'some sort of a thing' you'd probably get to hear about on the news come the *Scene Around Six* bulletin, or maybe sooner, in the form of a newsflash telling of the bombing or shooting up of an RUC station – there was always a reason. And nothing but the best of reasons, at that.

Mary, his wife, gave off every time she had the chance, of course, though her tantrums usually had little or no effect upon her husband and worked only to the detriment of her own mostly easygoing temperament. It was all right Seamus the older blaming 'those treacherous Brits and bastard'ne RUC' for the loss of half of his dole money, she'd say, as she passed him by in the hallway, threw on her own coat and scarf and made for the front door. But they were hardly makin' him buy gallons of the drink and pourin' it down his fuckin' throat, were they? Seamus the older would raise the palm of his hand like an angry traffic warden as she argued her point, then tell her in no uncertain terms that he was hardly going to stand in front of Dan McGeady, the CO – 'And you didn't hear me sayin' that, son,' he'd warn, with a shake of his finger, 'so mind you don't go repeatin' it' – and make out like he was some sort of a fuckin' miser, was he? And it wasn't as if she wasn't gettin' her money off him – which she was, he told her, pointedly. She just wasn't gettin' all of it, that's all. And it wasn't as if he was drinkin' as much as he used to, either – the Lord and Mary both knew that well in their heart of hearts – and, sure, he'd been near enough completely sober since the day he got involved. Ma's answer began, as always, with a derisive snort, followed, as if by rote, by her own standard verbiage.

'Now, Seamus Doherty – senior, mind you,' she'd reassure the boy, with a nod – 'you're up there pissin' good stews and a Sunday joint up against the back wall of the Telstar from mornin' till night whilst me and your son – your one and only son, I might well fuckin' add, because you haven't got it in ye to give me another – survive on champ, stews and sausages five, if not six, days a week. And I don't give a monkey's fuck about that Dan fuckin' McGeady either, because he couldn't instruct a dead hedgehog to lie still for an hour, never mind drill a load of yahoos into an army to take on the Brits, and those English bastards no more than a crowd of yellow wankers too! Huh, Dan McGeady?' she'd snort. 'Him and you and the rest of the Stickies and the Provies playin' at toy soldiers while their families are lyin' in their houses worried sick about whether they'll see them again. Well, fuck him, Seamus Doherty, and to fuck with you too! And if you don't get your fuckin' act together soon you wont have a fuckin' family! Besides, that drink's not doin' you any favours either. Have you looked in the fuckin' mirror recently? You've aged a thousand years in the last seven, and people are askin' if you're me da, for Christ's sakes! It's a demon, Seamus Doherty senior. A vile, money-suckin' leech of a demon that'll kill you stone dead before you're forty, the same way it killed your own da and his own da before that. And you're the only one who can't fuckin' see it!'

It was her standard answer, give or take the order of his da's alleged offences – the answer that always preceded the slamming of the door. It had always started with the word 'Now', Seamus remembered sadly. As if his mother somehow believed that particular word would bring what she perceived – or claimed to perceive, because she was as every bit as republican-minded as he; a fact, when she calmed, which she would never deny – to be the error of his father's ways immediately home to the man. Her words of advice had little effect upon his father's ways, for he was as stubborn as a mule – that, Seamus the younger would find out near to the end of his own life. By then, of course, he too had realised – though much too late for it to be of any help – that perhaps he should more often have heeded advice from better-informed people.

Stubborn as a mule, Seamus Doherty had been that all right. Because he wasn't afraid of demons now, nor had he ever been. At least that was what he'd one day tell his son as he swaggered into their house in Dunree Gardens. It had been around five o'clock one Sunday evening; young Seamus remembered it well, because his da had given him a soiled one-pound note and winked at him, tousling his hair and telling him not to let on to his ma. He'd breezed in with his now-standard carry-out of four beers in hand, dressed in his oldest Wrangler jeans and a faded leather jacket which were mucked and torn, a week-old growth thick on the hollows of his cheeks and his eyes black as coal under the rims. There was the familiar smell of stale drink on his breath, though, even with that fortification, he was barely able to meet and match his wife's stare. Instead, as a defence mechanism, he looked around him, sniffed the air and got stuck into Mary about not having a joint on the table. But Mary didn't want to know. She was just on her way out to bingo in the Creggan Community Centre, because she'd been stuck in the house all night, not able to go out because she didn't know where he'd been, and he'd promised her that he'd be back before one, no later. Anyhow, now she didn't really want to know, she said, with tears in her eyes, because what was the point? Just what was the fuckin' point? He'd tried to reply that day, but Mary had slammed the door behind her, muttering before she did so that, if he didn't fuckin' mind shutting up talkin' shite for a while, could he give everyone's head peace and keep an eye on the fuckin' wain while she went out for an hour and cleared her head!

His father had shrugged lamely, opened a Dumpy's and watched a thin snow of flaking paint descend slowly to the worn linoleum as the door settled into place. Then he had settled back in a chair and continued talking to Seamus as if he'd never been interrupted.

'Because demons drive a man, son,' he'd say, as he flicked a television channel loudly into life, to provide them both with black-and-white company that perfectly matched the rest of their black-and-white world, where splinters of genuine colour rarely reached. Demons gave you an anger that you needed to motivate and propel yourself forward in this bastard of a world, where it was dog-eat-dog and the British government was standing with a muzzle in one hand and a whip in the other, always ready to pounce on the winnin' mutt and drag him off to make some more money at the next fuckin' dogfight. Aye, and there was no point in bein' afraid of demons, because you needed them to help you fight other, more powerful demons – those who were better armed and ready to snatch the land of your fathers right out from under your fuckin' noses.

Seamus the younger had listened to him intently that particular evening, as he always did when his father spoke. The young boy sat down at the side of the easy chair, his legs curled beneath him. He enjoyed these talks with his father and it didn't matter about the commingling smells that could have made you nauseous if you had really concentrated on breathing them in. The smells of week-old lard in the chip pan, of old paint or of champ, that staple mixture of potatoes, scallions and margarine of which he would have grown readily sick if given the choice. The smells of stale beer and spirits on smoky breath, mixing with the new smells of freshly opened Harp in Dumpy's bottles and foul-reeking Woodbines.

The smells of a man who hadn't had time to wash in a week because 'the fuckin' Brits', as he called them, had been out there in the back fields again the last few nights and he'd had to wait until they left before riskin' his life by going up there along with Billy Flannagan to check if they'd been tryin' to sneak in en masse or merely pretending to do so for the umpteenth time in months. Him and Billy Flannagan crawlin' over cow-pats and through muck and shit, for Christ's sake, and they'd seen fuck all but a cow. A cow, for Christ's sakes, and it was lying down and Billy had tripped over it. Then it was runnin' mad all over the place and Billy had panicked, nearly shot it dead because it had shit beside him! And, just to put the tin hat on it, the person they'd thought to be an intruder had turned out to be a wee farmer and he'd nearly flaked it dead on the spot, Billy having to slap his face to bring him round. The night had been a balls-up, a complete and utter balls-up, and all they'd got was soaked and dirty for Ireland.

'But don't say a word of that, son,' his da had said then, laughing, finally seeing the funny side of it all. 'And there's your ma thinkin' I'm out enjoyin' meself all the time. Christ! But still, ye can't blame her for worryin',' can ye?' his da had added, frowning. 'She'll come round in the mornin', when she finds her tea and toast at the edge of the bed. Still, that other stuff's between you and me and the garden post, because I don't fancy gettin' myself tarred and feathered – or worse – for no man, do ye hear?'

And Seamus had nodded, listening intently as always, trying to ignore the smell of manure and lard and smoke and paint and beer. His father, who had for a very short time been a painter by trade, had taught him a long while back that you didn't have to breathe through your nose, anyhow, if you didn't want to. He didn't do it so much himself now, the older man declared, because if you'd spent your whole life working with strong paints and primers inside, say, a school building, and the windows had been nailed closed and fixed with metal grills in case someone broke in and stole stuff for the riots, then you wouldn't be long getting into the way of it, y'know? So Seamus the younger had nodded and easily learned how to do that. And he'd listened for a long time as his father had rambled on and on about the Brits and how they thought they were someone when they were really nobody at all. About how they'd taken over the whole world and they couldn't sort out a few fuckin' Paddies. But then that was because they were the same as the Americans, kid, Seamus senior declared knowledgeably. Give the Yanks a big-scale war where they could use their weapons from afar and they'd blow the fuck out of everythin' you put in front of them with their B52s and their napalm, their big navy guns that fired rockets in from miles out at sea, and shit like that. Same with the Brits, of course, though on a much smaller scale. But give any of the two of them somewhere like Vietnam or Northern Ireland, where the locals were prepared to defy the bastards to the last and you might have to get right in there in the middle of them and use your brains as well as your balls, then, hey, they hadn't a fuckin' clue.

Same thing, his father declared staunchly. Exact same thing, if you really thought about it. The Vietcong were fighting a guerrilla war, and so were we, and it was the exact same thing. The North against the South over there in Vietnam. Over here, the North against – well, *part* of the North of Ireland – the whole of England, I suppose. But aye, same thing really, give or take the colour of skins and clothes. And his father would laugh when he said that, so young Seamus would laugh too. Because this was what communication was about, after all, wasn't it? Or at least that was how Seamus always reassured himself. The communication between father and son that bonded them together throughout a lifetime. Or maybe turned them both into simple bastards.

Several years ago, however, his father told him through a screen of smoke, the Brits had been the saviours of the North. Sure even his own mother, Mary, would agree with him there, he'd said, and she'd argue a black crow white for the sake of it, son. See, she's well versed in politics, despite her hatred for a particular couple of the Boys here in Creggan. Better up on things, perhaps, than even his own da had been years back, and he'd been staunch as they come. Because her crowd went all the way back to 1916, see. Sure her grandfather had even known big Michael Collins, son, I kid you not. Great fella, right and civil, and him shot shortly after the end of the whole war. Terrible that, really was. Him sold out by that de Valera bastard, they reckoned, though they never said it openly. Sold out by the same boy he eventually helped bring to power as prime minister of Ireland. No sense of honour, some people, see. Some people have it and some people don't. Collins had it; de Valera didn't. His father had shrugged, as if he couldn't understand just why that was. And then he'd said that that was just the way it went in wars sometimes, that was just the way it went.

Seamus smiled and he shrugged too. He enjoyed hearing all about the Troubles. It was the only time he ever got into a real conversation with his father, he recalled, though deep down he knew that, like his mother, he mainly supplied the ears.

He had smiled and nodded when his da had asked him did he mind the Brits the first time they'd arrived in Derry the year before. The first battalion of the Prince of Wales's own, his da remembered. That was the crowd we had in here, and we thought they were great, son – thought that it was wil' nice of the young Prince Charlie to send his own men down from where they were stationed in Belfast to help us out after those B-Special bastards had gone on the rampage through the Bogside breakin' windows and kickin' doors in after that Orange march. That had resulted in the Battle of the Bogside, three days and nights of intense riotin' and sheer unadulterated madness, though that had only been the start of it, of course. And sure, then another crowd of Brits had had to intervene up in the Ardoyne district of Belfast as Catholics and Protestants fought pitched battles on the Crumlin Road, night after bloody night.

Aye, the boy had lied, he'd remembered them arriving at the edge of the Bog, because he'd seen it on the news, but as for the exact day he'd first seen them in the actual flesh, well . . . He was going to shake his head then, but he nodded anyway. And he just kept nodding as his da reminded him of things that the young boy had never seen. It was his way of feeling close because, if he nodded, then his father smiled and patted his head. Though he always ended up thinking when he was older that it probably wouldn't have mattered if he'd nodded if his father asked him did he remember the time the Dohertys all went to the moon, because he wasn't absolutely sure if his father had really been listening to him anyway.

He did remember the odd thing about the arrival of the army, of course, though not half as much as his father thought he did. He remembered his mother sitting glued to the telly the time they'd marched across the Craigavon Bridge, all right, and he wasn't lying about that, because she looked as if she was getting her Christmas presents early. Her eating her dinner with a smile on her face for a change, oohing and aahing as she listened to their commander talking on the television in his proper Etonian accent, talking over the officer's words as his father was trying to shush her and saying something about how naive and innocent they looked, and how they were just kids fresh out of school sent over here to fight a load of devious Orange bastards who were up to their necks in it with the B-Specials just for the money the Brits pumped into the North – *their* North – and loyalty to the Crown had fuck all to do with it. He remembered that incident because his father had sat there on the sofa, with a cigarette in his mouth, saying that now they'd all see what was coming to them, and if the loyalists thought they could fight against the might of the entire British army – an army that had conquered half the world at various times – then they'd soon get their fuckin' eyes opened, and that was a fact, if ever there was one.

And he remembered that, the very next day, his mother had been out there on the streets with the rest of the women watching in quiet bemusement as the first foot patrol crossed the perimeter of the Bogside. She'd taken young Seamus down the town along with Sadie, her nearest next-door neighbour, to visit Bernie Duddy, who lived in William Street. Bernie was a friend that Mary visited perhaps once every few months or so, though now Bernie had a whole platoon of Brits almost on her doorstep and that, sheerly by coincidence, had sparked genuine concern in the two women as to how she was coping with it all. They'd all ended up staring through the windows at the Brits for a time as if they were chimps in a zoo. Shyly at first, watching the soldiers moving sandbags and barbed wire aimlessly around the place, as if they were unsure of their purpose; as if that well-trained army didn't exactly know what they were supposed to be doing here in the second-largest city in the North of Ireland; as if they were unsure as to who was supposed to be fighting with whom.

Though an hour later, that shyness forgotten, Mary had been out in the street helping Bernie and Sadie to serve up tea and biscuits to the grateful troops, offering her own particular adopted squaddie a reassuring smile, telling him all about the way the Catholics had been trodden on for seven hundred years, maybe even longer, by power-hungry Protestants; by Orangemen who marched two or three thousand times a year in the North as a reminder that they'd once won a war; who marched several times a year along the length of Derry's walls, banging hard on their Lambeg drums, lofting their symbolic banners high and firing pennies into the Bogside as they called for the Catholic 'Croppies' to lie down in subservience to the might of Orangeism.

'Sure isn't it the same in your own country, wee boy?' she'd say, admiring his SLR, patting him on the rucksack and nudging her friend and next-door neighbour Sadie with an elbow and telling her to get a load of the wee lad's eyes. 'And look at his camouflaged helmet. Far too big for his wee head, bless him. How out of place does that look, eh?' she added, with a wink and a smile. 'Him wearin' the same stuff they'd been wearin' over there in Aden, probably his big brother's, by the look of it. You'd think you were off to the jungle again, son. And that bayonet affixed on top of your gun too. 'Christ,' she'd said, grinning, 'they must have given you some impression of us Paddies over there in England, son, mustn't they?

'Catholics and Protestants, and one keeping the other down. Sure isn't it the same over there in your own country, son?' But her squaddie had shrugged and offered a limp 'Dunno', and Mary had told him hurriedly that it was, and remarked on his accent instead, saying that it was lovely and that he was no more than a wee lad and what the fuck could he ever know about politics, sure? 'Hope my Seamus and your Jimmy grows up like that,' she'd tell Sadie, and both women would nod and smile, looking for similarities between the two lads, as young Seamus dropped his head, blushed and wished they'd stop talking about him. Mary and Sadie nodding like donkeys at a fair, happy to have met the lad, because he'd be away back home in two months' time when everything blew over, and maybe he'd write to their sons and maybe invite them over in a couple of years and stuff.

Less than ten minutes after they'd stepped back and allowed the Orangies – as she called them – to burn and terrorise the Catholics out of their homes up in Belfast, however, she'd declared that she'd seen the other side of them as soon as they'd arrived and they were all the sons of bastards. 'God forgive me,' she'd said, 'but you'd have to shoot them first, because every last one of them would stick a bayonet in ye as soon as ye looked at him. Sure ye seen that wee cunt that time he came danderin' up William Street to get his tea. Thick as fuck and he'd nothin' in his head, 'cause ye could see it in his eyes. He'd known nothin' about politics, she'd had to tell him everythin', and he probably still thinks a Jaffa is a biscuit. He'd probably been given time for rape or somethin', see, and they had nowhere to put him. Because they stick them in the army, y'know, when their jails are all full up. Oh aye, that's what they do with them, seen it on a documentary one night. Or he probably couldn't get a job back home because he was thick as a plank, so they stuck him in the army as a last resort, just to get him out of the country. Happens all the time.'

And she'd been out there banging the bin lids on the pavements with the rest of them every time a Saracen or a Sixer came into the street after that, and once she'd nearly taken the head off a Brit with a rolling pin during their internment swoop in August 1971 as he'd dared to get out of a jeep and take cover in her garden, her commenting that he was an evil wee bastard and had the eyes of the devil himself. He'd turned pure white at that and stuck the SLR in her face then, and she'd urged him to pull the trigger, to get it out of his evil wee system for once and for all, but apparently he hadn't had the balls to do it. She'd laughed in his face when she'd told him that. And she'd proudly boasted about the event to Seamus the younger with a cup of tea in her hand to steady her nerves and eyes standing out like those of a myxomatosis rabbit in her head. Seamus had shivered, seeing his ma angry like that, and he had led her back into the house in Dunree Gardens as some other thick wee fucker in green had helped the shivering wee Brit back into his Saracen and down Westway towards the sanctity of either the Victoria Army Barracks or the Strand Road RUC Station.

He'd always remember her eyes that day. She must have got a lend of them off someone else, he always remembered thinking. Because surely they had to belong to someone – anyone but his own flesh. 'But aye,' she'd say, when she'd calmed down, 'we're all Taigs and nothing else to that lot, nothing but that and Fenian bastards who thought the Pope was infallible when that was hardly possible and who believed in the Virgin Birth, which was utter nonsense.' Then she'd half-laugh, even as she started to cry, saying that not a one of them knew what a Taig was anyhow, and as for a Fenian, sure half of them couldn't even say it, let alone spell it. 'And there they were with their SLRs, ready to drop the first one that looked at them through angry eyes,' she'd continued, 'because someone up high had ordered them here in our streets. *Our* fuckin' streets, and them angry at us for wantin' them out of it?' It was, she declared sorrowfully, enough to make you fuckin' weep a bucketful.

And Seamus the younger had half-laughed and half-cried too that time as he took her cold and shaking hand in his own and rubbed a little warmth back into it, not wishing to ask the difference between a Taig and a Fenian, never mind the spelling, because he'd heard a whisper over in the Holy Child Primary School that, if you didn't know what the difference was, then you were no better than a black enamelled bastard yourself and the Boys would come around and tar and feather you. And that wasn't nice to watch, Seamus knew, never mind have it done to you. He'd seen a few girls being tied to lamp-posts over on Central Drive in front of the shops, them supposedly having had it away with the squaddies and thinking of marrying them. Their hair cut off and lukewarm pitch poured over them if they were lucky, and pigeon feathers or half an eiderdown over that – same thing, really, they said. And he'd seen boys having concrete blocks dropped on their legs or getting paint thrown over them for being hoods and doing antisocial sorts of stuff. He'd shivered then and Mary had started rubbing at his hands to heat him up.

Seamus the older had nodded his agreement with Mary the time she'd stood up to the Brit. He'd grabbed a rusty bedpost from out in the back garden, then run up the front steps and thrown it at the jeep. Then he'd run back inside the house as the vehicle stopped and the driver faked a reverse down the street and aimed a rubber-bullet gun at him before racing off down Westway. That was one of the few times they'd agreed about anything, as far as Seamus could mind. Lying back in another niche he'd worked into the black sofa, his father had agreed with his mother that the Brits would probably be here for no more than another six months now and you'd soon see the Catholics taking up arms against them, you see if they didn't. And he'd be out there with the rest of the Boys, he swore, as he cracked open a Dumpy's. And he swore it on his wee lad's life, because they had it comin' to them, every fuckin' last one of them.

Seamus Doherty had been right about the shooting war. It had been the riots at first and then the guns, just like in 1916. The IRA shot dead their first serving British soldier in Northern Ireland on the fifth of February 1971. In July of the same year, the British army killed two local youths who, they claimed, were armed with a nail bomb and a rifle; the IRA shot dead their first soldier in the Creggan estate the day after the introduction of internment in August of the same year. But Seamus the older hadn't joined up with the rest of the Boys at first, saying that there was no need, because the Brits'd be pullin' out right and shortly when the rest of the world saw what they were doin' to innocent Catholics over here – when they saw that we weren't goin' to lie down and let them walk all over the top of us like doormats. He didn't actually join up until about three weeks after Bloody Sunday.

A defenceless civil rights march of about thirty thousand people, protesting against the British government's introduction of internment, had marched through Creggan, the Brandywell and the Bogside and down to Free Derry Corner on the thirtieth of January 1972. It was an illegal demonstration, according to the British government, though the remedy to that perceived problem had been drastic even by British colonial standards. The marchers had been fired on by paratroopers from the junction of William Street, from the top of Stevenson's bakery and also from the Derry walls – those same paratroopers that the Catholic population of Belfast had warmly welcomed into the Shankill Road in '69 and given cups of tea to had now arrived down in Derry and shot thirteen people dead and wounded fourteen more, one of whom died of his injuries several months later. Seamus Doherty and the rest of the civilised world had been stunned into disbelief for weeks, if not months, afterwards, and the decision to join up had come easily.

Thirteen coffins lying in St Mary's Chapel and the whole of the Creggan – maybe the whole of Northern Ireland too – as silent and eerie as a morgue for days afterwards. Thousands gathering in and around the church for the funerals, their numbers swamping Fanad Drive, Iniscarn and the Bishop's Field, there to pay tribute to innocent civilians who had wanted to be treated as equals and nothing else. The world media there to catch it indelibly on film and in word, the entire city in mourning. The Provisional IRA would never know the strength they knew in the years immediately following that: the clamouring to join, to defend, to fight, to avenge. Seamus Doherty the older was as moved as every other man in the city, and his decision had been natural. There weren't enough triggers to go around yet, he was told, but there were enough people willing to pull them, and they'd keep him in mind. Three weeks later, true to their word, they did. During the two years that followed that unholiest of events, more Brits would die on the streets of Northern Ireland than ever before or after and, for the first few months, Seamus Doherty senior would play a hand in their demise.

Seamus Doherty had taken the defence of his country as seriously as the next man. It was then that he had actually allowed the demon to go on an extended holiday as more pressing matters – like the defence of no-go areas such as the Creggan, the Bogside and the Brandywell from the British army and the much-hated RUC – brought him temporarily back to his senses. Seamus the younger, now eleven years old, used to smile proudly as he and young Jimmy Duffy stood behind the small crowd that had gathered to watch the hooded-up Boys in the Watery Lane as they fired up into the rat-infested back fields at makeshift targets that each man there knew would some day very soon turn into real flesh-and-blood men that fired back. For, standing there beside the hedgerow of that narrow mucky and waterlogged path which ran between Creggan Heights and Circular Road, only he and Jimmy – and, of course, the rest of the Boys – knew that one of those men was his father. Young Seamus could nearly believe that his father, an almost dashing and heroic figure in his black army-surplus jumper and matching balaclava, black Doctor Marten boots and blue Wrangler jeans, was as normal as Jimmy's da – that at times he'd almost toy with the idea of throwing you a few shillings out of his dole money on the Thursday morning of every second week before he skipped on over to the Telstar bar in Central Drive to hook up with an old friend who'd just returned temporarily from his holidays.

Seamus the younger didn't know if that old friend of his had been with his da the night he'd been killed up in the back fields, however, though he doubted it, because his da had cut right down on the drink, despite the fact that Mary still got onto him about it. Yet no one seemed to have got the full story of things, his mother had sobbed, because the Boys had snatched the body right out from under everyone's noses and driven it across the border to a secret address in Letterkenny, where they'd kept it for two days. They'd taken a chance in doing that, she knew, because under the Special Powers Act it was illegal to conceal injured or dead persons from the government, and they had all faced years in jail.

The bullet had gone deep – a fatal wound that had splintered into shards in his gut. They couldn't save him. He had died on the second day. The Boys had taken a chance, it was said, but then so had Seamus Doherty senior. He'd taken one chance too many for them and, as grateful as his mother was for what they'd done for him that night, she also hated one or more of them with a passion afterwards. Now it didn't matter to her any more just who had done what in the name of what, or why. Seamus Doherty senior was dead, and it had almost broken his mother's heart.

His father's death had taken place shortly before the onset of Operation Motorman, a British military operation that planned to wrest control of the no-go areas from the Catholics and hand them over to the RUC. Seamus hadn't been around to see it. Having just completed his eleven-plus, he'd been whisked away to France under some sort of a scheme called the Holiday Projects, which took both Catholic and Protestant kids out of the country and allowed them to meet on neutral ground so each could see that the other was not anything like the horned beasts of legend which politicians on either side chose to promote them as. Mister Sharkey, vice-principal of the Holy Child, had told his mother that the boy had 'a hunger for learning' and that the whole thing would do him good, broaden his horizons and better prepare him for the world in general. 'A hunger for learning', those were the words he had used. And Seamus the younger would remember those words well throughout his lifetime, because no one would ever say anything like that to him again, ever. Sharkey hadn't liked Seamus all that much, but he was fair – very fair – and that made the compliment all the better. Many times afterwards, when things went horribly wrong for him, Seamus would find himself wondering just where that eager young boy with the then-elusive and long-forgotten hunger for learning had vanished to, and why that same hunger, of which he was supposedly possessed from such a tender age, hadn't warned him of the dangers to come.

His mother hadn't minded him going off to France, of course, because 'It was far better than him hangin' around here', she had told his father with a wink. 'What with this whole shootin' and bombin' thing going on at the moment up there in Belfast, what with the whole place ghettoised and everyone afraid to move out of their own particular estates. Same as here,' she had warned, with a frown. 'It's nearly as bad down here in Derry since Bloody Sunday, and if you think we can hold out against them forever then you're sorely mistaken,' she had said. But his father had objected, the way he always seemed to when Mary spoke. Because she'd argue a black crow white and he always seemed to see it as his task to put her right.

'Sure this whole fuckin' place is as safe as a row of houses, woman,' he'd told her. He was sitting at the fireplace when he'd said that, Seamus remembered. Sitting slightly hunched over, rubbing quickly at his hands as small, pale flames licked slowly at the furthest wall of the grate, him almost willing the small black jewels of wet coal to spark into a furnace of a fire. The house was cold even in the summer, drafts whispering in under gaps between the windows and the brick, the repairs that the housing association had once promised never having arrived. His father had never pushed the issue with them, perhaps never being fully aware of the problem, as he was never at home long enough to realise that problems – any problems – could arise there. Even now, he wasn't half aware that a young boy's immediate future depended upon his saying aye or no; he was seemingly more interested in the hypnotic flames that had barely found life, because they were running out of coal and no one had thought to hijack a coal lorry in ages.

'You're gettin' it all wrong, comparin' this place to Belfast, woman. Sure that place is a shootin' gallery, half-Catholic, half-Protestant, the Falls and the Shankill sittin' smack on top of each other. It's no fuckin' wonder they're at each other's throats. But down here's a different kettle of fish. Sure you've only those Jaffs up in the Fountain estate and a couple living in the Glen, some on the Foyle Road and Bishop Street. Couldn't be more than a few hundred of them in all. Sure, and Creggan's been a no-go area for nearly a year and those bastards haven't a clue as to how to get in. We've every road into the place guarded at night. A couple of vigilantes with guns on each, them sittin' it out in their wee corrugated tin huts and nothin' but a wee fire, tea and a few sandwiches to warm them, winter and summer alike. I'm fuckin' proud of them, every fuckin' last one of them.' Seamus had seen the older man's eyes misting over as he'd said it. 'They're takin' their lives in their hands and nobody seems to understand why. Ye seen what happened the other night, for example. The fuckin' Brits came down through the fields dressed as cows and we shot the arses off them. I got one in the hole, I'm telling ye, I hit him square in the arse with me Armalite and he nearly had a fuckin' blue fit tryin' to crawl back up through the field . . . '

'You're a spoofer,' Mary stormed. 'If you'd got one, sure it'd have made the news.'

'Aye well, if I'm a fuckin' spoofer then where'd you ever hear about cows shootin' back, eh? Some bastard put a hole in me coat.' His father showed Mary a hole that could have been either a bullet hole or, equally, a rip. Mary didn't seem in any way impressed. 'Hey, they don't stick everythin' on the news, woman, don't be an arse. It's all about disinformation, Dan says. Disinformation and misinformation. He reckons they're tellin' them fuck all on the news over in England, probably sayin' that we got pea-shooters and fuck all else, that they're winnin' everythin' and we're winnin' fuck all.'

Mary raised an eyebrow. 'Sure they'd have nothin' to gain from that. You reckon they're just gonna tell some wee woman over there that her son died for his country but she'll have to shut her mouth about it 'til the war's over?' The raised eyebrow was to signify that Seamus Doherty senior was the arse. 'I don't fuckin' think so!'

Seamus senior shrugged and took a slug from his Dumpy's – one of the few he'd allowed himself that night. 'They'll tell her that her son was killed on a trainin' exercise, that he froze or starved to death on a fuckin' yomp across the Yorkshire Moors, or some other shite like that. Or maybe they'll say that someone put live ammunition into their guns by mistake when they were out practicin' how to kill Paddies. Sure they're always sayin' that stuff – say it all the time. They're a crowd of sleeked bastards and there's nothin' beneath them.'

'You're the arse, Seamus Doherty.' Mary decided to say it out straight, apparently believing that her husband wasn't getting the message. 'You're out chasin' shadows but, sure, then that's the story of your life.'

Seamus turned to his son. 'They ran like blue fuck up there in the direction of Haterick's farm, son, and they haven't tried to come down since.' He turned back to Mary. 'The boy doesn't need to go away on any educational trip. He'll learn everythin' he ever wants to know here in Creggan, and I'll make sure of it. Sure he isn't goin' to get a job in this country anyway. He's the wrong fuckin' colour. Green, not orange, and you need to be orange to get ahead, and ye know that yourself.'

'He's goin' away,' Mary declared, thickly. She stood above her husband, arms folded, vying for his attention with piercing eyes that had once sent a wee Brit running into his jeep. But the hypnotic flames held his da's attention in the grate. 'He needs a chance to make a better life of it than we ever did,' his wife continued. 'D'you think I want him spendin' his life on the fuckin' brew the way you do? D'you think I want him workin' one week out of twenty and never knowin' anywhere but the fuckin' pub?' His father, never a man to be cowed , had made to rise but Mary had pushed him down onto the red pouffe. He relented, seemingly not in the mood to storm out of the house and away from the fire. 'He's gettin' the fuck out of this hole, even if it is only for three weeks,' Mary continued, 'and you – you're goin' to give him the money to go, because I haven't got it.' Seamus the older started to grumble about not having a red cent in his pocket. 'Well, you can go and get it all back off your republican friends,' Mary cut in, quickly. 'Those Stickies and Provies who you've been playin' cards with every night when you're supposed to be concentratin' on mannin' the barricades. I thought you lot hated each other, anyway.'

'We do,' Seamus senior huffed. 'Sometimes,' he added, with an uncertain frown.

'Huh! You're shootin' each other dead one minute and you're drinkin' and playin' cards the next. And every fuckin' night, too, whilst your son cowers in his bed. Us worryin' ourselves sick and wonderin' if you're ever goin' to come home of an evenin'.'

'I'm not out playin' soldiers, Mary, and ye know it as well as anyone,' his father barked. 'You're as republican as the rest of us, so stop fuckin' sayin' that. Christ, ask the kid. He'll tell you. I'm the finest shot up there.' Young Seamus hung his head low as his father turned to him for help. 'Well, he'd tell ye if he wasn't so fuckin' scared of ye. I know he would.'

'He's not scared of me, Seamus Doherty,' Mary barked. 'He knows me because I'm here for him every day. He's more like scared of you. Probably wonderin' just who the fuck ye are, if you really want to know.'

His father had risen quickly, his face contorted with rage. He leaned in close to Mary and the room crackled with electricity, but Mary didn't back off even slightly.

'Now you're being stupid,' Seamus roared. 'This is for you lot. That's the only fuckin' reason we're doin' it, you know! These no-go areas aren't just a load of boys standin' about with their toy guns, playin' at soldiers. There's an enemy out there, and it's as real as you and me. The Stickies and the Provies both are tryin' to ensure that our kid and every other kid in the place has a chance to get on in the world, instead of livin' under the yoke of Stormont, where we'll always be second-class citizens, if even that. They say they've suspended Stormont, that all power's now in Westminster. But there isn't a fuckin' difference. A hundred thousand of them cheerin' Brian Faulkner as if he was king of the fuckin' world. It'll be back, you take it from me. You'll still see that shower burnin' the Catholics out of their fuckin' homes in Belfast for years to come, no matter who holds the reins.'

He shrugged and looked hard at Mary, his voice softening slightly. 'We're just stoppin' them doin' the same here. We haven't had a Brit in this fuckin' place for a long time back, and it's only because of the boys and ye know it.' He sat down at the fire and waved a dismissive hand. 'Go on, send the kid away then. Ye want to send him away, ye send him away.' He turned to young Seamus, his anger leaving him as he looked into the young boy's eyes. 'Aye, I suppose it'll do you the world of good, kid. I'll stump up the dough for ye, too, so don't ye worry about that. And when ye get back, your da'll be a hero and even your ma'll like him.'

'I wouldn't count on you ever winnin' that war, Seamus Doherty,' his mother had retorted, frostily. But then she'd smiled and had even touched him lightly on the shoulder. That touch had had no significance to the younger Seamus then. Though when he grew older and his own black-and-white world knew many more shades of grey than he thought possible, that touch would bring sharply home the fact that his father, too, had once been made of flesh and that his mother had loved him more dearly than she ever admitted.

Young Seamus had smiled when his father had said that, not listening as his parents became engrossed once more in exchanging their ceaseless unpleasantries. He was going to France and getting the hell out of Creggan for three weeks. Jimmy Duffy, Paddy Monaghan, Mick Deery and Barney Ferguson would be jealous when he told them that, as would those other beings who congregated around the Creggan shops after six in the evening – those who didn't have a hunger for learning.

Aye, they'd all been jealous all right, he remembered that much. Seamy Doherty was going away to France and getting the hell out of Creggan with the school. How the fuck did he manage that, the bastard, Jimmy Duffy asked him in awe as he, Paddy Monaghan and Mick Deery smoked a few Park Drives in the dirty lane that ran behind the Creggan shops while Barney Ferguson kept lookout at the corner for adults or Brits.

Seamus looked at Jimmy. The red hair, the pasty skin, the kind eyes. Jimmy was happy for him. Then he looked around him, sensing the good-natured jealousy. 'A hunger for learning,' Seamus told them all with a smile, suppressing a cough.

'Eh?'

'Sure you wouldn't understand,' Seamus said, grinning. 'Ye're all too fuckin' thick.'

*

Two and a half weeks into the holiday, and they, along with everyone else in the estate, understood everything they needed to understand. Dunree Gardens was lit by weak auras of fluorescent orange light as the Holiday Projects van pulled up outside the Doherty house. A gaggle of silent, zombie-like neighbours watched as Margaret Stewart – his ma's younger sister – led her young nephew out of the van and into the packed house. Seamus was tired and confused. They'd passed dozens of soldiers on their way into the estate, more than he had ever seen before. Now the army were everywhere, their foot patrols, their one-ton Humber armoured cars and yellow Saracens overrunning the formerly IRA-manned estates. Now the entire Creggan was like a prison camp without the barbed-wire fences. Only a day earlier he'd been sitting on the veranda of the summer house in the Côte d'Azur, with the sun shining brightly overhead and not a Brit or an RUC man to be seen. Eating huge helpings of fresh French bread and salad, sipping at table wine and wondering just why he'd been born in Northern Ireland when he could have been born here, where even the dirtiest side streets seemed to possess a timeless beauty you'd never find anywhere else in the world.

And then the phone call had come. Mister Mechon, whom Seamus was staying with, had answered it, his face growing lined and more serious with each passing moment. He had cupped a hand across the phone and asked the rest of his family to go inside. 'Except for Seamus,' he'd said gravely, in his lilting accent, pulling the young boy back gently by the arm. 'If he could just sit here for a moment,' the kindly man had said in a sad whisper, putting down the phone, touching his shoulder and sighing deeply, as if storm-clouds were gathering in the face of his own private sun. 'It seems,' he'd said, in that same subdued and almost choking whisper, 'that there has been, 'ow do you say . . . an accident. Your father, he was, 'ow would you say . . . '

And then he'd said it out straight, proving to Seamus that he knew exactly how to say it and that it was perhaps the hardest thing he'd ever have to say in the English tongue, no matter how fluent he became in the language.

He'd been shot, his father. There'd been an, 'ow do you say . . .

an accident, and he'd been shot – shot dead. And Seamus had cried as the man had cradled his head against his chest. The trip in the plane back to the North had been a blur.

More faces had lined the hallway as he'd entered the house. He moved through them in silence. His father's coffin had lain there in the corner, the body in perfect repose. His hair blacker than ever, no real lines upon his face, his worries gone. Seamus had run to him, seeking to shake him awake from that most peaceful of slumbers, then had stepped quickly back as the coldness of his father's skin upon his fingertips had cut into both his brain and his chest like a hot knife. The next few days were also a blur, and not until a year, maybe two years, later would every moment come with perfect clarity back to mind. The sobering perfume of the flowers, the tear-streaked faces, the penitent mumbling of the Rosary. He would remember perfectly where every last one of them was sitting, what they were wearing, what most, if not all, of them were saying. His mother's face and words in particular would always remain. Sitting there on the sofa in the freshly cleaned room, with its new mats, its many vases of flowers and its trays of sandwiches hardly touched, she'd said nothing at first. In that foreign room, with its new lamps, its borrowed chairs, its helpful, doleful neighbours, who kept ruffling the young boy's hair, she seemingly hadn't had the energy to speak.

Aye, he'd always remember his mother in particular. Sitting there on that sofa like a broken toy, staring mournfully at the cold figure in the coffin as if she truly cared for the man she'd spent her nights shouting at, and her always leaving the house as soon as he entered it, as if she could hardly bear to be in the same room as him. For the man whom she'd told to reform now or move forever out of her life. It was hours before she spoke to the young boy in the privacy of his bedroom, thinking, at first, that it was enough to hold him close. It was years, however, before Seamus found out that she had really loved his father more than anything else – that she had only been trying to change him, because that was every woman's task in the world, no matter their social standing.

But by then the rot had set in and Seamus believed that he lived in a world where no one truly cared. Where little really mattered and every man was a hunter of that elusive monster, money, which glided fleetingly between council houses, staring into the windows and laughing at the misery there within as he passed by. Where life was what you took and not what you gave.

It was hard to crawl back from that, hard to learn anything different, even if you had a hunger for learning. Seamus, although he always believed in his later life that he had tried his best to do so, never would.

Two

At the age of eleven and a half, Seamus Doherty was to find out about life and death, about love and hate – and, more importantly, he was to discover all about shimmering shades of grey which existed where, often, no one thought they could. Equally disturbing, however, was the fact that he was to find out over time that, while children, given time, love and support, seldom have any problem adapting to the hard truths imposed by the world, adults often do – and it is usually they who decide to dwell within the realm of fantasy.

Time had moved very slowly after his father's death. The young boy had wished it away at first with a mixture of tears and prayers. Then he'd tried sleeping the pain away, even when tiredness had left him. And then he'd even tried exhausting himself by running the streets long into the night with his friends, playing knick-knock on the doors, letting down car tyres or setting hedges on fire, all so that he might get a cheevy from an angry neighbour, who might chase him until he dropped – and, hopefully, died from exhaustion. But it was all to no avail. The prayers remained unanswered, proving that God just didn't care about the amount of pain that He inflicted. The sleep provided him with lucid nightmares, which were, if anything, even more horrible than the long-drawn-out reality of daytime. And the neighbours, gruff and cursing like troopers at first, became quite placid upon spotting that 'Doherty kid who's just gone and lost his da' running off down the street, and they defeated the whole purpose of the exercise, because they didn't even bother to give chase.

His mother had helped him, of course, keeping him active in his most lethargic moments by making sure that he had done his homework and that his chores around the house were never neglected. She had neglected her own chores for a time, though, and Sadie had almost had to coerce her back into her own daily routine. Still, she seemed to recover quicker than Seamus did, which was about right for his ma, the young boy had decided. The woman had a certain strength and depth of character that Seamus had always known to be there. The strength that had helped her stand against his father in his angriest of moments, against his father's friends when they had come calling for him long after midnight or dropped into the house to hold an impromptu meeting about 'things to be done', and against the weight of the world when it bore down heavily upon the Doherty household and someone had to do something and she was all they had. And that character had helped to keep him in check for a time, too, though the young boy hadn't seen its true purpose back then.

He'd seen a tempered bitterness in her that wouldn't allow him to lie down, an anger-filled anxiety that hadn't let him forget that he was going to make something of his life. Because his father had fought for it in his own way, his mother declared sternly, as had so many others who were fighting still, even though this damned war seemed no closer to an end than it had ever been.

He had made it through to Saint Columb's College in Bishop Street after primary school with no apparent difficulty, though how he had done so he had no real idea, because it wasn't as if he'd gone out of his way to do such a thing. His mother had been a strong woman, certainly, and Mister Sharkey had been a good teacher – of that there was little or no doubt. But neither his teacher nor his mother had been so predisposed to such generosity that they'd allowed him an easy ride in the world. Mothers didn't allow you to lie down to life, no matter how tired you were of living, and teachers didn't allow no-hopers to pass their eleven-plus exams without making an effort. No, it must have had something to do with that hunger for learning that his primary teacher had once talked about – though Seamus couldn't think what.

The college had proven somewhat different from the primary school, however. No one, be they pupil, teacher or priest, seemed to have that same interest in anyone but themselves. The cruel initiation ceremonies – which the fourth- and fifth-year students at the college usually inflicted upon the new students – he had thankfully missed, making his newness at the college less stressful and the settling-in period easier for him than for most. Also, Barney Ferguson, another of the 'Creggan Shop Squad' – as they now liked to call themselves, because every small group was getting a name for itself these days, and apparently you didn't really have to be paramilitary by nature to qualify – had joined him there in the school.

Barney was pale-skinned, small and skinny, and he lived around the corner from Seamus on Fanad Drive. They'd been friends since long before he could remember, and their worlds were virtually the same, their natures not all that different. Easygoing, forever trying to get along without too much hassle, yet willing to take a chance and have a bit of fun at someone else's expense if they thought they'd get away with it. Though not if it really hurt someone, and they sort of knew that about each other without ever having to say it out loud.

So Barney knew everything that Seamus did and he was an

ally in this strange new world on that first day – two being stronger than one, and in fact as good as a regular army, paramilitary or otherwise. His presence there was a godsend, cutting down on the immediate need of the uninitiated to make himself a friend – and quickly, in case everyone got to thinking he was some sort of a weirdo because he was wandering around by himself during break. Before the bigger boys noticed that he was standing there out in the open like the weakest deer in the pack and turned on him, making his life from that moment onwards a regular hell on earth.

You didn't need problems like that to add to the rest of your troubles. Seamus was nearly twelve, and shades of grey were galloping at speed into his life. He was finding out that you had to file them into two boxes: one you'd previously allotted to black, the other to white. It was confusing, to say the least. The teachers were strict – stricter, certainly, than those in the Holy Child, and almost demonic compared to those up in Saint Joe's and Saint Pete's in Creggan, in both of which it was rumoured that a somewhat lackadaisical regime had taken hold over the last few years. Rumour also had it that you could throw things at the teachers and tell them to fuck away off to themselves without getting the strap, and if there was ever a shooting incident or a bomb went off, then both schools closed down as a matter of procedure, even if the incident was miles away. Not so the college. Two kids had nearly stepped on a landmine somewhere close by once and they hadn't even shut the damned place for an afternoon.

Actually getting into Saint Pete's or Saint Joe's was a fantasy that Seamus entertained every single school day – a dream that he hoped, from the moment he set foot in the college, would come true. Here they gave you the strap for the smallest thing. Like if you forgot your homework and maybe left it on the bus – if you came on the bus, that is, which Seamus didn't. His mother had encouraged him to take either the Sticky cabs or the Provo cars, because the people wanted the money to go back to the people and not into the government-run buses, which seldom turned up anyhow. If they did, they were burnt out and their blackened husks were left lying lengthways across the streets. As well as the strap, the dean of the college was forever patrolling the grounds, so you couldn't make it to the gate and down into the freedom of the town.

Seamus didn't realise how much he had liked the Holy Child until he'd left it. Encouragement had inspired him to read, and to enjoy reading – which were, apparently, two entirely different things. He had also learned to ignore the older boys who gathered across the main road behind the shops in their Crombies and their Wrangler jeans cut three-quarters of the way up the legs, so that they barely overlapped the boys' DM boots, waiting for the Brits to pass by so that they could, hopefully, stone or petrol-bomb them to a pulp.

For the Brits had taken Creggan now, and they weren't long letting you know all about it, either, what with their Sixers and their Saracens; their numerous foot patrols, complete with sniffer dogs, as they swamped seven or eight streets at a time, kicked in doors that weren't opened quickly enough and raided every house in their frenzied and often fruitless search for weapons; their roadblocks, where they held you for hours at a time if there were more than two in a car, and you all trying to get to school or work and nothing more; and their foul manners as they called you a little Fenian scumbag bastard under their breath as you passed by. They did this even as you minded your own business and crossed the road to get out of their way, always hoping that they wouldn't pull you aside and accuse you of rioting, 'lift' you and take you off to the nearest barracks, where they'd kick seven colours of shite out of you, or worse.

He had learned to enjoy books and, by and large, to ignore the squadrons of soldiers moving along Central Drive in a tight six-by-four formation, like Roman legionaries, some with their five-foot-long perspex shields held out to guard each side and the rest using theirs to form a roof as they advanced. A phalanx; a perspex box with rubber-bullet guns sticking out of the side; a regular war-wagon on legs. He had learned to ignore the clash of halfers – the technical name for half of a house-brick – bottles, petrol bombs and long metal stakes bouncing off the perspex shields and the sharp retort of smoking rubber-bullet guns as baton rounds were fired high into the crowds, seeking to maim. The stench of cordite, the cheers as a missile thrown from one or other side hit home. The angry cries of defiance as one obdurate group ran towards the other, and the rise in tempo as the second group faltered and ran off to find cover behind armoured cars or walls, behind hedges or jeeps.

His primary-school teacher had been a remarkable man, when Seamus really thought about it. Getting a whole class to avoid a war and find some solace in a bunch of words. He must have been something of a bloody genius. Most of the teachers in the college were less inspiring, however, Seamus found. They were lacking that same grand vision, or perhaps they had difficulty dealing with people who were more curious about life now. Who were maturing physically, if not altogether mentally, and finding girls and riots and dobbing school infinitely more interesting than academia. Of course, some of the teachers had that rare innate quality that enabled them to impart confidence with their visions and grand ideas with their words. Some of them could even make you believe that one day you would live in a city not at war, where both Catholics and Protestants would enjoy a decent standard of living by working together for the good of the community as a whole. It was only a year, they said – maybe two years, at the most – down the line. Yet not all of them were as observant as they might have been on a certain cold December morning during break – that much, Seamus remembered all too clearly too.

He'd been down playing handball – a game he was reasonably good at – in the courts across from the Nissans, when Hugo Doran ventured by. It was a game that the priests encouraged – because it was the national sport and apparently nearly everyone in Ireland had either forgotten about it or thought that hurling or Gaelic football should have been – though there were only two courts in the school and, as a result, there was always a queue to get on either.

Doran was a third-year, brawny and lacking in intellect. How he had made it here to Saint Columb's was anyone's guess, and it was generally agreed amongst his peers that someone, somewhere along the line, had taken a bribe, perhaps to maintain the compound fence or break out on some new lead-filled straps. Whatever the reason, Hugo Doran was there in the flesh, a bane of the lives of all first-years and even some of those in the higher grades. He bounced the ball at the edge of the court, then motioned with an almost casual thumb and accompanying grimace that Seamus should get off while he still had the power in his limbs to do so.

'I was here first,' Seamus retorted hotly, certain that, upon being reminded of the obvious, the older boy would come to his senses and get to the back of the disorderly queue. 'So ye can play the winner of the next game, or the one after that,' he continued. He slammed the red ball into the corner with an almighty effort and for seconds his cold breath was faintly visible in the air. His opponent failed to see the master stroke, missing his return swing by a mile and losing, leaving himself seven points down. 'Which'll be me, if ye just hold your horses.'

'I'm not waitin' anywhere for the son of a tout,' the third-year responded easily, smiling as his words hushed the rest of the gathering into an abrupt silence. He bounced his own ball slowly up and down on the concrete as all eyes widened and turned to Seamus. Yet Doran's eyes remained firmly on the ball and nothing else. Seamus should have found this fact somewhat disconcerting, as it showed that the boy had enough confidence to lead a nation and he wasn't in the least worried that Seamus would retaliate either verbally or physically.

Seamus laughed then, though he didn't know why. Looking back, he always thought that it was because his initial feeling was that the boy was mad. But deep down, his heart fluttered, and he knew or felt instinctively that his world was just about to change forever.

'What the fuck are ye talkin' about, Doran?' Seamus asked.

The older boy looked up and smiled thinly, the ball held fast in one hand, the other hand in his pocket. 'Your da. He was a fuckin' tout. Everyone knows it. Now get the fuck off the court or I'll knock you off.'

Seamus had seen red then. He wasn't a fighter – at least, he hadn't been until that moment. But all those eyes, judging, accusing, without even waiting for him to reply to such a ridiculous accusation. He dived at the boy and threw a half-hearted punch that was well off target. Something hit him hard in the eye and pain coursed through his head, his mind. He crumpled to the concrete floor of the handball alley, still and lifeless, the fight taken from him in that one punch. He felt his ribs crumble and his breath left him as a DM shoe bounced from his side. There was a faint cheering sound and then a strange silence. He looked up through teary eyes to see feet – perhaps twenty or more of them – standing around him. Moments later a passage through them cleared and a long black robe and highly polished shoes, that could only have belonged to the dean, flowed through.

'My office,' a dispassionate voice said. 'Both of you.' He didn't bother to help Seamus to his feet. Instead he turned away, and Seamus noticed the long leather strap held to his back – the weapon of the guard. A familiar pair of hands helped him up instead. Barney stood before him, holding onto him for a second after he stood and allowing him to regain his composure, his breath and especially his vision, which swam a little still. The rest of the pupils had moved hurriedly away as the dean had placed his strap into his waistband and clanged his hand-held bell. They resembling so many beaten-down prisoners, like those in *Escape from Colditz*, which ran in black and white on a Sunday night. They had folded in around the fight and then moved off as soon as a guard appeared. It was classical in its simplicity, and Seamus knew that the dean had seen nothing. To the priest, both boys were equally at fault.

'Why didn't ye help me?' Seamus found himself asking, as he pressed a hand against his eye, pulled it away and looked at it to see if there was any blood.

Barney regarded him with a pained expression which made him seem even more small and fragile, and Seamus looked away, knowing the answer even as he spoke.

'I wanted to, really. But the bastard's bigger and I was afraid. I thought . . . ' Barney dropped his head, ashamed. 'Well, I was just afraid, y'know?'

Seamus righted himself, pulled his black blazer into place and dusted off his trousers. He took a deep breath and winced a fraction of a second later. His lungs were on fire, his eye stinging like the devil. He put an arm around his ribcage, cradling his torso. 'It doesn't matter. I'll get him back sometime. The bastard did that for fuck all. I'll get him back if it fuckin' kills me.' He looked his friend square in the face. 'What the fuck did he say that for, anyway? Why did he say that?'

Barney shrugged. His gaze dropped once more.

Seamus raised an eyebrow and paled. 'You know, don't ye?'

Barney shrugged again and sighed, his frown deepening.

Seamus shook his shoulder roughly. 'Well, fuckin' tell me. I can handle it. Tell me why the fuck he said that about me da.'

'They say your da was a tout,' Barney said, without looking up. 'I don't believe it for a second,' he added, quickly. 'Sure he was 'RA. And none of the other boys believe it either – Paddy, Mick or Jimmy. But Eddie's da is Dan McGeady, *the* Dan McGeady,' Barney said in a hushed whisper, looking around to see if anyone was nearby. There wasn't, but Barney kept whispering anyway. 'He said it to Eddie and apparently he was once in the same group – or cell, whatever – as your father.'

Seamus turned away angrily. Barney was a good friend but he didn't have a notion what he was talking about. Seamus walked quickly into the central school building.

The wait in the cold little antechamber of the dean's office was long and funereal, though it probably lasted for no more than fifteen minutes. Thoughts turned in the young boy's head, even though his eye was watering and stung like blazes and he was sure his ribs were all broken. Still, he didn't know which pained him more, the physical pain or the possibility that his father had been a tout. Seamus couldn't believe that. Not after Bloody Sunday. Not after the Brits shooting thirteen of our own dead at a peaceful civil rights march and injuring many more, them fighting for parity of esteem – nothing more than the same international standards that afforded you the right to stand with your head held high amongst equals. Sure everyone in their right minds hated everything British and everything Orange thereafter. Sure everyone, his father included, had been clamouring to join the Provos after that; the IRA had never been stronger. No one had wanted anything to do with the Brits, because they were a bunch of murdering bastards, woman- and child-killers. Sure who'd want even to spit on them, never mind tout to that lot about anything?

Sure even at the funeral, most of the Boys had been there. Though not all of them, now that he thought about it. His da's CO had arrived along with Billy Flannagan – his da's best friend – and that had to mean something. It must have, surely. The two men ashen-faced, gravely white. Dan McGeady standing there outside the house and talking solemnly with one or two of the local figures, Seamus had noticed. Then Dan McGeady had come into the house and offered a hand to Mary. But Mary had recoiled snake-like – Seamus recalled that clearly too. Still, she'd never liked the man anyway; that was probably normal, what with her husband having been shot out in the back fields. And perhaps she had blamed him in some small way for leading his da to his death. Or maybe she'd blamed him for keeping the true cause of his death out of the papers. It had to have been something like that, *had* to have been.

Because they'd decided to keep the nature of his death a secret, apparently. He'd been killed during the run-up to Operation Motorman but they didn't want the Brits getting any more credit than the media in England had already given them. They'd taken out one gunman and one petrol-bomber – at least that's what it had said on the news, though the truth was somewhat different, according to the locals, who said neither of the two young teenagers were guilty of anything other than stepping out of their homes to see what was going on. But neither of those two innocents had been his da. His mother had told him this in his bedroom when everyone else was downstairs talking in hushed tones and he'd rushed up there to escape from them all forever. 'Your father was a hero, son, just the way he told you he would be. To you and, aye' – and she'd smiled ever so faintly – 'even to me. Aye son, even to me, just like he said he always would be. But we've decided to play the bastards at their own game now, same as they do to us. Misinformation and disinformation, that's what your da would have said. It's just another way of beatin' them out of our country, keepin' them from gettin' another one over on us in their fuckin' propaganda war.'

So they hadn't given him a paramilitary funeral, the way they did when any of the others had died, because someone somewhere had decided that this was for the best. The reason could have been that the whole area was saturated with soldiers, but then that would never have stopped them, Seamus knew. The real reason was because the Boys hadn't wanted it. And his mother had shrugged sadly, telling him that she hadn't wanted it either. She had wanted it quiet and dignified and Seamus had thought that a little funny at the time, her being the strong republican that she was and her crowd going all the way back to Collins and de Valera. And his da dying a hero as well, the way he'd said he would. But the young boy hadn't found it so strange as to make him think about it in any great detail. He just took it for granted that Mary must have been stunned and in shock when she'd agreed to that. Because she probably couldn't think about anything else, seein' as how the fuckin' Brits had killed her Seamus and her very world all in one and she'd loved him like the devil.

He was sure he'd heard her say that. As sure of it as he was that he was alive and breathing and that maybe his ribs were broken.

Though now, as he sat in the antechamber – which was cold even at the height of summer – he thought that maybe he hadn't heard that. It was funny, but here and now he couldn't even remember whether his da had died at all.

The dean was feeling somewhat generous today, Seamus noticed when he finally entered the office. Three weeks' detention after school; two if he told the dean exactly what had happened and why. But Seamus didn't want to say a word. His da had been a fucking tout, he sort of knew it deep in his heart, and he swore then that he wasn't going to end up like his fucking da, ever.

The theory became fact as soon as he stepped into the house in Dunree. Mary stood there in the kitchen and Seamus came straight out with it, nearly making her drop her teacup. His face was contorted with rage, his voice bitter. 'They sais me da was a tout.'

Mary seemed shocked by this strange outburst, which had interrupted her now nearly monastic daily routine. She'd been sorting out bulbs in their beds out the front and she was wearing her old gardening apron – the one she'd started using again only recently, with a little encouragement from Sadie next door.

'They sais . . . '

Mary seemed horrified and Seamus thought he could detect a shake in her hand. 'Who . . . who sais that?'

Seamus saw anger rising there but he continued, holding back his own tears. 'They . . . it doesn't matter who the fuck they are. Was he? Was he a fuckin' tout?'

Mary's free hand stung his cheek and the tears came to both of them. 'He was a hero, your da, Seamus, and don't you ever curse in front of me, never mind fuckin' say that again.' She took a deep breath. 'People say lots of things . . . ' Mary looked at his face and tried to approach him but he recoiled from her. She took another deep breath, hurt by his reluctance to forgive her immediately. 'I'm sorry. I didn't mean to do that. People are cruel sometimes, Seamus. I . . . they said a lot of things. I . . . '

'Then why didn't ye tell me?' His forehead took on a deep frown.

'Tell ye *what?* You were only a young boy when your da was shot. Christ, ye still are.' She paused as Seamus threw himself down onto the old sofa, the niche too large as yet to be comfortable. 'I couldn't bad-mouth your da to his one and only son, could I?'

Her expression matched his own, and she sat down at the old brown table, leaning an elbow on the wooden surface, where rings formed by hot dinner plates remained, despite the accumulating layers of Johnson's polish. 'Some said that he sais a few things to the wrong people – they didn't go into what – but I don't believe it,' Mary said then. 'They said he was a weak man because he was hard on the drink. Sure half of the fuckers in every army are,' she added, bitterly. 'And he was off it for a long time, only took an odd one. Them judgin' him. Where do they think they get the right?'

She shrugged and Seamus saw the years there in her face, in her movement. For a long time they'd been hidden. 'But I don't believe it. To me, your da was a good man. Sure we argued a lot but that's what marriages are all about. He was good enough to me and you most of the time, and that's all that counts. Maybe some of the things he did, you don't remember. And I'll tell ye about them someday, really I will. But not yet. I'm not ready to . . . '

Seamus looked up to see that his mother was crying. He got up from the sofa and went to her, placing an arm around her shoulder.

She held him close, then looked up. 'You don't believe it, do ye, son?'

Seamus shook his head, not sure what to say. He paused for a moment. 'No,' he said, finally, though he realised that his voice held little conviction. 'But everyone else does. I don't know if I can go back to that school any more.'

'Aye, ye can,' Mary said, soothingly. 'Ye can do it because you're a strong kid and ye take after me and your da both.'

Seamus wasn't that strong, he was soon to realise, even though he truly wanted to be. Kids could be cruel and, once they latched onto something and saw the discomfort it brought, they focused long and hard upon that Achilles' heel. It wasn't so bad in the Creggan. There the Dohertys were known as a family who came from a very strong republican line. His mother's family went all the way back to Dublin and Cork and, sure, they were still talking and laughing about some of the exploits her grandfather had got up to in his early years. That strong republican link helped to dampen down the effects of his father's shame. In Creggan Seamus still had a strong support group in his friends, his acquaintances, his family. So it was inevitable, really, he supposed, and quite understandable that he started skipping school and staying closer to home. And it was perhaps also inevitable that he ended up getting himself transferred to Saint Peter's. He liked it there in the new school, though not enough to give up dobbing completely.

Though he wasn't the only one who had decided that dobbing was the best way of passing a day. Barney Ferguson – who was still going to the college – had also decided that being part of an army of two had been fine but that an army of one just hadn't got the same ring to it. So he'd joined Seamus over at the reservoirs on the periphery of the estate, as had Paddy Monaghan and Mick Deery – another two of his friends who had found out that even the comparatively relaxed atmosphere in Saint Joe's could sometimes be too much for a young boy to take. Only Jimmy Duffy, who would turn out to be Seamus's closest friend in later years, hadn't joined up with them as yet.

But then, it was early on in the second term and the young fellas up in Saint Pete's, just off the end of Circular Road, were still winning their war of attrition against the teachers. In another few weeks or so, when the first strap was pulled and used against him, Jimmy Duffy would find that the 'resi' – as the younger residents of the estate called it – was one of the best places on earth to spend a school day. That and the local cemetery, but Seamus confided in the rest of the boys that he didn't really fancy going there. The place held too many memories, all now tainted and spoiled by the words of a gobshite called Doran. He wasn't ever going to go there again, if he could help it.

The resi was a series of three small reservoirs that provided the surrounding estates with their regular water supply. It stood on the periphery of Creggan, interrupted only by a series of unkempt fields that were then used as a rubbish dump by the residents. Small woods of pine and other deciduous trees surrounded the three bowls and, while they weren't what anyone would exactly have classed as forests, they provided plenty of hiding places for those who sought them. Across the reservoir bowls, on the furthest side of Creggan, a single high stone wall fenced the entire area off from the country roads that led off eventually in the direction of Killea and Letterkenny, both over the border in the south of Ireland. A thick mesh fence separated the furthest encroaching woods from the Glenowen housing estate, and the resultant well-defined area was patrolled by a watchie who even had his own hut.

So you had to be careful, especially when you were lighting

fires in the often damp loam – though sometimes you didn't really give a damn anyhow because the thrill of the chase would warm your bones on a cold winter's morning, when a fire never could. And there were many ways of passing the day. The jumps, the daring leaps, the climbs that you performed almost every day in a ritualistic way to show your improving strength and manly prowess to your friends. And it would set them laughing in admiration if you were in any way good – or sniggering if you fell into the small streams that ran between banks of loam-covered earth.

Seamus was growing to be bigger than the other boys and thus he was naturally stronger. It was a gift, his mother told him, that he'd received from her side of the family, especially her brother Johnny, who was now on the run in Buncrana because he'd forgotten to clean his prints off the rifle before returning it to an ill-concealed dump. Seamus could do all the jumps and nearly all the climbs across the fallen trees without slipping. He hardly ever fell and, even if he did, they'd almost all agree that it was an accident and they'd give him credit for it even if he never attempted to do it again. Paddy Monaghan would always get something in about him being a cheat and stuff, but then that was him all over.

Paddy Monaghan was a year older than the other boys – the self-styled leader of the group, though this was never officially talked about and certainly nobody had ever said it. And though he was never as physically strong as Seamus, he had a certain charisma about him. He'd lead them around the town, taking care to steer them away from the Brits and the cops. He knew the best places to steal lead, the scrapyards where you got the best prices. He knew the way into the old buildings down at the docks, into the old abandoned warehouses along the quay. He was always game to go looting the bombed-out shops for smoke-damaged goods days after the police had boarded the places over, and he'd think nothing of going on board the merchant boats that came in every now and then to Derry docks and asking the sailors for fags or drink, or anything they might have wanted to give away for free, had they a mind.

He should have made it to the college, the rest of the lads said that many times over when he wasn't there. But his particular strain of intelligence was more geared towards craft and a certain street-wiseness than academic abilities – towards how to do things and get away with them when others would simply never have taken the chance.

Seamus didn't really mind following after someone else. He wasn't a natural leader of men, anyway – he knew that, deep inside. Besides, natural leaders who forever thrust themselves into the limelight were seen warts and all at various times, usually when they were under pressure. And Seamus couldn't afford ever to get himself into that position. After the initial few weeks of being called a scab and a tout in the college – though he hadn't touted on Doran and everyone knew it, because he wouldn't have got himself detention otherwise – he'd decided to let the taunts ride. He'd made a go at a few of the braver offenders, clipping one or two of them around the head now and then and telling them never to come near him again, but eventually that had only served to exacerbate the problem.

Others were still saying things about him, despite the passage of time, even though it was now mostly in hushed whispers. And when he'd found himself in a small-group conversation and someone was talking about something or other that wasn't as yet public knowledge, he'd often see them stopping and looking in his direction before hesitantly continuing, actually considering whether it was safe to talk when he was about. In the end, it didn't matter if he was the son of an alleged tout or an actual tout, the shit was sticking and there wasn't a damned thing he could do about it.

The slur against his name was there, ever present – an undercurrent of knowledge available to anyone who wanted to use it against him. No, he'd never become a leader, he decided. He didn't want ever to step into the spotlight and have his flaws exposed. Leaders made decisions, decisions sometimes went wrong, no matter the experience and accumulated craft of an individual, and then you got it in your face. Or behind your back. The abuse, the criticism, the aggro. Seamus didn't need the ugly facts of his father's life rearing their Medusa's head every time he opened his mouth. He'd more or less made a general plan to conform with everyone, to ride life out as a sheep for a few years or so, until everyone took him for the person that he was trying so hard to be. It wasn't much of a plan, he knew, and it had a few quite obvious pitfalls. But then his da had been a fucking simple bastard for doing what he did – they said he'd done it, so he might have done, and that was that – and he'd gone and got his son into this whole fucking mess as a result. Now it was his son's turn to get himself out of it in the best way he saw fit, and no one could blame him about how he went about it, could they?

Seamus was prepared to take some chances, of course, because he wasn't planning on being a complete invertebrate for the rest of his life. Though he would take only those chances that showed him off in a good light. Paddy Monaghan had soon got sick of the small, confined world of the resi and had got bored with running the town, especially in the winter, when the cold got you deep in the bones, no matter how many trees you attempted to burn down. It was inevitable, really. Although it was a relatively safe place to hide out and you only had the watchie to think about, it was also boring as hell. So one cold January day, when Seamus was a third-year – and during the second week of their second major dobbing expedition that term – he declared that he was going to lead the small troop on a mission.

He couldn't tell them what it was, he said, as they gathered one evening behind the shops and cracked a load of flagstones into chunks while waiting patiently for a Saracen – or, better still, a few jeeps with heads poking out the top of them – to come by. Seamus nodded along with the rest of them. He didn't mind running the town at times and hiding out in the derelict houses and factories, but he often came home mucked to the eyeballs and it was getting hard to explain it away. Saying you'd fallen in the field on the way home or that you'd got caught up in a game of Gaelic, sure how long was his ma going to fall for that one?

Besides, he was having enough difficulty in the mornings hanging back for the postman and intercepting letters from the school that were starting to enquire just how long he might have the malaria and was there any chance he'd be back before the new year. But he'd go anyway, he decided, because if he strayed from the safety of the group then they'd start talking about him.

It would be a few comments on the first day – nothing too sinister or dramatic – and most of them would likely be forwarded by Paddy Monaghan, who saw Seamus, who was larger and more gregarious than him, as some sort of a threat, though Seamus couldn't think why. But then it would probably thicken into a plot – a plot in which he was likely being offered three months off school if he told the dean where everyone hid out during the school day. Barney Ferguson would stick up for him, of course, he was sure of that, but then Barney Ferguson wasn't the largest boy in the world and he hadn't been much use up there in the college. And Jimmy Duffy, his closest friend out of the lot of them, would be in there for him like a shot. But it was Paddy Monaghan and Mick Deery who were the people who swayed the group. Two against two: they'd win either physically or verbally. Seamus Doherty's name would be mud in a week and he'd probably get lifted by the Boys and shot a week after that. Such was the way things sometimes went in war situations, Seamus supposed dismally; sometimes that was just the way it went.

The jeeps came, and two heads were sticking out of each. It was an unexpected bonus, because now there was more to aim at. Paddy Monaghan was one of the first of about thirty or so to run around the corner, game as ever. Casting fist-sized lumps of concrete in the air and watching with baited breath as they bounced off the vehicles, which brushed slowly through the hastily erected barricade across Central Drive. Seamus Doherty came out with the next batch of assailants. Carefully, he stuck a flame to the petrol-soaked rag on top of the milk bottle, keeping to a half-trot to ensure that he kept it away from his clothes and perfectly upright. The clatter of concrete against the first jeep had been exhilarating, and it must have scared the shite out of the driver, because he'd nearly swerved the thing into the wall that ran adjacent to the shops. The sight of the petrol bombs as they found the side of the second Land Rover and engulfed it for moments in a solid wall of flame was truly mind-blowing, however, and had the soldiers panicking like mad. Them trying to crawl back inside their jeep and pull over the hatch as the wall of flame approached – you could have laughed until you cried. But then that pleasure was short-lived. The speed of the jeep hurtling along Central and off towards Westway soon blew the flames into nothingness, and the soldiers were rarely hurt. Seamus and the rest of the group moved back behind the shops. There he and the rest of his friends sat down against the dirty, whitewashed wall, sweating freely, hearts beating heavily in their chests.

'They didn't even fire a single fuckin' rubber,' Barney said, the disappointment heavy in his eyes. 'I've got six of the things but I want a dozen, 'cause I'm thinkin' of sellin' them to the tourists. I'm gonna get them mounted in a silver case, maybe get a fiver for each one. Seen them over in Liam Case's house. They look great, engraved and everythin'.'

'They'll be back,' Mick Deery reassured him, with a grin. Mick was tall, impressively tall, and therefore worthy of respect by those as short as Barney. 'Sure that'll be the first of them for the evenin'. We'll set the bastards on fire, burn them out of this fuckin' place again, just like our das did a few years back.'

Paddy Monaghan undid his Crombie, his cheeks flushed. His face was angular, his nose thin, giving him the look of a hawk. He looked around him. 'So you're all on for tomorrow, then?'

There was a general consensus of nodding.

'And you, Seamy? You with us?'

Seamus shrugged and smiled inwardly. What were they planning to do? The way Paddy said it, you'd swear the fifteen-year-old was thinking of taking a bank. 'Sure.'

Paddy nodded, and smiled as the familiar sound of a Saracen grew steadily nearer. He stood and grabbed a few halfers, then put a beer bottle in each pocket. 'Tomorrow, then.' He ran out into the street. The halfers flew as a red sea against the jeeps, Paddy Monaghan's lost amongst so many.

*

Paddy peeked cautiously in through the kitchen window. The rest of the boys stayed close to the garden hedges in case a neighbour happened to be looking out across the gardens.

'She's out,' Mick Deery, the second-in-command, said. 'She always goes up the town on a Wednesday. Sure I know her routine off by heart. She won't be back until five, and by then we'll be long gone.'

'Ye sure?' Paddy Monaghan asked, cupping his hand against the lowest part of the window-pane, to allow him to get a better view of the living room.

Mick nodded. 'Sure she's my aunt, isn't she?'

Paddy nodded towards the next house. 'Anyone at that other nosy bastard's window?'

Jimmy Duffy shook his head. 'Nah, you're all right.'

Paddy rose quickly, backed off a little and then approached the back door at speed, sticking his Doc Marten square in the frame. The wood splintered a little but the door held firm in the frame and he ducked low, as if hit by a rubber bullet. 'Am I still all right?' Paddy asked.

Jimmy nodded. The second kick opened the door, and Jimmy regarded the neighbour's kitchen window pensively. Then he winked and nodded again. The boys filed quickly into the bungalow. Paddy flung himself down onto the sofa in the neat little living room, which was made for one, maybe two at the most. He smiled exultantly, savouring the luxury of the most comfortable dobbing place ever.

Seamus went to the fireplace and picked up a photograph. It was a family photograph – a memory that someone held dear enough to keep forever in view. 'Ye sure this is right?' he found himself asking. 'This is some wee pensioner's bungalow.'

'Ye not up for it?' Paddy asked, raising an eyebrow and looking around him at the faces there, as if surprised. 'Ye not got the balls for it, or what?'

Seamus shrugged. 'Whatever,' he found himself saying.

'Good, then go and get the fuckin' tea on. One sugar for me,' he said, laughing. 'Mick?'

Mick laughed. 'Two. And lots of toast, with stacks of butter, just the way me ma does it. Hey, and you, Barney, keep the fuck away from that window. We don't want the fuckin' neighbours getting wind of what we're up to.'

'What about fingerprints?' Jimmy Duffy asked, lying back on the sofa. Seamus moved into the kitchen, an uneasy feeling in his gut. He listened for Paddy's answer as he filled the kettle. Jimmy had his head screwed on where that sort of stuff was concerned. He'd seen a few boys getting kneecapped for stuff like this, and he'd told Seamus and the rest of them all about it. It was bad enough the cops getting you, he'd said, but when the Boys got you they shot you in the back of the knee. Or maybe in the calf, if they knew your family and didn't want to damage you too much. A graze and no more. But they still fuckin' shot you, Jimmy said, and it had to have hurt like hell – had to. So who would you prefer to lift ye: them or the cops?

'We wont be leavin' any fingerprints,' Paddy said, easily.

'Sure, the place is probably fuckin' clattered in them already,' Barney Ferguson said, almost conversationally, not eager to invoke anyone's wrath.

'We'll not be leaving any, and that's that,' Paddy said, with a finality that ended the conversation. There was a moment's silence, then he added, 'Hey, Seamy, you finished with that fuckin' toast yet, or what? And give me in some biscuits, if you find any – I'm fuckin' starvin. Me ma thinks I like livin' on mince and Doherty's sausages, for fuck's sake. She hasn't a fuckin' clue.'

They laughed. Seamus joined them moments later, a tray of tea and biscuits and nearly a loaf of toast all heaped on a plate, well buttered. They told him the joke and he laughed too.

Three

The big man in the doorway was one of the Boys, Seamus knew that as well as anyone else in the Creggan, though he didn't know his name. Jimmy Duffy had pointed him out one day as he was walking into the Telstar bar, saying that you didn't want to mess with him, ever, because he was as tough as they came. His mother knew the man, though, and she was standing talking to him now, arms folded, a serious scowl on her face, though her stance was otherwise relaxed. Seamus found his stomach churning at the thought of seeing them both locked in such an earnest conversation.

Mary smiled at the man, even had a bit of a laugh with him. Then the man turned and walked away up the steps to his car. He drove off in the direction of Fanad Drive and Seamus crossed the street from where he'd been standing outside the doorway of John Curran's house. Mary stepped back into the kitchen and Seamus followed her. The brown mince-and-potato stew was simmering in the grey pot on the cooker and he grabbed a bowl out of the cupboard and helped himself to his tea. The young boy ignored his mother's almost frosty glare and poured some HP sauce into the bubbling brown dinner. He lifted a piece of bread out of the loaf that was already on the table and dunked it into the stew.

'What was your man here about?' he asked, as casually as he could.

'He's askin' about the streets. Wants to know if we know

anythin' about the fire yesterday that was over in an old pensioner's bungalow over in Westway. Sais a couple of boyos were seen runnin' off in the direction of the reservoir after it took hold. The kids wouldn't let the fire engine through the barricades at first, and when they did they started stonin' them. Bloody disgrace, that carry on!' she said, thickly. 'Those firemen might all be Orangemen all right, but they're here to put out our fires too. Sure we probably have more bloody fires than them if ye think about it, the way this city's bein' burned to the ground of late. Anyway, the firemen couldn't save it and that wee pensioner Sally has lost everythin' she ever owned. Her whole life down the Swanee and her husband only passed away a year back. Now I know you've been hangin' around over there . . . '

'Hangin' around where, ma?' Seamus frowned and blew on a spoonful of stew to cool it, not lifting his head. 'I wasn't hangin' around anywhere.'

Mary paused for a second and produced a piece of paper. 'And I know you've been dobbin' school again, too, Seamus Doherty, because I got another note this mornin', so don't even think about lyin' to me. That's why ye ended up in Saint Pete's in the first place, you dobbin' the college all the time, and now you're at it up there. Sure it's all blockheads go there and now you're up there in the middle of them. You could have lasted at the college if you'd tried harder, I know you could. Now you're never goin' to make it anywhere in the world, ever.'

Seamus wiped his mouth and rose from his chair. He stood beside his mother and threw on his Wrangler jacket. At fourteen and a half years of age he was taller than her now and he didn't concern himself that she might slap him one any more.

'I didn't choose to get in the dean's bad books, ma, if you remember rightly. He thought I was a troublemaker, but then he didn't have to listen to the shite that I did, did he?' Seamus was going to elaborate but he held himself in check. They'd had this argument so many times over the last two years and he always ended up shouting and mentioning his da. And his ma always ended up crying. Today he couldn't be bothered with the hassle of it all.

Mary lit up a Park Drive. It was a recently acquired habit that the last few years of seeing her son disintegrate into something of a renegade and a bully had brought on. She would never have thought it possible. If you had asked her years ago about her son, she'd have told you that he had a great future ahead of him. Once the Troubles were over, of course, which they would be soon.

'Well then, maybe you shouldn't have confirmed it for him by goin' around punchin' so many people, eh?' Her tone was sarcastic, meant to cut. Perhaps because it was the only weapon she had left.

'I wouldn't have if they hadn't kept tryin' to be smart. And the dean givin' me detention for weeks at a time every time I missed a few days. Christ, I was gettin' interned and I'd have been in there for the rest of me life if he had his way. That was hardly goin' to encourage me to learn, was it?'

'He was actin' smart because he *was* smart, Seamus. He was tryin' to discipline you, nothin' else.'

'Aye, well he had it in for me. No one wants the son of a tout at their school, not even the dean.'

'I told ye never to say that again, Seamus.' Mary's voice softened. It always did before the tears came.

'Ye told me a lot of things, ma. Doesn't mean you're always right, does it?' Seamus looked into her eyes and saw the hurt there. 'Look, I'll be fine up in Saint Pete's,' he sighed. 'I'm far better off there, ye know it yourself, sure.'

'If ye ever go there, that is. And doin' all right's not enough to get you by in the world, Seamus Doherty.'

'Aye well, it'll do me. It'll have to.'

'You were always a smart kid,' Mary persisted, knowing that the argument was lost but having to try anyway. 'You could have made a go of it if you'd stuck with it. Do you think that dobbin' school half the time and only goin' when it suits ye is goin' to get you a job when you're older?'

'I won't ever get a job. I'm the wrong colour, aren't I? Me da said that. It was probably the only truthful thing I ever heard him say.' Seamus snorted indignantly. 'Him and his talk of honour and being a fuckin' hero and shit. Load of crap, that was. A load of bullshit. He never said anythin' else of any relevance ever.'

Mary moved in the way of the front door. 'You're entitled to your own opinion about your da. I'll allow ye that, because you're much too young to know what he was all about. But just tell me you had nothin' to do with that fire and the trashin' of that wee pensioner's bungalow,' she almost pleaded.

Seamus could have pushed her aside but he never would have done. Despite his anger at the world, and at his father, he would never have hurt his mother. To him there was a boundary – a thin line that you never crossed, despite your pain.

He dropped his gaze. 'I didn't do it, ma. I was over in the resi, sure, but I always go over there, you know that. Sure there's fu . . . ' He took a deep breath and tried to remember that his mother knew pain too, despite her strength. 'There's nothin' else to do in this shit-hole. The place is a slum. You've got your disco in the community centre on a Friday night and that's about it.'

His mother moved aside, though not before searching his face. Seamus felt that her gaze was an intrusion. He dropped his head, put his hand on the doorknob and turned it. Mary moved aside. 'Will ye be back soon?' she asked, softly.

'Aye, I will. I'm just goin' over to the shops for a while.'

'Stay out of trouble then, ye hear. There was a blatter of shootin' just a wee while back. Sounded like it came from Glenowen or somewhere.' He nodded complacently. 'You see those British bastards, you get the hell way from them, because you're nearly old enough for them to put away now. They brought two Saracens up the shops the other day – one from each end of the street – to catch the wee boys who'd been doin' a harmless bit of riotin'. Then they sent a snatch squad down Little Lane. Brits runnin' down like the blazes in their slippers, and they pulled a few of our boys into the back of the Saracens and gave them a wild trunchin' with their batons. Ye want to see that wee fella Brown's eyes. He was lucky he didn't lose them.'

Seamus nodded wearily. 'Aye, I'll not go anywhere near them, promise.'

*

Seamus tied the white handkerchief across his mouth. The smell of the vinegar-soaked cloth nearly made him gag, but then he readjusted his breathing in the way his father had taught him, so that he was breathing in and out through his mouth. It was starting to rain now and that was good because it would dampen the grey-white cloud-banks of CS gas down to a minimum. He looked around him and smiled.

The barricades were set. A burning bus at the end of Carrickray Gardens. Pallets, rubble, a few trees and a couple of old sofas over at the top of Westway. Two recently burnt-out cars, still smouldering, lying at an angle at the top of Fanad Drive. The Brits would have to come up along Iniscarn or up along Circular and down through Creggan if they wanted to reach the shops. Seamus picked up on a rumour going about that the lowest of the barricades over on Westway had been booby-trapped by the 'RA because a couple of the Boys were standing around on the corner of Central and making sure that no one went near them. It was a well-known fact that they usually didn't mind if you kept on adding any old debris to the barricades, because the bigger and higher they were, the better. It just made it harder for the Brits to get in, and the longer they were at the barricades the longer you could stone them, petrol-bomb them or even shoot at them, had you a mind.

But this time the Boys didn't want that, and speculation was rife. Someone else informed Seamus that, about an hour before, there'd been a few shots fired up at a patrol on the back roads from the derelict flats above the shops. Another rumour sweeping through the crowds which had gathered behind the boarded-up shops was that this evening the Brits would come in force, maybe approach from two or three directions at once. They'd bring the Forensics with them, maybe swamp the area with cops and raid half the houses in the Creggan estate.

Seamus moved among the crowds gathered there, searching for familiar clothes and shapes among the hooded characters who were manning the petrol-bomb factory. None of his friends had arrived yet. The mood at the shops was tense but jubilant anyhow, and Seamus talked with a few boys he knew merely by sight. They had dozens of crates of petrol bombs at the ready, one of them told him excitedly, because one of the boys had hijacked a petrol tanker earlier in the day as it made its way along William Street. The driver had got himself lost looking for the town's arterial Strand Road and one of the boys had smiled, got into the cab and taken him into the Bogside, where several masked men had relieved him of his burden. There was enough petrol now to last a week.

The hypothesis about the expected attack from multiple fronts proved to be correct. Two Sixers came hurtling up Westway shortly after six o'clock. These were multiple-personnel vehicles that each held twelve soldiers, including the crew, and were heavily armoured, with a turret on top. The first, Seamus would learn afterwards, hit the barricade at full speed, the driver thinking perhaps that the piled-up sofas, trees and wooden pallets were nothing more than a slight hindrance to his progress. Seamus was standing at the front of the shops when that occurred. He had an unlit petrol bomb in his hands and was busy watching three of the bigger and more heavily armoured Saracens turning out of Iniscarn and driving across the Bishop's Field when he heard the explosion. A loud cheer went up from behind the shops and the Saracens seemed to stop dead for a moment in the middle of the field before spurring quickly back into life. As they made their second assault, the crates of petrol bombs were moved into place and lumps of concrete or bottles were lifted, one in each hand, with two more tucked inside jackets or coats, for what most hoped – if they were lucky enough not to leave them wounded – would be a second assault.

There was a loud cheer from the front of the shops as the meaning of the explosion slowly registered. The loud report of rubber bullets being fired came from the direction of Westway perhaps only a second later. Moments after that, a thick pall of smoking cordite rose over the houses on the furthest end of Central Drive, as clear from the front of the shops as a black blanket of smoke.

'Christ, they're going mad over there!' someone said, above the noise. 'It sounds like a fuckin' war's taking place. Maybe we'd better get the fuck over there and help them.'

'Aye, well you think that's bad, look over there.' A hundred faces followed the path of a pointed finger. 'Those bastards aren't even using the fuckin' road. I think we'd better hang around here.'

Seamus recognised the voice instantly and went over to the hooded figure, lifted the corner of the balaclava and smiled. Paddy Monaghan returned a crooked grin and pulled the balaclava quickly back into place. 'You want those bastards to finger me, Seamus?'

Seamus laughed and turned his gaze back in the direction of the Bishop's Field. 'They'll be able to identify us all by the smell of the shite soon,' he said, giving a low whistle as the Saracens skidded over the field. 'Look at those bastards go. I don't think they're plannin' on stoppin'. They'll probably drive over the fuckin' top of us.'

'We'll be all right,' Paddy assured him. 'Sure, look at the stuff we have.'

The rain was hindering the progress of the Saracen tanks only slightly, the muck and sods flying out from under their back wheels as the loud, whining engines strained against the quagmire of upturned earth. A breathless Mick Deery came running over Central. He was wearing a hooded-up Parka jacket that left little of his face visible, but the boys knew him immediately by his height. His eyes were wide with excitement.

'They've overturned a fuckin' Sixer over on Westway,' he said, quickly. 'Christ, you want to see it. It's lyin' on its side with the smoke belchin' out of it and the fuckin' Brits are crawlin' out of it, dazed as fuck. Someone says one of them is dead and the other ones are firin' rubbers like fuck at anythin' that moves. You can't get near them, and a couple of the lads are trapped near the wee bungalows across from Melmore. Maybe we better go help them.'

'We're gonna need everyone we have here,' Monaghan said,

dispassionately. 'We're gonna have our own war going on in a minute and if we run off now they'll chase after us and catch us in the middle. At least if we stay here we can fuck off up through the shops towards the Heights and scatter.' He ducked behind the wall of the shops as the Saracen stopped about halfway up the Bishop's Field and a dozen or so troops piled quickly out of the back, their perspex shields held high. They moved hurriedly into formation as the first gauging missiles were thrown: a dozen shields in a row, visors down over their faces, rubber-bullet guns poking out from the side. And then they began to advance.

And the rioters – mainly teenagers, though there were some adults present – came out from behind the shops, their initial timidity at seeing that the robotic Saracens contained merely men – and often less than men, they'd later remark – forgotten. An airborne sea of broken concrete and glass sailed against them, still gauging distance like the cannons of old – some hitting, though most missing. And then the rioters would quickly duck behind the low red walls which ran parallel to the front of the shops, behind the barricades – behind anything that afforded cover. Keeping themselves low to the ground as the first volley of rubbers came hurtling at them. Knowing that the Brits were supposed to bounce the six-inch-long missiles off the ground in front of their targets because they'd said that was the way they always did it when answering the claims of the human rights people on *Scene Around Six* when some poor lad lost an eye or was knocked into a coma. But they never did that. Here on the ground it was a war and they didn't fight fair. Though neither did anyone – especially the IRA, it was argued by the English papers, when they were blowing Belfast and Derry into smithereens – and you could set all the rules you wanted, it just never happened like that.

Nothing was ever settled by words, Seamus knew that as well

as anyone in the Creggan. The army had been here since 1969 and, even as the politicians argued their causes backwards and forwards on the six o'clock news like petulant children – and you laughed whilst eating your tea as they got stuck into each other, even though it was deadly serious and each round of words often resulted in someone losing their life – the rioting continued. The same scenes played and replayed a thousand times until you thought you'd finally seen them all.

This time was no different from many others. The first wave of Brits with their gas masks on, seeming to crumble back under the assault of concrete and flame, then carefully and slowly picking their way across the rubble-strewn field under the smokescreen of cordite and CS gas. The rioters stumbling back as the gas stung their eyes, as their ammunition ran out, as they sought the solace of the back of the shops where the air was fresh and you couldn't hear the bangs reverberating so loudly in your ears. Where twenty or more younger boys were busy in their makeshift petrol-bomb factory, hurriedly churning out the ammunition for the next assault. And sometimes the Brits would achieve their aim and the barricades would tumble. Or sometimes one of the Brits would get himself set on fire and you'd hear, even above the cheers, the approach of the green army ambulance with the red cross on the side. And the masked rioters would stone the ambulance as it made its way off the battlefield and would cheer, not giving a hoot about rules, because the Brits had assaulted the Knights of Malta on Bloody Sunday and, fuck them, they'd started it!

Sometimes the Brits would clip a few boys in the stomach or the legs with their rubber bullets and maybe they'd snatch a few of the ringleaders and give them the kicking of their lives or take them away and get them a few months in the Crum' – the prison on the Crumlin Road – or in St Pat's, the juvenile offenders' centre in Belfast. Or sometimes a Brit would stray from the pack and get himself kicked senseless by the baying mob before his comrades could get him out.

Seamus had seen it all and he was still only fourteen and a half. It was a game of sorts, and they all played it. A game that was sometimes dangerous, sometimes fatal – and often exhilarating. Sometimes you won and sometimes they did. On that particular winter's day the Brits fell back from the shops shortly after seven o'clock and just before it was getting really dark, because it was common knowledge that if they had waited any longer they'd have had more than a few petrol bombs to worry about. The snipers would have come out again and they'd have had a real war on their hands. All this to gather up a few bits of forensic evidence on somebody that they'd never get anyway.

Someone must have decided that it wasn't worth the hassle of it all on that particular day – someone in Brit HQ with a bit of common sense. Because they pulled their Saracens off the Bishop's Field and raced them down Iniscarn, past the enthralled audience of the wee old men and women who had gathered there, some with cups of tea in hand, to watch the battle. Away from the main front of the riot and back to the barracks to recuperate and ready themselves for another day. At least, it seemed that way to almost everyone gathered there at the front of the Creggan shops.

It took a while for the boys at the shops to cotton on to what they were doing. But Paddy Monaghan was one of the first to catch on. They weren't going home. They were going over to Westway, where the battle must have turned, to concentrate on getting their beleaguered men back to the RUC and army base on the Strand Road.

The crowds turned to run over in the direction of Westway when they heard this. It was perhaps only some three or four hundred yards away, and the general idea was to hinder the evacuation and maybe notch up a few more enemy injuries. From there, the reports of the rubber-bullet guns were still as loud as ever. Seamus ran behind the shops and grabbed two petrol bombs, then moved quickly around the corner to hurry across Central Drive. But as he did so, a figure stood in his way.

He recognised the figure immediately as that of Dan McGeady, the man who had become know to him over the years as his father's commanding officer in the early Troubles. At first Seamus thought he was in the man's way – that perhaps the man wanted to grab a load of petrol bombs too and make his way over to the riot. That maybe the man had forsaken his Armalite for a while to get himself involved in a bit of the basic, grass-roots war. But the man stepped in his way a second time and Seamus stood upright.

'Seamus Doherty?' the man said, casually.

'Aye.'

'I'd like a word, if you have a second.' Cordial, polite.

'I was just on my way over to Westway. Did ye hear the news? The Brits have a few men down over there and . . . ' Excited.

'If you have a second.' A trace of strength in the voice, though nothing too forceful. The man placed a hand on his shoulder. Seamus baulked. The man wasn't asking him, he was telling him. The young boy's eyes widened as two dark-clad, hooded figures stepped around the corner from the direction of the Telstar, one leading the lanky and dishevelled Mick Deery by the scruff of the neck. Dan McGeady feigned indifference at what was happening. He turned the young boy away and made to lead him in the direction of Carrickray Gardens.

'Do ye want me to call an ambulance, Dan?' one of the men asked, almost throwing Mick Deery to the ground. Dan McGeady removed his hand from the young boy's shoulder, then pointed with the other hand at his watch, tapped it and flashed his fingers twice in a signal. Ten minutes, Seamus guessed he meant. Then the older man shrugged casually, placed his hand on the boy's shoulder once more and turned to lead him away.

'You'd better take that mask off,' Dan McGeady said, easily. 'I don't fancy comin' across a stray patrol and havin' to explain that to them, do you?'

Seamus shook his head and removed the handkerchief. He coughed as they passed by the Bishop's Field, where the stench of cordite and CS gas still hung thick in the air. The gas stung at his eyes a little but he didn't rub them, knowing that this would have made them worse. Dan McGeady slowed as they left the thinning mists behind them. Seamus startled as, suddenly, a gunshot sounded. He made to turn but the older man prevented him from doing so. Seamus felt his shoulders sagging and his legs about to give way beneath him, but he walked on. The man patted his shoulder reassuringly and led him into a house about halfway up the street. Seamus hesitated as they approached the doorway.

'I only want a word,' the older man said, lightly. Seamus nodded, completely unconvinced. His heart was beating a mile a minute, trying to break free from his chest. His legs were barely able to function as he stepped in through the door. The older man led him into the living room and Seamus looked around. It wasn't abandoned, as he had feared, nor was it filled with a thousand devices of torture. It was an ordinary room in an ordinary house, neat and well decorated. The only thing that was out of place was a coat strewn lengthways across the sofa. Dan McGeady directed Seamus to take a seat on one of the armchairs, the one in the furthest corner of the room. The young boy found himself breathing hard as he sat down, licking nervously at his lips.

'I knew your da, kid,' the older man started, settling back in the other armchair. The one nearest the door. The man was relaxed, acting as if they'd known each other for years and were the best of friends. 'I was . . . '

'His . . . '

'His friend, kid, if you want to give me a title,' the man interrupted, sharply, managing a thin smile. 'His friend, and nothin' more than that, ye understand?'

Seamus nodded slowly, biting his upper lip.

'Good man, your father,' Dan McGeady continued, settling back into the chair, his head against the rest. He produced some cigarettes, lit one and offered one to Seamus. The boy shook his head. Dan McGeady shrugged. 'No matter what some people thought of him, he was one of the best men I ever knew. Me and him went through a lot of things together. I can't tell ye what – ye know the score. But take it from me, he was fearless, game as a badger. He had his principles, his morals. Sure he might have drank a bit too much at one time but then where's the harm in that, eh.' He eyed Seamus intently. 'Ye drink, yourself?'

Seamus shook his head gingerly, hoping the lie was concealed.

'That's good, kid. Time enough until you're thirty.'

'Did they . . . shoot Mick Deery dead there now?' Seamus asked, his voice fractured. The question was out of his mouth before he realised what he was saying. He frowned and dropped his head.

The older man blew off a smoke ring and watched it slowly whirl into a disfigured figure of eight before he blew it away. 'Dead?' he laughed. 'Christ, I hope not.' His friendly eyes became flint all of a sudden. 'But they hurt him a little, sure they did. He's been bad, Seamus. You've all been bad,' he added, pointedly. 'Though Mick's been worst than most. He's been doin' a bit of house-breakin', slashin' car tyres up and stuff. And he's supposed to have mugged an old man the other night down in Rosemount, beat him up real bad. Real, real bad. You know anythin' about that?'

Seamus shook his head quickly, truthfully.

'Aye, well I'll give you the benefit of the doubt on that one. "Yet I shall temper so justice with mercy, as may illustrate most them fully satisfied, and thee appease." The older man saw the look of confusion on the youth's face. 'Ye know who said that, Seamus?'

Seamus shook his head again, his mouth dry.

'Milton. *Paradise Lost*. Great wordsmith,' the older man declared brightly. 'Seems they don't give the lads the same education as they did in my day. Still, where was I at?' He paused a second and raised an eyebrow, contemplative. 'Oh aye,' he said, casually. 'Let's talk about this burnin' down of an old pensioner's bungalow and with it everythin' that she'd ever owned in the world. Fuck, that's bad too, kid! Real bad.'

Seamus felt his chest constricting. He went to speak, to protest his innocence, maybe to say it had been Paddy Monaghan's or maybe Mick Deery's idea, but the man put a finger to his own lips.

'I'd rather you didn't say anythin' about that, son. I don't want to ruin my first impression of you. You look like a good enough kid, y'know.'

Seamus found that he was labouring for breath. The man was right. It wouldn't have been so wise, he supposed, for the son of a tout to start acting like a tout. He wasn't like his da – wasn't ever going to be like his da. He'd decided that a long time back.

The man blew another blue-grey smoke ring into the air, as if he was suddenly bored. 'I'm hopin' to be a pensioner myself some day, kid,' he said suddenly. 'Hopin' to maybe live until I'm a hundred and thirty in a nice wee place in Donegal or maybe Cork – haven't decided yet. Haven't got the money for it now, sure, but it's a bit of a pipe dream of mine.' He smiled thinly and his gaze was upon Seamus once more, his eyes flinty and hypnotic. 'And I sure wouldn't like a load of little bastards like your lot burnin' the fuck out of it just because you were playin' hookey and you had fuck all to do of an afternoon, know what I mean?'

Seamus nodded, eyes wide, the pain in his chest increasing.

The older man nodded casually and took a deep drag of his cigarette. 'Aye, I knew your da, kid,' he frowned. 'I know your mother. Good woman, comes from a great republican family. Doesn't particularly like me all that much, but then that's her prerogative and I don't really give a flyin' fuck who likes me, if the truth be known. Because that's the mantle I've donned, kid. The cloak I've been given, nah, *forced* to wear. Someone has to do somethin' to bring this place out of the shite and I guess I've a part to play. And as Milton recognised, it's far better to reign in hell than serve in heaven.' He shrugged. 'But that's enough chewin' the fat. Go on over there to the sofa and lift that jacket up.'

Seamus rose with some trepidation. Was Dan McGeady going to shoot him in the back, he wondered, and then leave him here in a puddle of blood for some wee woman to find when she came home? He reassured himself quickly as he approached the sofa. First of all, the older man hadn't kicked the door in. He'd walked in here along with Seamus and someone had to have seen them, so the man was hardly going to do anything stupid, was he? But then again, a second voice cut in to his thoughts, who the hell was going to squeal on him if he did. Everyone knew who he was and they'd have to go on the run to Buncrana or even further south if they even thought about telling on him. Seamus shivered and pushed the thoughts aside. He quickly lifted the coat. He nearly fell over as he saw a shotgun underneath.

'Sit down again,' the man said.

Seamus sat down in the armchair, unable to take his eyes off the gun.

'That's yours, kid, if you really want it.'

'Mine?' Seamus's eyes widened.

The man smiled thinly and nodded.

'What do ye mean?'

McGeady laughed at Seamus's frown. 'Oh, I'm not offerin' it to ye as a fuckin' gift – not in that sense, anyhow,' he said, grimly. 'It's what you'll be gettin' – you and the fuckin' rest of them – if you ever pull a stunt like that again.'

Seamus pulled his eyes away from the gun and realised that the man was standing, his eyes piercing and seemingly as black as pitch. Seamus felt the goose pimples rising on his arms and quickly became aware that the room seemed suddenly very cold.

'Ye understand me, kid?' The man moved towards the window and pulled apart a couple of slats of the blind, something in the street having caught his atQtention. Seamus nodded, said 'Aye' and was sure he heard the siren of an ambulance in the distance, though he couldn't be sure. 'This is for your da and your ma, no one else. That wee woman over at Westway has fuck all left in the world and she's in the middle of a nervous breakdown as we speak. It's bad enough the fuckin' Brits racin' their fuckin' armoured cars up and down her street and shootin' at her sons and daughters, without toe-rags like you burnin' her house down. Now go on, get the fuck out of here!'

Seamus rose hesitantly from the easy chair. Before he made it to the door the man said, 'Hey!'

Seamus turned, though he didn't think he'd be able to.

'I was watchin' ye out at the riots this evenin', kid,' the older man said, easily. His original calm manner had returned; his eyes were brown once more. In the waning evening light that streamed in through the blinds, they even seemed to contain a little warmth. Seamus didn't know which was scarier. 'Ye were good, very sharp off the mark, you all were. With people like you on our side we might just have a chance of winnin' this fuckin' war, ye know?'

Seamus nodded.

'But ye need an education too, kid. Most people seem to forget that we're tryin' to beat the bastards on all fronts. We want the same as them, therefore we need to be as smart as them. Riotin's all right, sure, and it makes its own point. But havin' brains is where it's really at.' The older man pointed at his head. 'Havin' a bit of savvy, ye couldn't beat it. Do ye get me drift?'

Seamus nodded once more. It was all he could manage, as his legs were about to give way.

'Good.'

The man inclined his head towards the door, motioning him to leave. Seamus closed the front door very easily behind him and moved into the street, shivering as he remembered that the man was probably looking out at him. Out here, people were coming and going, able to move out of their houses now that the rioting had stopped. Things had returned quickly to what now passed as normality, the way they always did, but Christ, the young boy could hardly move his feet. He took a couple of deep breaths and walked slowly in the direction of the shops, listening for the familiar reports of the rubber-bullet guns or the comforting crack of a Garande rifle or an M16 in the darkening night. Nothing, he thought dismally, as the power came slowly back to his legs. The rioting was over and the rubble-strewn battlefield had been left for the men from the council to clean up come the early hours of the following morning.

After a minute Seamus found himself running in the direction of the back of the shops. There was a crowd there, the familiar figure of his friend Jimmy Duffy amongst them.

Jimmy turned and saw him coming, his pasty features whiter now than ever. He nodded grimly at the large pool of blood that had set some of the concrete dust into an almost obscene red cement.

'Is he going to be all right?' Seamus asked, in a hushed whisper.

'I dunno a fuck. The bastards didn't even call an ambulance for ages,' Jimmy whispered back. 'Someone said that the Boys that did it had never done it before and they didn't roll up the legs of his jeans or fuck all. And they left him lyin' for ages, so it's probably infected. Sure nobody heard the shot above the noise and everyone was over the street watchin' the Brits pull that fuckin' Sixer out of there with a crane.' Jimmy shook his head, eyes wide, unfocused, staring at nothing. 'Aye, he was lyin' there for ages.'

Seamus turned and made to walk away. 'Where are you goin'?' Jimmy asked him, pensively.

'I'm goin' fuckin' home, and I'd do the same if I was you. The Boys might be lookin' for ye. They just had a chat with me . . . '

'You're fuckin' jokin'.'

'Do I look as if I'm fuckin' jokin'?' Seamus walked across Central Drive in the direction of Lislane and Jimmy followed him. 'I'll tell ye about it tomorrow. If you're still about,' he added, ominously. Jimmy paled visibly. 'And tell that fuck-wit Monaghan to stay the hell away from me from now on,' Seamus added, angrily. 'He'll get us all killed someday, ye can bet your fuckin' life on it.'

Jimmy nodded uncertainly. 'I'll see you in the mornin' at the resi then, eh?' His tone was fearful.

'Nah, I don't fuckin' think so. I'll see ye in school. We'd be better off hangin' around where people can see us for a while.'

Jimmy Duffy nodded uncertainly. Then he turned and ran off up Lislane at speed.

Four

His mother hadn't all that much to say to him on his return, though the worried look on her face was real enough. She was sitting in the kitchen, a cup of tea warming her hands. She seemed to be staring at the table, perhaps beyond it, doing nothing much. She got up after a time, to stand silhouetted against the window, the sombre shadows reflecting her mood.

'They reckon he'll make it.'

'Aye.' Seamus poured himself a cup and made a play at drinking it.

'Though he might lose the leg. Somethin' about an infection, or somethin'.'

'Aye, so.'

'They went up to that Paddy Monaghan boy's house too, ye know. 'Cause his ma's just after phonin' me and she's in a right state. Says that . . . '

'Aye, ma, for Christ's sake. I get the drift.'

Mary didn't move a muscle. She'd long ago given up trying to knock the cursing out of him. 'I'm just tellin' ye. Ye better just lie low for a while, son, keep your nose clean. That Francie Burke boy wasn't jokin' when he called round earlier on, and he sais what he sais.'

'What did he say?'

'It doesn't matter. He was just right when he sais it, that's all ye have to know.'

'He was sayin' stuff about me and it doesn't matter?' Seamus tried to keep from rising and storming out of the door. '*How* doesn't it matter?'

'I've been told to tell you to keep your nose clean, son – that's all that matters. Ye do that and everything'll be grand. That Dan McGeady boy . . . so help me God, he makes my skin crawl and I can't bear being in the same room as the bastard!' Mary made the sign of the cross. 'But he came over here today too and he says that if ye keep your head low everything'll . . . '

' . . . be fine. Aye, sure ye sais that already.'

'Aye, well ye don't seem too fuckin' concerned about it all,' she said, angrily. 'It's your legs we're talkin' about here – maybe your life. I've done me best for ye. My word used to have a little weight with them and you. It hasn't had any the last few years.' Mary looked almost sorrowful. She took a deep breath and said nothing for a moment. 'You'll do that, then?' she added, uncertainly. 'For me?'

Seamus nodded almost reluctantly. 'Aye.' His tea was cold but he sipped at it anyway, to stop himself from saying anything else.

Mary moved away from the window and tousled his hair. 'I'm poppin' into Sadie's house for an hour. You'll probably be in bed when I get back, won't ye? You havin' school in the mornin' and all.' Hopeful.

Seamus lifted his head and noticed the frown. He nodded wearily. 'Aye, I was for doin' that anyway.'

She was smiling when she closed the front door behind her.

*

He was five minutes early the next morning. Jimmy Duffy was hanging around one of the gardens about halfway up Circular

Road, looking furtively around him as he dragged the life out of a Park Drive. He twisted his face up bitterly as the smoke from the unfiltered fag bit deep into his throat.

'He's gonna live,' Jimmy said. He seemed pale and somewhat drawn, Seamus decided, as if maybe he hadn't had a good night's sleep.

'Were the Boys up with ye?'

'Aye.' Jimmy trod his cigarette butt into the flagstones, grinding it angrily into nothingness. Seamus didn't bother pursuing the Boys' methods. The result had obviously been the same.

He nodded, lit up a fag and flung his school bag casually over his back. 'I think we'd better stay away from Monaghan for a few weeks.' He saw the concern on Jimmy's face. 'Well, it's up to you. I know what I'll be doin', anyhow. That buck eejit's gonna end up the same way as Deery, and I'm not stickin' me neck out for him any more.'

Jimmy had nodded and they'd left it at that.

*

The several weeks that Seamus had suggested went by and the height of their mischievousness was the riots down at the shops. Paddy Monaghan didn't show his face during all that time. At first that had worried Seamus, he confided to Barney Ferguson and Jimmy Duffy one night as they went for a walk out to the resi. But then he reasoned that it was because Paddy was probably concerned that a few of the Boys were still keeping an eye on him.

Barney Ferguson had dismissed that suggestion immediately. The Boys had got far more to worry about than Paddy Monaghan, he'd say. What with those black bastard'ne Brits droppin' into people's houses at any time of the day they fuckin' felt like – them shoutin' and screamin' their heads off, kickin' the doors in on top of ye, shuttin' the curtains and raidin' the place and nobody knowin' a thing of what they were at – sure we all had enough to worry about, did we not?

And it didn't matter a damn to them if ye were innocent or not, just so long as they got their body count. So everyone had enough to worry about without getting overly concerned about Paddy Monaghan. Those RUC bastards all anonymous in their blue overalls and you not allowed to follow them about from room to room. Sure what kind of a fuckin' way was that to go about doin' anythin'? They could plant anythin' they wanted on ye. And it didn't have to be much, because ye were guilty until you were proved guilty here in the North – or innocent until ye were proved Irish, as someone had once said on TV – and who'd believe ye were innocent anyhow if it was your word against the law? They found as much as a rubber bullet, the smaller boy assured the others, and that was you, interned forever. Them and their Special Powers Act. Christ, they were plantin' the stuff half the time in the homes of innocent men, sure, and even the civil-rights people were saying it on the news. And they were givin' off about the powers the Brits had, sayin' they could lock anyone away forever like the Count of Monte Cristo or the Man in the Iron Mask if they had a mind and no one could do a thing about it. But no one was listening any more. His da had told him that not even the people who were doing the talking these days were listening any more, not even to themselves.

He'd heard a good one about Peter Brady over on Blighs Lane though, he said, laughing, quite unaware from the looks on the other two boys' faces that his arguments were more centred on cataloguing the atrocities of the Brits and the RUC than on settling their doubts about the older boy. Seems Peter had had two Armalites in the house. So the Brits go in and they search the place but they find fuck all and then they leave. Peter's waving away to them as they go, wishing them all a good day, nice as ye like. Barney laughs even louder, getting ready to deliver the punchline. Seems they'd come in and shut the curtains, same as usual, but Peter'd had the guns stashed in behind two panels he'd built, one on either side of his living-room window. Right behind the curtains, Barney said gleefully. It was the only place they never searched during a raid. Was he a smart cunt, or what?

And they'd all laughed for a while, their concerns about Paddy Monaghan and the attentions of the Boys lost in their admiration of someone called Peter Brady whom two of them didn't even know. And then they had raced down through the pines and into the woods behind Glenowen, doing a few half-hearted jumps and paring a few branches with a couple of Stanley Knives they'd borrowed from Jimmy's da without telling him. But when they were exhausted and flopped down on the grass, the conversation eventually returned to the whereabouts of Paddy Monaghan.

Jimmy said he'd seen him out with wee Eileen Flannagan a few nights back. He'd been in a car going over Iniscarn Crescent, and Jimmy had thought it might have been a taxi, but he wasn't really sure. Anyhow, Paddy had smiled and waved, so he must have been all right, mustn't he? And Jimmy had also heard from one of the lads in the school that Paddy was hanging around with Dan McGeady's oldest son, Eddie. But that wasn't a fact and they'd never know until they talked with Paddy himself. Which they probably would do soon enough, because Creggan was a small place and they were bound to run into him eventually, weren't they?

They'd all nodded, calmed by the fact that Paddy was riding

wee Eileen and he was probably too shagged out to go anywhere, her being a quare wee half who apparently rode like a Trojan, because half of the town had been at her. Though no one was going to say that to Paddy, Jimmy said, because he was probably in love with her, would probably end up marrying her, that was the kind of him. Sure he might come out in a few days' time, they decided between them, when the power had returned to his lower limbs. And maybe he'd even get around to making a guest appearance over at the riots, they all agreed.

They'd laughed then, happy with that thought, because Paddy was a wild man and that was the sort of him to go missing for weeks and maybe months at a time, though no one there could actually recall when he'd done such a thing last. Sure he wasn't really missing anything anyhow, they agreed. The riots had calmed down the last while back because some wee boy from the Catholic Gobnascale area of the Waterside had got shot in the forehead with a baton round down off William Street and he was still lying unconscious in the Royal Victoria in Belfast, critical but stable, though they'd had to perform some sort of skin graft on him and he'd never be the same again. That would keep it relatively calm for a week or two, though things would be back to normal when something else even more startling hogged the news.

Seamus didn't know it then, but it would be nearly two years before the four lads met up again as a group. The other three lads still hung around with each other throughout that time, however, though by now it wasn't anywhere near as often. If anything, it was Seamus and Jimmy who maintained the closest relationship, though the three still spent their free time over in the resi, down at the disco in the community centre on Fanad Drive, and rioting – though now on occasions they even ventured down the town to 'Aggro Corner' in William Street or sometimes the Little

Diamond, attending the riots there to break the monotony.

Derry town centre had changed over the last few years and it would have been almost unrecognisable to, for example, the man who was returning to his homeland after being abroad for a number of years. Like Belfast and most of the major towns in the North, the heart of Derry city was now sealed in behind iron palisades, barbed wire, and brick- and sandbag-reinforced checkpoints, the entire place one big garrison fortress that allowed civilians just a little more access than an ordinary barracks. *An Phoblacht* declared that the Provisional IRA were fighting a war on several fronts, one of which was economic. The British papers declared that their forces too were fighting a war and that they too had an economic agenda to pursue. Though sometimes, when Seamus stared down the rubble-strewn side streets on the town's perimeter, with their bricked-up and mostly derelict houses, he wondered where all the money had gone and whether the economy hadn't just gone and died and maybe they'd all forgotten to bury it.

Like so many others, all he knew for certain was what he saw with his own eyes. Derry's day-to-day commerce had been disrupted by that war, with, at one stage in the Troubles, most of the city-centre businesses being temporarily or completely put out of action, and the remainder sealed up with metal grilles on the windows and doors. The disruption had been brought about by car bombs placed near – or sometimes inside – military targets, by bombs targeting specific buildings, by hoax calls, by rioting, by the planting of incendiary devices and the devastation they caused and the looting that often took place afterwards, by random shooting incidents, by killing, by dying.

The immediate outskirts of the city proper were marked by the remnants of factories and half-tumbledown houses, leaving the city reminiscent, the young boy would often hear older people say, of Coventry during the Blitz. The destruction was the combined result of economic deprivation and disruption by all sides. The evidence was clearly visible in the bricked-up factories; in the blackened tarmacadam and asphalt of nearly all the main roads, which were distorted and stained by burnt-out cars, lorries and vans; in the disused hoardings, that hadn't had a sign posted on them in years; in the cracked pavements and dilapidated shops, outside the cordon, which the council hadn't enough money either to repair or to raze to the ground; in the numerous heavily armed police and army foot patrols, the fortified lookout posts, the suspicious looks and often laboriously drawn-out enquiries concerning your personal details and your intended destination as you entered the city compound. The place was perhaps reminiscent of Saigon at the height of the Vietnam War, except for the fact that, in Derry, there was a somewhat strained feeling of normality in between the violent clashes.

Which the people somehow managed to maintain, with a resiliency that showed the strength of ancient peoples. There were many examples of that resilience, and the boys would laugh about them often. Like the way the rioters had learned to fire heavy catapults and ball-bearings at the army from a safe distance, thereby avoiding the stinging retort of the plastic and rubber bullets; like the way they strung fishing gut across country roads in an attempt to decapitate the Brits who stuck their heads out of the tops of jeeps as they drove past; or like the way they used sugar or thin strips of rubber inside the petrol bombs so that the flames would stick like inferior napalm to the missile's target. Or like when the riots were in full progress and the rioters were, say, attacking the small post on the corner of William Street and Great James Street from both avenues, you'd often hear a shout that some wee woman with a white handkerchief was coming through to go about her business. And the rioters would stop throwing their bottles and their bricks, the army would stop firing their rubbers or their latest weapon, the plastics, and they'd all let the wee woman through. And when she was through and everyone had made sure she was OK, someone would shout that everything was fine and the riot would start again, the hatred and the anger there just as strong as if it had never been interrupted. And at six o'clock on most days, give or take a few minutes, the rioters would go and get their tea and the Brits would go and get theirs. And they'd all be back at it around seven – if it was light enough or if they could sustain their anger and hatred – burning off their calories until midnight or long after.

Though it wasn't all riots. Sometimes, despite the over-whelming influences of their peers, they'd forsake the riots for an almost proper social life by going to the disco in the Creggan Community Centre on Fanad Drive. And every now and then one or more of the three of them would hook up with a wee bit of stuff who made them believe the world was wonderful, despite its often more serious realities. Seamus was sixteen and a half, though he looked much older, and he had got himself a place in Springtown Training Centre now. He'd been there a month and was an apprentice painter and decorator in the making. Jimmy Duffy was driving a van for Doherty's bakery, and Barney Ferguson – the only one of them who'd passed more than two O levels – was thinking of going over to a university in Liverpool as soon as he'd done his As.

It was only because of a chance meeting that Jimmy Duffy had one day with Neil McGuigan – one of Paddy Monaghan's nearest neighbours up on Creggan Heights – that the three friends realised how long it was since they'd seen each other last. That same night they were sitting in Seamus's house with a carry-out of beer, a gathering that was more by accident than design. His mother was out, though where she'd gone she hadn't said – but she had mentioned that he shouldn't worry if she was late. Now quite often she never said where she was off to, and Seamus couldn't ask without her asking him the same question when he went out. He didn't want to tell her as much these days, though he could think of no particular reason why. His privacy just seemed to matter more and more to him the older he got. Still, Seamus didn't mind his mother's refusal to elaborate on her comings and goings. They were her own business, after all. And it would allow him to have a few cans on the sly. She'd never smell the alcohol – she was long past trying to catch him out. Which was good. And when he thought about it, he sincerely believed then that their mutual silence was quite normal.

Jimmy Duffy had come down to Seamus's house shortly before eight that night, but neither he nor Barney was stopping long, as they were on their way to a disco in the Everglades Hotel, which was on the other side of the bridge. They hadn't planned this get-together, because Seamus had told Jimmy during the week that he had a date too, but now, due to unforeseen circumstances, it was off. Still, they'd called in on the off chance, because they'd been going this way anyway.

Seamus wasn't really in the mood for seeing his two best friends all spruced up. He was lying there in front of the television feeling sorry for himself because Una Mahon, a girl he'd been seeing on and off for the last six months – though more off than on – had phoned him and told him that they were finished, and she hadn't really given him a reason for splitting up. She'd merely said he was too pushy about trying to get her to have sex with him, that she wanted to remain a virgin until she'd met Mister Right. He'd told her that, according to all the lads up at the training centre, she wasn't a virgin before she met him and there wasn't much chance of her becoming one now. Then he'd hung up the phone, feeling for all the world as if his life was at an end. As it was, he just skipped over the reasons when Jimmy asked what had happened to have him in such a foul mood on a Saturday night, giving the two of them only the scantiest details of why *he* had finished with *her*.

For what seemed to be a very long time, Jimmy and Barney had sat and looked at him in silence, small hints of doubt in their eyes, though they had said nothing. 'I hear Paddy Monaghan's supposed to have been sayin' some stuff about ye,' Jimmy said, eventually.

Which was a somewhat childish thing to say, but Jimmy was like that at times. Normally Seamus would have laughed, but tonight he wasn't in the mood for anyone. 'Like what?' he asked. Thoughts of Mick Deery lying behind the Creggan shops two years ago suddenly came back to him, the memory as strong as ever. He shivered. It was amazing where time went, he thought suddenly. Mick had been in hospital for four weeks after the shooting and it had been touch and go whether he would lose the leg. He hadn't, in the end, and they'd all been grateful about that, but then that had been it. They'd all gone on with their lives as if he had never existed. Then one day about two months after that they'd heard that his mother had sent him off to Belfast to stay with an aunt for a little while to get him out of the way of the riots. They'd all laughed when they'd heard that. Belfast? Sure up there was worse than here in Derry, for God's sake, and it wasn't getting any better, despite the passing of the years. And then that little while had also turned into years. They'd all gone on with their lives and they'd never seen Mick Deery since.

'He sais that he heard you're runnin' around blamin' him for what happened to Deery,' said Jimmy.

Seamus started to laugh. Paddy's best friend had nearly lost a leg because of his own stupid ideas, though Paddy had been equally at fault, in Seamus's eyes. All right, so he'd told one or two people that he thought Paddy was responsible for it, but so what? Everyone had agreed with Seamus that Paddy was at fault – at least everyone Seamus had said it to.

'Fuck, that was nearly two years back, maybe more,' Seamus shot back. 'Why's he draggin' that shit up now?'

'Neil sais Paddy thinks that you blamed him for settin' the bungalow on fire. Sais you told it to a few people who he'd rather hadn't of heard it. Now one of them is askin' him questions and it was goin' to set his chances way back.'

'Chances at what?'

Jimmy and Barney looked at each other and shrugged. 'Fuck knows,' Barney said, sipping at his can.

'He did set it on fire, though I haven't mentioned that for ages,' Seamus retorted. 'At least, it was him told us to go on home, and that him and Mick would be along in a minute.' In a restrained show of temper, he kicked a cushion onto the new carpet his mother had got for a steal from the Pakistani who came round the houses giving people tick. 'Sure he was the one said about not leavin' the fingerprints. It was his fuckin' idea, wasn't it?'

Barney shrugged. 'He sais you sais it to that girl you're goin'... you *were* goin' out with, sorry.' There was a sheepish expression on Barney's face as Seamus frowned darkly. 'She sais it to someone else and it got back to Eddie McGeady's da or somethin',' he added, quickly. 'And it's probably him that's askin' the questions.'

'Ah shite!' Seamus said, with a nod. He remembered suddenly

that he had said it after all. Trying to impress Una Mahon so he could get the knickers off her, but she wouldn't bite, not even after six months. Christ, he thought then, he'd gone and wasted six months of his life! He bit the corner of his lip. 'So, erm, what's happenin' about it?'

Jimmy nodded uncertainly. 'Nothin', as far as I know. I think he talked Dan McGeady into lettin' it go. Said it was just someone blowin' their mouth off. But Paddy'll tell ye himself. He says we can go up to his house tomorrow night, bring a few cans. Sounds friendly enough, him sayin' that, doesn't it?'

Seamus shrugged and pursed his lips. 'Aye, maybe.'

'Don't think he wants to make an issue out of it, 'cause Neil sais he'd rather ye were talkin' to him than about him, us all bein' old mates and stuff.'

'Since when did Paddy Monaghan care that I was still talkin' to him? Sure we never see each other any more.'

Jimmy got up. 'Neil sais that Paddy sais we all know too much about each other ever to be enemies.'

Seamus nodded, though he said nothing. Jimmy went to the mirror in the hall to fix his hair. Then he and Barney bade their farewells, told him to keep his chin up, because there were more fish in the sea – and that one Una Mahon was nothing but a slag anyway – and they'd left as quickly as they'd arrived. Seamus lay there thinking. Paddy Monaghan was all right in his own way but there were times when he didn't give a fuck about anyone but himself. What did he think Seamus was going to do – go straight up to Dan McGeady and squeal on him, or something? Seamus paled slightly as the answer hit him square in the face.

Shit, it was there all the time, wasn't it? Talking to him rather than about him. The past was never going to go away. There would always be a doubt in the minds of others, no matter how much time elapsed, no matter how much they professed to be his friends. He cursed loudly and kicked the sofa hard, scuffing the already worn leather even more. Aye, he'd go and meet up with Paddy tomorrow night, he promised himself, and a team of wild horses wouldn't stop him. And if Paddy Monaghan wanted to say or do anything about anything, then so be it.

*

Paddy Monaghan lived in Creggan Heights, a long, winding road that marked the upper end of the estate. He was staring out through the front window at two young boys playing ball when Seamus and Jimmy called at the door shortly after seven the next evening. He answered their knock, a wide grin on his face. Seamus searched his eyes for some tell-tale sign of displeasure, though he could see no trace of hostility. Still, that meant nothing where Paddy Monaghan was concerned. He was something of a master at keeping his emotions under wraps.

Seamus wasn't in the mood for hidden agendas. Una – his now ex-girlfriend to stay – had phoned him earlier on that day, saying that she thought now that she'd made a mistake and maybe they could patch things up. But Jimmy had passed her by in another fella's car last night down the town, he was nearly sure of it, he had told Seamus that afternoon. Now Seamus wasn't really in the mood for anyone. As Paddy spoke, Seamus stood there solemnly, eyeing him up evenly for a second. If he was honest with himself, he didn't care all that much which way this conversation went.

'Ye lookin' to see me?' Seamus asked.

Paddy opened the door wide and stepped back inside the house. He seemed surprised. 'Jesus, Seamus, what's with the sour bake? You look as if someone kicked your dog into a coma. C'mon in.' He went to pat Seamus gently on the arm, but Seamus pulled away. 'Christ, Seamus!' he muttered, 'you'd think you were lookin' to fight me. What're ye goin' on like that for?'

'That thing that happened years back, you angry at me for slabberin' about it, or what?'

Paddy took a deep breath and smiled again. 'Don't worry about it, Seamus, it's all sorted. It's long over and we're both friends. Aren't we? He raised an eyebrow, that familiar charismatic smile of his bringing a thin smile to Seamus's face also.

Seamus found himself laughing, despite the fact that he'd been trying to keep a straight face. That wee fucker Una had him like this – uptight, angry; she'd turned him into a right old hate-the-world. 'Aye,' he said, relenting. 'Aye, we are. Always have been, right enough.'

Paddy looked back at the blue plastic bag in Jimmy's hands, and the cans straining against it. 'Hope ye got me some Harp, Jimmy boy. Ye know I don't like that other cheap shite ye drink.'

Jimmy smiled. He exchanged grins with Seamus and they both walked inside the hallway, passing by the closed sitting-room door and following Paddy through to the kitchen. Barney was there, staring out over the back fields in the direction of the Creggan Army Camp – best known to the locals as 'the Piggery' – on Piggery Ridge. When he looked out across those fields, Seamus always found himself thinking of his father and the gunmen who had defended the estate from the army earlier in the Troubles. He had faint memories of the army trying to break their way into the Creggan on one or more occasions in his early youth, shooting down into the houses from their Wessex helicopters, trying to crawl down through the back fields, SLRs cracking, seeking to regain ground that had been lost to them for nearly a year. Jimmy and Paddy used to tell him how a load of screeching cars would pull up into the Heights, each filled with Volunteers who'd be pulling on their hoods and loading their rifles at the same time, all eager to join the fight. Them lying up the gardens in the muck, their targets having finally become solid flesh and blood. The gun battles would rage long into the night, with no one ever really winning – and the 'RA never really losing. Now the army patrolled these same fields nearly all the time, and spotlights lit the area up at night. Black thoughts of his da always took precedence over any other memories, however, and he'd immediately blank them all from his mind.

Barney remained at the window as the other three boys sat at a table in the brightly painted kitchen. Seamus looked about him. He'd been in Paddy's house a couple of times before, stopping by on his way home from Saint Peter's school. It was a well-furnished house, with a matching sofa and chairs and a colour television. They even had a car – a real car, one with four doors instead of the more usual two. Paddy's father was an electrician by trade and he'd never really been out of work in his life or seen the poverty that a lot of Catholic families on the west bank of the Foyle river had endured throughout their lifetimes due to a lack of employment. Seamus found himself admiring the paper and the lacquered dado rail on the walls even as Paddy pulled out some Park Drive cigarettes and handed them around. The kitchen was papered; he'd only ever seen that twice before. 'Jesus, Barney,' the older boy said, lighting a match, 'will you sit the fuck down? Those bastards have been patrollin' up and down the backs all day. You're just invitin' trouble by starin' out at them.'

'They're a fuckin' shower,' Barney said, lighting his own fag. 'Every day you look, they have a new fuckin' base. One in Blighs Lane, one in Rosemount, one in the Essex factory, and now one up the back of the Heights. They've got the fuckin' Creggan surrounded, and down the town's like a garrison, what with their fuckin' iron railin's and their checkpoints. Christ, you can't go through those fuckin' things without the civilian searchers slappin' the balls of ye as they pretend to search ye. 'Cause that's what the bastards are doin' – pretendin'.'

'Aye, they're a bunch of sadis- ' Jimmy seemed momentarily perplexed.

'"Sadistic" the word you're lookin' for?' Seamus volunteered, easily. He winked at Jimmy and Jimmy grinned.

'Aye, sadistic bastards, that's what me da says. Homos and queers and sadistic bastards who just like feelin' you up. Searchin's got fuck all to do with it. Sure the Boys still get in there and plant their bombs and stuff, so a fat lot of good sealin' off the town is gonna do. Anyhow, there's word goin' about that they're takin' the things down soon. Any of yous'uns hear that?'

'That's a load of shite,' Jimmy retorted thickly, looking at the smaller boy as if he'd suddenly sprouted horns. He took a deep drag of his fag and cracked open a can. He leaned in close to Paddy. 'Hey, your da not mind us havin' a few bevvies in here, like?'

Paddy shook his head. 'Sure we're all the age, aren't we?'

'Aye,' Jimmy smiled. 'Near enough.' He passed the cans around and waited for the rest of the boys to take a drink. He ignored Paddy's raised eyebrow and took a slug of his beer. 'Hey, aye, you're on about those civvy searchers. One of them give me a wild hidin' one day. Cunt, he was. Hit me for fuck all and then tried to get the fuckin' Brit standin' next to him to arrest me for hittin' him. But the wee Brit was all right. Y'know the way they usually just pull out their wee wallet with the photographs of the people they're lookin' for in them, and they say they recognise ye, whether they recognise ye or not?' The others smiled and nodded. 'Well this wee boy wasn't too bad. He just told me to go on ahead out of there. So I sais to him that I want to make a complaint, but then the wee fucker says he didn't see the searcher doin' anythin'. Bastard!'

'The 'RA are startin' to sort that out,' Barney laughed. 'Sure they're shootin' them too now. And about time too, if ye ask me.'

'Aye, there's none of them all right,' Paddy agreed. 'Especially that fuckin' SAS crowd that they sent in two years back. Ye have them runnin' about at nights in their unmarked cars, shootin' anyone they want. A load of James Bonds with licences to kill. Good fuckin' laugh.'

'Hey, is it true you're runnin' around with that Stickie McGeady's son, Eddie?' Jimmy asked.

Paddy casually shrugged the question off. 'Sure we went to school together and now we're labourin' together on the sites. He's not the worst. I only go out for a pint with him now and then, nothin' else. And his da's not a Stick anymore, he's a Provie. Changed shop after Motorman, me da says. Didn't agree with their policies, and ye have to see his point there, don't ye? Sure us havin' a ceasefire isn't the answer, and them Brit bastards runnin' around with their guns, able to kill anyone they want and we just have to sit there and take it. Them cleared of torture in Strasbourg, it was on the news last week, and they're still fuckin' at it in Castlereagh Holdin' Centre. Torturin' boys into signin' confessions and some judge in a Diplock court lockin' them away in Long Kesh concentration camp on the word of some lyin' bastard of a cop. No jury, no rights, and that bastard Roy Mason sayin' that we're gettin' no political status for soldiers fightin' against an occupyin' force. No fuck all if you're a Taig. Some fuckin' truce that, all right,' Paddy said, drily. 'They get everythin' they want and we get fuck all but their dole money – a pittance handed to the croppies to make them lie down.'

'Ye sure he wasn't afraid that the Provies would wipe him out?' Jimmy mocked, referring to Dan McGeady. 'Sure the Stickies and the Provos were back shootin' the fuck out of each other last year. Four of them dead, about twenty injured. It was obvious who was gonna win. Christ, have they not got enough people to fight, with the UDA, the UDR, the RUC, the Brits, the UVF and fuck knows who else on the other side?'

'He's not a Stickie any more,' Paddy replied. He seemed a little on edge for a moment. He relaxed as he noticed Seamus watching him, the charismatic smile fixed firmly into place once more. 'That's all I know.'

Seamus nodded thoughtfully. Paddy had seemed very defensive when they'd talked about Dan McGeady; his tone when mentioning the man was almost reverent. When Seamus looked at Jimmy he wondered if his best friend was thinking the same as him.

'So are ye in there or what?' The question was out before Seamus had time to think about it. It was just so relaxing in the kitchen, and the drink was getting to him. He'd spent a night tossing and turning, thinking about how he had really liked Una Mahon, just to wake up and find that she was two-timing him with some fucker from down the Bogside.

Paddy raised an eyebrow and sipped at his can. 'In where?'

'In *there*,' Seamus repeated. It should have been obvious to Paddy from the expression on his face what he meant, but he elaborated anyhow. 'In with the Boys.'

Paddy smiled easily and dropped his gaze to the table. 'Sure if I was I'd hardly tell ye, would I?'

Seamus frowned heavily, his hackles rising. The past and the present suddenly merged into one. 'Why the fuck not?'

Paddy got the meaning immediately. 'I wouldn't tell anybody,' he said, raising his palms upwards. 'Neither you nor anybody else. Jesus, Seamy, lighten up and enjoy yourself! I know your form. Ye wouldn't say fuck all to anyone about anythin'. Sure I know that. But get a grip. You're goin' on there like a simple bastard. I'm just sayin' that if I was in with them then I'd hardly say to anyone, would I? Simple common sense says that.'

Seamus took a deep breath. Paddy was right. 'Hey, listen,' he said, turning his gaze downwards. 'I was goin' out with that girl Una for a long time, and I might have mentioned that fire. But I thought she was all right, y'know.'

'Forget about it.' Paddy's tone was genuine. 'We all say stuff to women to impress them – I've done it meself. I still do. Sure it's all straightened out now. No worries.'

'Aye, it's over,' Seamus agreed. 'Fuck it.'

'Hey, but it wasn't my idea to light the place,' Paddy said, with a frown. 'I'm just settin' the record straight here. I know I said I wasn't goin' to leave fingerprints, but then I'd planned to wipe the place clean with a rag, nothin' else. That's why I told the rest of ye to go on. It's no odds now, like I say, because it was years back. But it was Mickey's idea to torch it. Seriously. He had the matches and I thought he was jokin'.'

'Fuck it,' Seamus said. He looked down at the kitchen floor, not certain he wanted to hear the full story from Paddy in case a lie inadvertently revealed itself and ruined what was turning out to be a good evening. 'How is he now, anyhow? Ye ever hear from him?' He moved his seat around the table to make way for Barney, who had given up on his one-man vigil.

'Me ma phoned over to Altnagelvin Hospital that night he was shot, and they said he was serious but stable. I wanted to go over but she told me not to bother, because the Brits have a bunker on the fuckin' roof of the place and they were crawlin' the grounds, especially in and around Intensive Care, because three of them were seriously hurt when that Sixer piled over on Westway.' He began to laugh. 'Ye mind that?' he asked. 'Some fuckin' scream, that riot, wasn't it? Ye see the bastards runnin' up and down Westway like headless chickens after we chased them away from the shops, or what?'

'I wasn't there then, in case you don't remember,' Seamus retorted, pointedly.

Paddy nodded solemnly and took a deep drag of his fag. 'Aye, I hear Dan took you for a walk.' That boyish grin appeared then, as if by magic. 'He say anythin' to ye?'

'Did I say anythin' to *him*, you mean?'

The other boys laughed nervously. 'Jesus, Seamy,' Paddy said, grinning, 'we're gonna have to get that paranoia thing sorted out right and sharpish.' He grabbed the boy's shoulder and shook him playfully. 'We've been your friends for the last seven, eight years,' Paddy said. 'Even when others said . . . well, I hardly need tell you what they were sayin', eh?'

Seamus nodded, smiled easily and relaxed. That simple truth hit home sharply. 'Aye, he showed me what I was gettin' if I kept up the hoodin',' he laughed. 'An OBE. One Behind the Ear.'

Now it was Barney's turn to slap Seamus's shoulder. 'Thank fuck he missed me. Me ma would have had a blue fit if he had of showed himself at my door. She doesn't like bother. She reckons she's gettin' too old for it – that the Troubles will never be over in her lifetime.'

'That's stupid talk,' Jimmy said, with a shake of his head. 'Sure it's 1978 and the bastards have been here nearly nine years. They can't stay much longer. The world's gettin' wise to their antics. It's only a matter of time before they pack up and go.'

'Eddie's da says they'll be here for years to come,' Paddy said, solemnly. 'Sure the whole city's still tied up like a drum. And he knows. I get on all right with him now. Bit different from that first time he came round here, askin' could he speak to me da and the boy in the kitchen. Aye, me ma sais, no problem. So he's talkin' away and stuff and all of a sudden he pushes his jacket back a wee bit and the fucker has a short in his waistband.' Paddy began to laugh. 'Me da nearly had a fuckin' coronary. Your man's sittin' there cool as a cucumber, as if maybe it was an accident that his coat slipped back and he hasn't spotted it yet. Me da can't take his eyes of this gun, but Dan just sais what he's come for and then he pulls his coat together and heads off. Bids me ma goodnight as she's sittin' there in the sittin' room, and there's me and me da sittin' out here in the kitchen, mortified and not able to speak.'

They started laughing. 'Aye,' Jimmy Duffy said, eventually. 'My old boy says he's a mad bastard. Says he went down to some checkpoint in Belfast once and there's two cops outside of it. He's standin' around the corner all hooded up. Suddenly he steps around the corner, pulls back his coat and tells them to draw.' There were tears of laughter in Jimmy's eyes, and the rest of them were soon caught up in the infectious laughter. 'Aye, he's got two guns tucked into his belt and he's tellin' the fuckers to draw. They start fumbling with their guns, caught on the hop, like, and he shoots them both. Kills one, wounds the other. Mad bastard, or what?'

Paddy Monaghan nearly choked on his fag, he was laughing that hard. Barney slapped him square in the back with a fist until he started breathing near normally again. Seamus felt the drink coming down his own nose and he was nearly doubled in two.

'Aye,' Jimmy continued, his eyes red because he'd been rubbing away the tears of laughter. 'And there's a Brit in the lookout post up above the fuckin' place and two civilian searchers inside. The searchers dived to the ground, didn't want to know, and the wee Brit can't get his rifle turned to fire downwards, the place is that fuckin' small . . . '

Seamus couldn't stop laughing. The beer had gone to his head, the smoke was dizzying and he was dog-tired. But he couldn't stop himself. That night, after they had swapped a dozen more stories and smoked and drunk themselves nearly sick, Barney and Seamus headed on down Lislane and Jimmy waved to them both as he walked the short distance to his home across the street.

'Hey, Seamy,' Paddy called out as they left. Seamus turned, still sniggering at one of the stories. 'We're all goin' down the town on Saturday night. You fancy goin' with us?'

Seamus shrugged, undecided.

'Aye, go on. For the laugh. Sure we're takin' the car,' Paddy said, smiling.

Seamus frowned. 'Ye haven't got a car.'

'We'll get a car. Are you goin' out with us or not?'

Seamus nodded. 'Aye, why not.'

'Right, see you then.'

'Aye.'

He was alone and walking over Dunree when he realised that he hadn't laughed so hard and so much in ages. It had been like old times tonight, even without the rioting. But the laughter had also gotten something out of his system, and he felt relieved. Perhaps for the first time he realised that his friends – Paddy Monaghan included – had stuck by him completely over the past few years, despite the things that other boys had been saying about his da. It was a good feeling, and that night, after sliding under the blankets, he slept like a log.

FIVE

Seamus was looking good that Saturday night, all spruced up in a pair of light-blue parallels he'd bought with the rest of his training-centre wages after giving his ma his keep. The new trousers were set off to perfection by the obligatory DMs, which were shined until you could nearly see your face in them, a white grandad-style shirt and faded Wrangler jacket. He'd wandered down the town earlier in the day and had been talking to Jimmy outside McCool's newsagents in William Street. The red-haired youth had told him that Paddy Monaghan intended taking them to either a disco in the Embassy Court building on Strand Road or to 52nd Street – another disco further down the same road, just opposite the Strand Road RUC Station.

'Aye, and he's got a car,' Jimmy had told him with a smile.

'Has he fuck! Where'd he get a car? Sure Christ, he's only a fuckin' labourer and his da wouldn't lend him his, would he?'

'Nah, it's not his da's. Sure his da's is a green Cavalier and the one I saw him in today was navy blue. They must be payin' labourers well these days,' Jimmy had added, with a shrug. 'That's all I know.'

Seamus was curious. Jimmy told him that they'd drop by at nine, and Seamus was waiting at the window when the car pulled up. His mother was too engrossed in *The Generation Game* on the television to notice that he'd been standing behind the curtains for ages. She had a fag in her hand and a bottle of gin and the rest of her daily supply of forty cigarettes at her side. Seamus heard the car before he saw it. The vehicle was an old Vauxhall Viva, navy blue and with more smoke flying out of the exhaust than was perhaps normal. Still, Seamus was impressed. Paddy was the first of them to have driven a car legally – probably the first of them to have taken a car from A to B without sticking a match to it. He pulled on his coat and stepped outside, calling back to his mother that he wouldn't be late and not to wait up for him.

'And don't go gettin' too drunk,' his mother had called out. Her voice was neutral. These days she didn't raise her voice. Seamus had come to realise that, as long as she had her small bottle and her fags, she didn't need to.

He'd paled when she'd said that. She knew he'd been drinking and he thought he'd been keeping it a secret. He shrugged. He was growing up into a man and they both knew it. Sixteen and a half years old. His first bitter-sweet fumblings with the opposite sex had begun two years back. Back then he'd found out from a young girl who lived in the neighbouring housing estate of Rosemount that he had a heart. A few months later she'd taught him that it could be broken, when she'd dumped him for a better scrapper from Shantallow who could reputedly 'do' two boys at once. Since then he'd learned quite a bit about women, about their guiles and their sneaky wee ways of drawing you in with their flirtatious wee smiles – most of that education having been received down in the Creggan Centre. He'd learned about how they'd go on one date with you and then tell everyone how you were all going steady, and maybe them having been out with someone else the night before and them going steady with him too. It led to fights – to lots of silly wee scraps in which gangs of three and four roamed the streets looking for you and all your mates. And all because of women. Or girls, if you saw them as they really were. Silly wee girls.

He'd learned a lot since then, and he was slowly becoming a man. He'd seen what women could do if they put their minds to it, and he'd also seen what drink could do: the delights it could bring, the sickness it could bring on if you were still at a stage in your life where you didn't know which drink was wise to take with which, and which was better to avoid. He hadn't rushed into the drinking. He'd drunk a few cans and stuff out the resi on the best of the summer nights with Barney and Jimmy. He'd skipped down the town a few nights since joining the training centre with the lads in the joinery department. They were good fellas, nearly every last one of them, more than a couple of them level-headed and not liable to throw a wobbler when someone banged into them in the disco, either by accident or on purpose. He had learned how to enjoy drink and enjoy their company.

Aye, now he was well over sixteen and he'd experienced everything there was to experience in the world, he was sure of it. He climbed into the Vauxhall. Paddy was sitting there at the wheel, proud as a peacock, dressed in his best Wrangler suit. Jimmy and Barney sat in the back. They greeted him with a smile, revelling in the fact that they were just about to head off down the town for a cruise in their wheels.

'What do ye think of her, Seamy?' Paddy asked, as they drove off down Westway.

'Neat,' Seamus said, with a nod. 'Fuckin' cracker, right enough.'

'Neat,' Paddy agreed. 'We all goin' to the Embassy then, or 52nd Street?'

'Fifty-second Street,' Barney piped up. It was unusual for him to put forward suggestions so quickly, and Seamus turned to him, smiling, admiring his new-found confidence.

Paddy laughed. He leaned in close to Seamus in the front seat. 'He says the bouncers have him barred from the Embassy and he reckons the bouncers down in 52nd Street are thick as fuck, 'cause they don't ask him for ID. He doesn't realise that that's because he's with me.'

The boys laughed and Paddy took the car down through Rosemount and out over the Northland Road in the direction of the town. He cut off down William Street and took the car to a disused lot near the Stevenson's bakery

'I haven't got me licence yet,' he explained. 'So we'll walk the rest of the way and go in through the checkpoint at the bottom of the street. Don't want those bastard Brits stoppin' me and haulin' me off to the Victoria Barracks. Last time I was in there they had me standin' spread-eagled in the search position against the wall for a fuckin' hour and a half.'

Seamus frowned. 'I don't mind hearin' about that. When were you in there?' he asked. They moved down William Street. It was dark now, the sky leaden; it was just about to rain. The boys hurried, none of them wishing to get soaked.

'Ach aye, that's right. Sure I didn't tell ye the score. Y'know I was just thinkin', it must be a year and a half since we were last hangin' about.'

Seamus grinned. 'It's probably nearer two.'

Paddy nodded thoughtfully. 'They got me drivin' me da's car one night down in Shanty. So this black Brit stops the car and asked me me name. I sais Samuel Bow and he doesn't catch on … ' Paddy caught Seamus's own frown. 'Sam Bow,' Paddy explained. 'Sambo. Ye get it?' The other three laughed. 'So he catches on eventually. Fuck, he would need to have done, 'cause I said it three times. He hauls me off to the Strand Road Barracks, slaps the fuck out of me and says he's gonna do me with everythin'. Sais he's got photos of me riotin' and asks me do I want to make a statement. So I laugh, tell him me name, me address but not me date of birth, 'cause ye don't have to tell the bastards that, ye know.' Jimmy and Seamus nodded knowledgeably, though Seamus wasn't overly clued-in on his rights.

'Ye have to tell the cops but,' Barney cut in sagely. 'Ye have to tell them or they can do ye with obstruction and shit. Or somethin' like that.'

They stopped talking as they neared the checkpoint at the bottom of William Street, taking care to hurry along to the front of a few old-age pensioners. It was a precautionary method. If you had someone behind you then the civilian searchers wouldn't hold you back for questioning – like asking, "Who are you, Jimmy Duffy?" or, "What's your name, Seamus Doherty?" – or maybe try to fit you up with the latest in riotous behaviour because they were bored. And they wouldn't start making you hold your arms up really high and running their hands quickly up between your legs to whack you in the balls. Each of the boys knew the drill, without saying it. By now such evasive tactics had become natural to nearly every youth in town.

They passed through the checkpoint easily enough and made their way down past the tall Embassy Court building on the left, on the top of which the army had set up a gunpost. They moved past the crowds that were gathering outside, down past Wellworths and the Victoria Market Barracks, passing a foot patrol in silence and then turning to shout 'Up the Provos' after them, before hurrying on. About three or four hundred yards further down the Strand, opposite the RUC station, was the disco known as 52nd Street. Seamus had been there several times with the lads from work, but he'd never been there with his old friends. He savoured the thought, thinking that it might be a little more relaxed and maybe even more enjoyable with his friends than with his work-mates.

Paddy led them inside. He paid his money at the desk and exchanged greetings with one or two of the bouncers whom he knew well. The disco was packed, an intense darkness gently suffused with blue, yellow and red neon. Paddy ordered four pints of Harp at the bar without even asking everyone if that was what they wanted. Seamus smiled. That was Paddy Monaghan to a tee. He maintained that nothing ever changed in the world – that people always followed suit. Seamus took his cold beer and drank a little.

'So you still goin' steady?' he asked Paddy, as a couple of young Creggan women they all knew passed by, smiling, waving and exchanging ribald comments with the boys. Paddy, however, seemed momentarily distant, distracted.

Paddy smiled. 'Eh? Mmm, aye. Wee Eileen.'

'Nice, erm, girl,' Seamus said. On hearing that remark, Jimmy seemed to be having bother drinking his beer, though Paddy didn't notice that either. His attention was focused on someone at the other end of the disco. He nudged Seamus.

'Look at that wee thing over there,' he said.

Seamus looked across the dance floor and whistled softly under his breath. Three girls stood together, laughing and talking amongst themselves. The best-looking of the three was blonde, petite and – as far as Seamus could see – perfectly formed. 'Christ, look at the knockers on her. And that walk. God, she's a stunner!'

'She's a quare half,' Jimmy agreed, sipping heavily at his pint. 'Wouldn't mind givin' her one.'

'Or a couple,' Paddy laughed. 'Hey, Seamy, I'll bet you a five spot ye won't go over and ask her out for a dance.'

'Aye right, she'll go out for a dance with me,' Seamus puffed. 'She must be the best-lookin' bit of stuff in here. Her fella's probably with her, anyway, and he's likely enough built like a shithouse. You ask her out, if ye think she's that hot. I came here for a drink, nothin' else.'

'Sure she's lookin' at you,' Paddy smiled. 'Isn't she, Barney?' He nudged the smallest boy in the ribs.

'Creamin' herself lookin' at you,' Barney agreed, with a sly grin. 'Leavin' a trail like a slug after her on the floor, she's that wet.'

Seamus smiled and raised a condescending eyebrow. 'Aye, right.'

'Have ye no balls, Seamy?' Paddy said, seriously.

Seamus's back straightened ever so slightly for a moment, his chin raised. 'Aye, I've balls all right. Sure ye know that.'

Paddy cocked his head to the side and pursed his lips, as if to signify that he wasn't so sure. Seamus gritted his teeth. He had balls. He was Seamus Doherty, nothing like his father, and he had balls. He handed his pint to Paddy. 'We'll see.' He moved across the dance floor until he was standing near the edge, beside the girl and her two friends. Seamus steeled himself and took a deep breath, then fixed his Wrangler jacket into place, hands in the pockets, cool.

'Heaven must be missin' an angel tonight,' he said suddenly. And he winced inwardly as the girls laughed, knowing that this was the corniest remark he'd ever heard in his life, but someone had said it on television and it was all he could think to say.

The girl looked at him bemused. 'Your da teach you that one?' she said.

Seamus wanted to be offended by that remark but as he looked at her, standing there smiling at her own joke, he couldn't do anything but smile in return. The slow set began and he took another deep breath.

'Ye, erm, want to dance?'

She shrugged. It was a big decision and she had to act as if there was a long queue of suitors standing there behind him. She shrugged. 'Mmm, aye, all right then. I suppose. Maybe one.'

'They all your mates over there?' she asked, as Seamus walked her onto the floor. She put her arms around him, confusing his senses for a moment as she pulled him close. The subtle smell of her perfume accosted him; the way she moved, smiled, cocked her head and raised her eyebrow made him smile. Seamus didn't hear her for a moment, lost there on the dance floor.

'Eh? Oh aye. They are that.'

'They keep starin' over, makin' rude signs. They just out of Gransha madhouse for the weekend, or what?'

Seamus gritted his teeth, angry at his friends for taking the mick, and he moved her further into the huddle until they were completely surrounded by other couples. He introduced himself. 'I'm Seamus. Seamus Doherty.'

She smiled, and cocked her head. Seamus found himself thinking of a small, friendly spaniel. 'Elaine. Elaine . . . ' She went to continue, but then apparently thought better of it.

'Elaine what?'

She shrugged. 'Just Elaine. I don't know ye well enough, so no more questions. Let's just dance.' She leaned in close and he didn't know what to do for moment, the closeness was so sudden, so unexpected. So natural.

They danced for several songs – which seemed that night to be far shorter than usual – and even continued dancing when the faster songs came on. Seamus was no dancer, shyness usually forcing him to leave the floor directly after the slow set. But it was either dance or leave the floor, and he didn't want to leave her. She hadn't said more than three or four things to him but he felt he had known her forever. He struggled through the next six or seven songs, and she smiled at him.

'What?' he said, defensively.

'Very original dancin'. You takin' lessons from Quasimodo?'

He blushed. She was mocking him but he laughed, comfortable in her presence. And then she turned, about to make her way off the floor. 'I have to go back to my friends.' She nodded to the corner and paused.

It was now or never. 'I . . . I'd like to, erm . . . Well, will ye see me again sometime?' He dropped his head, butterflies in his stomach, realising that she could just walk away and that that moment would never be more than a memory.

She cocked her head and smiled, the seconds long. Then she nodded and gave him her phone number. He watched her walk away, smiling as she turned once before reaching the end of the floor, his heart thumping as she returned that smile.

'Christ, Seamy,' Jimmy said as he returned, smiling, victorious. 'Were you shaggin' her out there, or what?'

'Somethin' like that. Told her my face was leavin' here in ten minutes and she'd better be on it.' Jimmy nearly choked on his pint, laughing.

'He's got balls after all,' Paddy snorted, playfully. He slapped a five-pound note into the grinning youth's hand. Seamus stuck it back in his friend's coat pocket. 'Ye hang onto it,' Seamus said. 'Ye did me a favour. Got a fuckin' date out of that and everythin'.'

'Jammy bastard,' Barney said, jealously. 'Wish I'd done that. And I'd have kept the fiver too. Taken her out next week somewhere real nice.'

Paddy smiled. 'That's what friends are for, Seamy boy. And now, as if I haven't fuckin' done enough for ye in one night, I'm gonna do ye a bigger favour.'

Seamus smiled and took a long drink of his beer. Paddy

couldn't have done him a greater favour, he thought then, not even if he'd handed him the world on a plate. 'Oh aye?'

Paddy clasped his shoulder and turned him in the direction of the hallway leading into the disco. 'A friend of yours, if I'm not mistaken.'

Seamus followed the older boy's finger. His jaw tightened as he saw the familiar figure in the corner, standing there along with his girl. The man was tubbier now, almost fat beyond belief, though still recognisable five years on.

'Doran. That bastard Doran,' Seamus said, thickly. 'That cunt caused one hell of a lot of shit in my life for over two years. Christ, I haven't seen him in years.'

Paddy thumped Seamus playfully in the stomach. 'Well, you're seein' him now, aren't ye? Ye talked about him then as if ye hated him, I always remember that. Do ye still now?'

Seamus found himself nodding. He hadn't seen Hugo Doran in years, though for a long time after he'd left the college he'd found himself thinking about him. Whenever he was angry at someone for doing something wrong to him, for looking at him, for making him feel stupid, he always, funnily enough, found himself blaming first his father and, second, Doran. Which was stupid, utterly stupid, he knew. The incident in the college was five years past and it was silly to keep thinking about it. So much had changed. He was now in the training centre, he was earning a wage, having a few pints with the lads and going out on the odd date – when he found the courage to ask someone he fancied. People in the main now took him for himself – for what he was, and not for what his da might or might not have once been. He was happier, content, and he'd just met the most beautiful girl he'd ever laid eyes on – even arranged a date with her.

Or had things really changed, he wondered sadly. His mother's life had crumbled ever so slowly away over the past five years or so. Not so much that everyone would notice, of course, but the signs were there when you lived with the woman. The small bottles of sherry had been a Friday-night treat in his da's time. Now you could hear the sounds of glass clanking in the bin when a dog came through the hedges out the back of the house and knocked it over. Once Seamus had chased a dog off and stuck the rubbish back into the bin himself. He'd been alarmed by what he saw there. Bottles, and more bottles: gin, sherry, vodka. All expertly tucked away from the prying eyes of neighbours. And then there were the cigarettes. Seamus smoked himself now. His mother hadn't approved for a while, but then she could hardly have said anything to him, what with the way she sometimes had the living room like Brown's foundry. But then, those were just the outward signs, and in doing that she was really no different from thousands of others the entire world over.

The tears she hid from the rest of the world. The tears she cried so often at night as she lay in her bed. Mary Doherty, the strong wee woman from Dunree Gardens who could stand up against Brits and Provos alike, who had the respect of everyone who ever knew her – and not just because her staunch relatives went back to the time of Michael Collins and de Valera. Only Mary Doherty wasn't as strong as everyone thought she should be, and very few people knew it. Maybe Sadie, her next-door neighbour and best friend. And, of course, Seamus. Those two and possibly no one else. Seamus was beginning to learn that the compatible silence those two had once enjoyed was becoming a wall that neither knew how to break down.

Still, his father had messed his mother's life up – and Seamus's – initially, yet the young boy would never have known about it except for Doran. It wasn't Doran's fault that the world turned and people had the free will to do as they did – Seamus knew that. It wasn't Doran's fault that they sometimes messed it up for themselves and for others. But people like Doran kept the world turning at speed when others merely wanted it to drift by. They were the real demons, and they spurred a man to life against others who were bigger or smaller – those who fought for what they knew to be right or what they knew to be wrong, it didn't really matter. Always against others, creating anxiety and stress, havoc and mayhem. Always spinning the world at speed until it ended up spinning way out of control.

Seamus looked at Doran and his jaw tightened. He knew in that moment that, by realising the root of his problems, he had grown up. Though too, in a small way, he was like his father – although he would never have admitted it in public. Because he wasn't afraid of demons either.

'Aye. I hate him surely. What do ye reckon? I don't want to get in trouble with the bouncers. They look like stupid fuckers, but they're *big* stupid fuckers. I don't fancy gettin' into a tangle with them.'

'Drink up, then, and we'll go outside,' Paddy said.

'Ye can't do anythin' out front,' Jimmy put in quickly. 'Sure the fuckin' barracks is just across the road.'

'He lives down the Bog, doesn't he?' Paddy asked Seamus. 'You not tell me that once?' Seamus nodded. 'Well then, we'll get the car and follow him home. Sure he hasn't seen us and he won't know a fuckin' thing about what hit him.'

Seamus nodded. He didn't hate too many people, except the Brits and the Orangies, but he hated Hugo Doran and always had done. It didn't matter if the older lad wasn't expecting it. Seamus hadn't been expecting it either. That was the way things went sometimes. It was just the way things went.

Paddy took the car around the back of the quay and up the Abercorn Road. He drove across Bishop Street and over the Lone Moor. Once in the Bogside, he parked the car a little way from the Bogside Inn, facing it in the direction of Creggan.

'That's his house there,' Seamus said, pointing. 'The one with the big vase in the front window.'

'Aye, well you mind what I told ye,' Paddy warned. 'Keep in to the shadows. Those black bastards have a listening post on the walls, just to the left of the remains of Governor Walker's statue. Their microphones and cameras are trained on the Sinn Féin centre in Cable Street, but they're watchin' everythin' in the Bog, I'm tellin ye. Look,' he said, nudging Seamus in the ribs. 'Fuck, he was quick! Is that the cunt gettin' out of that taxi?'

Seamus strained his eyes. 'Aye, but his fuckin' girl's gettin' out with him. Maybe we'd better leave it.'

Paddy put a hand on his shoulder. 'Nah, look, she's just givin' him a kiss. There, she's gettin' back in. Go on,' he urged. 'Out ye get.' Paddy got out of the car, keeping his back to the couple, who were only about fifty feet away, in Abbey Park.

'Where the fuck are ye goin'?' Seamus asked, getting out of the car.

'We're your backin', Seamy. We'll just stand back out of the road, but we'll be in like a shot if anythin' goes wrong.'

'Aye, well there's no need. I don't need help, so just hang back. I'll sort it out.'

Seamus watched the youth moving across the street. There was no time to argue with Paddy Monaghan. Seamus moved quickly across the road. 'Hey!' he said. Hugo Doran turned.

Seamus had his head held low and the youth stood there outside his gate. 'Ye got a light on ye?'

Hugo Doran put his hand inside his pocket as Seamus neared, but then he stopped, catching sight of Paddy moving towards him. He made to turn into the driveway, fumbling in his trouser pocket for his keys, but Seamus caught up with him and grabbed him by the shoulder, spun him around and hit him square in the face. Doran fell heavily to the concrete path outside his house and Seamus kicked him hard in the ribs. He stepped back then, a feeling of immense satisfaction coursing through him. He had expected a fight but Hugo Doran had fallen, winded, his face screwed up in agony. Seamus shook his head. It had been an anticlimax of sorts. Almost immediately, Paddy Monaghan ran forward, his boot flying at the youth's head. With a sickening crack, it connected, and Doran's breath left his body in a groan. Seamus was momentarily startled. When the initial shock of the action finally brought him to his senses, he pulled Paddy back, though not before the older youth could deliver a second kick at the boy's head. Hugo Doran lay there unconscious in the middle of his own garden path.

'What the fuck are ye playin' at'?' Seamus said loudly, his face contorted in rage.

'Helpin' ye out, what do ye think?' Paddy said, thickly. There was a strange black glint in his eyes and Seamus regarded him quizzically for long moments, wondering at the strange lack of compassion there, the disappearance of the charm, the charisma. The spell was broken as a voice sounded out from within the house and the living-room lights went on. They both turned and Paddy's voice broke through the stalemate. 'C'mon to fuck, let's get out of here.'

They ran back to the car, spurred on by the other two youths, who had remained beside the vehicle throughout. Paddy keyed it into life, moving quickly through the gears as he aimed her up Westland Street and towards the sanctity of Creggan as an old man stepped out of the house. They could still hear him shouting as they neared the top of the road.

'Fuckin' great job, eh?' Paddy grinned as they neared the junction at St Eugene's Cathedral. 'That cunt won't ruin anyone's life again so quick. Fuckin' wanker!' he exclaimed. 'He'll wake up in the mornin' and won't know a fuck what hit him!'

Seamus felt his adrenalin levels rising and he was about to say something. He didn't mind fighting, God knew, because he'd had to fight his way through the last few years due to the stigma brought upon him by the acts of his father. But he'd always fought fairly, one to one. Paddy Monaghan's actions had shocked him. For a second he wanted to tell the older boy to pull the car over and let him out, that he'd walk home, and never to come near him again. But then he looked at Jimmy and Barney's faces. They were laughing too.

'Jesus, Seamy, you're gettin' to be a right simple bastard,' Barney said, the admiration easy to spot in his voice.

'You're a fuckin' wil' man,' Jimmy agreed, with a smile. 'A fuckin' Blue-Card, if ever there was one!'

Seamus frowned and then he too started laughing. Ah, fuck him, he thought suddenly. He got a bit of a kicking, but so fucking what? He'd been a bully and a coward for years and nobody had ever stood up to him. Now it was all coming back to him, the way it did to all bullies eventually. Fuck him! Seamus found himself laughing hard, even though his hands were shaking. He felt good, he realised, very good – and no longer as guilty as he had at first. He only stopped laughing as the glare of a set of headlights caught their attention as they drove up towards Creggan hill. The beam from the car behind them was full on and dazzling in the mirror. Paddy shielded his eyes as he looked quickly back.

'Who the fuck's your man?' he said irately, putting the car into fourth. 'The bastard's gettin' far too close.'

'Stop, and we'll get out and do him too,' Barney said, suddenly.

Seamus turned to the smaller boy. He would have laughed but the look on Barney's face said that he was deadly serious. God, Seamus found himself thinking, this bravery thing is getting infectious and Barney's confidence is growing by the day.

'Just drive on,' Seamus found himself saying. 'He probably noticed us back there and he's lookin' to stick his nose in. Just drive on. We don't need any more bother tonight. Go on up Westway. You'll lose him in the Creggan.'

'Hold on tight,' Paddy said. He suddenly slammed on the brakes and the Vauxhall screeched loudly to a halt. The car behind suddenly hit them square on and the breath left Seamus all at once as he nearly hit the dashboard. Jimmy let out a roar. 'Jesus, Paddy, what the hell are ye at?'

Paddy didn't seem in the least perturbed. He spurred the car forward again, moving through the gears as he drove up Creggan Hill towards Westway. 'Hope there's no more of those cunts in the Rosemount Barracks,' he said evenly. 'If there are, we're all fucked. Dead as maggots.'

Seamus felt his senses reeling. Jimmy and Barney didn't open their mouths. The fortified Rosemount RUC Station was directly ahead at the top of the hill, situated as it was midway between the Creggan and Rosemount housing estates. It was surrounded by a high, corrugated-tin fence and razor wire and, in the earlier years of the Troubles, had once been subjected to a three-day siege under near-constant gunfire. Atop a central mast in the centre of the fortification the army had erected cameras to spy on all the approach roads. 'What do you mean, more of them?' he asked, quickly putting his seat belt on and then clinging with both hands to the dashboard. He watched Paddy intently as the car approached the top of the road and swung quickly up Westway. His attention flickered back to the car behind. The lights were now dimmed, the car about two hundred yards behind and seeming to labour slightly as it crested the hill.

'Fuckin' SAS or undercover cops in that car,' Paddy said, biting his lower lip. 'It's a Ford Sierra. Souped-up like fuck. They could eat us up on the road if they wanted.'

'Eh?' Seamus screeched. 'Jesus, maybe we'd better stop!' He looked through the back window, the blood draining from his face. He raised an eyebrow. 'Or maybe . . . Hey, hold on, they've stopped,' he said softly. 'They've just stopped and they aren't movin' at all.'

'We're losin' them,' Jimmy said, in wonder. 'Shit, souped-up or not, you must have knocked the fuckin' engine out of it back there.'

'We're losin' nobody,' Paddy said tersely. 'They just aren't so keen to follow us up here without any backin'. But they will do in a minute. They'll fuckin' swamp the place, you'll see.'

Seamus looked at him and then back at the car, which had drawn to a halt at the bottom of Westway. It was now about four hundred yards behind, and they were turning into the top of Beechwood Avenue. Suddenly the headlights of the car were back on full beam and Seamus heard the heavy revving of the engine as it kicked into life. Paddy slammed on the brakes and the handbrake and turned the car until it lay at a peculiar angle across the middle of the road. 'Out,' he urged quickly. 'C'mon, everyone out. Hurry it up to fuck. And make sure ye roll down your windows. I want the air to circulate.'

Seamus looked at him perplexed, but didn't argue. He quickly did as he was told and then stepped out of the car. Paddy was around at the boot. The older boy slammed it hurriedly shut and Seamus noticed that he was carrying a petrol can. The older boy unscrewed the lid and poured the contents of the can in through the car windows. He pointed to the dimly lit waste ground that ran up between the side streets that ran parallel to both Westway and Broadway – waste ground that the local council had forsaken and which was now used mostly as a dump and, occasionally, for the setting up of the August the Fifteenth bonfires, which celebrated the Feast of the Assumption. 'Up there, and hurry! I'll be with ye in a minute.'

The three boys ran up through the waste ground. Seamus looked back. Flames were licking up through the interior of the car, nourished by the petrol and the highly flammable plastic seats, growing brighter and illuminating the night. Seconds later, Paddy was running after them. They heard a car screech to a halt only moments afterwards – and then the heart-stopping sound of the heavily revving engine of a Saracen following behind. Seamus was out of breath as he reached Leenan Gardens: his lungs felt as though they were on fire. The explosion of the petrol tank should have made him laugh, but he was too exhausted to care. He so wanted to stop; in fact, he was about to when Paddy caught up with them.

'Youse boys'd need to do a bit more exercise,' Paddy said, laughing. 'Get into the football. It'll pay off as ye get older, take it from me. Follow me.' He ran about halfway up Malin Gardens as the noise of the Saracen's engine intensified. 'Not to the end of the road, Jimmy,' he called after the red-haired youth. 'Ye want to do it properly – follow me.' He opened a gate and ran up the garden path, brushing some protruding rhododendron bushes easily aside. The other boys followed him through another taller gate and into a back garden. From there Paddy stepped over a low wire fence and moved into an adjoining garden. Moments later, they were in Leenan. Paddy mounted the steps that led to the road, and looked up and down the street. When he was sure there was nobody about, he crossed the road and repeated the exercise, moving through gardens into the parallel streets of Melmore, and then Dunree. He was running through forests of dock leaves, through long grass and unevenly layered back gardens one moment, jumping low fences and sprinting across well-tended lawns and through flower beds the next.

Jimmy got caught up in a tangle of brambles. 'Wish to fuck these fuckers would look after their gardens properly,' he said. They all laughed, nervously, until Paddy shushed them to silence.

'Four streets away and we never turned a corner,' Paddy said. 'That's the way the Boys do it,' he added, with a smile. 'Stick with me, I'll keep ye right.' He cocked his head suddenly. 'Quick, get over here.'

They jumped over a gate and hid in a garden in Dunree Gardens about three doors up from his mother's, the house belonging to old Mister Flaherty, a widower. Seamus wanted to rise up from there and lead them all into the safety of his house, but Paddy grabbed him by the shoulder and held him firmly in his place even as he went to get up. With his free hand, Paddy urged the others down behind the clutter of hedges, then put a finger over his mouth. They all ceased talking immediately.

Seamus went to ask why, but Paddy clamped a hand over his mouth. A jeep, the noise of its engines muffled, was moving up the furthest end of the street, a searchlight on top of it. The street was lit by orangey-yellow fluorescents but the blinding light above the jeep must have been about a hundred times brighter.

Seamus ducked down as the jeep moved slowly along the street, stopping now and then as it searched a garden. He nearly jumped out of his skin as a dog suddenly ran out from one of the gardens, barking ferociously at the jeep. One of the two soldiers who were standing looking out of the hatch shouted at it and waved his rifle threateningly at it. But the dog barked on and on relentlessly. Lights went on in various houses down the length of the street: the boys could see them through the hedges. Still, they didn't move a muscle. The jeep neared, though the Brits were driving more quickly now, their search hampered by the clamour of neighbours who were coming out of their houses and enquiring as to cause of the commotion.

Seamus found himself praying that old Mister Flaherty wouldn't come out and give their position away. His heart stopped for several moments as the bedroom lights came on above them. He saw the figure of the friendly old man peering out through the blinds in the direction of the jeep and then closing them as quickly. Mister Flaherty didn't want any trouble – probably hadn't seen anything, anyway. Seamus began to breathe out as the jeep neared the end of the street, quickly spurred on by the heckling shouts of his neighbours.

'Stay down for a while in case they come back,' Paddy whispered. 'And if they get us, ye all say fuck all, y'hear?' The other three boys nodded. 'Sign fuck all, say you want to see your solicitor, and don't let them pressure you into sayin' anythin', no matter what, ye hear?' The three boys nodded again.

Paddy seemed to know exactly what he was doing, Seamus thought, admiringly, as they sat there in the garden, near-motionless. After a few moments the women had gone back inside their houses. The boys sat there for a further ten or fifteen minutes. When it seemed almost certain that the jeeps would not return,

Seamus rose gingerly and led the other youths into his house. 'Ye all want to kip down here?' he asked. 'It might be safer.'

'Sure I'm only over the street,' Barney said. He looked at Jimmy and Paddy. 'What about you two?'

'Nah,' Paddy said. 'We'll be all right, won't we, Jimmy?' The red-haired youth nodded uncertainly. 'Sure those bastards haven't a fuckin' clue, have they?'

Jimmy didn't seem so certain about that one either, but he nodded again anyway. A few moments afterwards, Paddy went out into the street and did a reconnaissance. He returned some five minutes later and signalled to Jimmy that it was safe to leave. 'Some carry-on that tonight, eh?' he said to Seamus as he left.

'Aye,' Seamus agreed, with a half-smile. 'Some carry-on all right.'

'I'll get in touch with ye tomorrow.'

'Aye.'

*

Jimmy, not Paddy Monaghan, got in touch with Seamus two days later. It was that Monday, and Seamus had just returned from the training centre. He was up the stairs getting changed out of his yellow overalls when there was a knock at the door. Mary called up the stairs. 'Seamy, that's for you. Jimmy Duffy.'

Jimmy seemed pensive and agitated when Seamus came down the stairs. He was towelling himself off, the smell of turpentine still on his hands. 'What's happenin'?'

Jimmy looked over at Mary, frowned and forced a smile. 'Ah, nothin' much.'

Seamus searched his eyes and then led him out into the kitchen, closing the door behind them. Jimmy waited a moment and then said softly, 'Your man, did ye hear about him?'

'Who?'

'Doran.'

Seamus paled. 'What about him?'

'He's in a fuckin' coma.'

'Eh? Are ye fuckin' jokin', or what?'

'Aye, I'm fuckin' serious. He's in a coma and over in Altnagelvin in Intensive Care.' Jimmy was rising as he said it, agitated, moving towards the door. 'Paddy said to meet him later at the back of the shops, in about half an hour. We'll all be there. Make sure you are, eh?'

Seamus nodded as Jimmy opened the kitchen door. He didn't turn back and he let himself out. Seamus went up to his room. He dressed hurriedly.

'Seamus, I'm stickin' your tea out now,' Mary called up the stairs. 'It's stews. Ye ready for it, or what?'

'Nah, ma, I've a message to run. I'll get it in a wee while.'

'Sure ye must be starvin'. You've had nothin' since lunch.'

'I'll be grand, and it'll keep. I'll get it later.'

*

They were all standing there when he arrived. Paddy was joking about something or other but he stopped talking as Seamus approached.

'Ye hear the news?'

Seamus nodded, pensive.

'Aye, well it'll be all right . . . '

'How do ye reckon?' Seamus realised that there must have been fear in his voice, and he dropped his head. Paddy touched his arm lightly.

'They have fuck all on anyone, and he's gonna be all right anyway,' the older boy said, with conviction. 'Sure, do ye not think they would have lifted us by now. That old boy of his didn't see a fuckin' thing. We were all halfway up Westland Street when he came out of the house, and even you and I couldn't pick out a registration number at that distance. And those fuckin' SAS bastards, sure they saw fuck all either. Ye seen them stoppin' at the bottom of the street. Afraid to follow us up into Creggan, and them supposed to be the toughest soldiers in the world. They're a crowd of fuckin' tubes, every last one of them.'

Seamus nodded slowly. Paddy had a point. Today was Monday, and that had happened on Saturday night. If the cops or the Brits had known anything, they would have lifted the whole lot of them by now.

'Aye, you're probably right enough.'

'But I'm gonna tell ye all somethin' now,' Paddy said. His face had grown darkly serious and Seamus paled, though he hoped no one had noticed. 'They get ye in there in the barracks, ye have to know your rights. Ye sign fuck all. Ye give them your name and address, your date of birth if it's the RUC. Ye ask for a solicitor. They'll say they're gettin' ye one, but they'll wait hours before they do. In that time they'll play mind games with ye, try to fuck with your head. The way around it is to picture them with no clothes on, picture them having a crap or somethin' . . . ' Paddy paused as the others laughed, though his face remained impassive. 'I'm fuckin' serious. If they start hittin' ye, then just curl up in a ball in the corner. They usually hit ye at the back of the neck or in they balls, ye see, or whack you with a telephone directory, so they don't leave any fuckin' marks. Or if ye want, ye can get your retaliation in first. Hit them when ye get the chance.'

'What are ye tellin' us this for?' Jimmy asked. 'It's not as if we shot anyone or anythin', is it? Do ye not think your man'll come out of the coma then?' Now it was Jimmy's voice which had fear in it. No one was laughing any more.

'It's nothin' to do with that,' Paddy said, sighing. 'The car was stolen. You heard about that robbery on Saturday – the Northern bank down the town?'

Barney nodded but Seamus and Jimmy looked puzzled. There were that many robberies these days that they weren't talked about in more than a passing comment. They shook their heads.

'Aye, well there was a robbery and a wee bit of shootin' . . . '

'What do ye mean, a wee bit of shootin'?' Seamus said, incredulously.

'A few shots, nothin' else. No one was hurt, it's all right.'

'Fuckin' hell!' Jimmy gasped.

'Be quiet a minute, will ye?' Paddy said, thickly. The boys quietened. 'Everything'll be all right – you'll see. That was the car they used. It was supposed to be disposed of shortly afterwards but they had to hide the fuckin' thing in a garage in Rosemount because the fuckin' Brits were crawlin' the place. I was supposed to burn the fuckin' thing late on Saturday night, dump it across a road. What the fuck do you think I had a can of petrol in the boot for?'

Jimmy shrugged. 'I dunno. In case you ran out, or somethin'?'

Seamus looked at him darkly, then looked away. Jimmy was his best friend but he could be as thick as a plank sometimes. 'They,' he said. 'Who are they?'

Paddy looked at him for a second and then looked away. 'It doesn't matter a fuck who they are,' he said. 'All of ye just remember what I said. Ye know nothin' about the kickin', less about the car. Chances are ye won't get lifted, but if ye do . . . '
He let the words hang in the air.

Seamus looked at Jimmy and then at Barney. Jimmy looked to be deep in shock, though Barney had a thin smile on his face. But that was because the smaller boy was probably unaware of the gravity of the situation, Seamus decided. Either that or he'd been eating those courage tablets by the handful. He nodded then – they all did – and, as suddenly, the meeting was over.

'Me and Barney are headin' out for the night,' Paddy said then. The charismatic smile had returned. 'You boys fancy headin' out for a few pints with us?'

Seamus shook his head. 'Nah. If I go out tonight I'll never get up in the mornin'. And I'm savin' me money for tomorrow night.' He gave a beaming smile. 'I've a date, in case ye don't remember.'

The others exchanged smiles. Paddy made a few hand-signals that told the others what Seamus's date was getting.

'You, Jimmy?' Paddy smiled.

'Nah,' Jimmy replied. 'It's all right for you fuckin' labourers. Ye do fuck all all day. But some of us have to work for a livin'.'

'Work?' Paddy snorted. 'Drivin' a bread van? Sittin' on your hoop all day? Throwin' buns in and out of a lorry? Huh, my fuckin' dog could do that!'

'Talkin' about dogs, how's Eileen?' Jimmy asked, grinning.

Paddy laughed. He made another hand-signal at Jimmy to signify that Jimmy's sex life consisted of him and him alone. 'See ye's all later then.'

'Aye.'

When they had gone Jimmy turned to Seamus. 'Ye hear that?'

'Sure I was fuckin' standin' beside ye, wasn't I?'

'Ye know what I mean.'

'Aye,' Seamus said, gravely. 'I do that.' Paddy Monaghan was involved with some of the paramilitaries: it was as plain as day to both of them. Though neither knew which group it might be. It was either the Provos, which was more likely, or the INLA, an offshoot of the Official IRA who had their own particular brand of Marxism that no one – including them, according to the cynical reports of his mother – seemed to be overly sure about. He was getting rid of their cars, sweeping up after them. The connection between him and Dan McGeady, Seamus realised, must have been deeper than he had at first thought.

Six

Elaine was home when he phoned, just in from her work in the Rainbow Café, and they made plans to meet up at eight at the front of the Palace Picture House in Shipquay Street. He was early and expected her to be late but she arrived just as the hand of the clock met the hour. She smiled easily when she saw him, and paid the taxi driver.

'Hope ye aren't thinkin' of takin' me into that fleapit,' Elaine said, feigning a frown. Seamus blushed. Had his intentions been that obvious, he wondered. 'But it doesn't matter if ye are.' She scanned the billboard up above. 'I'm not into those Bruce Lee films, anyway. Are you? Because if ye are, I don't mind.'

Seamus shook his head. 'No,' he lied. 'Never liked him.' He wondered what she would say if she could see the posters on his bedroom wall, the nunchukas that he'd had one of the joiners fashion for him from teak. 'I'm not into violence and stuff.' Thoughts of Hugo Doran lying out cold on the garden path came to him, the boy's father tending to his son and shouting after the car as it screeched out of the Bogside and in the direction of Creggan. God, he was getting to be a terrible liar, he thought, despondently. He shivered briskly and broke into a cold sweat.

'Are ye all right? Ye look a little white.' She was genuinely concerned.

He smiled, pleased at that. 'Aye, I'm grand.'

She gave that lopsided grin again, and he blushed. 'Really, I don't mind where we go.'

'No, we'll do whatever you decide. That's good for me.'

'C'mon then, the Rialto it is. It's only a wee dander up the road, and *Grease* is showin'. I haven't seen it yet. Have you?'

He shook his head once more. The words weren't coming easily and he wondered why he was so nervous. And yet she seemed relaxed enough, satisfied with his company. That cheered him up and for a while his nervousness disappeared. Him, Seamus Doherty, and her, a quare wee bit of stuff! God, he couldn't believe his luck, after the last few dragons he'd been out with of late, especially that Una Mahon. He sat back and tried to relax, watching her every now and then as she silently mouthed the hit songs, laughing as she told him that she would love to have a voice like Olivia Newton-John and snorting as she went on and on about that John Travolta: was he a babe, or what?

After the film was over they went for a walk on the high, medieval walls that had surrounded the city for centuries, though these days – due to the effects of the Troubles – most of the old stone walls were barricaded off, army sangars positioned on top of them to overlook the entire Bogside, and only a little of their length open to the public. It was a warm enough evening, though thin, dark clutters of rain clouds scudded overhead, brooding.

'That phone number of yours,' he said, as they peered down a near-empty Carlisle Road in the direction of the Craigavon Bridge and the fortified, and mainly Protestant, Fountain Estate. 'Where exactly is that for?'

She smiled and dropped her gaze. 'I'm from the Waterside,' she told him. There was a worried look on her face – a strange frown had appeared there. Seamus nodded. 'Irish Street,' she continued.

'Oh!'

She smiled. '"Oh"? Is that a good "oh" or a bad "oh"?' The smile was strained.

'Whatever,' he said, with a shrug. They stood there silently for a time, Seamus having clicked onto the meaning of her frown immediately. Irish Street was a predominantly Protestant area on the other side of the bridge. Like most Protestant parts of the city, it was easy identifiable by its red, white and blue kerbstones and by its loyalist murals of King Billy and various others paramilitary emblems painted on the gable ends of houses. This tradition was, of course, diametrically opposed to that of the predominantly Catholic areas, where street murals were dedicated to various republican factions, to Padraig Pearse and James Connolly and others involved in the Easter Rising, all given that extra touch by their own green- white- and gold-painted kerbstones or flags. Seamus shivered again but tried to hide it. He had never been near the estate in his life but he knew well from often-unsubstantiated rumours that the Irish Street area was well out of bounds to all – or at least most – Catholics.

'You can't tell,' he said, smiling.

She regarded him quizzically, her soft blue eyes penetrating, expectant. Though what she expected him to add, he couldn't tell. 'You can't tell what?' she asked, softly.

'Me da always used to say that ye can tell the difference between us. He reckoned that he could do it just by lookin'. My friends reckon that they can tell by . . . ' He paused, aware that she was staring uneasily at her feet. He took her gently by the arm. 'I'm only sayin' what they say,' he said, easily. 'It doesn't bother me, because I don't know many Protestants, really I don't. A few of the instructors in the trainin' centre and a few of the lads in there too, but then they tend to stick together in the canteen . . . ' He cocked his head to the side, trying to make eye contact with her. When she looked at him she was smiling again. 'I don't mind, really. Do . . . ?' He could hardly finish his sentence.

She shook her head, her smile conveying an answer more genuine than words ever could. She took his hand and pulled her coat close together against the dusting drizzle of rain that was sweeping in from the west. 'I don't care,' she told him, firmly. 'I really don't. C'mon, let's walk a little. We aren't that different, I suppose. We can't be. Two eyes, one nose, no horns . . . '

He laughed. 'And ye don't eat babies, do ye?'

She shook her head, grinning. 'Rarely.' She regarded him for long moments and he turned out of the wind. 'I guess we don't really know anythin' much about each other, do we?' she said, softly.

Seamus shrugged easily, wondering if she was talking about the two of them in particular. That smile of hers was infectious and he felt deliriously happy. 'We know enough for now,' he told her, simply. 'I reckon we can spend a little time findin' out. What do ye think?'

'Umm . . . ' Undecided. She frowned, and for a moment his heart stopped. Then that mischievous smile was there once more. 'Aye, all right. I'll take a chance if you will.' He laughed, relieved.

The night passed quickly after that. They walked along the walls and then down Bishop Street, with no particular direction in mind. They took shelter in doorways as the rain gathered from a thin, soaking mizzle at first to a pelting crescendo as the night darkened perceptibly. They held each other close and she told him in between times that her father worked for the civil service in the Waterside, her mother was a schoolteacher and her two older brothers were painters by trade. He laughed when he heard that and they joked that one day they might end up working alongside each other. Once this war was over, of course, they both found themselves saying as one. And then they laughed again, knowing that that was unlikely to occur in the near future.

She also had a sister, she smiled; an older sister whom she adored though never saw much of now, because she'd married an Englishman a couple of years back and it wasn't really safe to wander about this city at the moment if you were an Englishman. So they'd moved. She hadn't wanted to, really, but she had done anyway. For him. Seamus nodded at that, commenting that it was a great sacrifice. He'd heard of people who were originally from the city coming back and them getting dragged into bar toilets or down dark lanes and quizzed for no more reason than they had a pale English accent that they'd gathered over their time abroad. And if you really were from England, then that was more trouble again. The squaddies stuck to familiar bars in the mainly Protestant towns here in the North, though often even their recreational time had been curtailed, due to the increasing number of bombings and shootings in the bars and nightclubs that dared to serve them drink.

And then Seamus had told her to skip the details about her family, and she'd been hurt by that remark, because she was telling him about herself – her life – and she'd thought he wanted to hear about it. But he apologised, saying that of course he wanted to know – but more about her than her family. And she had smiled that smile, pleased at the compliment, and he had relaxed almost completely, the tension all but gone. Then he'd listened intently as she told him that she was only working in the Rainbow Café on a part-time basis, mainly Friday nights and weekends. She was studying too, she told him proudly, doing her secretarial exams in the technical college on the Strand Road. Because she had plans, she said excitedly – plans to get the hell out of this country, because the Troubles were never going to end and everyone knew it; maybe go over to England to her sister in Newcastle and get a job there. And Seamus had felt his heart jump when she had said that and he wondered why and how she could have such an effect on him with only words.

He walked her to a taxi stand shortly after eleven, gave her a long kiss and told her he'd phone. He would, of course – he knew that as well as he had ever known anything in his life. He made his way through the turnstile barriers down in William Street and began to walk home. It was raining heavily now and he was almost soaked to the skin but he didn't care. He was delirious, almost ecstatic and couldn't believe his luck. She was the best-looking girl in the city, had to be – although maybe he was being a little biased on that score. But she wanted to see him again, and that couldn't be bad. He suddenly remembered that she was a Protestant and he wondered what Paddy Monaghan and the rest of the gang would say. Then he frowned angrily. What did it matter? He'd only met up with Paddy Monaghan again recently after a few years, and two days after their meeting someone was in a coma because of him. It hardly mattered what he thought at all.

Or maybe the fella is in a coma because of you. A dark voice cut through his thoughts. It's all right blaming everyone else when something goes wrong, Seamus Doherty, but you were the one who went over and hit him when he wasn't expecting it. If it hadn't been for you and your cowardly actions, then . . .

'Can I have a word with you, sir?' The accent was neutral. Northern Irish certainly, but Seamus couldn't place it.

Seamus turned and nearly jumped out of his skin. He hadn't heard the red Ford Sierra pulling up alongside him. Probably because of the sound of the rain dashing hard off the pavement, though more likely, he thought drily, because of the loud voice of his conscience, which was tearing at his brain. He noticed that the back door of the car was opened, and that a grey-haired, middle-aged man was beckoning him over. Seamus couldn't see who else was in the car because the windows of the vehicle were made of thick, tinted glass. His heart hammered in his chest and he badly wanted to run, but he knew instinctively that he'd never get away. A plain-clothes Brit, maybe a member of Special Branch, maybe SAS. Though that third option was unlikely. Too old, Seamus decided. Too fat. From the look of him, too slow.

'What's your name, son?'

'Brian Boru.'

The man sighed as if someone had placed the weight of the world on his shoulders, and shook his head slowly from side to side. 'Get in, son.'

'Nah, I don't want a lift,' he said, fighting the panic. 'I like the rain. Thanks, anyhow.' His legs were leaden but he went to try and walk on regardless. The car screeched ahead of him, nearly running over his toes. 'I'm not askin' you, son,' the man said gravely.

Seamus took a deep breath. 'What do ye want? I'm just headin' home.'

The man climbed out of the car and motioned to the interior with a hand. He was a few inches taller than Seamus. He was heavy-set, but a long, grey coat hid his physical shape. 'Get in.'

Seamus reluctantly climbed into the car. There were three other men in the car, each of them wearing police uniform. The fourth man climbed in beside Seamus, sandwiching him between himself and one of the other officers. 'We're goin' for a little run, son,' the man said, impassively. 'You like cars, aye?'

Seamus steeled himself, remembering Paddy Monaghan's words.

'You not talkin', kid?' The grey-haired man smiled and spread his palms. 'It's just that you look like the sort of kid who likes fast cars, who likes gettin' out for a spin now and then, when he's nothin' else to do. Maybe late at night when the bars and discos are over.' The man shrugged impassively. 'Whatever, son. Whatever. Let's go.' He tapped the policeman in the front on the shoulder.

The car shot off up William Street and Seamus baulked at the power of the vehicle. It turned at the roundabout, skipping along the Northland Road and off in the direction of the Buncrana Road. Seamus was panicking but he didn't want to imagine the man with no clothes on in case he started laughing. Instead he concentrated on the road ahead, on the sound of the raindrops bouncing off the roof, on the long black stretch of the Buncrana Road as it swept by in a blur, and he wondered just how the driver could see clearly through the darkened windscreen. Even with the windscreen wipers going full speed, the rain had to be hampering his vision.

'I've a bit of a thing for snapshots, son,' the man said, as the driver took them in the direction of the border checkpoint. 'You like photography yourself?'

Seamus shook his head and feigned a lack of interest. The man tapped one of the policemen in the front on the shoulder and the man handed him a file. The older man opened the folder and produced what appeared to Seamus to be dozens of photographs. He kept them tight to his chest and flicked through them, smiling as he did so, as if they were old family snapshots. He selected about half a dozen and handed the folder back to his stone-faced companion.

'Aye, birds mainly – and the feathered variety, at that . . . ' He winked at the policeman on the other side of Seamus and the man laughed momentarily, then transferred his gaze out into the night. 'But I do all other sorts of wildlife too, you know. Like vermin, for instance. Cockroaches, rats, snakes . . . ' He shrugged and turned to the youth. 'Few pieces of my work for you to look at, Seamus.'

Seamus nearly stopped breathing. The man had called him by his first name, yet he didn't seem to notice the young boy's shock. 'Like you to tell me if you recognise a few of these heads, eh?'

'I don't give a fuck what ye do to me, I'm sayin' fuck all!' Seamus retorted, hotly. He wondered if he should just lash out now and at least try and get his own retaliation in first, as he'd been advised.

'Well, we'll see,' the man said. He showed a photograph to Seamus. Seamus felt his breath stalling and tried not to show his alarm. It was an old photo – one of Dan McGeady walking across Central Drive with a masked rioter. Christ, how had they gotten that shot, Seamus wondered, hoping that his shock wasn't showing on his face. That was two years or more past and, from that angle, they would need to have taken it from the roundabout beside St Mary's Church, which was adjacent to the Bishop's Field. The second photograph showed the small boy with his makeshift mask removed. It was blurred and perhaps taken from a moving vehicle. Seamus recognised himself. He had been smaller then and he'd filled out a little since. He breathed deeply, instinctively feeling that such a picture would never hold up in court. And he'd been a minor then: that had to count for something.

The third photograph was of a masked man in full flight as a riot was in progress in William Street. Seamus knew the figure immediately, even beneath the makeshift mask. As usual, Paddy Monaghan was near the front of the crowd, his angular features making him somewhat hard to miss, despite his mask. Seamus spotted several other familiar figures in the background, each engaged in various acts of rioting. He suppressed a smile as he recognised the dimly visible figures of Jimmy Duffy and Barney Ferguson caught up in a smog of tear-gas in the background, and he smiled as the memories of that day came back to him.

That particular riot had occurred on the day that one of the Protestant paramilitary groups had shot two Catholics in Belfast in revenge for a bomb attack on a fish shop in which five Protestants had been killed. Jimmy had been wearing white parallels and he'd snagged them on a low wall as he and the rest of the rioters had run away from a Saracen into Glenfada Park. Seamus remembered that he himself had been standing some way off to the left of his friends, trying to smash a concrete slab into pieces.

That riot had been a particularly vicious one. Someone had thrown a nail-bomb at the army sangar at 'Aggro Corner'. The hand-held device had fallen short of its intended target, and the thick concrete, sandbag-reinforced wall of the sangar had thwarted the missile's lethal spray of metal shrapnel. It had been a dangerous game to play, because the army had been known to shoot dead nail-bombers, seeing as how that particular weapon was deadly. Still, the perpetrator of that action had achieved his desired effect: he had drawn the army out of their relatively safe bolt-hole and into the Bogside. On hearing the explosion, the rioters had immediately scattered into the safety of the Bogside, where other rioters had made their preparations. Some had stood high up on the roof of the Rossville flats with petrol bombs and scaffolding rods at the ready, waiting for the influx of Saracens, Sixers and foot troops to flood the Bogside; others had capped bottles of petrol, their intention being to saturate either the RUC or the Brits with as much of it as they could before throwing in a light.

It was a game at times. That day, however, the game had

resulted in three rioters being snatched and seriously beaten before being charged with attempted murder, a dozen or more being seriously injured – one critically – with rubber bullets and at least six Brits being treated for second-degree burns. It was a game, on the whole. But sometimes it was a lethal one.

The next two photographs, however, were the ones that would stick in Seamus's mind the most. Not that there was anything much to be seen in the first picture, as each of the photographic subjects was masked. But there *was* something – something that would only become clear to him over time. It was a clear black-and-white photograph of a paramilitary funeral – though which particular one, he had no way of knowing. There were six republicans in dark clothes and black berets, with dark hand-kerchiefs tied across their mouths, carrying a coffin. Seamus didn't know why they were showing him this one, nor the second, which was of the same funeral taken from a different angle. There was something there; he felt it, though he couldn't figure out what. And the man wasn't showing them to him for nothing. But he couldn't for the life of him figure out what it was. He turned his attention away from them, thinking that the police were either trying to trick him into thinking they were just showing him any old bunch of photographs or that perhaps they'd made a mistake in showing him those two pictures in particular. He wondered instead at how the police had taken such clear photographs. But then he realised that they had long-range lenses and access to the latest technology.

'Dunno them, any of them,' he shrugged. 'They aren't very clear.'

'They're clear enough, Seamus,' the older man said, with a laugh. 'And they're enough to convict a man, you take it from me. But I'm not interested in doin' that.' He handed the photographs back to the policeman in the front. 'I want us to be friends, Seamus, nothin' more. I want us to go beyond this thing. I could send you to Saint Pat's in Belfast or . . . no, now I'm thinkin' that you're under sixteen,' he smiled. 'But you're not, sure, are you?'

Seamus didn't reply.

'Nah, it'd be the big one for you, my son. The Crum'. In there along with the hard men who've shot and bombed and killed and maimed. But you see, I'm not really into that. I think if ye stick a baby in with the apes then you'll end up with a wee Tarzan sort of a figure. And sure, there's enough of them runnin' around the fuckin' place already, aren't there?'

Seamus turned away, only to find the policeman on his right staring deep into his eyes. He faced the front, silent and scared.

'We're not interested in you, Seamus. We don't think you're up to anythin' real bad, except for a bit of riotin'. And sure, that's a bit of a laugh most of the time, isn't it?' He regarded the youth's impassive face. 'Sure we don't lose out there either, kid. You barbarians are wreckin' the very fuckin' place you live in, burnin' and bombin' the very mud huts you live in to the ground. And we get to go home to our nice wee houses up the country that all you fuckers have bought for us with the danger money we get every time ye bounce a brick off our car. Fuck,' he exclaimed, laughing, 'sometimes we even get months off on the sick if we get clipped. Great laugh that – money for fuck all and a holiday abroad out of it. Sure who's losin' out there, kid?'

'I'm sayin' fuck all about nothin'. Ye can shoot me if ye want but I don't give a fuck!'

The driver was taking them at breakneck speed along winding back roads in the driving rain and the youth's mind was working overtime. They were going to kill him, he was sure of it, maybe take him out to a deserted field and torture him for hours. Then they'd bury him in a pit of lime or feed his body to the pigs on a farm somewhere, same as the Boys had reportedly done with undercover Brits and informers over the years. Knock you out, throw a bucket of swill over you, and in the morning you'd be lucky if they found your belt buckle. It didn't matter that these people were supposed to be enforcing the law in a fair-minded manner. Northern Ireland had never had that luxury in his lifetime – or if it had, he had never heard about it. Rumours had it that the upholders of the law had even tied and hooded suspects and then taken them for a ride in a helicopter. Once in the air, they'd push them out backwards, only for the screaming victims to find that they had been no more than three or four feet off the ground in the first place.

'D'you not want to be our friend, Seamus? D'you not want to help us out?' The man seemed at ease with the speed at which the curves in the road approached and disappeared, at ease with the rain dashing off the windscreen and blurring their vision, with the skidding of the wheels on the tarmacadamed surface of the road.

'Where are ye takin' me? Are ye gonna kill me?'

They laughed at him then and he felt foolish for asking. 'Are you goin' to help us out, or what?'

'I'm no tout. Ye can fuckin' kill me, I told ye that. But do it quick, 'cause I'm sick of your slabberin'.' He was angry now and he just wanted this to be over and done with, no matter which way it went.

They laughed again. 'We don't kill people for nothin', Seamus, despite what you might have heard. It's your lot does that. Sure you see it on the news all the time.'

Seamus wanted to say that he saw whatever the establishment wanted him to see, because that was the answer his ma would have given, every night when she was staring at the TV. But he said nothing. Giving his opinions on the cause and solutions to the Troubles wasn't going to earn him any Brownie points.

'Where are ye takin' me?' he repeated, as calmly as he could.

'Home, Seamus,' the man replied, smiling easily. 'Sure isn't that where you're goin'?'

Seamus saw lights through the rain. He didn't recognise the structure in the distance at first but then the green wall of corrugated tin sheets and the watchtower up ahead came slowly into focus and he recognised the even line of rooftops at the end of the unkempt, marshy field. The car slowed halfway along the road that led to Creggan Heights and Seamus knew he was on the back road that led to the Piggery Ridge army camp.

'Stop,' the older man said suddenly, tapping the driver on the shoulder. 'Just pull in here. We don't want too many people seein' him gettin' out, do we?' He turned to Seamus and smiled. 'That saved you from gettin' wet, didn't it, kid?' He smiled again and climbed out of the car. 'Go on, get out and away home with you.'

Seamus didn't move but instead looked the man directly in the eyes. 'Are ye goin' to shoot me? At least have the guts to tell me that, because I'll not be around to tell anyone, will I?'

'Nah, son, there's worse things than shootin' someone. I just wanted you to help me out a little. There's a lot of bad people out there in the world and I have to take a broom to them. Nothing personal against any of them, of course. To me, it's just a job.'

'Ye'll be hearin' about this,' Seamus said angrily, aware of his vulnerability, the shake beginning in his legs. 'Me ma'll be on the phone to a solicitor first thing in the fuckin' mornin'.'

'Ach, I don't think so, Seamus.'

'Why's that?'

The older man pulled the collar of his long coat up around

his face as protection from the now-driving rain and didn't reply immediately.

'Well?' Seamus urged.

'Out of there, son, and hurry the fuck up. I'll get me death.' He lifted his head as Seamus gingerly crawled out past him. The young boy was unaware of the ferocity of the rain just then, unaware that he was nearly soaked through, though he was sure that his peripheral vision was clearer than it had ever been. There was nowhere to run if they started shooting, nowhere to hide. He was standing on a back road that ran between two flat and untended rat-infested fields, the only life around here the occasional cow or horse. Vulnerable, in danger, shaking. The older man looked up at him as he stood there, uncertain what to do next. 'You want to know why you won't talk, son?' Seamus gritted his teeth and nodded angrily. 'Because I have some information for you.' The man laughed and got back in the car. 'You won't talk to me yet, Seamus,' he added with conviction, as he brushed the excess rain off his coat and out of the car door. 'But I can tell you with all certainty that some day you will, don't you worry about it. Now go on, away with you.'

Seamus turned and walked slowly away. His legs were jelly and he remembered that same feeling from over two years ago as he'd left Dan McGeady in Cromore and made his way back to the shops. Only then it wasn't the middle of the night, and there would have been witnesses. Now he had about four hundred yards to walk before he arrived at the Heights. One single shot, that's all it would have taken. And nobody gave a damn about a single shot ringing out in the back of nowhere. You heard a gunshot in the middle of the night in these times, you listened, then you rolled over and went back to sleep. Maybe if there was a gun battle in progress, you lay awake, trying to distinguish between the sounds of the guns, trying to pick out the sounds of the Provies' Armalites and AK-47s and the Brits' SLRs and Stens. But it wouldn't have made you get out of bed, because you'd hear about it eventually in the morning on the news – the next night at the latest. You always seemed to hear about everything that happened in Derry, because there were no secrets any more.

His mother told him that everyone knew everyone else's business. That was due, she reckoned, to the fact that everyone had to – that it kept strangers from wandering in and out of the estates at will. Here in Derry there was a network of information about everyone available to everyone. Detailing their sympathies, their relatives, those who were sympathetic to or against the cause – and people were rated more in terms of their staunchness than for their other more morally redeeming qualities. The war had brought that familiarity on, Mary had told him with conviction, and there was perhaps no other city in Europe where you were able to get hold of so much of information about relative strangers within so short a space of time.

A single shot and he'd be another statistic for whom the Boys would riot tomorrow evening, maybe for up to a week afterwards. A single shot, that was all it would take.

'Hey, and Seamus . . . ' the policeman called out.

Seamus was about two hundred yards away, consciously moving out of the glare of the car's headlights. He didn't turn, figuring that it would at least look bad for them if they had to shoot him in the back. 'What the fuck do ye want now?' he called out, hoarsely.

'This meetin' of ours, we'll be doin' it again. Except the next time, I'll be able to tell you all about your father.'

Seamus wanted to reply, to say something, yet he couldn't think of anything suitable. He didn't like the fact that the man had used the word "meeting". That implied something that had been implicitly planned, that was of mutual convenience to all groups concerned, and to Seamus this sudden unplanned get-together had been anything but that.

'Go fuck yourself!' he said under his breath, feeling that it would be stupid to push his luck at this stage.

'So I'd think very carefully about tellin' anyone, if I were you.' The man laughed and Seamus jumped as the door slammed shut.

He walked on down the road. Slowly, keeping his breathing in check. He heard the vehicle's heavy engine revving behind him and he watched as the headlights cut across his path to the right, then vanished as the car turned back up towards the back roads. Seamus ran then and he didn't stop until he was safely back home.

*

Jimmy was out driving, the receptionist said, and she'd let him know that someone had called as soon as he returned. In all, she must have said that about six times that morning, and she sounded quite ticked off with the caller's persistence. It was the seventh call that found him, and the red-haired boy was unusually angry when he answered the phone.

'Jesus, Seamus, what are ye at? They said some eejit's been blockin' the line all mornin' and they've lost a fortune of business over it.' Before Seamus could reply, he added, 'That's a load of shite and I know it, but Jesus, what the hell's wrong with ye?'

'I need to talk to ye, important like.'

'Is . . . is it about your man?' Jimmy's voice was subdued. 'Christ, is he . . . ?'

'Nah . . . I, well, I dunno about that. Good fuckin' question. But it's about somethin' else more important.'

'Christ, it must be bad if it's worse than that.'

'It is.'

Jimmy had hurried around straight after work, still in his white coat. Seamus didn't even let him set foot in the door. Instead he put his Wrangler coat on and said goodbye to his mother. Mary waved a cheerless, wordless goodbye to him as he wandered up the street, hands deep in his pockets. It wasn't cold but he shivered anyhow. When they reached the path that led down to the reservoirs he relaxed slightly and told his friend about the cops – one of whom he was sure was Special Branch – and the crazy drive along the back roads of Creggan, just to let him off at the top of Creggan Heights. But Jimmy seemed to be more interested in other aspects of the conversation.

'Aye, and they've a photo of me, ye say? Christ, I mind that day too! Bastards nearly ripped me leg off with a plastic. Tore me trousers an' all.'

Seamus snorted loudly. 'Ye ripped the fuckin' things on a wall. Sure I was there.'

'That's what I sais,' Jimmy retorted hotly. 'I ripped me trousers tryin' to avoid a plastic.'

'Are ye fuckin' listenin' to me, Jimmy, or what? The bastards were tryin' to set me up for somethin', I'm nearly sure of it.'

Jimmy nodded. 'Aye, maybe,' he agreed, pursing his lips and raising an eyebrow, as if he wasn't too sure. 'And you're sayin' your woman's a Hun?' he added, seemingly aghast. 'Fuck, that's a good one. You'll not be seein' her again then, eh?'

Seamus felt like clashing him on the side of the head with his balled fist. 'Jimmy,' he nearly squealed, 'what the hell has that got to do with anythin'? Christ, we're talkin' about my fuckin' life here.'

'Doesn't sound that bad to me,' Jimmy returned, with a shrug. He offered his friend a cigarette. 'They gave ye a lift, ye sais fuck all to them and then they sais cheerio. Sure where's the harm in that? At least ye didn't get soaked.'

Seamus stepped in front of him. 'Aye, and then when I asked them if they were gonna shoot me, they sais no and that they'd just done somethin' worse. Or they said somethin' about there bein' worse things ... or somethin'. Christ, I dunno what the fuck they said. What the fuck did they mean by that, anyhow?'

'You don't know what they said but ye want me to explain it, is that it?' Jimmy shook his head in disbelief. 'You're goin' on there like a space cadet, if ye want the truth. But sure, it's all easy enough solved. Ye go to Sinn Féin and they call a news conference. Sure they're at that all the fuckin' time. Ye get your photo taken with one or two of them, sure the cops won't come near ye again. Ye could nearly bet your life on it. Sure wasn't there one boy last week, they were doin' the same to him? He hasn't heard anythin' since.'

'I go to Sinn Féin and tell them that the cops gave me a lift home the other night because it was rainin'. Ye think they're gonna stick that in fuckin' *An Phoblacht?* The cops doin' some community-relations work and Sinn Féin givin' them publicity for it? Jesus, get a fuckin' grip, Jimmy, for fuck's sakes!'

'Sorry for fuckin' talkin'!' Jimmy said, in a huff.

Seamus took a deep breath, produced a packet of Park Drive and offered one to Jimmy.

Jimmy grinned at the conciliatory gesture. 'You're gettin' right and heavy on the blows, Seamy. Ye just put one out.' He took one anyway.

'Aye, sure me life's fuckin' as good as over. And those bastards have me worked up to high doh.'

Jimmy accepted a light. 'Aye, I see where you're at. But they do it all the time, ye know.'

'Do what?'

'Lift boys. Christ, sure they've lifted half – maybe all – of this estate at one time or another. They're just fishin', that's what me ma says. Fishin' to see if they can get someone vulnerable enough to tout to them. They get a wee bit of information on ye and they milk the shite out of it to make ye talk. And if ye don't, then they just move on and pick on someone else. I wouldn't worry about it, if it was me. Wouldn't give a monkey's, I'm tellin' ye now.'

Seamus smiled, thinking that maybe he had a point. 'Aye maybe, right enough.'

'Hey, but there's another thing, Seamy.'

'What?'

'Well, if ye think about it hard enough it'll come to ye. And maybe ye wouldn't want to hear it from me anyway.' Jimmy inhaled deeply from his cigarette, his eyes on the ground. Seamus hated the way he did that. He inhaled half a cigarette at a time and left the other half too warm and unsmokable, that being the direct result of a furtive time, not too long past, when he hadn't been allowed to smoke at all.

'Well, me mind's not functionin' the best at the moment. Go on, get it out.'

'Ye might not want to hear it,' Jimmy warned, pursing his lips and raising his palms. 'I'm tellin' ye now.'

'Jesus, Jimmy.'

'Aye, well on your own head be it.' He waved a finger. 'And, mind, this is not the way that I think, so don't go gettin' fucked up with me.' He took a deep breath. 'What if you did go to them?' he asked. 'Sinn Féin, I mean. And you said that the cops had given you a ride home, showed ye a few photos of you riotin' and stuff and then just let ye go. Just like that,' Jimmy said. Stopping and looking directly into his friend's face, he raised an eyebrow. 'Aye, they just let ye go. Do ye think the lads would believe ye? Do you think they'd believe anyone who came out with that story, never mind . . . '

Seamus nodded grimly. 'Aye, never mind me, the son of a tout.'

'Maybe they'd think ye were just coverin' your tracks. Ye know the way they think, suspicious as fuck. Those boys don't even trust each other these days. Maybe that's the way they'd see it.' The red-haired youth shrugged. 'That's only the way I'm thinkin', anyhow. Sure they said fuck all about your da, didn't they, Seamy?' Jimmy said, quickly. 'The cops, I mean. They never mentioned him, did they?'

Seamus wanted to tell him. He'd told him everything of real importance in his life – always had done. But the grey-haired man had been playing an ace when he'd said he knew something about his da. One sentence, thrown in amongst so many others, as if it hadn't mattered a damn – as if he'd just remembered about the boy's father and had ad libbed it for something to say. But there had been something about the way he had said it, something about that whole meeting – as the man had called it – that had the workings of a planned event. They'd known his name; they'd known that he lived in the Creggan. Deep down, Seamus felt they'd known far more than they'd let on about. He shook his head.

'Nah, well they know fuck all. Special Branch never do. Just tryin' their luck.'

'Ye reckon that's who he was?'

'Aye, probably.'

Seamus shook his head and sat down on a fence. 'Aye, that'd sound good all right, wouldn't it? Me goin' and tellin' them that, like. The Boys'd be thinkin' I fingered someone, especially if I said they had me bang to rights on riotous behaviour. That bloody wanker! That was what he meant when he said he'd done somethin' worse.'

'Aye well, ye ask me, that's just one of your problems. You're goin' out with a Hun. And her from Nelson Drive too. Christ, what do ye think Monaghan will say about that?'

'Fuck Monaghan!' Seamus snapped. 'What the fuck does it matter what he thinks? She's a left-footer all right but sure that's fuck all. I'm workin' with them every day of the week. Big deal.'

Jimmy shrugged and handed him another cigarette. 'I don't care myself. I like them, actually. Couldn't eat a full one, though.' He smiled at Seamus. 'Couldn't eat a full one. Get it?'

Seamus smiled thinly, despite his mood.

Jimmy shrugged. 'Just tryin' to lighten the load. I'm just sayin', that's all. Hey, and her family wouldn't take it so well either, you sittin' there with the Boys, and them Huns. Sure maybe the wee woman herself would finish with ye. Not that she'd want to,' he added, quickly. 'But they might make her. I'm not sayin' they're sectarian or nothin',' he continued, 'but they'd probably reckon ye weren't picked on for nothin' and that ye must know somethin'. That'd be the way they'd think. I reckon, anyhow.'

Which was the argument that finally swung it for him. 'Aye, well I've decided that I'm not sayin' fuck all to anyone about anythin', and neither are you. Ye hear me?'

Jimmy raised three fingers of his left hand. 'Scout's Honour. If that's what ye want, that's fine. Dunno if it's what I'd do but . . . '

'Aye, well it's what I'm doin'. And you were obviously never in the fuckin' Scouts, because that's the wrong fuckin' hand, you eejit!'

Jimmy grinned a stupid grin. 'Just kiddin' about. C'mon, we'll go get a pint. My treat.'

Seamus shrugged. 'Aye, I could do with one all right. Ease me nerves.'

They walked over Central in silence, nodding and waving to a few friends on their way to the bar.

'Aye, it's your own bearpit, Seamy,' Jimmy said, eventually. 'I'm tellin' ye now, it is. I'll say fuck all about the girl and I'll swear I never heard ye mention a word about the cop thing. It's probably better anyhow, right enough. But what if that boy lifts ye again? What if that was just the start of somethin'?'

Seamus shook his head. 'Those photos were taken two years back and there's nothin' he can do about me now. It's obvious – he was just tryin' to scare the fuck out of me. I'll lie low for a while and it'll blow over. You'll see. It'll all just blow over as soon as Paddy gets a grip and gets away from whatever the fuck he's mixed up in. We'll all be grand then, you'll see.'

Jimmy shrugged. 'And that boy Doran?' he asked. His face was once more lined with concern.

'I've never heard of anyone called Doran,' Seamus returned, easily, as they entered the Telstar.

Jimmy laughed. 'Aye, you're a fuckin' head case all right, Seamy. A fuckin' Grade A head case.'

*

Despite that outward show of bravado, for the next three days Seamus worried himself sick. Thoughts of the unconscious Hugo Doran lying out cold in Intensive Care kept coming back to him, no matter how he chose to occupy himself, and he was convinced that it was only a matter of time before the youth died. At night he found himself lying awake, waiting for the front door to be shouldered in and the Brits or the cops to come hurtling up the stairs, batons drawn, charge sheet in hand. Attempted murder, maybe even actual murder: he envisaged the worst. The only thing he could be certain of was that if the youth's condition deteriorated any more, it would be in Friday's edition of the *Journal*. He found himself humming a song one evening; he knew that he knew the tune but he couldn't place it. It came to him on Wednesday morning. It was the tune of 'The Men Behind the Wire' and the words swam in his head:

> *Armoured cars and tanks and guns,*
> *Came to take away our sons,*
> *But every man will stand behind*
> *The men behind the wire.*

Thoughts of spending an eternity in Crumlin Road Jail threatened to engulf him and he hardly spoke to anyone. His mother was concerned, of course, because he seemed to be off his food and she said that she thought he was coming down with a bug: 'Might have got it comin' back in on Monday night, you havin' to walk it home from the town, and ye should have asked me for a lend of the money to get yourself a taxi till ye got your pay.'

Though she didn't believe it for a minute and Seamus knew it. It was what she hoped was happening to him. She could read him like a book and she knew immediately when her boy was in trouble, because she'd told him that so many times over. She just wanted him to be sick, to be maybe as ordinary as wee Marty McSwine from down the street, whose mother had only just told Mary the other day that he was going off to Maynooth to become a priest, God bless him, just as soon as he got an A in all of his exams. Seamus agreed with Mary anyway and, when she furthered her diagnosis, he even feigned a headache just to please her. She gave him a few Anadin, though she didn't hang around to watch him swallow them.

And for a time she was his mother again, wee Mary Doherty,

as strong as they came. Mary Doherty who had fought the Brits and stood up to the 'RA, who had always said her piece and to hell with anyone who didn't agree. Also, there was communication there and Seamus and his mother actually began to talk for a time. The conversation was superficial, perhaps, and it dealt with the mundane things that pressed heavily upon those moments of their time together. But it was conversation and Seamus relished that, not realising until then that he had missed her words, her thoughts, her ideas. And not realising that recently he had hated the companionable silence until the moment that she sparked ever so briefly into life.

He met up with Elaine that Thursday night, having been looking forward to seeing her all week. She was the only thing he had going for him at the moment, though he'd never tell her that. You didn't do that, according to Jimmy Duffy. You never let that secret out of the bag with women, because then they'd walk all over you. She was the first to let the secret slip.

She told him that she felt like she was in heaven every time she met him. Even though at times they did nothing more than walk around the town, or go to the latest release in the Palace, the Rialto or the Strand cinema, or even to the occasional disco – although the discos were always down the town, and they'd both agreed that not going there together too often was both wise and safe and ultimately in both their interests. And for several weeks afterwards everything went well and Seamus started to believe that he was in heaven too.

SEVEN

Hugo Doran was making a slow but marked recovery – that was the good news. Seamus and Jimmy had learned that from the local paper, not having the nerve to ask around. But the bad news was that Paddy Monaghan had gone to ground.

In one way Seamus was happy about that because hanging around with Paddy Monaghan was a mixed blessing. He was good fun to be with, and yet he always seemed to thrive on danger, to live his life on a knife-edge. Yet in another way Paddy Monaghan's disappearance was also slightly annoying. Monaghan seemed to have a habit of doing that, of hiding when things got too much and then reappearing with that beguiling smile on his face, the one that charmed you into believing that nothing had occurred – that everything in the garden was rosy. Seamus wasn't really sure which scenario he preferred and this ambiguity made Seamus decide that he was going to forget certain things. Like the 'meeting', as the Special Branch man had called it. And the fact that he was going out with a Protestant girl. A Protestant girl whom he now loved more than life himself; it scared him, he loved her that much.

He had been going out with her for several months now and everything had been wonderful. He even found himself hanging around in the Rainbow Café every now and then on the days that he wasn't seeing her. That fact didn't escape the notice of the proprietors, an elderly couple who had been married for years and who ran the café in a relaxed though very efficient manner. They took an instant shine to him, even gave him the occasional cup of tea and maybe a scone for free, saying that they remembered him from years ago when he used to come in with his mother and, my, hadn't he grown up to be a handsome wee lad, or what?

Elaine Rogers was a quiet, unassuming girl by nature and Seamus was starting to believe that their relationship was about as perfect as any he had ever known. He found that now, in contrast to his initial date with her, he could talk to her about nearly everything. There were one or two subjects which they both broached tentatively – though those same topics weren't exactly off-limits either. Like religion and politics, for example. Like how it would have been nice to meet up with each other's families if they ever had the time – which they always seemed to have, but one or the other of them invariably had an excuse at the ready. Or how Seamus always seemed to meet up with Elaine's friends and she never met up with his.

In lots of ways she was very like him, he had decided. She tagged along with other people's ideas, never thinking to disagree, even if she felt she had a valid point to put across. She was quieter when stronger people were in her company, always game for a laugh, so long as it didn't hurt anyone. Only when it came to her career did she show an inclination to push herself forward – a true determination to succeed that bordered almost on religious fervour. She knew where she was going in her life and Seamus found himself slightly jealous of that. Yet he knew that this jealousy of her determination lay in his own sad personal belief that some day she would leave the town and make a better life for herself abroad. In one way he admired her for that, but he hated her for it as well. And he felt stupid thinking the way he did, because he'd only known her for a matter of weeks and her future really had nothing to do with him, after all.

But he admired the way she handled everything else. The way she asked about his mother, truly concerned about her drink problem – which only three people in the world knew about. As if she'd known the woman all her life and truly cared about her, even though they'd never even met. Seamus felt guilty about that. He felt guilty about the fact that her friends were fun to hang around with in the discos and that she didn't know that his own friends could quite often be the same. He'd thought about introducing her to Jimmy Duffy – because Jimmy was safer than the others in that, mostly, he knew when to speak and when to keep his mouth shut – though he was afraid that, if the red-haired boy said something out of turn about religion or politics, Elaine would see Seamus in a different light. It happened at times – that much he guessed to be true. So, to be on the safe side, he didn't bother introducing her to any of his friends at all.

Of course, Seamus and Elaine had talked briefly once or twice about religion and politics. They lived in a country where both topics were foremost in everyone's lives and thus it had been practically inevitable that they would discuss them. In the sixth or seventh week of their relationship they had tentatively broached the topic of the Troubles, discussing how it affected their day-to-day routines. They were talking casually about the barriers that the army had put up around the town and the recent relaxation of security. Static checkpoints had been opened only recently in the centre of the city, which meant that pedestrians and motorists now no longer had to stop and be searched upon entering the town centre. Instead, snap searches were carried out at random by foot patrols. It had been a relatively quiet year all round and the move was being made to try and bring a sense of normality back to both traders and shoppers.

Seamus had said that it was good to see the city coming half back to normal but that some things would never change. It wouldn't make a blind bit of difference to him and his friends, for example. The Brits and the cops looked upon them all as enemies, no matter how quiet things became, and they'd all be stopped and searched anyhow. It didn't matter a damn how many barriers came down, he'd concluded, because one would always remain – and that was the fact that they were Catholics.

Elaine had blushed when he'd said that. She wasn't politically minded, she assured him softly, and she didn't understand why people were fighting over bits of land and why everyone couldn't just live in peace with each other. It was a naive dream, perhaps, to believe that it could ever happen in their lifetime, she knew, and she told him she was intelligent enough to realise that life wasn't ever going to be a bed of roses. But it was a nice dream, all the same, and it was a pity more people didn't share it. Because violence was futile, she said. It was a continuous cycle spurred on by mindless people who, when they had sated their own hatred by killing or hurting others, left those same others to fight that none-too-noble cause because of the hurt that had been inflicted upon them. An endless, futile cycle, and it all boiled down to fear in the end. Us being afraid of them, and vice versa.

Seamus had laughed at that, thinking the idea preposterous. He wasn't afraid of anyone, he told her, and he never would be. That was a lesson he had learned a long time back. Show people that you're bigger and stronger, he smiled, maybe hand out the odd thrashing, and people usually got the message in the end. But Elaine had giggled when he'd said that, causing him to blush. She didn't doubt his personal courage, she told him, but she was talking about the courage of acceptance – the courage to live beside others who weren't the same and accept the difference. After all, the Catholics were always going on about how rough they were getting it, but the Protestants were afraid that they would be downtrodden one day too, that their rights would be shunned because, in this city at least, they were in a minority.

Seamus had laughed at that, saying that the Catholics never walked over or intimidated anyone, sure everyone knew that. And then Elaine had mentioned the bombs, the hoaxes, the shootings, the beatings of her friends if they ever dared venture across the Craigavon Bridge and walk up the centre of the town on a Saturday night. She'd mentioned the fact that, although Protestants outnumbered Catholics in the North of Ireland, Derry's Protestant population was small. They had to live under threat of intimidation in the besieged Fountain estate and, ever so slowly, were being forced from their houses in the Glen into the Waterside. Sure if that wasn't intimidation, what was? And Seamus had thought about what she was saying, thinking maybe she had a point. A small point, right enough – because he still believed deep down that they'd started it – but a sort of a point nonetheless.

Seamus listened with admiration as she spoke – a true pacifist, it seemed, with no real love for one side or the other. He'd heard priests talk of peace, naturally, and most politicians had called for peace and calm at some stage in their career – though usually shortly after their own side had committed an atrocity. Then again, they often spoke for war when the other side did the same. But hearing those same words coming from someone he loved, he found that he could bring himself around to thinking a little that way too.

Elaine was a gentle girl who wouldn't harm a soul, he knew, yet she was also strong and courageous – not afraid to say her piece in her own, gentle way. In many ways she reminded him of the way his mother was now. He liked that, and marvelled at it too. And it was after hearing her say those words that he decided that maybe his mother and Elaine might get on well after all. He arranged a meeting between the two of them for a Sunday afternoon and his mother seemed pleased that he had decided to 'bring the wee girl home', as she put it.

That particular afternoon had gone better than he could ever have hoped. Mary Doherty wasn't all that used to having guests around for tea on a Sunday but she made a special effort for Elaine. She had even laid the table in the kitchen – the walls of which had been freshly papered, for the first time ever, by the wee man from across the road about a week before – and a selection of Swiss rolls and a plate of biscuits had been placed there in the centre, as if part of some ritual. Seamus had smiled as his mother had done that, feeling a strong yet slightly sorrowful affection for her as she had told him to get away with himself when he offered to help. Because it was 'No bother, no bother at all', and he should just 'Go and get the girl over here as soon as ye can, sure, 'cause I'm dyin' to meet the one who has our Seamus spendin' all of his free time and money on her, 'cause she must be a right wee cracker!' And he'd laughed even as she had at that remark, and savoured that small, fractured moment of bliss – in which the troubles of the world took leave of the Doherty household – for a long time afterwards.

Mary Doherty was the complete hostess that day: charming, charismatic – and none of it false. Seamus knew that falseness didn't exist in her heart: it never had. She was enjoying the girl's company as much as Elaine was apparently enjoying theirs. The tea was hardly touched and stories were exchanged about how Seamus was doing at work, about how he had done at school, about his plans for the future. And they'd laughed often, like two girls laughing about some wee fella in a disco, and Seamus had blushed, embarrassed slightly, but enjoying being the centre of attention too. Mary had disappeared for a short time that afternoon and there had followed the noise of some heavy shuffling up the stairs. Seamus had shrugged it off, saying that his ma was doting, or something. But Elaine had giggled, telling him that his mum was the nicest person she'd ever met and that he was a lucky man.

Seamus had smiled, realising that she was right, and he'd felt sad also. Very sad indeed, because he'd almost forgotten that fact, what with the way his life had been pressing down on him of late. Mary had appeared then, just as Elaine had leaned over to kiss him, and they'd both blushed. His mother had merely smiled. An introspective, reminiscent smile; a sad smile. She'd had an old biscuit tin in her hand, and Seamus had wondered if she wasn't going a little too far with the hospitality when he'd suddenly remembered that it was the one in which she kept her old photos and newspaper clippings. Seamus had tried to take it from her, but she'd pulled it away with a grin

'Ye aren't gettin' away that easily, Seamus Doherty,' she'd told him, her grin widening. 'The wee lass wants to see a few photos of ye when ye were younger, I'm sure of that. Isn't that right enough, Elaine?'

Elaine had nodded eagerly, giggled and slapped his hand away. 'Aye, I do that. I'm sure he was just beautiful when he was a baby.'

He had dropped his head, embarrassed, though smiling still. 'Aye, right.'

And Mary had pulled the photographs up to her chest and sorted through them. Seamus had shivered, remembering briefly how the Special Branch man had done the same. Then his mother had offered a few photographs around. One of Seamus when he was six months. Black and white, torn at the edges, slightly crumpled. One of his granny, who had died two years before he was born, and wasn't he like her?

Elaine had nodded, though later she said that he didn't resemble her in the slightest. And then one of his da, quickly offered and then taken back. Seamus saw the neutral look on Elaine's face. He hadn't told her much about his da, only that he'd died a few years back of a disease – a rare blood disease. Which was true, in a way, he'd convinced himself, so he wasn't really lying to her, which he hated doing. Lead poisoning was a blood disease after all, wasn't it? Though maybe it wasn't so rare in this country, he mused. Still, it was only a small lie – a white lie. Nothing to worry about.

He was definitely like his da, that was all Elaine had said – same cheekbones, chin and hairline. She'd seemed a little puzzled by the lack of response from Mary and Seamus, by their silence, by the speed with which Mary had passed Elaine other photographs of her own family and talked more of them than of his father. Still, Elaine hadn't said anything else about his father, and that was good. That wasn't the sort of her, and that had always pleased Seamus. She could sense when people didn't want to discuss something – at least, that always seemed to be the way when she was with him and he was in a silent mood.

His mother hadn't shown her feelings about the subject of his father – which Seamus appreciated greatly – though Seamus had seen her frowning slightly and passing one or two newspaper clippings skilfully under the box as Elaine had examined another photograph of Seamus when he was only ten. His girlfriend had laughed loudly and he'd blushed, pretending not to notice that Mary had stuck the clippings to the bottom of the box under the other clutter of memories before joining in the fun.

The afternoon had passed quickly after that. More photographs, more idle banter, and laughter devoid of either politics or religion. Though Seamus was quite certain that, by the end of the afternoon, both women could probably have handled those particular subjects excellently, such was the way they had taken to each other.

Later that evening, Seamus rang Elaine a taxi from Sadie's. He'd stood outside with her for a while at the side of the house, holding her close, laughing, kissing, each happy with how successful the afternoon had been. Mary had passed them by, saying that she was just on her way to bingo, telling Elaine to call back anytime – and she didn't have to wait for Seamus to ask her over, either. Elaine had laughed, said she would, thanked her for the tea, the fun. And standing there with Seamus she had said that she must return the compliment some day. Seamus nodded, saying it would be nice, though wondering if it would be. The taxi arrived and he kissed her and told her he'd ring her the next day, before waving goodbye and watching the taxi all the way over the street.

He was in a jubilant mood. The afternoon had gone far better than he had expected. It was shortly after eight and he made his way upstairs to his room intending to listen to some music, tired despite his exhilaration. His mother's bedroom door lay open, however, and Seamus pulled it shut. He was about to go into his own room when he remembered the biscuit tin and the newspaper clippings that she had ever so dextrously passed under the box in the kitchen.

He entered his mother's bedroom and felt immediately guilty about doing so. It wasn't his usual form to do such a thing but he felt that there was something in that box that was of relevance – something that he too had a right to see. He searched the wardrobe: above it, in it. He searched under the bed; in the clothes locker at the end of the bed. Nothing. He stood there thinking for a time. His mother was skilled at hiding things – he knew that much, to his chagrin – so where could she have put something of that shape and size? He clicked his fingers and his gaze went immediately to the bottom of the wardrobe. There was a small gap there and there was no way that Mary could have pushed the tin underneath the front. But the back, that was a different matter altogether – and that would possibly account for the shuffling noise he had heard earlier in the day, when his mother had gone upstairs.

He prised the wardrobe carefully out from the wall and rummaged around in the dark space underneath until his hand located the box. He pulled it out and pushed the wardrobe back into place. Then he went to his room.

*

'Ye shouldn't have been goin' through me things, Seamus. Christ, ye know that.'

Seamus had prepared an answer in his head, knowing what she'd say as soon as he showed her the newspaper clippings. It was about his right to know everything about his past, about his right to know about everything that had concerned his life until this moment. But the words wouldn't come to him now that he needed them. He saw his mother's red-rimmed eyes and the words were lost in the pain.

'I know,' was all he could manage to say in return.

'They're my things – my personal things. Ye had no right. Give that to me.'

She snatched the thin and very old newsprint from his hand, taking time to straighten out the edges carefully, to regard the picture sadly.

'It's me da, isn't it?'

His ma frowned sadly and smiled an almost winsome smile. 'Aye, that's your da. You would know that fat figure of his anywhere, even under that mask and beret.'

Seamus laughed nervously and then lowered his eyes. 'I'm sorry. Yesterday, when ye were showin' the photos to Elaine, I saw ye slippin' that . . . '

She nodded and sat down at the kitchen table. It was half past seven in the morning and she was dressed in her nightgown, her hair a mess. She'd usually get him up, put his breakfast on the table and go back to bed for an hour. She lit a cigarette and offered him one. He took it, lit it, then put it down on the edge of the ashtray as he slipped his overalls on. Anything to divert his attention away from the look in her eyes.

'Ye want tea?' he asked. His tone was conciliatory. 'I've time for a cup meself.' She smiled, knowing that he hadn't really. He rarely ate all his breakfast, his life was such a rush these days, what with work and going steady.

'Aye,' she said, after a moment. 'But ye'd need to get a move on.' She held the newspaper up to the light coming in through the window. The photograph was blurred, the newsprint smudged. 'Aye, Stevie McAdam's funeral, that was . . . ' She paused, deep in thought. 'Aye, sad, that was. Real sad. And that's Billy Flannagan on the other side of the coffin. He . . . '

'Aye, I mind that name,' Seamus said. 'That was the boy me da says was up in the back fields with him one time, wasn't it?'

Mary looked at him and dropped her head, her gaze thoughtful. 'Aye, you've a good memory for some things, Seamus. Always the wrong things, now as I mind. Still, aye, Billy Flannagan . . . he was your da's best friend. Committed suicide, he did, about two months after your da was . . . killed.' Mary seemed to have difficulty with the word. 'Married, he was, with five of a family. Just came in one night after a drink, went out to the backyard and blew his brains out in the shed. Never left a note.' Mary shrugged and looked at the photo once more. 'But aye, gettin' away from that, that was definitely Stevie McAdam's funeral. Aye, it was. Ye wouldn't mind him, 'cause that happened when ye were away on your holiday, about ten days or so before Motorman. But he was never out of our house. Him and the rest of the boys. Stickies one night, Provies the next. Christ, that was some fuckin' carry-on.'

She paused thoughtfully for a moment, then her face lined. 'Good fella, he was. Shot dead as he came back from an op along with your da and a few others . . . ' Mary's voice seemed distant and she shrugged again. 'One of many who lost their lives for the cause, I suppose, and you'd get a lot who wouldn't mind him now, there's that many have died. Anyhow, he was a good friend of your da's and your da was one of the colour party. That's him there, all right, large as life. McGeady behind him. Big Sean Cassidy behind him again, and on the other side that's John, Niall, Gerry – aye, they were the other four. Provos every one of them, except your da. Strange that, considerin' the Stickies had called a truce that May, him bein' allowed on their colour party. But he was the bomb expert and they let him tag along. And . . . ' Mary stopped, shrugged. 'I'll not go into it now. But Christ, aye!' she said, drawing deeply on her cigarette and sipping at the tea. 'That was a hairy one all right, that funeral.'

'Aye?'

Mary nodded. 'Aye, see, the place was still a no-go area then and we were all afraid that the helicopters would shoot into the crowd. The Brits couldn't get in any other way, see. They'd tried comin' in over the Lecky Road from Nixon's Corner one time that day but they were beaten back. So we huddled in together, got a Dutch news team to film the whole thing in case they tried anythin' funny, like. They never did, right enough, lucky for us. The press helped. Them takin' photos of the Brits shootin' into a crowd, sure it would have looked bad in the eyes of the world, wouldn't it? And ye can say what ye want about the Brits, but they weren't that stupid. If they were goin' to shoot ye they'd have done it on the quiet, because they'd hardly want the world to see it again, would they? Not after Bloody Sunday.'

Mary's face brightened momentarily. Seamus smiled and sat down beside her. 'And then the Boys lowered the coffin, stepped back, took out their pistols and fired off a few shots into the air as the helicopter came in right and low, tryin' to scatter us. God, ye talk about pandemonium! I fell to the ground, some eejit stepped on me hand. But we all held firm, stood our ground and pulled out the umbrellas, and they could do nothin'. Aye, Christ, that was some funeral all right.'

'That photograph, who took it?'

'God, now you're askin'.' Mary paused for a second. 'It wasn't that news team, sure all they had was a video camera. That's all they were allowed that day. Only certain photographers were allowed near the funerals. Only those known to the crowd, just in case the Branch slipped one of their own in amongst them. But I'd say the *Journal,* probably . . . *Telegraph,* maybe. Nah, son, I couldn't really say for certain.' She looked up at him briefly. 'Why?'

He shrugged as casually as he could. 'Ah, just.'

She held her tea in one hand, running the other beneath the cup to warm it up. Then she looked at him. 'Y'know, your da was a good man.'

Seamus shifted uncomfortably and sipped at his own tea, even though it was the last thing he wanted first thing in the morning.

'Aye, sure ye've told me that before a few times.'

She nodded. 'Aye, I have, and I'll likely tell ye a lot more too. He was a good man, despite what everyone else saw. The outer skin – just a façade, nothin' more. It's there in the eyes, you see, Seamus. Every man or woman's thoughts are written there in their eyes, visible for the entire world to see, if ye know what it is you're lookin' for.' She sighed, then took a sip of tea, a slight shake in her hands. 'He was a good man. He lived hard, that was his only fault. But that's because he was human, he was real. Your faults tell that to others, y'know.' He nodded and lowered his gaze. 'But he was never bad. Though now I'll tell ye why I keep tellin' ye that. Because you'll never hear it from anyone ever again, that's why.' She looked at him and he saw the years had gathered there in her face. She was starting to look old and he hated her for doing that – for growing old and for allowing time to wear her down. 'I'm the only one who'll ever say it to ye, y'know,' she repeated, sadly. 'And I think, by rights, that someone has to.'

Seamus nodded, gave her a kiss on the cheek and left the house. He wanted to hold her then – to hug her close and tell her that she should accept the truth. But then, halfway down the street, he started smiling. Mary Doherty was still a strong wee woman inside, he decided. Strong despite her own outer façade, because she still believed that his father was something he had never been. Time would only wear down her outer skin. She believed as strongly in her husband's innocence today as she had always done.

He thought then that he should have told her about the meeting with the Special Branch man. It had been almost two months ago now and was more of a funny memory than anything, though it had scared him silly at the time. Yet his mother wouldn't have seen it like that. She'd hardly see the funny side of someone from Special Branch telling her son that he knew something about his father. Nor too would she find it amusing that the same man had shown Seamus the original of the very picture she now held, with one other, tightly in her hand.

And then Seamus had frowned, forgetting all about his mother for a moment. It suddenly dawned on him that it had been no accident that he'd been shown those particular photographs.

*

Planning for Seamus to meet up with Elaine's parents proved to be a little more difficult. Not that Seamus would have minded if he'd never met them at all. He was happy enough with the way things were going and he had his reservations about going to his girlfriend's family home. First of all, they were a little more well-to-do than most people he knew – he'd gathered that from the way Elaine had talked of them. And second of all, he had an idea that they wouldn't take to him very well. He was a Catholic, after all. Though he then told himself that Elaine had done the same thing and no one had eaten her. It wouldn't have been fair to refuse her on those grounds – it would have been utterly sectarian, he knew that too.

It was Elaine who had finally set a time. She'd met up with his mother, after all, and it was only fair that he did the same. She arranged it for a Tuesday night some five or six weeks later – a night she assured Seamus that her brothers would be out playing snooker. She didn't want anyone else there in the house other than her parents, and he was grateful about that. But when the night finally arrived and they took a taxi over to the house, Seamus found that he was shaking at the knees. He would discover to his joy that he had nothing to worry about in the end. They were perfectly normal people – cordial, amusing and seemingly a lovely couple who were proud of their daughter and supported her every ambition and goal in life, just so long as she was happy. Seamus took to them immediately and ended up chastising himself for wondering why he had ever been nervous about meeting them.

Decent, ordinary people from across the river, and he'd been afraid of them because they lived in a notoriously Protestant estate. He laughed when he thought about it. They most likely thought the same way about him and his family. Catholics from Creggan or the Bogside. Two heads each and they all ate babies, prayed to an inverted cross. One of Elaine's two brothers, however, had a rather different attitude, he would discover. They arrived back home shortly after eleven, just as Seamus was about to get into the taxi. They passed him in the garden, and the girl's father – who was now standing at the door, pipe in hand – introduced the youth to them both. The younger one, who was perhaps the same age as Seamus, shook him firmly by the hand, genuine, smiling. The older boy, however, merely nodded, his glare anything but friendly.

Seamus lowered his head and got into the car, waving goodbye to the rest of them. I have a lot of work to do there, he thought as he rode home in the car. A hell of a lot of work.

But Elaine didn't take him home with her after that, and he was really rather grateful she didn't. They were good people but Seamus had still felt the barrier there. There always seemed to be, these days. Even when he was in the training centre and he got to know someone. Someone who was great fun to be around, as genuine as they came. And then you'd discover that they were one of the other lot, and your guard would go up. You'd watch what you were saying, the same way they would when they were talking to you. And every sentence, no matter how innocuous, would take on a hidden meaning. Seamus often wondered why that was.

Was he conditioned now into being like that, he wondered? Maybe he was as ghettoized as Elaine had told him he was, he thought with dismay, and maybe it would only be a matter of time before it showed through his false exterior as clear as day. In front of Elaine and her friends and relatives, if he ever got into a deep conversation with them. And then he'd stand there, unmasked, his faults showing him to be as real as any man could wish to be.

He shivered at the thought, hoping that day would never come.

*

He'd heard the shots that night and thought them of little or no relevance. Two of them, both from the same gun, definitely not an exchange of fire, because they'd come too close after each other, just after eleven o'clock in the evening. He'd been lying in his bed. Having an early night, because Elaine had kept him up the night before with her antics, the way she'd been doing the last eight and a half months. Though he hadn't complained. He never did, believing then that he never would.

Two shots, as clear as a whip cracking. He couldn't determine how near or how far they had been fired from. Or at whom. But he guessed that it was most likely that the Boys had been targeting a patrol or jeeps. Or maybe it had been a kneecapping, a punishment shooting, some hood getting his just deserts. They came from a pistol, that was all he knew for definite, easily recognisable from the more distinctive cracks. A handgun, but he couldn't figure out for the life of him what type it was. It was a

Browning, as it turned out. But he couldn't have known that then, nor would he have realised the deadly significance of the fact, so he'd just rolled over and gone to sleep.

But then he'd heard the screaming, so loud that it could only have been coming from the other end of the street. And lights had come on and there had been shouting, the screech of tyres and a car roaring off into the distance. Mary had come running up the stairs. She'd been drinking, Seamus could smell it on her breath, but the sounds of the gunfire had sobered her up immediately. That and the sounds of heavy engines roaring up Fanad Drive from the direction of St. Mary's. Saracens, Sixers, jeeps – a mixture of all of those, and all of them in a hurry. The noise was so great that it would have been impossible to determine just how many vehicles there were. The shouting, too, intensified and Seamus thought he heard one or two screams, though he couldn't be sure.

He was climbing out of bed, hurriedly throwing on his clothes, when she came in the room. 'The noise is comin' from over on Fanad,' she told Seamus. She seemed scared. 'The Brits are crawlin' the fuckin' place. I think they might be raidin' the houses. Don't you be goin' out there, Seamus. There was shootin' too and there's someone down there at the end of the street screamin' their head off.'

Seamus took her gently by the shoulder. 'I'll be all right, ma. I'll just have a wee look and I'll stay well back, promise.'

She nodded uncertainly and he put on his trainers, tied them quickly and went downstairs into the street. A crowd had gathered at the far end, just across from St Mary's School, and they were venomously heckling the Brits and the cops, who were there in huge numbers. The soldiers, in return, were pushing the crowd back into the road. Seamus moved cautiously to the back of the crowd, noticing that the Brits had effectively sealed off the entire top of the street and that there were about fifty of them swamping the area around Barney Ferguson's house. He recognised old man Flaherty from the back and pulled him by the tail of his half-buttoned shirt to get his attention. The old man turned.

'What's up?' Seamus asked.

'They shot the wee lad,' Flaherty said. There was an anger in his voice that was foreign, strange to this peaceful wee man. His hands were visibly shaking.

Seamus frowned. 'Who?'

The old man turned to him, his eyes misting over slightly. 'The wee lad from over the road there. Sure ye used to hang around with him yourself. I saw ye hidin' in me garden one night. What do ye call him?'

'Barney?' Seamus's voice was a whisper. 'Barney Ferguson?'

The old man nodded sadly and Seamus caught a glimpse through the heckling crowd of a body lying on the pavement. It was his friend, a guitar case at his side. The eyes were open, a stream of blood running from his head, another pooled on his chest. Seamus couldn't breathe and nearly fell over.

He didn't remember the walk back to the house and he was suddenly unaware of the purpose of the clamour: the shouting, the cursing, the crying. There was an arm on his, that much he remembered, old man Flaherty for once seemingly quicker of step than he. And his mother was waiting there at the door. She noticed his tears and then she too began to cry.

EIGHT

'Jesus Christ, I still can't fuckin' believe the way they dragged his body into the back of that fuckin' Saracen!'

There were tears building in Paddy Monaghan's eyes, and Seamus turned away, afraid that he too might start to cry again. It was raining lightly and they were standing in against the tall, unadorned red-brick wall of the community centre, just down the road from the Ferguson household, watching the steady procession of people who had been making their way in and out of the house to pay their respects. Most were gathered in and around the hallway, though a few stood outside, their hooded-up coats adding a disquieting feeling of anonymity to the scene. The hospital had released the body two days later, their autopsy complete. Barney Ferguson had died from two bullet wounds, one directly to the heart, the other to the side of his head. There was little disagreement about who had been responsible. The work bore the standard marks of an SAS attack. They never shot to wound.

'The bastards didn't even allow anyone to go over and help him,' Seamus said, thickly. 'They could have saved him,' he added, softly. 'Maybe.'

Paddy shook his head, the disgust apparent in the tight clench of his jaw. 'That was never gonna happen. Never.'

'They could have arrested him,' Jimmy said eventually. He looked between Seamus and Paddy, his incomprehension visible in his red-rimmed eyes. Seamus looked at him for a few seconds, then frowned and looked away. He didn't have an answer for his friend.

'They never go for an arrest,' Paddy said bitterly. 'And they always shoot to kill, the murderin' bastards! They were up there in the roof-space of St Mary's School just across the road. Probably watchin' the entire fuckin' area for suspicious signs for days, maybe weeks. Sure there was one wee woman over there in Central woke up in the middle of the night about three weeks back, sees one of the fuckers all dressed up in black in the middle of her livin' room, him searchin' the place with a pencil-torch for Boys on the run.'

'In her house?' Jimmy shook his head in disbelief.

'Aye, you can imagine what he was goin' to do if he had of got them, can't ye?' Paddy kicked a crushed Coke can hard up along the flagstones. 'Aye, they're takin' chances now, sneakin' in everywhere. They see him comin' out of the house with a guitar case. One of them comes out of the school grounds – out of fuckin' nowhere – and challenges him. Barney panics and tries to get away . . . ' Paddy's head slumped and his jaw tightened, his eyes misting over again. For long moments he didn't say anything, reflective, his brow heavily furrowed. 'They're only takin' those chances because they're sayin' the Boys are a spent force. They won't be sayin' that soon, I can tell ye.'

'That's the part I can't understand,' Jimmy said softly, paying no heed to Paddy's cryptic threat. 'Sure he was never musical.'

Seamus, in turn, ignored Jimmy. 'Why, what's gonna happen?' he asked Paddy. 'Ye reckon the war's gonna get worse?'

'Aye, it is, Seamy. In the next few months it's gonna get much, much worse.' Paddy stubbed his butt into the dirt and pulled his navy-blue Crombie in tight against the rain, watching as two as-yet-indistinct figures walked across the rainswept road in their direction.

'Ye never answered me,' Jimmy said. 'Was he in a band, or what?'

'Aye, well that instrument he was carryin' only played the one tune – a death dirge.'

Jimmy raised an eyebrow and looked at him, puzzled.

'Look,' Paddy said, as the two figures neared, 'I have to go. I'll see ye both tomorrow at the funeral.'

Seamus and Jimmy nodded half-heartedly. Seamus recognised the taller of the approaching figures and then lowered his head. The second figure, he didn't know. He was a gangly youth. He remained halfway up the road as the first figure approached. The man smiled thinly, obviously having spotted Seamus.

'Ye all right, wee Doherty?'

Seamus looked up. 'Mister McGeady,' he replied, half-heartedly. Out of the corner of his eye he noticed Jimmy paling and turning away. 'What about ye?'

'Don't be so formal, son.' The tone was friendly, genuine. 'He was a good wee man. I know he was a friend of yours. Good wee fella. I'm sorry.'

Seamus nodded heavily.

Dan McGeady sighed wearily. 'There's nothin' I can say to make it easier, but he died fightin' for what he believed in. That's the noblest cause of all, y'know.' Seamus looked at him. 'I was a teacher once, y'know, kid.' There was a spark in his eyes, as if of a precious memory savoured. 'I taught a lot of bright kids before the onset of the Troubles. And some of them died before their time, kid. Long before their time. They got caught up in the Troubles because they'd watched their parents gettin' dragged out of their houses and jailed for bein' a Catholic, for standin' up for the ordinary, everyday rights that other people across the water in England take for granted. People over there don't realise that we don't want this, son.' He nodded up towards the gathering outside their house.

'None of us wants the self-sacrifice and the martyrdom, despite what they think. None of us really wants to see anyone givin' his life to the cause, because we all die when one of our own dies,' he said, gravely. 'But what if we didn't fight? What if we just lay down and let them walk over us the way they've been walkin' over us for centuries?' He shook his head and his eyes misted over. 'That could be my son lyin' up there one day, and I know that too, though heaven knows I'd die at the thought. Him lyin' in a cold wooden casket surrounded by neighbours, by relatives, by those who knew him from afar. That boy up there belongs to us all.' He frowned heavily. 'I can't say I knew him all that well but I know why he did as he did. I know his reasons.' Dan McGeady regarded Seamus gravely. 'Just remember, kid, time is the subtle thief of youth. It seems to trickle through your hands like so much sand and ye think ye have control of it, but just try holdin' it back.' He sighed another heartfelt sigh. 'Anyway, I must be goin'. I'll see ye later.'

'Aye,' Seamus said, nodding, hands tight in his pockets, head low. Uneasy. 'Right then.'

'Fuckin' teacher, all right,' Jimmy said grimly under his breath as Dan McGeady walked off. 'Fuckin' lecturer, more like.'

Seamus managed a thin smile and watched as the man put a hand on Paddy's shoulder and led him out through the gates of the community centre. They met up with the third figure and made their way up Fanad Drive towards the wake-house, their conversation obviously serious. Paddy pulled away for a second, ran back through the gates and called Seamus aside. 'Just want to have a word, Jimmy. Somethin' sort of personal, between me and him, like. Don't be offended.'

Jimmy smiled, then lit up another cigarette to while away the time. He wasn't that easy to offend – never had been.

Paddy led Seamus over to the railings that bordered the centre. 'Ye still goin' out with the girl?' he asked. Seamus stiffened and Paddy sensed his mood. 'Hey, it's great if ye are,' he added, quickly. 'Good wee girl that, and I don't give a fuck about her kickin' with the other foot. That's between you and her and, sure, if we all had that arrangement there wouldn't be fuckin' messes like this to contend with.'

Seamus nodded. 'Aye, must be the guts of eight months now,' he said, feeling a surge of happiness sweep through him, then mentally pushing it aside as he remembered the stark reality of this otherwise black moment. 'She's me signed up for the Tech down the Strand. She reckons that the old education's easy carried and that someday I might not want to be a painter.' Seamus turned his eyes upwards and smiled thinly. 'She's tryin' to change me already. Hardly know her a wet week.'

'Sounds like she's got her head screwed on to me. She's a good girl.' Paddy chewed on the corner of his lip and paused a second, as if wary of offering any further comment. 'But I, erm, just wanted to help ye out with somethin', y'know,' he said, after a moment. 'Us bein' friends and stuff.'

Seamus nodded again, cautiously. 'Aye? What's that?'

'Ye meet her brothers yet?'

'Aye, just for a second or so. I didn't get chattin' to them, like.'

'Watch out for the older boy. Martin's his name. He mixes heavily with the other lot. Very involved.' Paddy raised an eyebrow. 'Know what I'm sayin', Seamy?' Seamus nodded. 'If ye go over that way at all, just keep an eye, that's all I'm tellin' ye.'

'Thanks,' Seamus said, sorry that he had thought to doubt his friend. Paddy had always tried to help him out, he knew that. It was just that sometimes the older boy seemed to approach things from the wrong angle. Forcibly, with little thought as to the consequences. 'I will.'

'Good.' Paddy winked at him, turned and ran back to join up with Dan McGeady. 'See ye both later,' he called back, before making his way up to the house.

'He's runnin' around with your man,' Jimmy said, nodding after Dan McGeady. 'Paddy Monaghan and Dan McGeady – what's the story there, then?'

Seamus shrugged his uncertainty, a sudden weariness settling upon him. He found it hard to believe that Barney Ferguson had joined the Fianna Éireann, the youth wing of the IRA. Too young for 'active service', they were used mainly for driving or hijacking cars, taking messages, acting as lookouts and doing other minor duties. 'I don't know anythin' these days. Barney Ferguson in the 'RA. Jesus, I can hardly believe it. Him quiet as a mouse, wouldn't harm a bird.'

'Who says he was in the Fianna?' Jimmy asked. 'I never heard anyone sayin' that.'

'Christ, Jimmy, do ye ever listen?' Seamus snapped. He turned away, more angry with himself than with his friend. Jimmy dropped his head and frowned. 'He was carryin' a gun in that guitar case,' Seamus explained, gazing at the wet concrete. 'A rifle, maybe takin' it to a job for the boys. The SAS saw him comin' out of the house with it, must have had their suspicions. Sure he didn't have a fuckin' hope.'

Jimmy looked up at the roof of the school. 'Ye reckon they're up there now?' he asked, pensively. 'I'd go up and shoot the fuckers meself if I thought so.'

Seamus smiled at the false bravado. 'Ye'd need a gun to do that.'

'Aye, well there's probably enough of the things floatin' about. I could get one off that eejit McGeady.'

'He hears ye callin' him that, he'll give ye one all right. One in the fuckin' head.'

Jimmy grinned thinly. He lit his fifth cigarette in a row. 'Paddy's right and close to him right enough, isn't he?'

'Aye, sure he hangs about with his son, did ye not hear him sayin' that?' Seamus closed his eyes, a dull pain throbbing in his head.

Jimmy snorted. 'I'll say fuck all. But between you and me, I never took Barney for 'RA. Paddy, though . . . ' Jimmy dragged at his cigarette, letting the thought hang in the air.

'Aye, we know each other years,' Seamus said, accepting his friend's cigarette and taking a drag, even though the build-up of heat in the thing took all the enjoyment out of it. 'But we obviously don't really fuckin' know each other at all – at least not as well as we thought we did – do we?'

'We know enough about each other,' Jimmy said. 'At least you and me do, anyway.'

And Seamus nodded wearily. They knew enough. He'd said that same thing to Elaine once and he'd been correct there too. Maybe they did know enough about each other – maybe they knew all they would ever know. They were just all growing up in their own ways, each susceptible to new ideas, to different pressures, dreams and hopes, and yet they were all still friends, in spite of the changes. Seamus realised that he probably couldn't realistically hope for anything more that that. Jimmy motioned to the house. 'Are ye goin' up to show your face?'

Seamus was nervous, his mouth dry, his stomach acidic. He'd never seen a dead body before and he had been reluctant about entering the house with such a big crowd about. Now there were a lot of people standing about outside, umbrellas slanted, to guard against the driving rain. He nodded slowly. 'Aye, I'll have to go in sometime.'

'Aye,' Jimmy said. 'And sure I'll be standin' alongside ye as usual. It won't be so bad.'

Seamus bit softly on his lower lip and managed another thin smile. He turned the collar of his coat up and began to move in the direction of the house. 'Aye, I know, Jimmy. Sure aren't ye always?'

*

The coffin lay there on the raised dais in front of the altar. St Mary's was packed to capacity, with some people standing at the door and many more outside in the grounds, behind the railings, on the road. The sky was grey-black, reflecting the mood of the mourners. There was a heavy police presence at the top of the New Road and Bligh's Lane, along Iniscarn and down Broadway, black flags tied to every lamp-post, the estate mourning its dead. The Divisional Commander of that time had dictated that such a show of strength was necessary, as the family had not complied with the RUC's wishes that they guarantee there would be no paramilitary involvement in the burial.

During the time that the Creggan estate had been a no-go area, Agnes Ferguson had once tried to save the life of a Brit who had driven into the area by mistake. A gang had set upon the soldier, taken his rifle and nearly beaten him to death with it, only to have Agnes and several other women throw themselves across the curled-up young man to prevent him from coming to any further harm. It hadn't worked. One of the Boys had come along and shot him dead. Agnes had cried that day for the young soldier – cried because, despite her efforts, she hadn't been able to save his life. She was a republican – that she had always avowed – but she was also a woman of compassion. Now it was her turn to see tragedy laid on her own doorstep and now, she told the RUC man who stood before her, she expected that same compassion returned. Their son had fought for what he believed, she declared, and, while she didn't exactly want a paramilitary funeral, she wasn't going to sully her son's beliefs by lying down to the whims of the cops or the army, no matter what her personal feelings were.

She spoke angrily, passionately, proudly, despite the solitary nature of her pain. Still, her dignity intensified her words, until even the policeman's stern gaze had dropped to the pavement. It wasn't right, she said, that the army and the police had nearly besieged the house the previous night so that no colour party could stand over the coffin. Her son had made the decisions of a man, he had fought like a man in the little time that the good Lord had allotted to him, and now he had the right to be buried like a man. He'd believed in what he'd believed, and that was that. The troops and the cops could swamp the entire estate if they wished: it wouldn't do them any good. The colour party would turn up. They'd march beside the coffin and fire off a few shots to mark the passing of their comrade.

It always happened like that, she told the RUC man neutrally, so she didn't know why they even bothered to show up. Except to gloat – to see another Irishman being lowered into this largest of all graves that was now Ireland. And they were all Irishmen, she said, Protestants and Catholics alike, and they were fighting each other over the stupidest of things – most people couldn't even tell you what those things were. The Divisional Commander hadn't replied to that. He'd ordered his men into the area at first light, though the crowds that now gathered thereabouts still outnumbered the police by roughly two to one.

Seamus had listened to her talking to the policeman the night before: few words, though spoken with the grace of a stateswoman – quietly, purposefully. He was willing to bet his life that what she had predicted would come true.

*

The priest had advised them beforehand not to put a tricolour on the coffin inside the chapel. It was disrespectful to God, he said, and it was probably for the best that they didn't. Someone had shouted from the back of the crowd that God never seemed to be offended when they did it in other countries – or even when they did it here, providing it was a Union Jack. Aye, it was only when they did it in the Catholic areas of the North that it seemed to offend anyone, including God, someone else had called out, and someone else again was heard to say that God wasn't up to much if He thought about picking on one of the smallest countries in the world over such a tiny wee thing when we'd all been praying earnestly to him for years, despite the sorrows He'd inflicted on us all. Sure it wasn't as if it was a slaughtered chicken and black candles we were layin' up there on top of the casket, was it? The priest, however, was unrepentant.

The tricolour and beret and gloves went on outside the chapel just after the requiem mass, and the RUC, seeking to divest the corpse of those flimsy pieces of cloth made up of the colours the young man had died for, pressed forward against the crowd that had gathered outside on the road. The crowd responded by linking arms, and the news people who had gathered to film the republican funeral allowed their cameras to roll as the play began. There were brief scuffles, shouting, heckling from all sides – the angry vehemence lost beneath the droning of the two helicopters which hovered less than two hundred feet up above, rotor blades whipping the air.

For a moment there was a stand-off, and someone went forward to talk with the officer in charge. But then someone else decided angrily that they were going ahead without the permission of the police, and the crowd surged forward to reinforce that argument, the air heavy with the threat of violence. The RUC retreated several yards: there was nothing they could do except watch. It was a small walk down from the chapel towards the cemetery – perhaps two, three hundred yards in all. The crowd formed a human chain and, even amongst the weakest, there were no truly weak links. Seven armed and masked men in dark uniforms appeared beside the coffin from out of the crowd. Six of them hoisted the casket high upon their shoulders at the seventh's command in Irish. And the seventh led the cortège and the closest relatives of the dead man through the chain.

Jimmy and Seamus stood together. Both were freshly shaved and dressed in their best trousers – and in leather jackets they'd had to borrow from a neighbour: the coats too big, that fact perhaps too obvious to others. Seamus had remarked about Paddy Monaghan's absence, but Jimmy had suggested that he was probably up the back of the crowd with his girl, maybe having met up with Mick Deery, who'd just came down from Belfast when he'd got the word. Seamus didn't speak after that, caught up as he was in the heavy and uncertain atmosphere, the promise of violence there at every step. They walked behind the coffin, still not believing that this was their friend and that he had dared to become a stranger to them all before dying. Grim faces staring into the crowd; grimmer faces staring back. He kept his own gaze upon the ground all the way down to the cemetery, and that walk seemed to take forever.

The RUC were there in the cemetery too, their grey, heavily armoured jeeps lined across the far side of the cemetery like grotesquely distorted daleks, perhaps a hundred feet away from the Volunteers' graves. There were three or four photographers along with them, and Seamus had no doubts that the helicopters too were filming everything from up above. The crowd gathered around the graveside and the coffin was lowered and placed beside the grave, the black-clad Volunteers standing to attention, eyes front, their faith in the crowd absolute. The priest gave an oration that was barely audible above the whirring blades of the helicopters, though no one was listening anyhow, their minds lying there in that long, dark slot carved out of the earth, each wondering as to breath's purpose and reason. The Bible closed minutes later and the Volunteers suddenly produced six pistols and rapidly fired off three shots each. The crowds nearest the back cheered, the crowds nearest the front − mostly relatives and close friends of the family − were comparatively silent, the significance of such defiance temporarily lost on them. The police on the outskirts of the crowd jostled and jeered, attempted to move forward, but the crowd never gave way. Finally the Volunteers stepped back and saluted as the coffin was lowered into the grave.

And then it was the women's turn to act. A cluster of umbrellas were drawn, opened and placed over the huddle of masked men as an awning so that they might disrobe. The crowd surged forward into that temporary shelter, becoming after seconds an indeterminate, writhing mass of human limbs, heads and bodies. Within seconds the uniforms were passed out through the throng, secreted in buggies and prams; the guns carried off by others − old men, young women: those who, in another time and place, might seem to be model citizens. The British army helicopters had caught the entire event on film but, as usual, they had seen nothing. They would never prove who had fired the shots, who had worn the clothes. No guns, no fingerprints, no uniforms, no evidence. They would have their long list of suspects, of course – faces they had picked out from the crowd with a well-aimed long-range lens. But the men had simply been there to pay their respects, and no one could prove otherwise. They were rarely, if ever, caught and charged for firing guns and wearing IRA uniforms at Volunteers' funerals.

Both Jimmy and Seamus had seen it all before, of course – quite a few times, in fact – and they too had cheered and clapped as the shots had been fired, understanding nothing more than the defiance of that action. Though this time it was more personal and they had merely started a little as the shots had rung out.

It wouldn't have been right to gloat, to exult, Seamus thought. Because this time it didn't seem to matter who revelled at the end of this protracted game of death. No one had really won. He saw Paddy Monaghan emerging from the huddle and he knew that he should have been surprised, but he wasn't. They were all going their own ways – Barney had proved that – though the three remaining boys were friends still, probably always would be. Seamus shrugged inwardly. He couldn't judge Paddy for what he believed in, he decided then, nor Dan McGeady for what he had said the day before. As much as he hated to admit it, there was some truth and sense in what they believed, said and did. Just as there was truth in Elaine's words, in his mother's, in Agnes Ferguson's. There was also a partial truth in violence, in pain, in death – a partial truth that joined perfectly with that other fractured truth found in the retreat of love, happiness and the joy of life.

The older boy's hair was slightly dishevelled and he was dressed in jeans, a black bomber jacket and Oxford shoes with tips. He shrugged almost apologetically. 'Best I could do for him,' he said, with a frown. Seamus didn't know what to say, so he didn't reply, merely nodded. Jimmy offered them both a cigarette and they accepted. He then handed a lit match around in hands that were carefully cupped to protect the flame from the breeze that was getting up. There was a strange unity in that action, Seamus knew – if you had tried to talk about or explain it, people would have thought you mad. They both accepted the cigarette, accepted each other. That action was significant to him then, though it was one they had performed on reflex a thousand times before.

'He would have appreciated that,' Jimmy agreed, solemnly. 'Christ, but ye took a fuckin' chance. Those black bastards were nearly in on top of ye all.'

'Aye,' Paddy Monaghan said, gravely. He dragged deeply on his cigarette, reminding Seamus then of Jimmy. Paddy's eyes were focused on the build-up of grim-faced RUC personnel around the cemetery gates. 'I took a chance but, sure, we all did. And some day those fuckers are gonna storm one of those funerals and shoot the Boys dead there and then. That's inevitable and we all fuckin' know it. But if we give in to them . . . ' He shrugged. 'Then what? They walk over us, keep us down. I dunno. I don't agree with the violence of it all, but it makes them think, it makes them look for compromisin' solutions, it makes them know they don't own the fuckin' world any more. Those days are gone, long gone,' Paddy said, throwing half his cigarette onto the grass as the crowd began to file out of the cemetery in a mass huddle, tramping and scrunching the black-and-white chips of marble that coated the aisles heavily underfoot. 'And they're the only fuckin' ones who don't know it. C'mon, we better stay in the middle here. I'm gonna shoot off as soon as I get the chance, so don't be surprised if ye look around ye in a wee minute and I'm not there.'

Seamus and Jimmy nodded.

'Ye all right, Seamy?' Paddy asked. The hand was there on his shoulder again, firm as ever.

'Aye,' Seamus said. Stunned, shocked. 'Christ, I'm shakin' like a leaf and me face must be as white as a sheet. It probably just hit me there now.'

'It hasn't hit me yet,' Paddy said, gravely. 'This time tonight, I'll be the one shakin' like a leaf. Good job wee Eileen's so good with her hands. She'll keep me right.'

'Hey, I hear Mick Deery's about,' Jimmy said. 'Ye see him, Paddy?'

'Aye, but he's with his aunt. Doesn't want to know me, for some reason, though ye might get a chat with him later on yourselves. If ye do, tell him I was askin' for him. Don't let the old girl hear ye, right enough. She might take a swing for ye.'

They smiled then, recognising the cleanliness of a foreign – if only momentary – emotion that had been missing for days. Then they filed into the crowd as it moved with dignity along the carefully cut paths between the graves, walking straight out past the stone-faced policemen, their heads turned away. Not taking them on, not recognising their right to existence. Straight ahead and onwards. Paddy left them, heading off with a wee old woman who had latched on to him like a motherly figure, someone who had bother standing up herself without help, someone who had needed his every attention there at the graveside. As if he had never left her side during the whole ceremony.

Seamus and Jimmy eventually split up and went their separate ways. It was Jimmy Duffy who ended up bumping into Mick Deery, though he wouldn't tell his best friend about it until later that night. By then, however, Seamus wasn't in the mood for hearing how well other people were or were not doing. He had enough problems of his own.

*

His head was splitting and he was lying down on the bed when Mary called out that there was a phone call for him next door in Sadie's house. Sadie had got herself a phone about six months back and she'd let both Mary and Seamus know that they were free to make use of it because, sure, that was what neighbours were for. Seamus got up from the bed and looked at the clock. It was half past six and he'd been lying there thinking since getting back from the funeral over three hours ago, the headache not allowing him the comfort of sleep. He went sluggishly down the stairs, stepped over the thin wooden fence that separated the two properties, and walked through the opened front door of Sadie's house without knocking. The wee old woman had closed her living-room door to give him some privacy.

'H . . . Hello?' He could hardly bring himself to speak.

'It's me.' Elaine's voice was hushed and his immediate thought was that she too was standing in her own hallway, though perhaps someone was close by and she couldn't speak normally.

'Aye.'

'Did ye see the news?'

Seamus tried to think. The day had been a blur. 'No, erm, nah . . . Why?'

'That funeral was on and your face was there, up at the graveside . . . '

He sighed heavily, the significance of that remark lost on him for a moment. 'He was my friend, I told ye that the other day, sure. We were at school together, we hung around together.'

'Aye, well our Martin saw you and he told me ma. She told me da and now they're all sittin' out there in the kitchen having a conference. And you're the main topic.'

'Christ, Elaine, he was my friend!' He bit his lip. He'd never cursed at her before. 'I had to go to his funeral. I'm sorry but, Christ, what was I supposed to do?'

She didn't speak for what seemed to be a long time and Seamus sighed deeply, cursing under his breath. When she did speak, she said, 'Aye, I'm not sayin' you shouldn't have went. But our Martin says that there were a few people he knew standin' around you. Said they were all Provies. It's his mates have him up to that. They've convinced him that you're up to your neck in . . . stuff. Now he's convinced me ma and da into thinking that maybe I . . . that maybe we . . . '

'What are ye sayin'?' he cut in. He fought to keep his voice even but his stomach was churning. 'Don't go sayin' things like that, Elaine, please.'

'We might have to stop seein' each other for a while, Seamus.' He could hear the pain in her voice and he knew that she was close to tears.

'I don't want to stop seein' ye. I . . . I . . . ' He wanted to tell her, but he was afraid that she might not want to hear about the way he felt, about how she was everything he lived for. You didn't tell that to women, anyhow, because if you did, they'd walk all over you. His friends had taught him that, but it was common enough knowledge.

'We have to. I . . . I don't really have a . . . We have to. I'm sorry.' The phone clicked down.

Seamus stood there for a minute, looking at the receiver, wondering whether he was sleeping, maybe in the middle of yet another nightmare. He dialled her number and said, 'Elaine . . . '

'It's not Elaine,' the voice on the other end of the line said. Gruff, serious. 'And if yeknow what's good for ye, ye won't be phonin' here again.'

'Let me talk to her, please.'

'We know your face, Doherty. We know what ye do and where ye go. We know all about you and your fuckin' Provie friends. Ye won't come back over here again to this side of the water if you're wise, ye hear?' The line went dead.

Seamus left Sadie's house and went straight back home and up to his bedroom. Lost, despondent, never having known the depth of betrayal the last twenty-four hours had shown him. The blindingly selfish betrayal of death; the confused betrayal of love. Mary came up to see him later that evening. She sat on the edge of his bed and ran her fingers through his hair. She hadn't done that for years – for too many years. The gentleness of her hands and her fingers as they drew small, incomplete circles upon his collar said everything.

'This world is the hardest, cruellest place at times,' she said, eventually. Her voice was clear, concise, soft. She hadn't been drinking and that was good. Seamus knew the difference now. 'At times I don't know how God can make us suffer like this, if He's possessed of so much love. Sometimes I wonder. Though I'm sure we all do,' she added, softly. 'But there has to be a reason for it all, doesn't there?' He didn't move; the tears came, blurring his eyes until they stung. 'Maybe we were all sittin' there in heaven one day long before the beginnin' of the world and we all agreed to take part in this grand play, take the good and the bad in our stride, no matter the level of the pain or the joy. Just so that we could get to know the difference, ye know? Just so that when we knew one dark extreme, we'd all fully appreciate the other, brighter side, knowin' that a particular joy had a time limit and it'd never last forever. It might be just a game – a throw of the dice, and nothin' more. Then again, it might not. But it's better to tell yourself that it is, I always think. That way ye get back up quicker when life kicks ye in the teeth. Well, that's what I always say to myself, anyway,' Mary said, smiling sadly. 'Silly wee way to think, I know that. But I have to tell myself somethin' – I have to. I have to have a reason for goin' on, and that's the only one I think makes any sense.'

'She says she can't see me again. Her brother saw me on the telly, told her ma and da I was a Provie . . . '

'But you're not, are ye?' Uncertain, an inflection of fear there. 'Though you'd still be my son if ye were, mind.'

He shook his head.

'Nah, I'd know if ye were. Mothers know things. Like maybe that you and her will be back together sometime. And that, even if this is a game, it's a bloody hard one. The hardest I've ever played.' She hugged him closer to her, and a small time later her tears mingled with his own.

*

He tried ringing the café several times, but the kindly old man who ran it said that Elaine had phoned him earlier in the week and told him that she'd had to leave. Not for any particular reason that he knew about, right enough, because she'd been happy as a lark there for the last two years, and he'd never heard her complaining once. The fact was that there was an opening in a fish shop in the Waterside and it was nearer to her house, the old man had explained. She was probably getting the same wages, he had added matter-of-factly, because wages for waitressing were more or less standard, but if it meant her saving on the taxi fare, then . . .

Seamus had thanked him for his help, but then he'd gone down there that Friday night anyhow and looked in through the window to make sure that the owner hadn't been told to say what he'd said. The old man had spotted him, even called him inside and offered him a job. Seamus had smiled at that, shook his head, then thanked him and left.

He went to the technical college on the Strand Road and enrolled for two night classes, one in O level French, the other in O level Spanish. He'd have four if he got them – along with his English and Maths. He was only really going for her, however, he convinced himself – to let her know what he should maybe have told her a long time back. But he didn't know if she was attending there at nights, and after a few months he was sure she wasn't. He went anyway, not knowing why, perhaps because he had nothing much else to do at nights and it became routine.

He thought about going down there during the day, though he never seemed to get around to it, and he wondered if it was because he was afraid of some final closure, some painful rejection – that he might find out that the idea had been in her head all along and that the funeral had been the perfect excuse. No mess, no fuss. A good time had by all, and away with someone else. He'd had it done on him before and couldn't think of a good reason why it wouldn't turn out like that again.

The passing of time seemed to strengthen those beliefs. She had a mind of her own, he chided himself. If she had really wanted to see him, she could have done so. They could have arranged to meet each other secretly and things could have been the way they were at the start, when they hadn't truly cared if anyone else existed. He wanted to see her and he didn't want to see her. To see her and thwart her plans for moving on by telling her that he was studying for her, that maybe she could try and convince her parents that he was someone who was trying to get on in the world, someone who minded his own business and just got on with his life.

But at the same time, he didn't want to see her, because he didn't know if he shared his mother's conviction that life was only a game you either won or lost, depending on your throw of the dice. He didn't want to lose, but then, he wasn't playing. Then again, he knew he was losing anyway.

Mary tried to help him. She'd been going out with a man from Demesne Gardens for a week or two now – a widower whose wife had died suddenly over two years ago of a heart attack. Seamus was really happy for her. Seeing her walking about the house with renewed zest for life pleased him no end but, inside, his own heart was breaking. For a time afterwards he didn't go out much.

Paddy Monaghan called around a few times and asked him if he wanted to go out for a pint with him and his girl, which he did three or four times. But Paddy's visits were soon to be limited. He'd gone and put wee Eileen 'up the spout', as he wryly put it, and thereby caused a bit of a furore in his family home. Seamus had laughed when he'd heard about that. Paddy's family were very staunch. They'd had Free Derry Radio in their house on many an occasion during the earlier Troubles and apparently they'd all been involved with helping out the various paramilitaries at one stage or another, even the sisters. Seamus couldn't fathom how Paddy's father could think his son was old enough to join up but too young to get a girl up the skite. Presuming he knew, of course, which he likely did, though Seamus couldn't be certain.

Jimmy was always there, of course, because Jimmy's love life was even worse than Seamus's. The red-haired youth couldn't just have one girl, and his list of exes was beginning to run like a phone directory. Women apparently loved him – at least, that was what he claimed – and he was always on the lookout to get Seamus fixed up, telling him that he was the only one of the old Creggan-shops gang who wasn't going steady these days. Sure even Mick Deery was gettin' himself hitched right and soon, Jimmy told him with a smile. To some wee girl from Andy's town up in Belfast too, and him all respectable now. Him workin' in a shoe shop and her a nurse. He'd filled out a little and, except for the smallest of limps, sure you'd never have known that anythin' had ever happened to him.

Seamus had tried to change the subject. Did Deery hold anything against Monaghan for that time about the bungalow? Jimmy had shaken his head, said he didn't hold anythin' against him now, though he did once, because it had been Paddy's idea and he'd told him not to do it. But his aunt and the rest of the family down in Derry, well, they were death on Paddy, wouldn't entertain him, said they'd better never see him again in their lifetime. Then Jimmy and Seamus had discussed that for a while, saying that it didn't really matter any more anyhow, so long as the big man was healthy and happy, sure that was all that mattered.

Aye, Jimmy had said. Mick had told him that the shooting was the worst thing that had ever happened to him and, in a funny way, the best. Because he wouldn't have met up with the wee nurse otherwise. And then the conversation had turned full circle from that to Seamus again. He was single, nearly eighteen, and it was looking as if he'd never get himself hooked; maybe he'd be left on the shelf forever. Jimmy's latest girlfriend's sister was available, the red-haired youth had then told him, with a nudge. Maybe she'd let him go all the way after a few dates, though she wasn't the hottest-looking thing in the world. Seamus declined that offer, though he did manage, on occasion, to talk

Jimmy into going to 52nd Street on the Strand Road.

But the reason that he went there was never there. She'd moved on, and so easily – at least that was what he had convinced himself – and she'd never be back. He thought of her getting onto a plane or a ferry and making her way over to her sister in England and it nearly broke his heart. He drank to forget her now, finding solace there in that disco most weekends. A first love, Jimmy had called it, and it was no more than that. Nearly a year – give or take a month or two – of passion, of laughter, of love, and then it was over. Sure Jimmy had been through it a dozen or more times himself, he boasted, with all the conviction of a modern-day Casanova, and there was always another one out there, better-looking and sexier than the last. And if not, there was always wee Una Mahon, the girl whom Seamus had been going out with for a while before he'd met Elaine. She was available at the moment and always good for a shag if nothing else showed up, wasn't she?

Seamus always laughed when the red-haired youth said that, because Jimmy wasn't laughing when he said it. It didn't ease the pain, but it helped him through and he found that it often gave him a reason to go on.

NINE

Christmas seemed to come and go in the blink of an eye, passing Seamus by almost completely. He was too busy at his work and his studies – which he now quite enjoyed – to notice what was going on in the rest of the North, never mind the world in general. The IRA had mounted a bombing campaign in Belfast only months earlier. They had planted incendiary devices in Ballynahinch and Downpatrick, in Dungannon, in Newry. The Dirty Protest in Long Kesh was still going strong, the first pictures having been released only weeks before, and now prison officers were being targeted by both the Provos and the UVF, due to reports coming out of the jails that the officers were engaged in the systematic abuse of prisoners. In Derry a large cache of ammunition was recovered from the Brandywell, three explosions had caused massive damage in the Ulsterbus depot in Springtown and, in England, five towns were bombed by the IRA.

It was late February 1979 and Seamus had turned eighteen on the seventh of the previous month. His mother had given him fifty pounds; this was a lot for someone who was struggling her way through the world, though Seamus reckoned that Mister Stewart – the widower whom his mother was now seeing on quite a regular basis – had helped her out there. Seamus was grateful for that gift, equivalent as it was to well over a week's wages in the training centre. He had expected several cards but got less than half the number he'd wished for. One from a girl he'd met up with in night classes and whom he'd been out with several times over the last few months. And one from Una Mahon, who was a changed girl now in many ways, her old ideas about virginity and marriage going together like a horse and carriage, changed by either loneliness or temptation. The card that he wanted he didn't get, however. And his birthday – as enjoyable as it turned out to be, because both Jimmy and Paddy called around and took him around several of the bars in the town that night – wasn't quite as brilliant as it could have been, because of that.

It had been a cold winter and it had snowed heavily over that period, Seamus recalled. It was mainly Jimmy who had kept him company, his mother who had provided the solace when the memories became too much, and Una who had kept him warm. He had met up with Mister Stewart several times by then. He'd been surprised at how much he'd liked the man, expecting initially to hate him for having intruded into what was becoming a very cosy life with his ma. But then he slowly realised that it was this man who was bringing his mother out of her despair and he had willingly allowed those feelings to disappear.

The man was pleasant, easygoing and generous, and he had an attitude to life few of the people Seamus knew possessed. And the man made his mother happy, which was something he hadn't seen in her for a very long time. Seamus was glad of that; he had little reason to be pleased about anything else.

He often went down to Una's house in Rosemount, despite the weather, kicking through drifts of snow that were the result of near-blizzards. He found that she concentrated his mind perfectly with her new-found lust, and that inquisitiveness helped them both in different ways. One blustery night, as he was walking up Westway, a car pulled up behind him. It was after one in the morning and Seamus hadn't intended to stay out so late but Una had been exceptionally pleasing that night. He turned and his heart nearly somersaulted in his ribcage. Cops; a blue, four-door Sierra. Seamus noticed the man in the back through the half-opened window and recognised him immediately. He gritted his teeth, drove his heels hard against the snowdrifts for better purchase and went to walk hurriedly on.

'Don't have me run you down, Seamus,' the man said.

Seamus stopped and walked back to the car, hands deep in his pockets, head down. 'What do ye want?'

'It's a bad night, Seamus. It always seems to be like that when we meet up, don't you agree?' The man smiled, his voice even and containing no trace of mirth.

'Aye, it's always a bad night when we run into each other, I'll give ye that.'

The man shook his head. 'Sarcasm is the lowest form, Seamus, ye know that. C'mon, get in.'

'Nah, you're all right. I'd rather die of frostbite.'

'You know the drill, Seamus. I'm not fuckin' askin'.'

Seamus looked at him through bitter eyes. 'Are ye arrestin' me? 'Cause that's the only way I'm gettin' into that fuckin' car. Ye'll have to fuckin' shoot me this time.'

The man pursed his lips for several moments, as if considering the offer. Seamus lowered his head again and swallowed hard, waiting. 'Ah, that's a toughie,' the man replied. 'But aye, all right, I'm arrestin' ye. C'mon, get in.'

Seamus frowned. 'Arrestin' me for fuckin' what, you fuckin' arsehole?'

The man got quickly out of the car and grabbed Seamus by the coat lapel, swinging him easily around in the direction of the door. 'Bad language,' the man said, pushing him into the vehicle. 'Bein' a pain in the hole in a built-up area. Whingein' without a fuckin' warrant. We'll think of somethin'.'

'Aye, well stop fuckin' pushin'. I'll get in me fuckin' self.'

'Good boy, Seamus. Now you're gettin' the hang of it.'

There were only three other people in the car this time: two cops and the man in the grey coat. They drove in silence for a time, the Sierra coursing easily through the slushed-up streets. Seamus tried to duck his head down low as they went over Central Drive, hoping to God that no one would spot him and get the wrong idea. The man laughed and watched him with amusement. 'We could stay up here all night,' the man told him. 'Wait until someone spots you, y'know. Then we could send in a raidin' party in the mornin' to a few of your friends' houses, lift them all for a few days, knock the crap out of them down in the barracks. A right few of our boys have done that for a laugh at times, I can tell you. You'd be right in the shite then, wouldn't ye? Right up to your hole in it, big time.'

'Do what ye fuckin' like, ye don't scare me. I don't give a fuck.'

'Or maybe wait for one of your lot to petrol-bomb us. That's some laugh, that is! "Throw Well, Throw Shell", isn't that what they say?' Seamus looked away, jaw clenched. 'Or, better again, let them shoot at us,' the Special Branch man continued, airily. 'You ever wonder what that's like, Seamus? You drivin' along, mindin' your own fuckin' business, y'know, and some fucker comes out and riddles your car. It's all right for a laugh, as they say, but it's no fuckin' joke. The smell of crap in the car afterwards and everyone shakin' like a leaf for days. It's very hairy, very hairy indeed. Words can't really describe it. That's why it might be better if you got the feelin' first-hand, as it were.'

'Do what ye like.' Seamus thought about what Jimmy had told him. The man was fishing, looking for someone vulnerable. All

Seamus had to do was act cool, unconcerned. When the cops saw that they weren't getting anywhere, they would go pick on someone else.

'Aye, it'd almost be worth the experience just to show you what I have to go through of a day. Still, lettin' a few people see you might be enough for now. Your lot would lift you, take you away for a chat. And then when they'd finished with you – shootin' you in the head and leavin' your hooded body all tied and bound on a lonely border crossin', or whatever way it is they handle their disciplinary procedures these days, I don't know – they'd have crowds throwin' stones through the windows of your mother's house, maybe even petrol bombs, dependin' on just how many of the lads were swooped. Aye,' he said, quickly. 'They'd be chasin' your ma out of the same home she's lived in all her life . . . '

'You leave me fuckin' ma out of this!'

The man shrugged. He shifted heavily in his seat and Seamus noticed that he'd put on a little weight and he was wearing his hair slightly longer than when he'd last seen him.

'It's just an idea. But you wouldn't be there to see it, of course. You'd be lyin' in a field or a ditch somewhere, all wrapped up in a cape of plastic and someone shovellin' the clay over the top of ye. Maybe you bein' used as a mulch for next year's spud crop. And all your neighbours unaware of how you died, and them eatin' the spuds and sayin' they taste more of shite this year than last.' The man started laughing as the car turned down Fanad Drive; the two cops in the front joined in. The car slowed as they passed Barney Ferguson's house.

'Shame about the wee lad, eh?' the man said then, turning to stare evenly at Seamus. Seamus felt his body chilling, even though the heat in the car was intense. 'A great pity. He would have made it to university in England, so I hear. He liked askin' questions about the law, about people's rights – at least that's what a couple of his teachers said when we asked about him. Had a bit of an interest in all things legal, might have been good at it even. Aye, you could just see what would have become of him. Him comin' back from England, gettin' himself a wee practice down there in Clarendon Street, defendin' all the wee Provies against the might of loyalist and British imperialism.

'Or maybe he'd have went the other way. Sometimes they do, y'know. They go over there to England and see things a little more clearly. They meet up with a nice girl, settle down, realise that there's no cause worth a single life, no piece of land worth a single soul. Aye, great shame about him, right enough. Another fallen son of Ireland, another working-class rebel, another back-lane lurker prepared to strike at the forces of the Crown in this endless war of attrition. Another sole arbiter of Irish and British innocence and guilt – judge, jury and executioner all rolled into one – and him martyred in the prime of his life too. Him tryin' to reverse the partition of Mother Ireland with a gun in a guitar case.' The man grinned lamely. 'A bit Bugsy Siegel-ish, if you ask me, but still, it's not for us to judge him, I suppose. He could have gone any way at all.'

Seamus looked at him, then looked away. He felt an anger rising within him, but he knew the man was trying to bait him, trying to get a reaction – any reaction – out of him. The car turned down the New Road. 'What do ye fuckin' want?' he said.

'Seen ye at the funeral, Seamus . . . '

'There were a lot of people at the funeral,' Seamus cut in, hotly. 'Did ye fuckin' lift all of them too?'

The man regarded him through serious eyes. 'Not yet. But we'll have to get around to that over time. Still, you were there. Sad, wasn't it?'

'Why don't ye go and take a flyin' fuck to yourself?'

The man feigned surprise. 'God, Seamus, there's no need for that. I'm only takin' ye for a spin, tryin' to become your friend. Sure where's the harm in that, eh?'

'Ye want me to become a tout, fuck all else. Well, there's more chance of the Guildhall sproutin' wings and flyin' off into the sun. Go pick on some other poor bastard, that'll help get ye through the night.'

The three men exchanged glances, smiling at each other.

'I don't know if I like what you're inferrin', Seamus. I'm only here to help ye out, exchange a few pieces of information, that's all. I don't know why you're goin' on there like some sort of an idiot, really I don't.'

'What could ye possibly tell me?'

Looking back, he realised that that was the exact moment he fell for it. The moment that he took the hook in his mouth, bit down hard on it and swallowed. He should have remained quiet, let the Special Branch man rattle on for a while; he would have got bored when he saw that he wasn't getting anywhere. Instead Seamus had asked that question. The man had smiled and looked away into the blackness of the night, as if pondering his next words.

'In 1972 your father was shot dead,' the man said, eventually. 'Shot for toutin', wasn't it?'

Seamus looked at him through hate-filled eyes. 'I'm not the same as me da, that's all I know for certain.'

'Never say never, son.'

'I'm not your son. And I'm me da's son in name only.'

'You might be the exact same as your da, son. Depends on exactly what sort of a person you think your da was.'

'I know what he was. We all do. So well and so good. I'm me.'

'Nah, I'd say you're exactly like your da. You see, I took your father for a few lifts in my car a couple of times. Liked a drink, he did, though he always seemed to maintain the same fuckin' stubbornness, despite his state of drunkenness or sobriety. Wouldn't say a word. Not even his name.' Seamus turned to the man, trying to keep his features expressionless, knowing that it was a trap, but feeling the lure anyhow. 'A couple of us thought he was a deaf mute at first – a regular Harpo Marx. Had him in the barracks and he wouldn't take so much as a drink of water, a fag, advice about gettin' himself a solicitor. Wouldn't take fuck all! He actually impressed me, really he did.'

'Are ye finished talkin' shite, or what?'

The man raised an open palm and Seamus flinched, securing himself against the door. The man grinned and withdrew his hand. 'You see, Seamus, if he'd even had the forethought to parrot the same three or four lines you have at your disposal, we might have kept him longer than we did. "I want to see my solicitor, officer." "I haven't a clue as to what you're gettin' at, orifice." "Could ye just fuck away off, you piece of shit, and give me head peace." Anythin' like that would have brightened the place up no end – had us at least sayin' what an illiterate sod he was, y'know. But he didn't open his mouth, and that bored the fuck out of everyone in Castlereagh. After the first few days we had him, we had to get a doctor from Derry – someone that he knew personally – to drive up and check his food and water. He would probably have gone and died on us otherwise, staunch bastard that he was.'

'It's not workin'.'

'What's not workin', Seamus?' A raised eyebrow, the eyes sharp. 'You think I'm tryin' to fool you?'

'Why don't ye just let me out and save your fairy tales for your wains. If ye can have them, a man in your state.'

The man laughed loudly. 'You see, your father wasn't a tout. He was a member of the IRA, nothin' else. He never touted on anyone in his life.'

'Don't start fillin' me full of crap,' Seamus said. He remembered Paddy Monaghan's words from so long ago. *They'll play mind games until ye don't know whether you're comin' or goin'.* 'I can accept my past. I know what I am. I know what he was. But it doesn't matter any more. The past is past, dead and gone. I only care about now. So what do ye want?'

'You hang around with some shifty people,' the man said, coldly. 'And they hang around with shiftier people still. Sometimes I think you're like some giant magnet and you attract them to your side.'

'You can fuckin' talk. Ye ever take a good fuckin' look around ye when you're in the fuckin' barracks? There's some shite clingin' onto the desks down there.'

The man yawned, as if suddenly bored. The car was being driven aimlessly along the Northland Road, and Seamus experienced a feeling of déjà vu. The older man ordered the driver to pull up in front of the fire station. Outside, the snow was falling hard, a bitter wind sweeping it back up into the air and in the direction of the cathedral. The man turned to Seamus, his left arm extended across the back of the seat. Seamus pulled away out of reach, watching the hand.

'My name's Dave, kid,' the man said, eventually. 'You're a good kid, and if it wasn't for the bad language and this awfully belligerent attitude of yours, I could see you doin' all right for yourself in the future. But the truth is, I need to know one or two things very quickly and I have a few things that I can give ye in exchange. Might alter your whole perception of the world – your whole perception of your friends, of the people who live around you.' He yawned again. 'I'll tell you, son, I'm tired, and I don't just mean I'm tired now. I'm tired of this fuckin' place, this fuckin' country, the same old attitudes, the same old hatreds, people tellin' me they're called Brian Boru or Rick O'Shea, shit like that. You think I like listenin' to that crap every day? You think I fuckin' like that? Eh?' Seamus looked down at his knees and didn't reply. The man sighed wearily. 'They hate you in this place and they don't even really know why. Half the people in this country couldn't even tell you who the fuck they're fightin' for . . . '

'They can tell ye who they're fightin' *against*,' Seamus interrupted, bitterly. He narrowed his eyes, wondering if they in any way resembled his mother's that time she'd gone at the wee Brit with the rolling pin. Black, opaque, filled with hate. He could tell from the man's expression that they probably were.

'Ach aye, they can tell you that all right,' the man agreed, with a sigh. He talked as if the ocean tide was rolling in against him and all he had with which to hold it back were words. 'They know exactly why they're fightin' – at least, they think they do. They can all recite history from the angle that suits them, forgettin' that history is written by men who, despite their claims of neutrality, discriminate proudly in favour of roughly half of their ancestors – the half they believe to be right and true, or the half they were spawned from. Same thing, really.

'Or if these same would-be heroes are a little impartial – which none of them ever really are – they're only very proud of themselves as storytellers. Regular Hans Christian Andersens, the lot of them. They can turn a sniper attack into the Tet Offensive. And we believe them, no matter the inaccuracies, because we all need somethin' to live and die for. It's human nature. We're all fightin' a war that should have died three hundred years ago, along with its many victims, though it never did. Aye, we're about to land in

Northern Ireland, please set your watch back three hundred years, isn't that the old joke?' Dave grinned sourly. 'Aye,' he sighed, heavily, 'history's written by contradictory, fallible men who omit the weaknesses that they'd rather never have happened and embellish the acts they think great and noble. And those differ greatly, dependin' on who you are, how you think and which side of the garden wall you're lookin' over. The past, eh? You're tellin' me about the past? I've an idea about mine, but you, you don't know fuckin' anythin' about yours.'

'I know enough,' Seamus snapped, lamely. 'More than enough.'

'You don't, Seamus. Otherwise you wouldn't have called your da a tout.'

'I know enough. The past is gone. It can't be changed by any man's words.' Seamus clenched his jaw, tense.

'Well, they reckon that even God can't change it, though there are many who'd tell you that you were wrong there, because historians and politicians can. They're the people who have us in the mess we're in, Seamus. They're the people who will conclude their fancy speeches or writings by tellin' you that violence has always been a catalyst for change in society, even though it inevitably leads to the collapse of society and the horrific death of innocents. And they're the people who'll tell you that civilisation will always develop faster because of that same violence, though nobody ever really gets what they wanted in the end, and we all lose, because there's nothin' fuckin' civilised about it all in the first place. If we only knew at what stage of this mad blood-feud the party was supposed to begin, then we might feel a little better, but they always forget to tell us that important fact, don't they? At least, that's what I find.'

'You're playin' your part. Why don't ye get out?' Bitter, angry. 'If nobody was takin' part then there'd be no fuckin' war, would there?' Elaine had said that to him once; his stomach churned as he thought of how much he missed her.

'Why don't I get out? Good question, Seamus, really,' the man said, smiling easily. 'And the answer is that I believe that what I'm doin' is right, the same way a lot of people on your side do. And I have to agree: my methods are sometimes no better than theirs. Aye, I too have sinned, that is true,' he added, ruefully. 'But I have to go on, despite my tiredness. Despite the fact that I stand here in the middle, with Gaelic and Celtic romanticism on the one side and fuckin' Rule Britannia on the other. And it's always the innocents in the middle who end up sufferin', because ultimately it's all about power. How long before our saviours don the mantle of the oppressor, Seamus? Eh? That's the question your lot should keep in mind when electin' them boys on your side to office. How long before they wear the boots and crack the whip? A fresh face and fresh ideas – we tend to think that things are goin' to get much better, but it isn't like that. It never is. Every last one of us fails to realise that patriotism is the last refuge of the scoundrel and every man with a gun in his hand can tell you by rote *what* he's fightin' for but he never really knows *who* he's fightin' for. He usually only finds out when he looks in the mirror or sees the bulge of money in his own pocket.' The man sighed deeply. 'Aye, the sooner it's all over, the fuckin' better. Still,' he said, 'I'm lucky in one way. You know what that is?'

'I don't give a monkey's fuck!'

He smiled thinly. 'No, you probably don't. But this is it, anyway. I know all about my background, my parent's loyalties, their loves, their hates. The things that made them what they are. As a result of that knowledge, I was able to grow up lovin' one parent and hatin' the other, same as anyone normal in this world. But you – your head's fucked up, halfway up your arse, if the truth be known, and you don't need to be a psychiatrist to see it. They tell you your father was a tout and then they bury him without honours?' The man shook his head sadly. 'And him fightin' for his country the best any man could.' He raised a palm-heel.

'Don't get me wrong, kid. I've no love for someone like that, though I have to show a begrudgin' respect for anyone who fights and dies for what he believes in, no matter how wrong they are. And he did just that. And you probably hate him because people told you otherwise, though maybe you should have loved him. Your whole life might have been very different as a result. It still might. Think about it. You knew him, didn't you?' The man waved a finger and Seamus heard the central locking system operate, the lock of the door springing open. 'You can go now if you want, but one more minute, kid, that's all I want. One more minute of shite, eh?' He smiled. 'And then I won't bother you again.'

Seamus looked away, but he was listening intently. He had one hand on the handle of the door and he could have opened it there and then and just walked away.

'Of course, you knew him, didn't you?' the man called Dave continued. 'I bet you all he ever talked about was the fuckin' 'RA and how great they were, about everythin' they did. Sure how could he just suddenly change with no provocation? How could he just change, and why would he? What had we on him, a mere foot soldier who was never charged with anythin', ever?'

Seamus opened the door and climbed out. 'I'll be talkin' to you again real soon, Seamus,' the man called after him. 'Real soon. Somethin' big is about to happen and we need a lead. You can help us, maybe save a hell of a lot of lives in the process. I'm countin' on the fact that you aren't really a bad kid, Seamus, that maybe you want to find out about a few things you don't really know about. An exchange of information, nothin' more. No harm done.' The man smiled and pulled the door shut. The car skidded through the slush and drove off.

Seamus spat after them. Me da had a problem with the drink, his mind told him curtly, that's most likely why he did as he did. But then he recalled that his da had actually cut way down on the drink near the end of his life and had been as strong a personality as ever – near as strong as wee Mary Doherty herself. Though she'd had her weaknesses too, pushed to the limits as she had been by fate and circumstance. Everyone, it seemed, had their strengths and weaknesses, and it was hard to know how their minds worked from day to day. Still, Seamus thought angrily, somehow or other that bastard has just discovered a weakness of mine – a chink in the armour I've been building for years.

Had he discovered it by luck, Seamus wondered. Did he have a capacity to read minds – to know people better than they knew themselves? Or had he planned it all from the start? Taken out a file somewhere and said to himself that Seamus Doherty was a vulnerable kid if ever there was one – an isolated loner who could never be trusted because his da had been a tout, so he'd instinctively do and become the same? Seamus sighed, perplexed. How would he ever know? He shrugged mentally and, pushing the turmoil from his mind, ran home.

*

'He's plantin' seeds in your head, nothin' else.'

Jimmy sprawled back in the armchair, hands behind his head. Seamus looked at him hard. He had a cup of steaming hot tea in his own hands, and two well-buttered, floury baps that Jimmy had brought with him at the end of his shift. He'd decided to tell Jimmy everything, even the things he hadn't mentioned the last time. Because the past was past and nothing had come of it. It didn't matter.

Jimmy's reaction had been unexpected. He'd whistled a low, soft whistle, to show that things weren't all that good in the Seamy camp. Then he'd said that maybe Seamus should have gone to the Sinn Féin centre after all the last time. Them showin' him pictures of his da, sure that was fuckin' harassment, if anythin' was.

Seamus had wondered then how Jimmy's mind worked. Jimmy seemed to have forgotten that the Special Branch man had also shown him pictures of the lads rioting. The red-haired youth hadn't classed that as harassment. Sure if that wasn't harassment too, then what was? Seamus had launched a further attack on Jimmy, saying that it had been Jimmy's idea in the first place for him not to go to Sinn Féin. Jimmy retorted that he hadn't heard the whole scenario then, so Seamus could hardly blame him for his advice, which was well-intentioned. Seamus relented with a despondent nod, knowing that he should have told his friend everything. Now he was doing so, he explained. He expected Jimmy to come up with an immediate solution, even though this was hardly fair.

'Ye reckon?'

Jimmy laughed. 'Aye, he's windin' your clock. I'm fuckin' sure of it.'

'He says that somethin' big's gonna happen soon. Sure ye heard Paddy sayin' that too, before the funeral.'

'Hey, I heard fuck all,' Jimmy warned, with a wag of his finger. 'And you'd be as well sayin' that ye heard fuck all too.'

'Aye, you're right. But that aside, I reckon he was fuckin' serious. He wants me to tout to him and he's tryin' to do some sort of a trade.'

Jimmy regarded him thoughtfully. 'Sure how would ye know

if he was tellin' the truth or not. Now I don't mean any disrespect here . . . '

Seamus waved a hand, his mouth full, telling him to continue.

' . . . but if your da was a tout, then who did he tout on and how exactly did they find all that out? *If* they found it out, that is,' Jimmy added, quickly. 'Because now ye don't know a fuck if he *was* a tout, do ye?'

Seamus shrugged. 'Aye, you're right enough there. I dunno what he was supposed to have done or said. Nobody ever told me.'

'And ye sais your man talked about your da bein' in Castlereagh Holdin' Centre up there in Belfast. Sure, do ye ever mind hearin' that from your ma?'

Seamus tried to think. Not once had he ever heard that. He shook his head.

'Then you'd better find out, hadn't ye?' Jimmy said, brightly. 'It'll give ye ammunition, just in case the bastard does lift ye again. At least you'll have an idea of when he's tellin' ye the truth and when he's not. That way he won't be able to fuck with your head any more.'

Seamus nodded. 'Aye, you're spot on there. Well, I'll do that then. And I'd rather ye didn't say fuck all about this again.' He regarded Jimmy strongly. 'I don't want to have to go explainin' this thing to anyone. If I do find out, then that'll be enough. Your man'll be off me back in no time.'

Jimmy nodded and sipped his tea. 'Aye, well how are ye gonna find out?'

Seamus looked at him, thinking. There were two people he could ask. He was going to ask his mother, he knew that, though it depended on getting the timing exactly right. The other person who knew a lot about his da was Dan McGeady. Seamus put that name to the back of his mind. Whether he would ask McGeady depended on how much success he had with his mother.

*

'Do we have to talk about this, Seamus?'

Seamus nodded, hoping, fingers crossed under his thighs. He sat forward, waiting, expectant.

He'd waited two weeks, all of that time gauging her moods, waiting for her to be alone, waiting for exactly the right moment to ask her. George Stewart or Sadie always seemed to be about, or his mother was in the middle of rushing here or there. Out to bingo, out to the shops, out for a date. Tonight seemed to be the perfect opportunity. It was a Wednesday night, the only night that Seamus knew his ma nearly always had to herself. He was doing nothing much himself tonight, anyhow. Night classes were on a Tuesday and Thursday night; he usually went out at the weekends. Tonight was perfect.

She'd usually throw her feet up on the new pouffe, watch a few cookery and gardening programmes, read a few women's magazines and smoke a hell of a lot of cigarettes. The only consolation for them both was that nowadays the drink was missing. Seamus hadn't seen the effort she was putting into her life these days, though he was sure it was there and he sensed she was doing just fine. He had his reservations about asking her, of course, because he didn't want to throw her into a deep, dark mood. Not now, not ever. After all she'd been through, she didn't deserve that.

'Ye sais you'd tell me sometime.'

She frowned and lit a cigarette. 'I don't remember sayin' that.' Dismissive, half-lost in *Gardener's World*. Or trying to get lost in it. The eyes weren't far enough away, the gaze temporarily distracted.

'It's a while back now. Ye said that me da was a good man, that he did a lot more for us than I should ever know. I'd just . . . well, I'd just like ye to tell me all about him. If ye don't, then maybe I'll never know.' He lowered his head. 'I have to know some things. I have to know a bit about me past, and you're the best one to ask.'

She nodded and frowned. 'Aye, it's been seven years, near enough – six and a half, anyway.' Her eyes were pained, her voice a subdued whisper. He looked away. 'Long enough, though only a whisper of time if ye think about it. Still . . . ' She took a deep breath and clucked her tongue, the past deep in her eyes. 'I was tellin' you about Stevie McAdam's funeral just before Motorman, wasn't I?'

Seamus nodded grimly. 'You told me about the actual funeral, aye.'

'Well, just a few days before that, the Boys had decided after a number of meetin's that they weren't goin' to try and defend the estates from tanks and Christ knew what else. So most of the ASUs were hidin' their weapons in dumps, gettin' ready to ship across the border into Buncrana and places like that until the whole shebang had quietened down. But, knowin' that the Brits were goin' to saturate the place and raid it within a matter of days – or maybe a week at the most – they decided to take the war to the Brits, as it were, in a sort of last-ditch effort to show them that we weren't goin' to lie down completely. So they decided to go and bomb the Ebrington Barracks in the Waterside, believin' as they did that that was where the Brits were keeping most of their heavy armoury for the invasion.'

His mother rolled her eyes again and shook her head, a slight smile telling him how ludicrous she thought the idea was. Seamus, slightly hunched in his seat, smiled thinly, fidgeting with his fingers.

'Aye, well that operation didn't go all that well,' Mary continued, with a sigh. 'Stevie was shot on the way back and the bombs were discovered and defused. Stevie died. They shot him twice, not a one of the others hurt at all. A terrible waste of a good man. Young, a family of one. A wee girl who never got to know her da. Wee Mary McAdams, ye probably know her to see . . . ' Seamus shook his head: he couldn't place her at all. 'Aye well, great shame, anyway.' Mary shrugged and stubbed out her cigarette hard in the ashtray, her gaze lost within the ashes. She quickly lit another and handed one to Seamus but, smoked out, he declined with a wave of his hand.

'But the rest made it back,' Mary added, brightly. 'And they decided to have one more go at the Brits. Stubborn, proud men, every last one of them, decidin' that they'd have to avenge a friend, though this one wasn't sanctioned and it was goin' to be done completely off their own bat. Their blood was up after that funeral, y'see, and your da had been heavy on the drink the whole night afterwards. Still, I couldn't blame him for that one last blow-out, could I? He'd cut it way down the last while before that. Way, way down. And I know what that's like,' Mary said, with a thin smile. 'So I have to give him credit for that, really I do, because it couldn't have been easy.

'Anyhow, where was I . . . ? Oh aye, they were supposed to slip off across the border to join up with the rest of the lads, but they decided to have one more go at the Brits. They just got into a car and drove off to meet up with a few boys from Shantallow who were plannin' some other operation. But the Brits were out in force that particular day, stoppin' everyone they could see. Your da, Billy Flannagan and Dan McGeady were lifted as they drove along the Greenhaw Road, taken away to Castlereagh Holdin' Centre just outside Belfast and held for seven days. It was a good job they had nothin' on them – no guns, no paramilitary clothin' of any kind – because they were supposed to collect that later on, y'see. A real good job, that was. They just claimed they were three workies on their way to a paintin' job, nothin' more. It was a good job for all of them,' she repeated, softly. 'A real good job indeed.'

Seamus wanted to tell her that he already knew about his father's exploits in the holding centre, that he'd already been told by a Special Branch man. But then, he mused, he didn't really know anything, did he? He knew what the man called Dave had told him, nothing more, and it was probably a tissue of lies, interwoven with bits of truth to make it more credible.

'He was in Castlereagh?' Seamus feigned surprise.

'Aye, oh aye. They took him away and gave him a wil' old time of it. Gave them all a time of it, as far as I hear. Your da says they made him run barefoot through rows of baton-wieldin' soldiers at one stage. Another time, they went at him with the sensory deprivation. A hood over his head, standin' in a search position, a bread-and-water diet, no sleep, white noise in the background. The three of them got that, only your da refuses food, water, the lot. Aye, he was a wil' man,' Mary said, a trace of admiration in her voice. 'Sure they had to get a doctor for him, him thinkin' they'd drugged the food to get him to talk. The doctor came, and he started to eat then. But after seven days they released him. After seven days they released them all.' Mary looked at him, her eyes searching.

He knew from the look on her face that she was wondering if she could stop there – if he would allow her to do that before it got all too real, too painful. But his gaze held firm and she knew what he was expecting. Everything. The warts-and-all version; the version that gave her nowhere to hide.

'It was about three days after their release that the Brits invaded,' Mary went on, sighing resignedly. 'But the boys were apparently in a state of alarm over somethin' or other and nobody seemed to know what. Someone had talked – that was the word that came in from Dublin. Someone had given the Brits the wire that there'd be no real resistance, had informed on the dumps where some of the weapons where to be found and, more importantly, had told them where some of the Provies were hidin' out, stuff like that. Your da, of course, got the blame, because he was the hardest drinker of the bunch. McGeady was the respected one – butter wouldn't have melted in his mouth,' Mary said, flatly. 'And Billy Flannagan, well, there's not a thing I could say about him. Good fella, he was. I liked him a lot. It's a pity he ended his life the way he did, because, by doin' that, he brought suspicion on himself. And that's not fair. Judgin' someone when they can't reply to your accusations, that's not very fair at all.'

'And . . . ?' Seamus blanched, even now feeling the heartache for the man he had hardly known. Though he knew he wouldn't cry. It was seven years on – way too late for crying.

'A couple of boys took him away for questionin' over the border. A couple of the boys from up the country, mind ye. They wouldn't have known him from Adam, y'see – that's the way it worked. No attachments, no sympathy, y'know.' Seamus nodded gravely. 'It was rumoured that he said he was innocent, but apparently he never said a word after that. They obviously didn't believe him. They shot him, of course,' Mary said, in a dull whisper. 'They just went and shot him in the back of the head, the way they do all informers.'

Seamus released a pent-up sigh. Gruesome pictures of his da lying dead in a field spun through his head. A bullet to the head, and death – instantaneous, final. He shivered. A cruel death. Any death must be hard, he thought then, but shot to death by someone you knew . . . Or anyone, really, come to think about it. He shivered again. 'And Billy Flannagan and Dan McGeady, didn't they stick up for him? Didn't they do or say anythin' for him at all?'

'They both spoke up for him, aye, but what could they do? They'd all been in different cells in the holdin' centre. They both said that the Branch were comin' in to each of them, sayin' stuff that they could only have got off one of the three. Stuff about their own four-man cell, about the attempted bombin' of the Ebrington Barracks, about how they'd thought about doin' the bridge, and stuff like that. Stuff they could never have guessed at in a thousand years. Sayin' one of them sais this and maybe you'd better say the same, though it really could have come from any one of them. But they released them all, despite their claims about knowin' everythin',' Mary said, shrugging. 'And everyone thought that was the end of it. Then your da gets shot for informin' soon after, and then your da's best friend, Billy Flannagan, goes and kills himself two months later for no apparent reason . . . '

'Aye, it wouldn't look the best, that, right enough.'

'Aye, and only a matter of weeks afterwards. A shot to the head, the gun at his side. No note, no explanation. And then people began to talk, the way they always do. To speculate, to insinuate, to put two and two together and come up with twenty-two, because it looks better. To believe whatever they fuckin' wanted to believe, because that's just the way some people are!' Mary said, coldly. 'Guilt, they sais. A guilt-racked man who couldn't bear the thought that his friend had died for somethin' that he didn't do.'

'So why do ye hate Dan McGeady, then?'

Mary shrugged, her forehead deeply creased. 'He's like a buzzard. He invites death to his side, despite his claims to savour life. I'm not sayin' he's not a good man in his own way. Maybe he is. And I know for a fact that he has the interests of his people at heart. Ye can tell that from the way he talks, the way he speaks. There's a feelin' there, a compassion for the people he's fightin' for, an intensity. But every time I looked at him after your da's funeral, I hated him. I despised him. Maybe because people like him can talk, maybe because they can rally people to them, make them commit themselves to a cause and then make them die for it. Make them throw their lives away, even if it is for the sake of what is right. But I think I hate him because it's always people like him who live on, who win. They never seem to die themselves, and somehow that isn't fair.'

'I thought ye always believed in the cause.'

'I did then,' Mary said, nodding. 'Oh aye, we all did, in our hearts, and I suppose I still do now – probably always will. Though I don't believe it's worth a single life any more. Ye never realise that stark fact until it's one of your own lyin' there. Ye must have felt that. You standin' there at wee Barney's graveside. The people at the back cheerin' as the shots are fired. The people at the front not knowin' why it's them has to suffer for a cause.'

Seamus nodded gravely, frowning.

'Nah, none of it's worth it. And I'm not sayin' that we were wrong in doin' what we did. Not one of us thinks like that. We all did what we had to do – we still do. Except there must be another way. There has to be. I just don't know why no one can figure it out after so long a time. Christ, it's been ten years! Ten fuckin' years, and it'll probably go on for another ten. And we're still no further on than ever.'

He sat there in silence and offered her a cigarette. She took it, the tremble in her hands just visible, but nothing like he had seen before. And she was still smiling. It was a sad smile: the resigned smile of a woman who had accepted everything that life had thrown at her and who was now prepared to get on with it, despite her deep inner pain. But it was a smile still, no matter the slight distortion, and Seamus was glad of that.

She took the cigarette and lit it, offering him a light too. It was an important ritual – one he'd shared with others in harder situations than this. He looked into his mother's eyes then, and he knew from her faint smile that she realised the significance of the moment too.

Ten

There were several cars sitting across the road when he came out of the training centre. One, a small white Peugeot, stood out from the rest, but only because Seamus could see who was driving it. The colour drained from his face. Elaine was behind the steering wheel, an uncertain smile on her face, her eyes flickering between his eyes and the windscreen. He was talking to some of his friends and blushed slightly as they noticed his interest, then cheered and laughed at him as he crossed the road. He dropped his gaze and approached the car, half-distracted by the jeers of his companions. Elaine smiled.

'You think we should get out of here a while?' she asked, hesitantly.

He shrugged non-committally, went around to the passenger side of the car and got in. He'd gone through every conceivable scenario in his head over the past few months, imagining what he would say to her if she should turn up out of the blue – if he should run into her one day as he was walking out the town. In each of these scenarios he'd been the hero: he'd been the one to walk away with his head held high after cutting her dead with dry, witty remarks that pierced her soul. And she'd been the one who ran after him. Lost, sorry that she had ever let him go, knowing that he could have had anyone he wanted in the world, because he was Seamus Doherty, and that he'd chosen her that first night in 52nd Street out of pity, nothing else.

But it was different now that he was here beside her in the car. His mouth was drying up, his heart thumping madly against his ribs, as if trying to tumble free from his chest. He concentrated on breathing deeply, the way he'd seen his mother do when she was having one of her mild panic attacks, the effects of retreating from the haven of drink causing that alarm. Elaine seemed calm enough about the whole thing, however. Completely in control and at ease. She drove the car down through the Springtown estate and onto the Buncrana Road, in the direction of the border. Not looking at him, aware only of the road, the steady flow of traffic.

He cursed inwardly and bit his lip hard. God, he thought, how could she remain so calm while he sat there going to pieces, her acting as if they'd never been apart. He couldn't think what to say and, even if one of his many prepared speeches came to him now, he decided that he wasn't going to say anything, because he didn't believe he was the one who should speak first. Yet the long-drawn-out silence was getting to him.

'I live in the Creggan, in case ye forget.'

She turned to him, her eyes showing hurt at that remark.

An impact. He savoured the hit but hated himself for saying it. 'It's the other way.' He couldn't stop, even though he half-wanted to.

'I'm sorry,' she said, convincingly, her concentration divided between him and the road. 'Really I am. I . . . ' She sighed and turned back to the road.

He could smell her perfume; he knew he should have turned away then, telling her exactly what he'd been practising for weeks – months, even: It's your loss. I'm fine now, never been better. Sure look at me. I've got ye out of me head and there are women galore lookin' to have me for themselves. Always one prettier and more willin' than the last, Jimmy and me both know that to our joy. And it's fun flittin' from one women to the next, interviewin' them and findin' that we have nothin' in common but lust and an ability to breathe in sequence.

'Why?' he found himself asking instead. Neutral, detached. A cat who loved its owner, though never showed affection. 'Sure ye got what ye wanted.'

'Why am I sorry?' The familiar raised eyebrow; a serious gaze – sorrowful, loving. He wanted to laugh, to hug her tight. He didn't answer. 'Because I am. You might not know I am, but I am. Really. I didn't want things to work out the way they did . . . '

'Why can't . . . Why couldn't . . . ?' He took a deep breath, listening to the familiar sound of the helicopters flying overhead, engaged in their twenty-four-hour surveillance routine. He looked up into the gun-metal-grey sky and guessed that one of the helicopters was just about over Creggan, the other somewhere nearer the town centre. He turned his gaze downwards, the daylight blinding, suddenly finding the Templemore Sports Complex and the athletes on the track there momentarily fascinating.

She raised her palms slightly off the wheel, her bunched shoulders betraying her tension. A little girl lost, a strange frown on her forehead. 'I live in my parents' house. I have to do what they say. I didn't want to leave you, because I miss you.' Her deep-blue eyes misted over slightly. Unable to look him directly in the face, she turned, then took the gearstick tightly in her hand.

He'd been bending a thumb backwards and forwards for a while for something to do with his hands, and only realised it then. 'I know,' he said, eventually. 'I miss you too.' He smiled then and caught her eyes brightening, even as a film of tears descended to cover them. 'And drivin', are we? God, that's a new one.' A change of subject: temporary relief for them both.

She laughed, beautiful, radiant despite her tears, and he clutched tentatively at her shoulder. She released one hand from the wheel and placed it gently around his, the fingers interlacing. 'That's the reason I'm here,' she told him. 'They can't keep such a good eye on me now. I can more or less go where I please.' She smiled, the tears held in check. 'Well, I can go anywhere within reason,' she added, quickly. 'And I'll have to say I'm goin' somewhere else from now on. Well, that's if . . . ' That frown again – the one he wanted to brush away from her forehead with a soft touch, to erase forever.

He nodded, completely happy, never having realised that she could bring such happiness into his life with so few words. 'I've been goin' to the Tech,' he told her, proudly. 'Doin' a couple of O levels, tryin' to better meself, like ye suggested.'

Smiling. 'Aye, I saw you a few times.'

'And ye didn't come over?'

'I was afraid to. My brother has a few friends in the Tech. He's told me ma that he's goin' to be keepin' an eye out for me. I've told them that it isn't necessary, but . . . '

'Aye, sure I suppose they're only lookin' out for ye,' he said, not believing this in the least. 'Sure that's what families do, isn't it? Look out for one another.' He pictured her eldest brother in his mind: he hated him as much then as he had once hated Doran, and he didn't even know him.

She shrugged, as if she too had no faith in that remark, then dropped through the gears as they approached the Buncrana Road checkpoint. There were two long lines of traffic gathering there: one coming over the border from the South, the other going in the other direction. There were, as usual, both RUC men and soldiers manning the checkpoint. Vehicles and their occupants were searched here, details of individuals' names and addresses were taken and logged and car registrations and car colours were computerised for use by the army and the RUC in their bid to keep an eye on the comings and goings of suspects. The border crossing points were also monitored by radar and buried sensors, and quite often the SAS lay in the hedgerows and ditches nearby to protect the outlying areas. Sometimes the traffic came to a crawl and it could take ages to get across the border, depending on the mood of individual British soldiers or RUC men. Today it wasn't so bad and the car was across the border in less than ten minutes, the policeman on duty perhaps enamoured by Elaine's beguiling smile and cheerful manner.

'Where are we headin'?' Seamus asked, relaxing into his seat. He often felt the tension leaving him as he crossed the border, as if entering a different world altogether. He'd heard his ma say that most people – 'Be they Catholic, Protestant or Dissenter, son' – felt the same. That small stretch of road beyond the checkpoints offered release from a situation and an environment that you always thought you had gotten used to, though obviously you never did.

'We're goin' on a mystery tour,' she smiled. 'Don't you like goin' for a spin in cars?'

He placed his hands behind his head, stretching his legs as far as the space in front of his seat would allow. 'Of course I do, Benson,' he smiled, her grin infectious.

He watched her for a time as she drove along the country road, taking a right at Bridgend and heading in the direction of Buncrana, a nearby town that was famous for its amusements and slot machines, its hotel lunches on a Sunday afternoon and its late drinking hours on a Sunday night. He stopped smiling then and she caught his sombre mood.

'What?' she asked.

'I kept thinkin' that you'd be in England by now,' Seamus said, with a frown. 'Thought I'd never see ye again, ever.' He felt his stomach churning ever so slightly, feeling vulnerable for admitting that – now no longer a family cat but a dog with a wagging tail. 'Ye still goin' to the Tech as well, then?' A stupid question she had already answered – not the one he wanted to ask her. Seeking to regain neutral ground, afraid, pensive. His whole dream could unravel in seconds if she said something he hoped she wouldn't.

'For now.'

She sighed and turned to concentrate fully on the road, her eyes misting over once more. For a time she didn't speak and the mood was serious: her concentrating on the road, him on the approaching Fahan Beach coastline, a scatter of boats bobbing about on the grey-blue water, a variety of coloured sails. The long stretch of speckled yellow and grey sand on his left was devoid of life except for a man walking his Labrador dog, a peaked cap low on his forehead, his collar held high to shield himself from the blustery February winds.

Elaine drummed her fingers on the wheel, as if vying for his attention. 'I'm not goin' to be here forever, you know,' she said, softly. 'I can't live my life with people watchin' over me, tellin' me what to do. Don't get me wrong,' she added quickly, 'I know my family are tryin' to do what they think is best for me, but . . . '

Seamus bit at his lip. 'Then why don't ye move out of the house? Why don't we . . . ?' He was thinking of Paddy Monaghan and Eileen, and the fact that they were looking for a flat, and was wondering if he was prepared for such a momentous step. He thought he might be, if it meant not losing her.

She smiled, not unkindly, and sighed. 'How could you and I

survive in this place on the money we get. Me workin' in a takeaway, you an apprentice painter. We wouldn't last a wet week on our wages. We'd end up fightin' to the end, hatin' each other, the way every couple do who never think about what they're gettin' into.'

He hated the way she always let her head rule her heart; the way she thought things through logically; the way she was nearly always right. 'I won't always be a painter, y'know,' he said, trying to reassure her – and himself, perhaps more so. 'I'm tryin' to go somewhere in life. And I will, even if it kills me, really I will.'

Her eyes sparkled, flashes of illumination there that made him want to hold her tight, never let her go. His insides were turning, heaving like the waves that were crashing into cold, bubbling spume on the shore below the road. 'I don't doubt it for a second. I know you're capable of doin' anythin' you put your mind to. But it's all goin' to take time – a hell of a lot of time – and I'm not sure . . . '

'Then how do ye hope to survive in England?' He knew the answer but he didn't want to hear her finish what she was saying. She wasn't sure of what? That she could survive that long in her situation? That she loved him enough to hang around? That it was even wise to consider a Protestant girl and a Catholic boy having a future together here in the city, never mind anywhere else in the North? 'Your sister, I suppose,' he added, heavy-hearted at the thought and wishing she had no lifeline there across the water.

She nodded. 'I can stay with her. I phone her all the time. That's why she left here, you know. Not because she was goin' out with an Englishman. Because there's life there, because there's more than fightin' and hatin' everyone, when we don't even know them.'

Seamus raised his palms, seeking to calm her ideas with empty reason. 'But sure, it's the same over there. They hate the blacks, the Pakistanis, the Germans, the French . . . Come to think of it, they fuckin' hate everyone in that country. A bunch of hate-the-fuckin'-worlds, that's the way they come across to me.' Stupid, empty words. Blaming the entire English nation for problems that were his and his alone. Yet it was all he could think to say. He wondered if he could hold back from releasing his every learned hatred if he was given cause. Looking once more into her eyes, he thought he might be able to do so. If she would let him; if she would allow him time to do so.

She shrugged, then smiled, aware of his pain. 'Maybe they do. But I'll have my privacy there. I won't be forced to live in one area and believe that all people are bad just because someone else says they are. I'll be able to make my own decisions, be myself . . . '

'And you'll be alone too,' he said, under his breath, not believing that for a second either. She was much too pretty ever to end up alone – too interesting, too motivated, too trusting. Too everything that he had ever seen or known in a person. He dropped his head, as if the wind was attacking him also, feeling an empathy with the man they'd left behind on the deserted shoreline.

She pulled into a car park beside the beach, stopped the car and removed her seat belt. Unrestricted, she turned to him. He didn't look up, embarrassed by his tears.

'You could go with me,' she said. A hopeful lilt in her voice, soothing. She tried lifting his head with a finger, despite his resistance, the other hand winding around his neck. So close that her perfume made his senses reel. 'We'd get work, both of us. We'd get a place too, far cheaper than we'd get here. We could make a life.'

He lifted his head a fraction, coughing to hide his pain, still not daring to look her in the eyes. She kissed him then, on the forehead, on the nose, on the mouth. 'I don't want to go away myself, Seamus. I want you to go with me.'

'What about the English over there?' he asked, knowing that it sounded ridiculous. 'I've heard they give Irish people a hard time because of the bombin's and stuff. What about the fact that you and me are different religions? What about school, your classes? What about your ma, my ma? What about . . . ?'

She lifted his head and kissed him on the mouth, the taste of salt tears on both their lips, a red, nail-varnished finger in between the two of them gently wiping the tears away. 'We take one problem at a time, Seamus. Not all English people are bigots. Sure there's as many in our own country as there are over there, we all know that. Different religions?' She shrugged easily and pouted. 'What does it really matter? You aren't overly Catholic – your ma was tellin' me that. Says you miss Mass through lyin' in every other Sunday, if I remember rightly. And I know that I'm not the most staunch Protestant in the world. Me ma and da are easygoin' enough that way.' She smiled, causing him to return that gesture thinly. 'And as for the classes, sure we've exams in June. We could head away after that. That'll give us three months or more to settle in and set ourselves up for next year's classes. Now,' she smiled, 'have ye anythin' else?'

He had a million questions coursing through his mind. In the last half-hour his life had suddenly turned somersaults, and now he was lost in confusion. Could he leave Derry? Could he just get up and walk away from his life – from everyone and everything he knew? Could he leave his mother all alone? What if he went to England and they didn't accept him there? Or, again, what if he didn't accept them? If all his hidden fears turned themselves into a protective, defensive wall through which he would never allow anyone access and over which he himself would never be able to climb?

He'd have Elaine there to guide him, of course. Elaine: the only person who could possibly make sense of such a gigantic and mentally overwhelming move. She'd help him adjust, help him gently forsake one set of ideas for another, softly blot out one culture, so heavily ingrained in him, and replace it ever so slowly with another. Yet he didn't know if such a dramatic change was possible. All he knew for certain just then was that he couldn't think straight, that she was holding him close, that her perfume and her ideas had sent his mind reeling.

He shook his head. 'Let's not decide now,' he told her, softly. He dared to look her in the face now, her smile and the light in her eyes strengthening him, when he hadn't even known that he was weak. 'Let's just be together and take it as it comes.'

'I do want you to be with me,' she told him, seriously. 'Really I do.'

'I know. I've always known.'

She nodded, smiling. 'So have I, Seamus Doherty. So have I.' She placed a finger on his lips once more, this time to silence him. 'But we don't have to decide now.' She kissed him, and in that fleeting moment his millions of uncertainties were answered and the decision was made.

*

His mother wondered why he wasn't coming straight home after work these days, of course: why he was staying out at the oddest times of the evening on a Saturday or Sunday, when he'd usually only ever sat in and watched television. Seamus was reluctant to tell her, at first, feeling that, if he did so, things might go drastically wrong, the way they did at times if you ever dared to dream, hope or plan. But she'd guessed the reason after a time and had told him so one evening over dinner. He'd said nothing, confirming her suspicions. Then she had patted him on the shoulder, telling him she hoped that it worked out this time, because he deserved to have as much happiness as she'd found of late. The both of them havin' been through so much in their young lives, sure they both deserved it, didn't they, she said.

The times when Seamus and Elaine could see each other had changed – but still suited both of them. Yet he wouldn't have cared if she'd wanted to see him in the middle of the night, just so long as he could be with her. She usually had an hour to kill after school, then a couple more after her dinner and before she went down to work in Brendan's takeaway, and he too was available then. She was down in her friend's house, if anyone asked, though she always made sure to let her friends know her precise plans, confiding in them that she was goin' out with someone new – not the boy she'd been goin' out with last year. Just as a safety precaution, mind, she told Seamus, with a smile. Because one of them, Ashlene, was right fond of her Marty, and you'd never know what she'd say if pressed. Or pressed against, Elaine laughed. What with her apparently havin' the morals of an alley cat.

Saturday evenings were better for the two of them, in that she could say she was going off for a jaunt around the town. Sunday evenings took a little more planning. She gave a different excuse each time she left the house. A make-up party, a lunch with the girls from the Tech down over the border – just in case her car was spotted – or a trip to see a friend who lived in Limavady town whom she hadn't seen in ages. Mary had offered them the house, because she was spending a lot of time in either Sadie's or Michael's, but they had declined the offer, feeling that they didn't really want to hide away from the world, when they spent so little time together anyway.

So Elaine would drive them to Buncrana, mostly, or to the Redcastle Hotel or, further down that road, to Moville. It didn't matter where they ended up, and most of the time it was a spontaneous decision. They enjoyed their time together, feeling closer now then they had ever done: happier, content. And the inconvenience that surrounded their meetings was always balanced out by the fact that they had made a mutual decision to move away.

They had told nobody, of course. Seamus often thought about that. He wanted to tell Jimmy, because he eventually told Jimmy everything in his life that was of consequence, and he felt guilty holding that secret back. But even more so he wanted to tell his mother. He found himself watching her more diligently in the days after he and Elaine had finally agreed to leave. He tried to gauge the depths of her happiness – to see whether she would be able to handle the departure of the second Seamus Doherty as well as she had handled that of the first.

He didn't think he had anything to worry about, in the main. His mother, he decided, seemed very happy these days; she hadn't touched a drink in months. She was happier still when Michael was about, and he was always hanging around the house of late. Seamus found that adapting to having another person around the place wasn't as hard as he'd thought it would be. As Michael felt the same way now, he expected that it would be only a matter of time before the older man moved in. At least, that was what he imagined would occur if things went on the way they were going. And so it was on the first Sunday of March that she called him into the living room and asked him to sit down.

He was out in the kitchen at the time, hurriedly slurping at a hot cup of tea and trying not to burn his mouth in the process, while pulling on his parka coat, as it was raining heavily outside. As usual, he was spruced up, in his best jeans and denim jacket – though the reason for his dressing well had nothing to do with the fact that it was Sunday. He looked pensively at his watch. 'Aye ma, no bother. But I hope ye tell me whatever it is right and quick, because Elaine'll be here in a minute. We're headin off over the border, maybe goin' down to Buncrana to play the slots.'

Mary ushered him into the living room. Michael was sitting there in front of the television. The older man, sitting nervously on the edge of his seat, smiled as Seamus came in. Mary took a seat, but Seamus moved to the window and pushed his hand into the slats of the blinds, pulling them apart.

'Aye, I'll not keep ye a moment,' his mother began. 'I've just somethin' to say, that's all.' She sat there for a time, looking between him and Michael, trying to appear serious. Trying hard, it seemed to Seamus, not to break into a smile.

Seamus looked between them. 'Right, I'm waitin'. What is it ye have to say?' Nothing; the eye contact between Mary and Michael flickering back and forth. There was warmth and affection there – happiness – tinged with mild nervousness. Seamus laughed. 'What? Are youse gettin' married, or somethin'?'

Mary laughed then and nodded uncertainly. Michael blushed, head down, not knowing whether he should smile or wait for Seamus's reaction. Seamus heard the car pulling up outside, the tooting of the horn. He stepped away from the window and moved towards his mother, who was rising, uncertain whether she should wait for his reaction or go and answer the door. He caught her in a bear-hug and gave her a kiss on the cheek. 'Aye, well I'm very happy for ye, ma,' he told her, seriously. 'Ye deserve it.' She returned the hug, pulling him in close, nearly knocking the breath out of him. 'Jesus, ma, you'd want to get on the television with Mick McManus and the rest of those wrestlers,' he said, surprised at her strength.

She released him, her eyes moist, but continued to clutch his hand. 'Ye don't mind, then? I mean . . . ' she added quickly, 'it's as big a change to your life as it is to mine.'

He shook his head and grinned, sincerely happy for her – for them both. Michael was answering the door as Seamus turned, and seconds later Elaine entered the room behind him. He shook the man's hand, and they exchanged honest smiles.

'Not in the least, ma. Sure ye know I'll not be here forever meself, don't ye?' It was the first time he'd broached the subject: now was as good an opportunity as ever, he thought.

'Naturally, son. Though there'll always be a place for ye, no matter what ye do in life. Ye know that, don't ye?'

He wasn't sure if she knew something then, but he remembered thinking that she was wiser than he'd ever given her credit for – that she'd told him once how mothers knew more than they let on. 'Aye, sure I know that. And I'm not away anywhere yet, so don't be rentin' out me room or nothin'.' He turned. Elaine stood there, hands held in front of her. 'Elaine, me ma and Michael are gettin' married.' Elaine's eyes widened and she took the older woman's hand and embraced her warmly, giving her congratulations and shaking Michael's hand at the same time, wishing him the best in the future and saying that, God, that was great.

'Aye,' Seamus said, catching his girlfriend's eye once more, 'they're gettin' married and they're goin' to be together forever.'

Elaine laughed then, fathoming his meaning immediately. Seamus didn't have to worry about his mother being alone when they went to England. She sensed his joy and she was as happy about the news as he was. 'That's wonderful,' the girl said. 'Really,

I think you'll make a lovely couple.'

'Do ye want to go out with us to celebrate?' Michael asked then. Seamus looked at Elaine, who shrugged politely. But then Mary caught Michael's hand in hers.

'There'll be time enough to celebrate later on,' Mary said, with a twinkle in her eye. 'The wains just want to go out and spend a wee bit of time together, sure. Don't ye?'

Seamus blushed. 'We aren't wains, ma. We're grown-ups and, aye, we'll go out with ye if ye want.'

Mary laughed, then waved a hand in the direction of the door. 'Go on out with yourselves. Ye never get enough time to yourselves these days anyway. We'll get out another day. Anyhow, me and Michael want to chat about the plans for the big day and stuff.'

Seamus smiled, raising his eyes to heaven, and Elaine took his hand. They waved goodbye to the older couple as they stood there on the doorstep, Michael's arm around the shoulder of Mary, who was smiling. Seamus and Elaine drove off towards Buncrana, not knowing then that, if they'd taken his mother up on her offer, they'd have saved themselves a lot of trouble.

*

It was five o'clock when they came out of Colm's Amusements, the car park packed with cars, the traffic on the road moving in and out of the town at a crawl. Elaine suggested getting something to eat and Seamus agreed, neither of them having eaten since breakfast. They'd won fifteen pounds on the slot machines, and Seamus, in his excitement – he'd never won that much before in his life – had wanted to stay on and try and win more. Elaine, as sensible as always, told him that his run of luck would end and that no one ever won if they kept on playing. Reluctantly, he agreed. She went into the fish-and-chip shop beside the depot; he decided to wait outside. Elaine had no idea how prophetic her last statement would prove to be.

Elaine had parked the car in an alley that ran alongside the amusements. Seamus was half-sitting on the bonnet of the car, not wishing to leave a dent in the side, when he suddenly felt himself being pulled backwards, pain exploding in his head. He hit the ground at speed and the shock of the impact surged through his right elbow. He couldn't break his fall after that, and his head banged off the tarmacadam surface. His vision swam for a second, and he fought the tidal wave of unconsciousness that threatened to wash over him. Shaking his head quickly – and fully aware that he was in some sort of danger – he sought fully to regain his vision quickly, but to no avail. Still, his vision, blurred as it was, allowed him to catch sight of a leg swinging backwards. He had only a second to cradle his head in his arms and curl up in a near-foetal position, to protect himself from the succession of kicks that then rained in on him. He cried out – a disjointed whimper of pain that he was sure nobody could have heard. Then he couldn't breathe, the boots having caught him in the gut, the back, the arm.

'Ye were told to stay the fuck away from her,' an angry voice barked. 'Maybe now ye get the fuckin' message.'

His vision swam; his coordination was in ruins. He couldn't answer. Another boot hit him in the ribs and he lost his breath – breath he thought by then he hadn't got to lose.

'We've lost one sister to a Brit – we'll not lose another to no fuckin' Taig. Ye go near her again, I'll blow your fuckin' head off, I swear to God!'

He heard the warning but the sky and the earth were blurring together in a patchwork of blue and brown and black and grey, and it didn't seem to matter who was saying what. Running, the sounds of feet racing away. The sounds of other feet approaching. Shouting. A car skidding on the roadway, people crowding the sky out, the patchwork blurring at the edges, darkening.

And then it was all replaced by the questionable comfort of total blackness.

ELEVEN

'And ye didn't even get a thump at him. Christ, that's bad for you, Seamy!' Jimmy Duffy shook his head in amazement, as if he could think of nothing worse that could have befallen his friend. Jimmy rubbed his hands in front of the fire and stared into the flames, reminding Seamus momentarily of a scene that had occurred years before.

Seamus went to lift his arms in protest – an action he'd also seen his father perform a hundred times or more at least – but the right one, heavily bruised and swollen around the elbow and upper forearm, refused to rise. He winced at the pain, then said, 'Sure I didn't see a fuckin' thing. He kicked the shite out of me before I had a chance to know if I was comin' or goin'.'

Paddy Monaghan took a sip out of his can – his second that afternoon – wiped a hand across his mouth and settled back into the sofa, legs outstretched. 'Fuck's sake, Seamy, you're in some mess all right. Those bloodshot eyes of yours make ye look as if ye were on the drink for a fuckin' week. And that nose . . . ye sure it isn't broken?'

'The doctor says it's only swollen.'

'I'd say it's broken. Looks broken to me.' This was said with all the conviction of an expert on broken noses.

'You'll be off work for a while, then?' Jimmy asked, with a smile. 'And you'll not be gettin' paid for it, either. That trainin' centre's a fuckin' joke, anyway. Crap wages, shit jobs. I don't know a fuck why you're still there. You'd be better off on the brew.'

'I'm there 'cause it's a job – the only one I've been offered so far.' Seamus shifted uncomfortably in his chair and propped his pillow under his right arm to lift it a little, using his left arm, which was barely in a better state than the right. 'I'll be fit enough to go back tomorrow but it won't be for much longer, if things work out. Sure it's a doddle in there, anyhow. They let ye do nothin', if that's what ye want. I only work in there to pass the time.'

Jimmy snorted, though he didn't elaborate on which part of the explanation he was casting doubt upon. 'And what did the wee woman say? Paddy asked, leaning across and prodding, with a childlike curiosity, at the black-and-purple swelling, clearly visible beneath the short arms of a T-shirt, on his friend's elbow.

'Jesus, Paddy!' Seamus exclaimed, moving back sharply into his seat on reflex. 'Will ye stop proddin' me like that. Ye think I'm some sort of a fuckin' cow or somethin'?'

Jimmy laughed, enjoying the moment. 'Aye, what'd the old doll say about it all?' he asked, enjoying a can of his own.

'Me ma was a bit shocked at first, what with them ringin' her from the hospital and tellin' her that they'd be keepin' me in overnight in case I came down with the concussion,' Seamus said. 'But she's grand now. It looks far worse than it really is.'

'Aye, 'minds me of the time that Hugo Doran boy got his beatin',' Jimmy said, and laughed.

'Aye well, that fucker deserved his,' Paddy Monaghan said, grimly. 'Seamy didn't. And I wasn't askin' about your ma, Seamy. No disrespect to her, of course,' he added, ''cause I'm sure it was a right shock. But I'm on about the other wee woman. How did she take it?'

Seamus rolled his eyes and clucked his tongue. 'Aye, well she was far from all right. She got someone to help me into the car and drove me to the hospital, but I mind fuck all. She went home when she knew I was all right and had an almighty row with her family over it – told them she was seein' me and it was up to her to do as she wanted with her life, stuff like that. Her own brother followin' her around in the family car. Christ, she was angry as fuck about that! Her ma and da sais he did it off his own bat, like. Still, she's stickin' by me, the same as I am by her.'

'Good on her,' Paddy said, raising a thumb to show his solidarity. 'Hey, you sure ye don't want a can of beer, Seamy?'

Seamus thought about that, uncertain. The doctor had told him not to drink along with the tablets he was taking. He looked at the carry-out, deciding. 'Nah, dunno.'

'I was goin' to have a few more meself,' Paddy continued, encouraging him. 'What with me and her arguin' like fuck about everythin' these days, I was gonna stay out for badness tonight. But maybe that's not such a good idea, her near ready to calve.' Paddy grinned inanely. 'Maybe I'll just go home half-tubed instead of blocked out of me head. That might be lesson enough.'

'That's right and decent of ye,' Jimmy said, drily.

'Aye, I'm a regular fuckin' Samaritan at the best of times.'

They all laughed at that. Paddy and Jimmy had come into Seamus's house that Wednesday at around six. Callin' in, as Jimmy put it, just as soon as they got word about their mucker gettin' a wallopin'. They'd discussed that for a time, going into vivid detail about how he'd taken every last boot and thump. About the reactions of the locals who had run to his rescue. About how the Guards had arrived on the scene, only to find that Marty Rogers – and perhaps some of his friends, though Seamus couldn't be absolutely sure of that – had escaped back across the border. About the startling fact that, for all the people who were about that evening, nobody had really seen anything. Though Seamus had explained that away by saying that he'd fallen behind the car and thus been out of sight of everyone except, unfortunately, his assailant – or assailants.

When the two visitors had recounted that scene from every viewpoint, to make sure they hadn't missed anything, Paddy had opened a can of beer and gone off on a downward tangent, explaining that he and Eileen hadn't been getting on all that well the last few weeks. Apparently, she blamed it on the fact that he was going out at night more often than usual, but Paddy had said that he'd been going out no more than usual and that maybe she was gettin' paranoid because other girls fancied him, what with her now bein' half the size of a cow, and just as attractive.

'Well, do ye want a can, or not?' Paddy said, smiling. 'Eileen'll thank ye if ye take one. It'll mean one less for me.'

'Nah, better not. I'd murder one but I'm not supposed to drink with these tablets and shit in me. It'll send me loopy.'

'Ye are fuckin' loopy,' Jimmy interjected. 'You're a fuckin' spacer! A Blue-Card, for some of the things ye get yourself into, I'll tell ye.' He shot Seamus a knowing look, then glanced away when Paddy turned to look between them.

'Why, what else are ye gettin' into these days?' Paddy asked, easily, looking between the two friends. 'Am I missin' somethin'?'

'Nothin' more than ye know about already,' Seamus said, casually, waiting for Paddy to turn his head before giving Jimmy the death-glare.

Paddy shrugged dismissively. 'Aye well, that sounds like more than enough, if ye ask me. So go on then,' he prompted. 'And then what?'

'Eh?' Seamus raised an eyebrow. He was conscious of doing that, because it was one of his ways of teasing Elaine – raising an eyebrow every time she did the same. He smiled as he remembered her concern as she had found him lying there, as she had lifted his head and kissed him until he came around. A kiss of life that she'd invented herself: her kisses covered not only his lips but his entire face.

'You're grinnin' there like a Cheshire cat, Seamy. I'm askin' ye what happened then, when the wee woman lost the bap with her parents?'

'She was about to walk out. About to go get her savin's out of the bank and head straight across the shuck to her sister in England.'

'Christ!' Jimmy said. 'And what did you say when she sais that?'

'I had to calm her down, tell her to think about what she was doin'. Sure she has to stay here and finish her exams before we can . . . '

Paddy looked puzzled. 'We?' he interjected.

Seamus shrugged, then winced at the pain. 'Aye,' he replied, sheepishly. 'Well, I was thinkin' of goin' too. I haven't told anyone yet, not even me ma, so you're privileged there. But say fuck all, eh? I just haven't found the right moment to break the news to her, y'know.'

Paddy held out his hand and shook Seamus's left hand ever so gently. 'Ye do right, Seamy,' he said, sincerely. 'Sure there's never goin' to be the same calibre of work her in the North as there is over in England. You'll be better off out of it, the two of ye.'

Seamus felt immediately guilty because, no matter what, he always found himself looking for the underlying meaning in what Paddy said – for the undercurrent that told Seamus that Paddy hadn't meant a thing he'd said. Seamus could never really tell if Paddy was being completely genuine. 'Thanks. I reckon – we reckon – you're right.'

'Aye, more power to ye,' Jimmy agreed, raising his can in a salute. 'Sure there's fuck all here. No jobs, nothin'.' He looked at his watch. It was nearly six o clock. 'Hey listen, I have to go. I've a date tonight with that Laura one from Chamberlain Street.'

'The one with the big tits?' Paddy said, smiling.

Jimmy snorted and shook his head slowly from side to side. 'Aye, that's her. Her a well-known hairdresser with a long-established clientele, and you remember her for her tits. Christ, Seamy, what kind of a boy are we hangin' about with here?' Seamus laughed, then bent forward a little as the laughter hurt his ribs.

Paddy held out a beer to Jimmy. 'Ye want a can or not, smart-arse?' he said, grinning.

Jimmy waved his hand, eyeing himself up in the mirror. He took a comb out and, vain as ever, fixed his hair, despite the fact that the wind was rising outside. 'Nah, two's enough. I don't want to be gettin' this brewer's droop they're all talkin' about. Not tonight, anyhow. I reckon tonight's the night.' He made a clenched fist and thrust it in the direction of Paddy's face. Paddy laughed. Seamus didn't dare. He felt it would have fractured another three ribs, and two broken ones was enough for anyone.

'Aye, well give her one for the boys,' Paddy said, as Jimmy put on his coat and made his way to the front door.

'I'll do that.' Jimmy popped his head back in the front door. 'Hey, Seamy, ye want to go get that fuckin' arsehole Rogers, I'm in there for ye. Ye just give me the wire, I'll be in there, same as last time.'

'I don't mind you doin' fuck all the last time,' Paddy Monaghan snorted, derisively.

'I was there in spirit. I always am.'

'I'll give ye a shout, aye, when I'm well enough,' Seamus told him, holding back a grin. The red-haired boy nodded, gave him the thumb – his latest cool sign – and left.

'Wil' man,' Paddy said, laughing. 'Shaggin' everythin' with a pulse ever since he found out his dick was for more than pissin' with. Wish to fuck I'd stayed single, same as him.'

'Ye are single, sure.'

'Ye know what I mean. Women, ye can't live with them and ye can't shoot them. I wish I was ye, Seamy, really I do. Anyways, talkin' of shootin' and stuff.' Paddy started looking around him and caught sight of what he was searching for on Jimmy's now-vacant seat. He grabbed the remote and flicked on the television. 'Just want to see somethin',' he said. 'The news is on now. Bear with me just a wee minute.'

'Take your time, Paddy. I'm goin' nowhere, sure, am I?'

Paddy grinned and flicked through the channels until he got the Ulster news. He seemed irritated. 'I'd rather watch the RTÉ news,' he sighed, sipping heavily at his beer. 'It's nowhere near as biased. But sure ye don't get it, do ye?'

'Nah, aerial's not good enough down here. The . . . '

'Shush a minute.' Paddy put a finger to his lips and belched. 'That's it now.'

'That's what?'

'Shh!'

Seamus raised his eyes and listened as the newsreader spoke. Security forces had uncovered their biggest cache of home-made bombs ever in Northern Ireland. A huge haul of forty-two gas cylinders, each filled with about ten pounds of explosives and timing devices, had been found in the early hours of that morning in a lean-to in the Short Strand area of Belfast. The security forces had been led there after a tip-off but, despite a surveillance operation, no one had as yet been arrested. In other news, some old Vetterle rifles and a Thompson sub-machine gun had been found in a well-constructed concrete hide under a farm building just outside Aughnacloy. Paddy shook his head despondently and cursed under his breath.

'What's the score there, then?' Seamus asked.

'The bastards have got half of the haul,' Paddy retorted, hotly. 'That stuff . . . ' As if suddenly aware that Seamus was there, he paused, a frown on his face. 'Nothin'. Nah, nothin's the matter, Seamy. Everythin's gonna be just fine. Just fine.' Paddy took another sip from his can. 'So when are we goin' to sort this bastard out, then?'

'Who?'

'*Who?*' Paddy exclaimed. 'The UVF bastard that has you sittin' there lookin' like a fuckin' butcher's shop. Christ, Seamy, get with the fuckin' programme here!'

Seamus regarded him squarely for a moment. There was no doubt in his mind that Paddy would have been the one to sort Martin Rogers out, him being as game as any man he had ever met. But Paddy had gone and mentioned a deadly-sounding combination of letters in amongst the expletives.

'UVF?'

'Aye, sure I told ye he was one of theirs the time of Barney's funeral.' Paddy's face was deadly serious, as if the gravity of that sentence had brought back the memories of a few months earlier. 'Ye probably forgot. Did ye forget?' Flat-toned, neutral.

Seamus shook his head quickly. 'Nah, I . . . well, ye didn't say exactly what he was messed up in. I knew he was one of the other side, as ye put it, but . . . '

'Aye, UVF, up to his balls in it. When he says he was goin' to kill ye the next time, the chances are that he wasn't just mouthin' off. Cunt's been at that stuff for the last two years at least. So . . . ?' Paddy let the question hang in the air.

Seamus looked him straight in the eyes, a chill running through him, because he instinctively knew that Paddy was serious. He'd seen what the older boy was capable of, and now he knew that he was perhaps capable of much worse. It could have been the drink talking, but he doubted it. Sort him out, Paddy had said. Sort him out with a wooden overcoat, he probably meant. 'I don't know if that's really such a good idea then,' he told Paddy, screwing up his face. 'Nah, maybe I should just chalk it down to experience – be a bit more careful in the future.'

'Careful about runnin' around in your own country. Christ's sakes, Seamy, that boy goes into the South, a country that him and his folks don't want – your country, I'll say it again in case ye weren't listenin' up – and he attacks ye there. Him a foreigner, an Englishman at heart. You an Irishman. Him invadin' your territory – and on a fuckin' Sunday too, a day of rest – then knockin' the shite out of ye on your own turf. Aye, that's a fuckin' act of war and it deserves to be dealt with as such.'

Then again, Seamus thought, it may have been the drink talking. Irrational, irresponsible chatter about war amongst nations when it was a simple one to one that Seamus himself would sort out, given the right time, space and opportunity. He wondered how he was going to get out of this conversation, onto more neutral ground. 'We mess with those boys, we're talkin' serious stuff,' he told his friend. 'That's all right for the Provies but . . . '

Paddy nodded, his thoughts once again hidden behind an inscrutable façade. 'Ye seen the girl since?'

'Elaine?' Paddy nodded. Seamus shook his head. 'Talked to her on the phone, just. We're lettin' it die down a bit.'

'You're plannin' on seein' her again though, right?'

Seamus nodded, hoping they were moving onto another topic. Even love. Even Eileen and the perceived faults Paddy saw in her now that he'd never seen in her until she fell pregnant. 'Aye, definitely. She's the one I want to be with.' He nodded. 'Aye, definitely.'

'Then he's goin' to come after ye,' Paddy reasoned. 'And he won't be lookin' to just give ye a kickin' the next time out, will he?'

Seamus turned white and shook his head. He hated to admit it but, once more, there was a grain of truth in what Paddy was saying.

Paddy shrugged. 'Then it's up to you, isn't it? It's either you or him. Obvious as fuck. A blind man could see it.'

Seamus feigned a pain in his arm. He didn't like where the conversation was going and he didn't want to say anything that might be construed as a signal for Paddy to do what he wanted to do, and then to hear on the news about the untimely demise of Marty Rogers. He'd felt guilty enough that time he'd hit Doran, and didn't think he could go through it again. Now it was definitely time to change the subject, no matter how unsubtly he did so. 'Sure we'll talk about it later, eh?'

'Up to yourself, Seamy boy, but we don't have that long. This is goin' to be a busy month for me. Eileen's about to calve and I'm up to me balls in other, bigger stuff, besides me work. It'd need to be right and soon.'

Seamus saw the opening: the slip road that led off Paddy's motorway of revenge. 'Why do ye keep sayin' that somethin' big's gonna happen, Paddy?'

Paddy smiled dreamily and closed his eyes. 'I can't tell ye, Seamy. And it's nothin' to do with anythin' about not trustin' ye, just in case ye bring all that old shite up again about your da. That's all before your time – all in the past. You're Seamy Doherty, a good friend of mine, and ye always will be. The past doesn't matter a fuck. You're a good man and I could tell ye anythin'. I know that.' Paddy lay back further into his seat and kicked off his shoes, savouring the heat of the fire on his feet.

'Then why don't ye?'

Paddy opened an eye. 'Why don't I what?'

'Tell me anythin'. I'm a good friend, ye said it yourself. What am I gonna do, put it in the fuckin' paper?'

Paddy closed his eyes again, took a sip of his beer and rubbed at his forehead with his free hand. 'Ah sure, I can't. It's for your own good as well as mine.'

Seamus shrugged gently, the threat of pain ever present. 'Ah, whatever. I was just askin', one friend to another. It's no fuckin' odds, I suppose. Probably catch it on the news some night right and soon anyway.' Back on even ground, happy.

Paddy laughed out loud, his eyes open once more, a glint of light there. 'Don't be like that about it, Seamy. I'm your mucker, you're mine, end of story.' He looked at the younger man's solemn face and released a pent-up sigh. 'All right, Seamy. Ye want to know? Ye really want to know?'

'Nah, I was only seein' if you'd tell me. I don't give a fuck one way or the other.'

Paddy laughed loudly. 'I know ye don't, Seamy, that's why I'm gonna tell ye. Mind ye, if ye tell anyone, I might have to shoot ye, that fair enough?'

Seamus laughed but Paddy's face was serious. Seamus stopped laughing.

'Only jokin', Seamy. This whole place, Derry and Belfast – Christ, half the fuckin' North! – is goin' up in smoke in about two weeks' time, round about the end of the month. Commercial and legitimate targets, mind, just like they used to do here in Derry years back. No innocents are gonna get hurt, same as years ago. It's all very well planned, very strict. If those Brit and RUC dicks think they got the whole haul today, they couldn't be more fuckin' wrong. They think they've got the Boys by the balls, but come the end of the month they'll know what's stickin' to them.'

'Sure how'd you know that?' Seamy feigned disbelief.

'Words from the horse's mouth. They won't know a fuck what hit them.' Paddy put the beer-can between his legs and threw his arms up to simulate an explosion.

Seamus shrugged easily, trying to make light of the fact that he'd probably just heard about the IRA's battle plan for the next month. 'Nothin' new there then,' he said, easily. Paddy frowned, a questioning look on his face. 'The explosions, I mean.'

'Ye think not, Seamy? I'm talkin' big. Real big. You just keep an eye on the news – that's how big I'm talkin'.' He regarded Seamus for a time and shook his head.

'What?' Paranoid.

'Ye say fuck all, y'hear? He wasn't supposed to tell me and I'm hardly supposed to tell anyone else – ye know the score.'

'I didn't hear a whisper. I told ye, I don't give a flyin' fuck about stuff like that – never did. I just want to get married, have kids, stuff like that. What other people do doesn't really concern me.'

Paddy shrugged. 'Aye, well we all have our own ways of goin' about stuff. I didn't want to stick me head in the sand and watch, that's all . . . '

'Ye think I do that?'

Paddy looked at him, sensing the mild offence contained in his remark. 'Nah, Seamy, you're one of the gamest boys I've ever known. Ye just can't hurt people any more than ye have to, that's your form. But sometimes the only way to fight fire is with fire, even if you're not an arsonist. Someone has to do it, and I just hope ye don't judge me wrongly because that's the path I've chosen. I'm defendin' me country, nothin' more. Same as the many who've gone before me. And just 'cause the Brits say it's wrong means fuck all. Sure they've said that everywhere they went in the world. They take your country by force and then brainwash ye into thinkin' that you're wrong to try and take it back the same way. Sure where's the fuckin' logic in that one?'

Seamus nodded sincerely. He understood why his friend thought as he did. In some ways, Seamus too thought like that. He had always had mixed feelings about the Troubles. Often when he heard the bombs going off in the town, when the windows shook in their frames and thick palls of black smoke and licking flames rose above the city in the dead of night, he used to shake his head in disgust, never comprehending why republicans were bombing their own town. But there was always the explanation about the targets being economic, about the bombs being a sign of determined resistance: that Irishmen weren't going to lie down to the English, no matter how much money the Brits claimed to be pumping into the economy.

And often when he came out of his house to see a blacked-up Brit in behind the hedges – with more of them in every gateway along the street, with intimidating scowls on their boot-polished faces, glowering, aiming their rifles at you as you walked up the street and calling you a paddy bastard – he'd know that this was no normal society, that they had to go, one way or another. That they had to be pushed out of the country from within, no matter the methods used, because they were foreigners – an army of occupation, with nothing to offer except hatred and death – and they shouldn't be here, regardless of the reasons they put forward to explain why they were. But he'd always believed deep down that peaceful protest was better – that there had to be a better way than killing and dying. Rioting was the exception, of course. Rioting wasn't that bad: it was an acceptable form of resistance, in the main. Though attending the 'Troops Out' rallies, the annual Bloody Sunday march and other organised demonstrations was perhaps the best approach of the lot.

'I don't blame ye,' Seamus said, at last. 'Seein' ye there the day of Barney's funeral, Christ, I admired ye . . . '

'Ye did?'

'Oh aye. But it's not my way, y'know. Me ma's seen enough tragedy. I just don't . . . '

Paddy held up a hand, stalling him. 'Ye don't have to explain it to me, Seamy. We're mates, end of story. But that's enough of that crap, eh?' Seamus laughed, the tension leaving him. He nodded as Paddy winked. The older youth sat and drank for a while, watching Seamus making himself comfortable on the sofa. 'Shit, he made a real mess of you,' Paddy said, eventually. 'I'm gonna have to sort that out too.'

Seamus rose gingerly from his seat. 'Ye want a sandwich?' he asked, once more eager to diffuse that particular conversation.

Paddy got up and placed the half-empty can gently on the ground at the side of the chair. 'Sit yourself down, Seamy lad,' he said, smiling. 'I'll be your maid for the evenin'.' Just then, there was the sound of a key in the lock, and they both turned their heads towards the front door. Mary came in, shaking the rain from her coat and hanging it over the stair banister in the hall.

'Ach, Paddy, good to see ye.'

'Mrs Doherty.' Paddy held out his hand and Mary took it, smiling as he kissed her ever so lightly on the back of it. 'I hear congratulations are in order. You're gettin' yourself hung, I hear, though in the nicest of all possible ways, mind.'

Mary gave him a winning smile, walked over to the fire and

stood with her back to it, fingers outstretched into the heat. 'And you're doin' the same yourself. When . . . ?'

Paddy's own smile diminished slightly. 'Another few weeks yet. End of the month. When's your own hangin'? July, isn't it?'

Mary nodded proudly and showed him the engagement ring Michael had bought her.

'Nice.'

'That'll settle your runnin' for a while,' Mary chastised him gently.

'Ach, sure I'm never out.' He grinned at Seamus and gave him a conspiratorial wink. Seamus raised an eyebrow, telling him he was the biggest liar he'd ever met.

'Well, ye may as well go out now, while ye still can,' Mary warned. 'It's all nappies from here on in. Up in the middle of the night fetchin' bottles, the wain cryin' its eyes out like mad and maybe you only havin' got it over to sleep. Then you tryin' to snatch an hour before headin' out to your work, cranky as a cat in a tumble-dryer. You and her at it like cats and dogs, day in, day out, for weeks on end.'

'That's a very pretty picture you're paintin' of it, Mrs D.' Now it was Paddy's turn to raise an eyebrow. 'Can't see why I didn't do it sooner.'

'I'm just bein' truthful,' Mary said, a hint of malicious joy in her eyes. 'Aye, it's all ahead of ye, right enough. I don't envy ye a bit of it.' She watched Paddy shifting uncomfortably from foot to foot. 'Ye lookin' to use the bogs?' Mary asked, concerned as to why he was screwing his face up.

'Nah, I was just gonna make your wee boy a few sandwiches.' Charismatic, charming, having a playful dig at Seamus. Mary grinned inanely, Paddy having moved ever so smoothly off the subject. Seamus admired the way he could do that, and wished he had the ability to do it himself at times.

'Ach, away out of that,' Mary flustered. 'Just sit down there, the both of ye, and make yourselves comfortable. I'm throwin' the dinner on, anyhow.'

Paddy winked at Seamus, sat down in front of the fire and raised his can to Mary. 'Ye don't mind, do ye? 'Cause if ye do, I'll chuck it in the bin.'

Mary smiled easily, the drink no longer the threat it once was. 'Not at all. Keep him company. I'll get the food. Stews all right?'

Paddy smiled. 'From what I hear, that'll be the best food in the estate.'

'Ah, away in there with ye.' Mary smiled again and went out into the kitchen.

'You've got her wrapped around your little finger,' Seamus said, grinning.

'Aye,' Paddy muttered. 'But sure, if only I had me own woman the same way, then things'd be fuckin' grand.'

The conversation turned to various other subjects after that, as the three of them sat in the kitchen and ate their dinner. They talked of Michael Stewart – of how he was helping Mary in every conceivable way. Then Mary deftly changed the subject back to all things maternal, saying how Eileen and Paddy had best save a little for a rainy day, the way she'd done herself when she'd heard wee Seamus was on his way into the world. They spoke of politics, of religion – Paddy and Mary were both as well up on those subjects as each other. In fact, they talked about everything except what had recently happened to Seamus and Elaine in Buncrana; Mary had probably not yet fully accepted that her son could fall foul of religious intolerance and bigotry.

Shortly after eleven, Paddy declared mournfully that he had to go up and join wee Eileen in her mother's house, because he'd been out long enough and she'd be phonin' everywhere lookin' for him. And he didn't need the mother-in-law on his back just yet, he joked, as he made his way out the door, several cans the worse for wear. There would be plenty of time for climbing into that bearpit in years to come.

And as Seamus climbed gingerly into his bed that night, he wondered just why he had had doubts about introducing the boy to Elaine after all.

*

Seamus didn't return to work until the following Monday morning. He was still sore, but he knew that the instructors – themselves former painters who had been lucky enough to stumble onto a gold mine of a job – would hardly push him to his limit. It was while he was walking by himself along on Northland Road that Thursday morning – just one of many green-and-yellow-overalled apprentices making their way slowly in the direction of the training centre – that a car pulled up alongside him. He cursed, recognising the Special Branch man named Dave in the back seat. Seamus became aware of eyes watching his every move. He looked around him at the sea of faces that were carefully studying the situation, while conceivably minding their own business.

'That's some face ye have on you, Seamus.'

'Did ye ever take a look in the mirror of late?' Ignorant, though not overly so, as he was in a hurry to get to work before the bell, as he hadn't been early yesterday either.

Dave laughed good-humouredly. 'You're a very hard man to keep a track of, Seamus. You'd make a pretty good terrorist.'

'I don't hate anyone enough to be a terrorist,' Seamus replied, acidly. 'Except you, maybe. I can sort of understand why they'd want to shoot you. You're a fuckin' pain in the arse.' The tolerance just wasn't there: it was too early in the morning.

Seamus went to walk on. It was an almost useless act of bravado, but he was the focus of everyone's attention and he had to do it: such defiance, while never directly spoken about in public, was expected from – and readily given by – every Catholic youth in the city. As the car rolled alongside him, he cursed under his breath and went to walk across the road. The cop in the front passenger seat got out of the car, quickly intercepting him. He ordered Seamus back to the other side of the road. Seamus dropped his head, as a line of traffic slowed to watch the scene. The Special Branch man got out of the car and ordered Seamus to turn around, making a show of searching him slowly.

'We all have the potential for hatred, Seamus,' he whispered into the youth's ear. 'Get to know someone long enough and you'll end up hatin' them enough to kill them. Sure that's a premise that marriages have been based upon for years.' He grinned broadly. 'That's a nice girl you have. Seen you both goin' over the border one day. Could have dragged you into a search bay, kept you there for the whole day, but I didn't. Let the young have their fun, that's my motto. You thinkin' of gettin' married, yourself?'

Seamus tried to turn but the Special Branch man wouldn't allow him to do so, ordering him to turn out his overall pockets. Loose change, a lighter, cigarettes, aspirins, a handkerchief. 'Why me?' he asked, with growing impatience. 'Why the hell are ye pickin' on me? There must be hundreds of others.'

'You're in a unique position, that's why. We have somethin' you want. You know the people we want and you can find out exactly what it is I want to know. C'mon, turn around there, get your hands up. We don't want anyone thinkin' that I'm talkin' nicely to you, do we?'

'You're tryin' to fit me up to look bad in the eyes of me mates. Well, fuck ye!' Seamus said, venomously. 'I'll be goin' to the papers today as soon as I get home. I'll be tellin' them what a bastard ye are and how you've been tryin' to get me to squeal on people the last two years. So stick that in your fuckin' pipe and smoke it!'

He made to turn around again but the policeman pushed him back against the wall, then turned to another youth who was walking slowly by. 'Get along there, son, unless you want to spend a day in the barracks.' The youth looked the officer up and down, muttered something under his breath, then walked slowly on. Seamus recognised him as Gerry McElhinney, who worked across the hall in the brickie section.

'Ye all right, Seamus?' the youth called over his shoulder.

'Aye, I'm grand. They're just checkin' to see if I'm takin' me rocket launcher into the centre, that's all. I'll see ye in there.'

The Special Branch man allowed him to turn around. He wasn't smiling any more. 'I'll be in the car park in the grounds of Magee University tomorrow night, Seamus,' he said, softly. 'I'll be alone and I'll be there at half nine. Why don't you come along? I have a file to show you.'

Seamus laughed then – a victorious gesture. 'I know how me da died,' he said. 'I know that maybe he wasn't a tout after all, that maybe you bastards talked his friend into squealin', that me da got the fuckin' blame and that his friend committed suicide a few months later. I know all of that, so ye can tell me fuck all.'

'Suicide?' Dave laughed, drily. His face turned to stone. 'They told you it was suicide? That's a good one, it really is. I have a file with an autopsy report in it that says different.'

The uncertainty must have shown on Seamus's face, because the Special Branch man broke into a relaxed smile. A few words, and that emotion was dragged once more from the depths in which he'd thought he had buried it for good. God, Seamus hated the way the man could do that. And with such ease, too.

'You're a fuckin' liar.' Seamus looked around the road self-consciously. The sea of faces had all but evaporated; the traffic had thinned to the occasional car, lorry or half-empty bus. No one seemed overly interested in what was happening, their apathy having been brought on by the deeply ingrained knowledge that getting involved in someone else's problems only brought problems your own way. Many people in Derry and other cities throughout the North just didn't need the hassle any more. Only Gerry McElhinney stood on at the end of the road that led into Springtown, fag in hand, watching.

'Ye finished now?' Seamus pulled free of the man's grasp and went to walk on. The man called Dave didn't resist but allowed him to walk off.

'I'll see ye tomorrow night, then.' He sounded certain of it. 'I'd rather we met up, Seamus. I don't want anyone to know that we've had several meetin's the last few years or so, but I can be a wil' man when people let me down. I might say somethin' to the wrong person about ye – let somethin' slip. Aye, Seamus Doherty, I meet him all the time. He doesn't say much but he says enough. And that wouldn't be a lie, would it? You do say stuff. All of it rude, I grant you that, but you do talk. And that's all I'll say. Seamus, he talked. Aye, I reckon that should be enough, don't you?'

Seamus cursed under his breath and quickened his pace without looking back. He wasn't sure if the car was coming after him or if it had done a U-turn and driven off in the opposite direction. But he didn't care. The man had said what he had intended to say. He'd achieved his aim, and they both knew it. At the corner of Springtown Industrial Estate, Gerry McElhinney offered him a cigarette and a light. 'What was that about?' he asked, with a frown.

'I wish to fuck I knew,' Seamus said, his hands visibly trembling.

'Aye, they do that all the time. Fuck all else to do. Pick a face, give the owner a hard time. Shower of fuckin' shite, the lot of them!'

'You fuckin' said it.'

They walked into the centre, punched in their clocking cards and went to their separate sections. Halfway through the day, Seamus recalled that Gerry McElhinney was a good friend of Dan McGeady's son Eddie, who was, in turn, a friend of Paddy Monaghan's. He cursed when he remembered that, feeling that the world was becoming a very claustrophobic place of late and wishing that July would hurry up and arrive.

TWELVE

Elaine had phoned Sadie's from the fish shop when he'd returned home that Thursday night. She'd told Seamus that she probably wouldn't be able to see him until Saturday afternoon, that time being suitable only because her brother Martin was heading off on a fishing trip across the border with his friends. The good news was that her brother would be away until late Saturday evening, which meant that no one would be keeping too close an eye on her – a fact which relieved them both.

They'd talked for nearly thirty minutes, and Seamus had smiled as Elaine had told him that she missed him. He'd told her he missed her too and had reminded her that it was the eighth of March and that they only had three months to go before they headed off to England. And next week, if he could get the timing right, Seamus was going to tell his ma all about their plans. Elaine had gushed at that, saying that when he did so it would be the second-last hurdle they'd have to cross. The final one, of course, concerned exactly what she would tell her own family. They knew she was planning on going away to join her sister; they just didn't know when. Neither, of course, did they know she wasn't planning to make that journey alone. She was going to withhold that last fact from them until she and Seamus had actually stepped off the plane in Newcastle. She could hardly wait for that moment, she'd told him, and found herself daydreaming about it even in the middle of her favourite classes. Seamus too could hardly wait, though he never told her the exact reasons why that was so. After what had occurred that morning, he was looking forward to the trip to England more than ever.

He'd just had his dinner – a rushed affair, because Mary was heading on out again, her own life's plan in full swing, her social calendar a whirl these days. Now he was lying on his bed, hands behind his head, the static-filled music of Radio Luxembourg playing in the background. He wasn't so worried about the pain in his limbs and torso any more – because that was receding with every passing day into no more than a series of dull aches – as he was about the pain in his head. Or, more to the point, the searing pain he imagined to be clawing strips from his brain.

He'd always thought that his da had been a simple bastard. A robotic man who had no ideas of his own, and someone who weakly followed in everyone else's wake when his common sense had been tarnished by the drink. A simple bastard, Seamus had often called him, when things weren't going as smoothly in his own life as they should have gone. A drunken puppet, a boggle-eyed robot, a drunk. Until recently, he'd never viewed him as an ordinary man, a human being who – no matter what anyone thought – had his own particular goals and ideals, who had a wife and son that he loved as dearly as any man in his situation could. A man who'd never allowed anyone to taper down his dreams, to whittle and chip away at his beliefs. Seamus had never known him, he realised, despondently. He'd spent so many years under the umbrella of one illusion that he'd never even thought about getting to know his father's better qualities. What with all his swearing that he'd never end up like his da, he'd never thought his da had actually possessed any better qualities.

The Special Branch man had set him thinking about every-thing he had ever held to be true. Now the man had something to show him. A file. A file that might perhaps prove that his father had been a brave man – nothing more but, more importantly, nothing less – and he was hanging it like a baited hook in front of Seamus. Information, he had promised. Information for information. A trade. Nothing to do with touting, of course, because that was a dirty word here in the North – a word that tainted souls and memories forever. A word that told people that you had turned. Against your own people, against your own religion, against everything you knew in your heart of hearts to be right and true. No, it was to be an exchange of information. You tell me what I want to know, I tell you. And in the process, you get to hold your head up high again and have the chance to take the weight of the world off your mother's shoulders – to remove the stigma that, despite the strong republicanism on his mother's side of the family and the respect that it had attracted – had never really vanished. And Seamus would get to save lives, to save property, to save the expenditure of many more millions in the ongoing cleaning-up and rebuilding process that you heard about so often on the TV or the radio here in the North of Ireland.

A few simple sentences exchanged between two people, and no one had to know. They're goin' to bomb the shite out of half the fuckin' North near the end of the month, in another two weeks or so. At least, that was what they thought they were going to do – what they'd been planning to do, until wee Seamus Doherty came along. Now they'd be able to stop them – to arrest them. Aye, that's grand, son. And now it's my turn. Your da hadn't said a thing. Not a word escaped his lips. Sure didn't you hear me when I said he was as staunch as they came? And I'm sure you heard others sayin' it too. Your ma, perhaps. No food, no water, and they'd had to get a doctor up from Derry, because he was going to fight it out until the bitter end. Sure how could he have done anything like that? Your da? He was a hero – he always said you'd end up regarding him like that. Not in those exact words, maybe, but that was what he had said, all right.

It was so attractive a package that it would have made you swear that Christmas was coming early. But then Seamus wondered why he felt such a bitter aftertaste in his mouth every time he thought about doing it. Like bile, rising up from his gut to choke him, and his mind spinning like a top, demons having the time of their lives pushing it out of control.

There was the deceit of it all. He hadn't told Mary a thing about the Special Branch man. He knew now that he should have, though at what point he wasn't really sure. He'd been trying to protect her – to keep the past from rearing its ugly head when she had been so vulnerable and unable to cope. Reality would have killed her back then. But now, Seamus knew, reality merely brought fond tears to her eyes and made her weep with both joy and pain – a handsome, admirable mixture that was perfectly normal in any person who had been through what she had been through. She had seen Seamus Doherty senior in both a good and a bad light, had noticed both his faults and his assets and had loved him, despite everything. She could hack it now, he felt almost certain of that, but then what was the point in saying anything to her, when her world was now the most pleasant of all dreams?

He hadn't told Paddy Monaghan either. And Paddy had told him information that, if it had been leaked, could have cost the older youth his own life. He'd most likely found it out from Dan McGeady, because Dan had risen through the ranks over the last few years and, though Seamus didn't know his correct title and position within the republican movement, he knew as much as the dogs in the street: Dan was the man. One of the main men, so it was said, and if anyone had his finger on the pulse, it was him. Paddy had definitely found out from him, or through someone else who had been one of the few who were privy to such information.

Now Seamus felt guilty, because the older boy had trusted him enough to tell him his most important secret. Seamus, basing his instinct on his knowledge of the Paddy Monaghan of old – the young Paddy Monaghan, who burned down bungalows and blamed other people for his actions thereafter – hadn't ever completely trusted him after that. Yet the truth was that Paddy had always been there for him. He'd helped him go after Doran; he had wanted to take out Marty Rogers too. Always there for him, and Seamus should have told him a long time back about his dilemma. Paddy would have sorted it out for him. If anyone could have done that for him, it was Paddy Monaghan.

But most importantly, he hadn't told Elaine. Though there had been nothing to tell, in one sense. He'd been lifted a few times by a Special Branch man – a snooping low-life cop who had known a little about the uncertainties and ambiguities surrounding his father's life, which now presented themselves as a stumbling block in Seamus's own life. How the man had known about those weaknesses was anyone's guess. He could have been there when they lifted his da: he was old enough, after all. Then again, he could just have been reading through some long-forgotten files, seen the one that had marked his father out as an informer, read it and spotted the advantages it offered. A truth, a half-truth, a mixture of lies and deceits all lost in time. Something that no one else knew about, that nobody even cared about any more. But something that a young boy might just want to hear about if he wanted to clear his father's name. Something that could be bartered – that might leave a youth vulnerable and susceptible to betraying his own people. Seamus didn't know the origin of this madness. He guessed that he would never know, unless . . .

He pushed that thought out of his head and replaced it with the one that was spinning in and out of his consciousness more often than the rest – the one he'd tried denying to himself at first. His mother had told him that his da had been arrested and taken to Castlereagh Holding Centre along with two other men: Dan McGeady and Billy Flannagan. The Special Branch man had told him that his father hadn't talked and his mother had confirmed that, by saying that he wouldn't have talked had they kept him in there forever – that maybe he'd have gone and died first. Then Billy Flannagan had committed suicide two months afterwards. A sign of guilt? Perhaps.

If it had been suicide. Maybe it hadn't. And what did that mean? Who did that point the finger at? Seamus shuddered every time the thought of Dan McGeady came into his mind. He asked himself why the Special Branch man had put such an idea in his head – what he had to gain by doing such a thing. The answer, of course, was the retrieval of valuable information. But then, why had he picked on Seamus? He must have had a preconceived notion that the youth was involved. Because the Special Branch and the RUC apparently had a fair idea at times – a better idea than most people thought, despite the fact that, on occasion, they seemed completely unable to deal with particular situations. That had to be the explanation.

He had assumed that Seamus was involved merely because of his friendships with Paddy Monaghan and Barney Ferguson. Because, perhaps, of the photograph he'd seen of Dan McGeady walking off into Cromore with Seamus on that evening several years ago when the Boys had shot Mick Deery at the back of the shops. Seamus smiled wryly at that thought. The Special Branch man had probably thought he'd caught the exact moment on film that Dan had recruited Seamus into the rank and file of the IRA. Two and two becoming twenty-two. It had happened to Seamus Doherty senior: he'd been associated with the drink and having a loose mouth. It had happened to Billy Flannagan, when he'd gone and shot himself – or been shot. Now it was happening to him. Guilty by association, and how did you go about proving yourself innocent of that?

This jumble of thoughts turned ceaselessly in his head, allowing him no respite. He didn't want to go to the meeting the following night, yet he had no choice. The Special Branch man had fucked with his head, just the way Paddy Monaghan had once warned they could do, and he didn't see that he had an alternative.

Though maybe there was one way, he thought, suddenly. It was going to involve taking a big risk, but no bigger than the one he had been asked to take already. He got up then, went downstairs and put on his coat. It was raining when he left the house and made his way up to Creggan Heights.

*

'Aye, Seamy, what's, erm, happenin' with ye?'

Paddy Monaghan seemed more than a little surprised to see Seamus standing on his doorstep at about eight o'clock that Thursday night. He was so surprised, in fact, that for a moment he forgot himself and didn't invite the younger youth inside, despite the heavy slant of rain that was dashing onto the carpet on which he stood. Seamus nodded to the sky, raindrops bouncing off his nose as he did so, running in zigzags across his cheeks.

'Oh aye, c'mon in. But ye got me at a bad time, Seamy.' He looked at his watch and rolled his eyes upwards. 'The wee woman reckons she's about to drop the sprog any time now, and she doesn't want me out of her sight. At least, that's what she's sayin'. Christ, Seamy, don't you ever go gettin' one up the spout, I'll tell ye. They're a fuckin' handful, every last one of them.' He regarded Seamus for a moment. 'So what's with the long face, Seamy? Ye look as if someone murdered your fuckin' cat.'

'I need to talk.'

Paddy moved aside. 'Aye, well c'mon in then. But like I say, I don't really have all that much time, what with . . . '

Seamus bit at his lip. 'It's really important. Really fuckin' important. But we can't talk here.'

Paddy frowned, catching the seriousness of Seamus's mood. He reached for his coat off the hanger and crept over to the door. 'C'mon, we'll head out then. Quiet, like. The battleaxe is in the kitchen. We'll get out and . . . '

A high-pitched voice – female, young – sounded from the back room. Seamus recognised it immediately and smiled a bemused smile. 'Paddy Monaghan, what the hell are ye at out there? I think me waters are about to break . . . '

Paddy rolled his eyes and went over to the kitchen door, urging Seamus to go on outside. 'What is it, wee love?' he said sweetly, shaking his head at Seamus, to signify his displeasure.

'Me bloody waters. They could be breakin' when you're standin' out there.'

'Aye, well me ma's in the sittin' room. She might know a thing or two about that, I'm not sure. I'll just slip out and get us some fags and some crisps. For later on, eh? Just in case your water does go, like, y'know.'

'Don't you be too long, Paddy Monaghan,' the voice warned.

'Ye know what might happen if you're away too long.'

'Aye, I do that.' Paddy Monaghan smiled a false smile into the kitchen and Seamus chuckled, despite his dark mood. The older boy closed the door and buttoned his coat. 'Ye might fuckin' run off and never come back,' he muttered, under his breath. 'With a bit of luck, anyhow.' He closed the door after him and called Seamus back from walking up the street. 'C'mon, Seamy, let's go in me da's car. It's too wet. Christ, I'm glad ye arrived when ye did. That fuckin' witch is puttin' years on me.'

They climbed into the green Cavalier and Paddy keyed the ignition. 'Ye might not be so glad when I'm finished tellin' ye what it is I have to tell ye,' Seamus warned.

Paddy didn't reply to that. He looked at Seamus oddly for a moment, then nodded. He drove the car along the Heights, down past the roundabout towards Westway and on down through Rosemount, then out along the Northland, cutting across the junction at the Buncrana Road and turning into Shantallow, going nowhere in particular. The roads were quiet enough – the rain enough to keep most people indoors. It was a while before Seamus could speak. He didn't really know where he should begin, thinking that maybe he was throwing himself off a cliff to fall on jagged rocks below. But when he started, it all came tumbling out. The first meeting, as the Special Branch man had called it. The second, the third. The threats, the harassment, the information about his da, the implication that perhaps Billy Flannagan, his da's best friend, hadn't committed suicide after all. That maybe someone had killed him – though Seamus didn't give a name. He didn't have to. He noticed Paddy's face growing white, his tongue curling up around his upper lip, his frown.

Seamus was shaking as he said these things, though more because he realised the enormity of the situation than because of who he was saying them to. It hadn't seemed all that bad when he was thinking it – when the memories had been merely in his head. Saying it out loud was a different thing altogether. Now the situation was as real as it could ever be. Now Seamus had stepped over the cliff, and he was waiting anxiously to see if Paddy was going to push the trampoline into place down below.

He talked for nearly an hour, not missing a single detail. Throughout that time, Paddy Monaghan just looked, with growing incredulity, between him and the rainswept road.

'Jesus,' Paddy Monaghan said, at last. 'Seamy, you're a fuckin' simple bastard, if ever there was one.'

Seamus dropped his head. 'Aye, don't ye think I fuckin' know it?' He looked away, expecting the wrath of the world to fall upon him then – certain that Paddy was just about to unleash a mouthful of venom. He wouldn't have blamed the older youth then. He expected it. He felt a hand on his shoulder: no roughness there.

Paddy took a deep breath, removed his hand from his friend's shoulder and then, changing tack, quickly pulled a packet of cigarettes out of his jacket pocket and handed them to Seamus. Seamus removed two from the packet, lit them both and handed one back to Paddy.

'Don't fuckin' worry about it, Seamy,' Paddy said then. 'You're in a tight fuckin' hole but don't worry about it.'

'What do ye reckon I should do, then?' Muted, pensive, drawing the consoling nicotine deep into his lungs.

'Leave it to me, Seamus. I'll sort somethin' out, don't ye worry.' While Seamus had been talking, they had travelled through the Shantallow housing estate, up along the Greenhaw Road and then down onto the Strand. Now they were approaching the bottom of the Rock Road, which led up past Magee University. Paddy drove the car up there at a crawl and they both found themselves staring into the car park, surveying the general area. Students – smiling, carefree, books in hand – were making their way in and out of the wide door of the old blanched-stone building, with its ornate windows and angular turrets.

'Aye, I'll think of somethin',' Paddy said. 'I'll get in contact with ye tomorrow evenin'. Earlyish, to give us time to talk. All right?' Seamus nodded, suddenly very weary. 'You'll be grand, don't ye worry about it,' Paddy said, with a wink.

They were the last words he said before leaving Seamus off home.

*

The green Cavalier was parked across the way when Seamus came out of the training centre the next day at half past four. Paddy Monaghan was behind the wheel. Seamus went around and climbed into the front seat without speaking a word. Paddy drew off into the heavy flow of traffic. 'You're to go there tonight,' Paddy said.

Seamus looked at him, eyes wide. 'Are ye fuckin' serious? I thought ye were gonna get me into a press conference sort of thing, or somethin'.'

Paddy glanced across at him. 'Aye, I'm serious. I've been given word that you're to go there. I've sorted it out for ye.'

Seamus gave a short laugh. He hadn't expected to hear those words. If anything, he'd expected to hear a different solution all together. 'Who gave ye the word? And how are they goin' to sort it out?'

Paddy didn't answer him, that familiar impassive look on his face.

'Ye didn't go to Dan McGeady, did ye? Christ, Paddy, I told

ye the score there. I told ye what the Special Branch man said.'

'I never went to McGeady,' Paddy said, a trace of anxiety in his voice. 'But I can't tell ye who I went to. Ye know the score . . . '

'No, I don't know the score,' Seamus said, angrily. 'It's my fuckin' life we're talkin' about here. I know fuck all.'

Paddy drove on a further mile or so, saying nothing. He pulled the car in at the side of the road, opposite the Glenowen housing estate. 'Aye, and it could be my life too, if I start sayin' any more stuff I shouldn't. I've told ye I sorted it out. Now, do ye trust me or do ye not?' he said, thickly.

Seamus inhaled deeply and dropped his head. 'Aye, of course I do.'

'Aye, well you're not actin' like ye do.'

Seamus looked up, frowning. 'I'm sorry. I do,' he repeated, softly. 'Of course I do.'

'Then it's sorted. One of the Boys is gonna take a few pictures of you and your man together. The thing about it is, those bastards deny everythin'. Every time someone goes to the press they say a complaint has been made and they're lookin' into it – that an internal investigation is under way. But ye never hear a fuckin' word about it again and they just move on to someone else. Sure that's like gettin' the fox in to audit the eggs in the hen house after the raid the night before, isn't it?'

Seamus managed a thin smile.

'Aye, Seamy, they're conductin' a never-endin' war of intimidation against the nationalists, and this time we're gonna have proof.' He looked at Seamus and returned the thin grin, his hand once more on Seamus's shoulder. 'You're gonna have to trust me on this one, Seamy. You've trusted me once already; you're gonna have to go with it again. Ye reckon ye can do that?' Seamus hung his head, biting his lip. He nodded uncertainly. Paddy patted him on the shoulder and keyed the car once more into life. 'Good. You'll be there at half nine tonight, then?'

'Aye.'

'Good.' Paddy turned the car off Westway into Dunree Gardens. 'Just keep him talkin' for a while, Seamy,' Paddy said, as Seamus got out of the car. 'That'll give the Boys a chance to get a few photographs. No more than ten minutes. Then just say you've changed your mind, get out of the car and go straight home. Don't let him intimidate ye into stayin'. If he starts threatenin' ye, just tell him to fuck off and run out of there. All right?"

'Aye, no bother.' Listless, half-hearted, not believing for a second that this was the only possible solution to his problems.

'And listen, Seamy.' Paddy bit his lip. 'I said a few things last week I shouldn't have said. I had a few drinks too many in me, 'cause I was a bit fucked off with the way wee Eileen . . . '

'Don't worry about it. I'll say fuck all. I never intended to, anyway. Sure that's why I told ye.'

Paddy smiled, then nodded. 'I know that. You're a good mate. I'll get a chat with ye tomorrow night around seven, if the dragon's waters still haven't broke, eh?' A reassuring smile. 'All right?'

Seamus nodded, closed the car door and entered the house. He ate his tea in near-silence. Mary, perhaps thinking he was tired and still sore from his beating, allowed him that, talking excitedly once more of how the date of the wedding was approaching and how much she still had left to do. Seamus smiled when needed, grunted 'Aye' where necessary and shook his head when a negative was required. Then, when Mary had left the house, he went to his room.

*

He left the house shortly after nine. It was dark and cold, the ground still wet from where it had rained earlier, but it wasn't raining now. Seamus wore his parka coat anyhow, the hood up, partly to protect him from the chilling wind blowing down from the direction of Sheriff's Mountain, but mainly to prevent anyone from seeing him – from looking into his eyes and maybe catching a glimpse of the blackness of his soul. He went briskly down Westway, down Creggan Hill and along the Northland, his heart fluttering as he made his way down the Rock Road.

The car park of Magee University was badly lit, with too few lamps having been placed unevenly around the campus, though the old building itself was lit by a series of upturned floodlights, the stonework yellow-gold. Some students were making their way in and out of the grounds, going, Seamus guessed, either to the library for a bit of late-night studying or, more likely, to the small green Students' Union cabin at the back of the university – the cabin was apparently too small by far to serve the numbers who used it. Seamus walked slowly down towards the car park. There were perhaps a dozen cars there in all and he wasn't sure what he was supposed to do next or where he was supposed to stand. He was thinking about turning around and going home when one car at the furthest – and perhaps the darkest – end of the car park flashed its headlights quickly twice. Seamus felt his heart thumping as he cautiously approached the car. One figure inside, though he couldn't be sure who it was. As he came nearer, he realised it was Dave – the bulky man dressed in a dark, worn suit. Seamus walked around to the passenger side of the vehicle, opened the door and got in.

'You decided to come, after all.' Dave was smiling, totally at ease with the situation. 'I had a feelin' you would.'

'Did I have a fuckin' choice?' Irritated.

The man laughed. 'We all have choices, Seamus. Sometimes they're limited, but they're always there. You, erm, didn't tell anyone about this, did you?' For a moment the man's voice was guarded, uncertain.

Seamus let him wait a moment, savouring that small chink of weakness. Then he said, 'What do ye think I am – a fuckin' simple bastard? Ye think I want anyone to know what I'm doin' here tonight?'

'You think that what you're doin' is wrong?' Completely relaxed once more.

'Of course it's wrong.' He felt edgy, nervous, cold. He took out a cigarette and lit it up, not offering the man called Dave one – not bothering to ask if it was all right to smoke in his vehicle. Not caring.

The man smiled and shook his head. 'There's nothin' wrong about it, Seamus. We're both out to set right the wrongs that others have inflicted – or would inflict – upon their own people, nothin' more.'

'The wrongs accordin' to you, ye mean. You could be tryin' to turn me against . . . ' He was about to mention Dan McGeady's name but hastily thought better of it. 'Against other people. Against my own people.'

'You think they're doin' what they do for *you*, Seamus? You think that when they plant a bomb in their own town, they're actually doin' that for their own?' The big man snorted in disbelief. 'Them and their economic war they're always spoutin' on about. You try tellin' some wee woman from Creggan that they're fightin' an economic war when they bomb the shit out of Littlewoods and Wellworths and she has to go elsewhere for her groceries, pay way over the odds for what she was gettin' right and cheap before. Sure who's losing money there? The Brits, who get that money back from the insurance companies a couple of months later, or the wee woman, who has to cut back on necessities to get by another week, who has to walk through a town full of rubble on her bad legs because someone has set the buses alight, who has to watch her son bein' kneecapped because he stole a few shillin's somewhere, while others think it's all right to steal thousands from banks and scran half of it for themselves, so long as they call themselves by a group name?'

'I know exactly who you're tryin' to turn me against,' Seamus said, pointedly. 'It won't work. I'm not as stupid as ye think. Not all of us fuckin' are.'

Dave laughed, then pulled out a packet of cigarettes. He offered one to Seamus. The youth declined with an abrupt shake of his head. The man shrugged and lit one himself. 'Aye, you're no slouch in the brains department, Seamus, I know that. At the college for a time, weren't you?'

Seamus didn't answer but stared at him hard. The man had done his homework. Still, Seamus wasn't overly surprised. That was his job.

'Aye, you were that. But I'll tell you somethin', Seamus. There's a lot of people out there with brains to burn – aye, and Dan McGeady's one of them, to give him credit – but not every one of them has the common sense that God gave a turkey. It's a funny thing about suicides. You see detectives on the television investigatin' them all the time. They find a gun in someone's hand, a note sayin' that the victim couldn't take any more – that he had to take his life because he couldn't stand the cruelties that the world had imposed upon him.

'But it's not like that a bit in real life, y'know. Most people who shoot themselves in the head don't end up with the gun in their hand. That's a load of shite. The gun usually flies off a little ways across the room – dependin', of course, on the power of the recoil – and the body itself usually spasms and flies away a little in the other direction, because of the force of the bullet rippin' into the flesh. The gun-in-the-hand bit makes good television, of course, 'cause it lets the less-than-bright viewer know what's happenin' almost immediately. But Billy Flannagan, oh, he was lyin' there with a gun in his hand. Fingers wrapped neatly around the grip, one flat against the trigger, gun facin' the head. Good television, that would have made. Oh aye. If you're a fuckin' brain-dead monkey, that is!'

'You're sayin' he was murdered?' Seamus said, contemptuously. 'And you're tryin' to tell me that Dan McGeady was responsible? You'll probably say that Billy was about to talk to the 'RA. That he was gonna tell them that it was Dan who had squealed and not me da. I can see through your ploy a fuckin' mile,' Seamus sneered. 'It's not workin.' He looked around the car park, wondering if he could go now – if the people who were supposed to be taking the photographs had done so.

'You nervous, kid? You're head's swivellin' around there like Linda Blair.'

'I wish you'd get to the fuckin' point, that's all.' Terse.

'It's a two-way street, Seamus, and I'm not ready to drive my car down it yet while your car's stuck at red, y'know? Now, I want to tell you a little about McGeady – the boy you think's everythin' that a good Che Guevara-type freedom fighter should be.'

'I don't particularly think anythin' of him. He's all right, but that's about it. I've no real love for him.'

'I wish everyone thought like that, Seamus, I really do. But people tend not to see him as he really is.'

'Oh aye, and what is he?' Sarcastic, dry.

'An umbrella, Seamus. Same as all those people in the IRA, Sinn Féin, whatever the fuck you want to call them. A fair-weather umbrella, though – one that's only lofted when it isn't rainin' shite from the heavens. People like him, they sell their soul for fifteen minutes of fame, believin' completely that they're better than the last man who raised the banner and marched to war for Ireland. Believin' that God has chosen them because they're special – because they're smarter, stronger, better people than every last one of their predecessors. Better than their cloned counterparts on the other side of the political fence, and better even than the people they're always claimin' to protect.

'And they get the young and the impressionable – those with fire in their blood – to follow after their guts-or-glory speeches. Only thing is, the young and impressionable almost always find it hard to live within the fixed constraints of other people's ideologies, because that's what it is to be young. They're full of energy, excitement and enthusiasm and they always have their own ideas as to how to hurry situations along, never seein' the bigger picture. So off they go by themselves at times to do their own thing – a wee robbery here, a wee murder there. Y'see, once you release the dogs of war into the battle – any battle – their bloodlust is hard to control. The umbrella then has to be lofted in foul weather, and those people don't like that, Seamus.

'People like Dan, they don't like that even a little. The disclaimers are thrown into the ring, the denials voiced, the distances drawn up, their own people forsaken. Even though the mouthpieces started the ball rollin' themselves. Even though they set the precedent, claimin' that, if you kick someone's door in long enough, they're bound to answer sometime. And the umbrella remains down in the shite storm, tucked away until it's all over. Then the young and the innocent have to go it alone in the H-blocks and the Crumlin, wonderin' why only some sorts of violence are acceptable – why it's only all right to kill or ruin a man forever for someone else's reasons, and not your own. Huh! People like Dan McGeady, they've prostituted themselves but, like prostitutes, they want power without responsibility.'

'That's a load of crap.'

'Is it?' Dave said, with a short laugh. 'Unfortunately, the truth isn't always starin' you in the face. They're weak men, these men who crave power and attention – any attention, no matter how it's bought – so they can spout off their pie-in-the-sky ideologies to all and sundry. They don't really care who dies or gets hurt, so long as they remain at the top and others speak their name with pride. And the more people fall under their umbrella and the more people they let use their name, the less power they have,' the Special Branch man continued. 'They're the weakest men in the world, Seamus, the men at the top, because ultimately they have no say over what goes on in their own organisations. They become guy-ropes that hold the ship in place as it rises and falls on the tide – as it founders or threatens to crash on the rocks. They aren't fuckin' individuals at all. They're names to be used in bad times, to be praised in good times. They don't have opinions – they *become* an opinion. And they quite often end up as an opinion that they themselves would never have dreamt up in the first place.'

Seamus laughed drily. 'Then why are you goin' after Dan McGeady, if he's such a weak man? You sound pretty afraid of someone who, in your eyes, is nothin' but a name.'

'Because not everyone can see what these people are immediately. The youth of the world more than most, unfortunately, due to their lack of experience in how devious some people can become. They join up, they follow their chosen flag – green, white and gold; red, white and blue; the one they believe to be better than a thousand others the world over – only to perform their deeds and, over time, to become filled with remorse and sorrow for their actions. And there's always remorse, Seamus, there's always regret, even when the hardest of the hard says there isn't. Though sometimes that remorse only comes long after their masters have got what they wanted – after their masters have decided that enough fightin's been done, that the war is over, because they got what they personally wanted.

'For some people, though, it's never over, and that's the part the IRA, the UVF, and all those other bundles of letters never understand. They plan to take what they want by force, then, when they've gained it, they fail to understand that other people will also fight to take those same possessions back. And the violence has been legitimised by their own brutal methods, so how the fuck can they complain when someone else does the same? How the fuck can they even argue with splinter groups who break away from their own primary cause to pursue a near-similar secondary cause, the logic of which sounds equally as convincin' when recited to the masses of ill-informed in the guildhall of cuckoo-ville? Fight your cause, back it up with a thousand good reasons that are never halfway reasonable, throw in a thousand rounds and a few bombs and then cry foul when someone else does the same. Aye, they all do it, and I'm tired of it all. It's a perverted fuckin' merry-go-round, nothin' else, and in the end-up it's wee Mrs McFenian or wee Mr McJaff that suffers – no one else.'

'Why don't ye get the fuck off it, then?'

'Like I sais, with some it takes longer than with others to get a view of the bigger picture. And the thing is, here in the North there's a never-endin' supply of people ready to jump on the merry-go-round when others have decided they're feelin' sick and have to get off. It's up to people like myself to slow the thing down, so that we can all get the fuck off it together. And I can't always do it by the book. That's why I do what I do – why I do it the *way* I do.'

'And your flag is better than anyone else's, ye think that?' Sarcastic, condescending.

Dave smiled thinly. 'My flag's the one that's flyin' from the ramparts at the moment, Seamus, and I have to do my best to see that it remains there. It's a flag of convenience, the same as every other – I'll grant ye that in confidence. But it's the best compromise that'll ever be reached in this fuckin' land, because Dublin, for all of their posturin' and preenin' at times, doesn't want the fuckin' North, and neither do the Brits. Only thing with the Brits is that they haven't the excuse to give this shit-hole up so long as the loyalists keep declarin' their questionable loyalty to the Crown.

'Nah, they want out – they've always wanted out. They just can't be seen to be gettin' pushed out, that's all, but they'll go some day, you take it from me. But until that day – and maybe long after it, who knows – it'll go on ad infinitum. To the victors the spoils; to the victims the soil. Death and more death: a relentless cycle that can only be broken when one man relents. And aye, I'll admit it,' Dave said, with a sigh, 'that man won't be me, for I too have that flaw of believin' that my flag's the best, Seamus. I too am the same as the others in believin' that I'm right. Only difference is, I'm workin' within the law so we can all have the one law, fair and just.'

'Within one law?' Seamus snorted. 'We live in a country where nearly half the people believe your laws are wrong, where your laws have been anythin' but just and fair. You're only the law now because ye fought and conquered others into submission – at least, that's the way I see it. You said it yourself: you're no different to anyone else.'

'You seem to believe you have a fair idea about politics, Seamus,' the Special Branch man said, admiringly.

'I know nothin' about politics – nothin' at all. I only have a good idea about common sense. And I know the two don't ever go together.'

'Aye, maybe you're right,' the man said, laughing. 'So the answer to that one is that these are the laws that prevail, Seamus. And I've chosen to follow them, believin' them to be near all-inclusive, near all-prevailin' – the best of a bad bunch. Anyhow, that's enough of the good-hearted banter. Why don't ye tell me what ye know about Dan McGeady, about Patrick Monaghan, about the movements of other boys in your area who are fightin' for their own particular cause and, more importantly, about what it is they have planned for the end of this month? Because we know there's somethin' goin' on – somethin' big.

'We know that, if you don't know now, you should have little bother findin' out, movin' within the circles that you do. And then, when ye do that, we'll work out a way of gettin' your father's name cleared, of gettin' him recognised as the soldier that he was, eh? Maybe get the Boys to creep into the cemetery up there in Creggan at midnight some night, fire a belated round or two over his grave. Maybe get a lone piper up there to deliver an even lonelier address, stuff like that. That'd be a nice wee touch, wouldn't it? Romantic, in a sense. A working-class rebel belatedly praised. Maybe there wouldn't be so many would know about it, but it'd be nice for you and your ma, eh? Somethin' to maybe tell the kids about when you get older.'

Seamus couldn't work out whether Dave was being sarcastic or not; he didn't even attempt to fathom his fatuous remarks. Instead, he replied, acidly, 'I think you've overestimated my capabilities. And I thought ye were supposed to have brains.'

'I have an idea about people, Seamus. I'm not too far off the mark most times – never have been.'

Seamus looked down, silent for a moment. 'Aye, well you're well off it this time out. You start first. You tell me about Dan McGeady,' he said, eventually. 'Ye didn't answer me question. Did he kill Billy Flannagan?'

'What have you got for me, Seamus? The lights are forever stuck on red, are they?'

Seamus sighed deeply. The talking was over and he was going to have to produce something, and fast. Either that or get out of the car and run. He sat there, momentarily lost in thought. As he did so, his eye caught a flash of movement to his immediate right. There was something in the hedges beyond the window on the driver's side. A flitting shadow, black, of indeterminate shape and size. Dave turned hurriedly, following the youth's eyes, sensing the alarm there. As he did so, he reached a hand inside his jacket, seeking to release a gun from within a leather holster secreted under his armpit.

'You plan this, Seamus?' he said gruffly, struggling to release his gun. 'Damn,' he cursed, unable to release it completely. 'The fuckin' . . . !'

Seamus saw the flashes, bright, blinding. He heard the bangs: two, three – he couldn't be sure. Ear-piercing, disorientating, causing his bowels to loosen slightly, his face to whiten, his body, on reflex, to drop for cover. At that exact moment, seemingly in slow motion, the window shattered into a hundred shards, the splinters spraying forward across their bodies, some catching Seamus in the side of the face, in the arm of his coat, stinging, numbing. His eyes closed for a split second and then opened. Dave slowly slumped forward into his seat, blood spreading across the front of his suit, running down along the side of his face.

Seamus put his hands quickly to his ears and huddled down between the front seat and the dashboard, shaking violently, jumping as each successive bang resounded loudly in the confined area. When the shooting had ceased, he dared to look up as the dark shadow moved purposefully around the front of the car, approaching the front passenger door.

A tall figure dressed in black, wearing a dark balaclava, gun in hand. Coming around to his window. Seamus wanted to move – to push open the door and run into the blackness of the grounds beyond, to become lost there forever. The figure, however, had this escape route covered. He stood outside the car for a second, eyeing his work. Dave wasn't moving. Seamus saw a thick river of blood pooling beneath him on the floor. He wanted to throw up, to die, to be able to breathe normally. He wanted the terrible claustrophobia that had engulfed him to end as quickly as it had begun. The hooded figure stood there and then raised his gun and pulled the trigger.

Seamus ducked down low, knowing that he was about to die. But the gun clicked with an empty sound. Jammed or out of ammunition, he didn't know – or care – which. The figure tried again, and once more. Seamus ducked low again, a prayer on his lips. Then, on the wind blowing in hard through the shattered window, the sounds of a siren, maybe two. The dark-clad figure raised his head slowly, as if gauging the distance of the approaching jeeps. Then he tucked his gun into his belt, took one last look at Seamus, turned and walked slowly and coolly away up the car park, in the direction of the students' union hut. From there, he vanished into the shadows, a couple of escape routes open to him.

Seamus only realised then that he was crying, shaking, unable to move. Beside him, Dave groaned almost perceptibly and opened his eyes, fighting for breath.

'Go . . . Seamus,' he said, with a great effort. 'But remember what I said. Dan McGeady . . . it was him who touted. He was quotin' Milton, talkin' . . . talkin' like the devil about everythin'. You go . . . you know . . . that your da didn't . . . ' Dave slumped forward, the breath leaving him in one long-drawn-out sigh.

The sirens were growing louder. Seamus knew there was nothing he could do. He was about to get out of the car when he noticed the gun lying on the floor in front of the dead Special Branch man. He lifted it, made his way out of the car, the gun held to his front, sweeping the grounds in an arc, knowing that this was a ridiculous thing to do, as he didn't know the first thing about guns. He placed it in his waistband and pulled his coat around him, flicked the hood up over his head and ran across the car park in the direction of the Rock Road. He narrowly avoided being knocked down by a car as he crossed the Northland Road, and he was aware that, behind him, the heavy-engined police jeeps had turned up the hill. Daring to look back for a half-second, he saw blue flashes of neon atop the grey Land Rovers, the vehicles racing up the Rock and into the car park at speed.

On the furthest side of the Northland Road there was a dark alleyway that ran up between the houses and an old abandoned church which led ultimately, through a criss-cross of lanes, to some old garages. The area was perfect for him at the moment in that it was ill-lit and rarely used at night. Seamus raced up the lane and lost himself in the blackness. At the top of the furthest laneway was Eden Street, a sharply winding road known locally as the Gander's Neck, which went through the centre of the Rosemount housing estate. There was a telephone box on the corner nearby. Seamus waited for a while in the shadows, watching.

A couple of cars came by, minutes apart. Seamus glanced up and down the road and then scampered over towards the booth.

Inside, his hands were shaking as he fumbled in his pockets for a coin. Once he found it, he inserted it in the slot and phoned Jimmy Duffy.

Thirteen

The bread van pulled up outside the laneway, Jimmy Duffy's eyes warily scanning the area. Seamus watched him for a while from the long shadow thrown by an outbuilding, his own gaze sweeping the well-lit road beyond. Jimmy Duffy, completely unaware of the urgency of the situation, tried to adjust his vision to the blackness. He rolled down the window and threw away a stub of cigarette. 'Seamy, ye there?' he called, loudly.

'Shh!' Seamus snapped, irritably. He was about to step out of the laneway when he spotted the headlights turning off the Northland, making up into Rosemount. A car. Its driver, he quickly ascertained as it neared, was an elderly man. Innocent enough, though it had his heart in a rage, beating madly, him tight against the moss-traced wall of the garage. Seamus waited for the man to drive past, then quickly ran out of the laneway and around to the passenger side of the van, scrambling up into the seat.

'Right, get us out of here!' he snapped.

Jimmy was smiling thinly, bemused. Seamus had phoned him to say he needed help, and fast. Jimmy had asked him what was wrong. Had someone beaten him up again? Did he need a backing? Seamus had told him to listen carefully, as he hadn't got much money. Jimmy had sensed the urgency in his tone and had told him to go ahead. Seamus had then told the red-haired youth to phone Elaine for him and ask her to come to the house in Dunree and wait for him there. She was to pack a few things and bring some money and her banklink card; he'd explain to her later just what was happening. There was an extra key in the grey vase just beside the flowerbed so that she could let herself in, placed there after a time, years before, when his father had been out for a night on the tiles and forgotten where he'd left his own. Jimmy had tried to question him about the situation but Seamus had warned him that this was perhaps the most important thing that had ever happened to him in his life and that, if Jimmy was really his friend, as he always said he was, then he should get his fuckin' arse down there, pronto. Jimmy claimed he was putting on his coat even as they spoke.

'Are ye gonna tell me what the hell's wrong with ye or not? Ye need a backin', I'm your man.' Jimmy pushed up a sleeve and balled a fist to show his solidarity. 'I'm here for ye, aye.'

'Ye hear that shootin' there now?' Seamus took a deep breath, the events still flashing through his mind in slow motion like some nightmarish Sam Peckinpah film. The masked figure, the bright flashes, the three bangs. Splintering shards of glass and blood spraying over and around him in a jagged rain. Dave slowly toppling forward onto the dashboard, blood seeping from a wound at the side of his forehead, another in his torso, his last words before he fell a curse because he couldn't pull his gun out of his underarm holster in time. Then, after the gunman had run away, rising slowly, racked with pain, a bloodied Lazarus, to tell him in a pale whisper that Dan McGeady had betrayed the republican movement and that he was responsible for his father's – and maybe even Billy Flannagan's – death.

There was a puzzled frown on Jimmy's face. He shook his head so slowly that Seamus felt like throttling him. 'Nah. Never heard a thing, why?'

'Turn the van. Just turn the fuckin' van and get us the fuck out of here, before . . . '

Jimmy raised an eyebrow. He'd been lying out on the sofa, relaxing, preparing for an early night, because he had to get up at six to start his deliveries. He looked dog-tired, his hair tangled, stubble on his chin. 'Jesus, Seamy, you're fuckin' sheet-white.'

'I just got somebody fuckin' killed. You'd be sheet-white too, wouldn't ye?'

'Are ye sure ye haven't been on the drink, or . . . ?'

'Just turn the fuckin' van around,' Seamus cut in, thickly. 'Jesus, Jimmy, this is fuckin' serious. I'm fuckin' serious, can ye not tell?' The tremor in his voice, audible even to himself, eyes moist, wide, staring. Jimmy didn't hesitate. He swung the van around, turning it in the direction from which he'd just come.

'Aye, no bother, Seamy. But are ye gonna tell me what's happenin', or what? Christ, I only want to help ye, nothin' else. I can't help ye if I don't know, sure.'

Seamus told him, blurting out about the meeting that Paddy Monaghan had arranged for him – the one that was supposed to provide an opportunity for photographs to be taken to be used in a press release, though which instead had led to the death of the Special Branch man.

'Jesus fuckin' Christ!' was all Jimmy Duffy could say in return. 'Jesus H. fuckin' Christ!' Jimmy was now fully awake. He took another long look at Seamus and meshed the gears, spurring the van up towards Creggan, his own eyes wide now, that familiar whistle of disbelief coming softly from between his lips. 'What do ye mean, killed?' he asked, eventually. 'As in killed dead, or nearly killed . . . '

'Aye, fuckin' killed dead,' Seamus barked. 'Now hurry up and get this van out of here, or we're both fucked.'

'Jesus, Seamy, you simple bastard!' Jimmy said, his hand having bother making the gearstick move like sheet lightning in its housing, the crunch of metal and his guttural curses attesting to that fact. 'What the hell have you gone and done now?'

'The Special Branch man . . . he . . . Jesus Christ, it's all my fuckin' fault!'

Jimmy seemed stunned – so much so that he had to blink twice before he properly saw the car coming down the road towards him. Seamus grabbed the steering wheel, and just in time pulled the vehicle out of the path of the oncoming car. 'Jesus, Jimmy, do ye not think I'm up to me neck in enough shite without ye gettin' us killed in a car accident.'

'Christ, Seamy, you're a simple bastard!' was all the red-haired youth could say in return. For a moment he regained his senses. 'Hey, where are we goin', anyway?'

'To Paddy Monaghan's house.'

Jimmy nearly crashed the van again. 'Do ye want me to fuckin' drive?' Seamus said, angrily. 'Can ye not even do somethin' as simple as that yourself, for Christ's sakes?'

'Aye, well I was hardly expectin' ye to say somethin' like that, was I?' Jimmy snapped in return. 'And why don't ye take your fuckin' hood down, while we're talkin' about you bein' a simple bastard. Ye not think that looks a wee bit suspicious, like? You with a hood up in the van and it not rainin'.'

Seamus looked at him, exhaled and pulled down his hood, loosening the coat. 'Christ, I'm sorry, Jimmy. I can't believe what happened back there.' He slapped his forehead with the palm of his hand. 'God, I don't believe I could have been so stupid.'

'Aye, well I've just gone and done somethin' stupid too,' Jimmy said.

'It wouldn't be a patch on anythin' I've done over the years, would it?'

'You'll not say that when ye hear it.' Jimmy looked at him, then checked the intersection at Creggan Hill before driving on up Westway.

'Then get it out.'

'After ye phoned, I thought you were in deep shite . . . '

'I fuckin' am!'

'Aye, well I thought ye'd got a kickin' or somethin', so I phoned Elaine for ye, just like ye said . . . '

'And?'

'Ach aye, that's all sorted,' Jimmy said, firmly. 'Her brother answered but I told him I was phonin' from . . . '

'What brother?'

Jimmy looked at him, raised an eyebrow and shrugged. 'Her brother, I dunno. Why?'

'Was he civil enough?'

'Nah, ignorant fucker, right enough. He wasn't goin' to go get her for me, until . . . '

Seamus exhaled deeply. 'Aye, that'll be her Marty. I thought that cunt was away on one of his fishin' trips. He didn't hear ye talkin' to her, did he?'

Jimmy smiled confidently. 'That's what I'm sayin'. I was right and crafty about it all.' Jimmy pointed to his head, then his feet. 'Up there for thinkin', down here for dancin', eh! He wasn't goin' to go get her until I said I was phonin' from the Rainbow Café. I sais I needed to talk to her about her shifts and shit. Then she came on and I told her the score. Well, I told her what I knew, which was fuck all. But she sais aye, she'll do as ye sais, 'cause it sounded bad enough. But then I went and phoned . . . '

Seamus hit the dashboard a slap with a balled fist.

'Christ, Seamy, what the hell's wrong with ye now?'

'Ye said ye were phonin' from the Rainbow about shifts. She

doesn't work in the fuckin' Rainbow any more, she works in Brendan's. Now the cunt'll be wonderin' where she's off to on a Friday night, won't he?'

Jimmy raised his palms. 'Aye, well that's not the worst of it. After I phoned her, I phoned . . . ' He paused a second, sheepish.

'Ye phoned . . . ?' Seamus paled even more as Jimmy looked away guiltily. 'Ye phoned Paddy Monaghan's house, didn't ye?'

Jimmy nodded tensely, biting at his lip.

'And?' He could hardly bear to ask.

'He wasn't there. His mother answered the phone, sais he was away on an errand. Sais he'd be back soon, could she give him a message.'

'And what did ye say?'

'I sais that I was away to see you.'

'Aye, that's fuckin' great!' Seamus shook his head, breathing heavily, thinking. An errand? What kind of an errand would that have been? He tried hard to ignore the answer that came into his head first.

Jimmy seemed afraid to speak. 'Ye still goin' up there?'

Seamus became aware of the gun in his belt. It had been sticking coldly into his leg as he climbed into the van but he hadn't been overly conscious of it until now. 'Aye, we're still goin' up there.' He looked into Jimmy's searching eyes and saw the uncertainty there. 'Well, I'm goin' up there. Ye can let me off outside your house, sure, and ye can head back to your bed. I'll go over and have a chat with him meself.'

'I'll go in with ye, no bother.'

Seamus felt a closeness to him then – the way he always did when Jimmy offered to get in over his head for him. 'Aye, thanks, but maybe ye better not, eh? I'll go over meself. He might not want anyone else to know the score, like.'

Jimmy nodded, then looked at him hard.

'Stop fuckin' lookin' at me like that,' Seamus said, angrily. 'Christ, you'd think I was a corpse at a wake!'

Jimmy shrugged glumly. 'Do ye, erm, reckon he'll be chattin', then?'

Seamus sat there for a moment, thinking, the gravity of that question making him feel claustrophobic. It was something he'd been thinking about as he raced across the car park, as he stood in the laneway, as he drove up the road in the van. That question was orbiting there in his subconscious, regardless of the other thoughts that spun out of control around it. He'd never truly been able to figure out Paddy Monaghan. He had known him about eight years now, the two boys having met, somewhere along the line, through Jimmy Duffy. Paddy had spoken to him last night and earlier in the day, his tone even, his eyes containing no deceit. Anyone else, he would have trusted implicitly if they had talked the way Paddy did – if they had offered the same protection, the same solutions. But he knew Paddy Monaghan like a brother now, and there was always something lurking behind the façade with him – you never really knew what it was. Had Paddy Monaghan set him up? Or had he simply been relaying a message – as blind to what was about to occur as Seamus himself? Sent perhaps by Dan McGeady – although he said he hadn't told the republican figure anything at all – unwittingly to set him up to be killed as a tout.

Or, even more chillingly, had Paddy Monaghan actually pulled the trigger himself? That possibility too was not inconceivable. The hooded figure had been a blur there in the darkness of the car park and, from the angle Seamus had been viewing him, it could have been anyone, as he had no clue as to the figure's exact shape or size. Seamus couldn't begin to think of an answer to those questions and he wasn't really sure he wanted any answers anyhow.

He was bigger than Paddy Monaghan, that much he did know, and he had always been physically stronger, though Paddy had always been a better runner, because he'd played a lot of football. The older boy had more stamina and it was true that he was craftier than the average man. Seamus shrugged inwardly. He wasn't afraid of him, never had been. The gun, however, was an added protection – it would balance out any differences betwen them, should there be any. If he could use it. Which he wasn't exactly sure about either.

'Aye, he'll talk. That's what he'll do. He'll talk.'

Jimmy nodded uncertainly.

Seamus had heard the doubt in his own voice and he understood Jimmy's silence. If that had been Paddy Monaghan down in the car park, he thought suddenly, then he had taken one life and tried to take another. A moment's hesitation, no more, and then he had tried to fire at Seamus, not once but twice. And if he had tried then, what was there to stop him trying again? A chill ran through Seamus's bones and he pulled the zipper of his coat up even further.

*

Paddy Monaghan was standing outside the front door when the bread van drove up the street. The older youth threw his cigarette into the rainswept street and came out to the gate to meet the approaching van. Jimmy waved to Paddy from inside the van, then took one long last look at Seamus and drove off.

'Christ, Seamy, ye all right? Jimmy said that ye were in bother. Did ye . . . ?'

Seamus looked tensely around him. It was nearly twenty past ten at night, the streets deserted, lights on in nearly all the houses on both sides of the street, an occasional stray dog running in and out of the gardens. He took a breath and eyed the other youth evenly. 'Ye want to go inside, or will we go somewhere quiet, like?'

Paddy looked at him for a moment, frowning. 'What the fuck happened down there?'

'Ye don't know?' A raised eyebrow – one that Elaine would have been proud of – the tone otherwise even enough.

'I'll get the keys,' Paddy said, gravely. He went into the hallway and pulled on his jacket, searching for the keys in the pocket. Seamus went out to the street and leaned against the bonnet of the car, becoming aware that his legs were weak – there was a shake there. Becoming aware that the bonnet was warm to the touch, despite the raindrops that ran down to gather in a black puddle on the dark bumper. Paddy left the house, closing the door after him. He walked to the car, opened the passenger door first and allowed Seamus to get in. Seamus did so, conscious that the gun was digging into his upper thigh once more. He sat down carefully, not wishing to dislodge the gun. As Paddy climbed in the driver's side, he half-unzipped his coat, the tarnished silver gun still concealed beneath it.

'Where are we goin'?' Paddy asked.

'You tell me.'

Paddy shrugged, then drove off down towards Westway. 'You don't look the best, Seamy. Are ye all right? Jesus, will ye tell me what happened down there tonight?'

Seamus looked at him, wishing for once that he had the ability to read minds. 'There was a shootin'. The Branch man's dead. I thought they were only goin' to take fuckin' photographs . . . '

'Jesus, Seamy, are ye fuckin' serious?' Paddy's face was lit for a moment by the orange-yellow fluorescents. Then shadows fell across his face as they left the lights behind, and Seamus shivered, seeing nothing but faint pinpoints of light in the other youth's eyes.

Seamus looked away, confused. 'Aye, I'm fuckin' serious. Do ye think I'd joke around about somethin' like that?' Hoarse, a lump in his throat, the sense of betrayal all too real. How could they have done this to him?

'Ye want me to do anythin' for ye?'

'Nah, you're doin' enough.' You've *done* enough, maybe I should say, he found himself thinking. Maybe more than enough. 'Where are we goin'?'

Paddy turned the car down the by-wash road, turning in the direction of Glenowen as he reached the top of the rise. 'You'll have to trust me, Seamy. I know that's the last thing ye want to do after tonight, but you'll have to trust me.' He looked across at Seamus. 'Ye trust me?' he asked, after a moment.

Seamus searched his eyes, seeing nothing there, but believing that he would if he dared to look long enough. Which he didn't. The gun dug once more into his upper thigh and he shifted to the side a little, relieving the pressure. 'Aye, I'll trust ye, Paddy Monaghan. You've done nothin' wrong on me so far.' Sounding as truthful as he possibly could. Or trying to.

Paddy nodded and drove the car on out the dark, back-country roads that led off around the top of Creggan, taking a right as they reached the fork that led either into the army barracks known as the Piggery or off down into the Heights. Paddy took the lower road, completing a ragged circle. He drove straight down along the Heights in the direction of Circular Road, past Saint Peter's Secondary School and further down into Rathkeel. He pulled the car in at a telephone booth on the corner.

'I have to get somethin' sorted here. Make a phone call. Ye all right there a second?'

Seamus nodded, suddenly more tired than he had ever been in his life.

Paddy got out of the car and went into the phone booth. A minute later he climbed back into the car. 'I'm takin' ye to see someone. Ye all right with that?'

Seamus shrugged as casually as he could. The world was turning at a phenomenal speed, flashes of the shooting incident piercing his mind like angry splinters, replaying the same scenes over and over, and he was certain it was never going to stop. Paddy returned a minute later, keyed the car into life and drove off along Rathkeel, down Southway, through the Bogside. It was about another twenty minutes before he reached the house, just off the Greenhaw Road, though it seemed no more than fleeting seconds or, equally, forever. Paddy got out of the car and opened the door for Seamus. Then Paddy went up to the front door of the house and rang the bell. When the door opened, Dan McGeady stood there, framed large in a pool of light that spilled out onto the road.

*

This time it was Seamus who hung back, allowing Dan and Paddy to enter the sitting room of the mock-Tudor home first. He felt he needed to maintain some authority, no matter how slight. This time, however, Dan McGeady acquiesced, and immediately Seamus's authority was lost. In giving way, the older man had shown his power – the power that declared that Seamus was no threat at all. Seamus cursed inwardly.

The older man didn't speak as Seamus entered the room. He

directed a hand to the settee, indicating that the two youths should take a seat. Seamus instead sat down in the armchair nearest the door, readjusting his position once more, to stop the gun barrel digging into his thigh. He kept his eyes on the older man and Paddy, who took the settee in the centre. On the tall, thin youth who entered the room and sat on the armchair in the furthest corner – Eddie McGeady, the older man's son, calm, impassive. On Paddy Monaghan, whose own eyes were flitting here and there between the others, uncertain, settling finally, deadly serious, upon Seamus. Seamus was aware that the atmosphere was cordial though restrained. Dan McGeady was the first to speak.

'Ye want tea, Seamus?'

'You're offerin' me tea after tryin' to fuckin' kill me?' Seamus barked, not having planned to start like that. 'Are ye fuckin' serious, or what?' The momentum lost. An accusation against one of the most powerful men in the republican movement. He should have maybe put it another way – maybe never said it at all.

'That wasn't supposed to happen,' Dan said, evenly. His face was impassive, unreadable. 'A bit of a mistake.'

'Aye, some fuckin' mistake. Didn't seem like a fuckin' mistake. Seemed right and fuckin' intentional, if ye ask me.'

Dan's eyes shifted to his son and then back to Seamus. 'Someone didn't do what they were told to do. They did a little bit more than they were asked to. It happens occasionally. People panic, take the initiative themselves.'

'Did ye think I was gonna squeal, or somethin'? Ye asked me to do somethin', I did it. Christ, what did ye fuckin' want?'

'This is a war, Seamus. Sometimes things go wrong, ye know that yourself. And sure, ye know nothin' anyhow . . . '

Testing, his eyes flickering between Paddy and Seamus. Now it was Seamus who remained free of emotion, his eyes too full of hatred to fall for that one, to feel afraid. Paddy's eyes, however, dropped to the carpet. Dan McGeady smiled a mysterious smile then and nodded softly. Seamus felt his stomach churning, unsure whether Dan McGeady had seen what he was looking for. 'But I was talkin' about war and the effects of war,' he continued. 'You're the same as the rest of us. You too have had more than your fair share of experience about what can happen.'

'Aye, so have you.' Quickly returned. Hoping to take the older man's attention off the dangerous information he may have gleaned in that protracted silence. The information that could, at worst, cost a further two lives.

Dan McGeady laughed easily. 'Dave Connors fillin' your head with shite, eh, Seamus?'

'How will I ever know?'

'That's a fair point, all right.' Dan McGeady shrugged and sat back in his own armchair. 'Good man at his job, was Dave, but dangerous too, very dangerous. Worked on the Criminal Intelligence Unit, providin' information for the Regional Crime Squad. Nice fancy names there, eh? Roy Mason and Kenneth Newsman's attempt to criminalise the IRA, that idea, and Dave was a product of that school of thought – a tool, in more fuckin' ways than one.

'Y'know, that fucker Mason wanted to have a news and media blackout of Northern Ireland when he took over the reins, give the army licence to do whatever the fuck they wanted. Intern, shoot, murder, break the will of the people, fill the H-blocks to overflowin' with anyone who had an original idea, who dared to fight back against the system. Can ye believe that, Seamus?' The older man raised an eyebrow. 'Us supposed to be livin' in the free world alongside one of the supposedly most civilised countries in the world, and them tryin' to throw up an iron curtain? Huh!

Now he's tryin' to bribe the Boys off the dirty protest by givin' them remission of sentence, the same remission that they give to ODCs. Behave like an ordinary decent criminal, they're sayin', and we'll treat ye well enough. Oh aye! Bribery, corruption, and us with a quarter to a third of our men on the blanket the last few years – they must be fuckin' jokin' if they think we're gonna fall for that one.'

Dan rubbed at his forehead and stretched back a little in his seat. 'The fuckin' Thought Police, Seamus, that's who he wants runnin' the country. Orwell's *1984*, that's the way he sees it all happenin'. Aye, and Dave Connors was a part of that too, God rest his bitter and twisted soul. Could turn a half-truth into a full-blown perjury in a matter of moments – often did, in the courthouse, him and the rest of his goons. Sent many an innocent man away, did Dave. The Boys tried to get him quite a few times. Guess this time his luck ran out. It always does in the end. I bet ye he had a field day with my name, eh, Seamus.'

'Aye, he mentioned one or two things.'

'I bet he did. Probably mentioned your da too, eh?' Seamus said nothing. 'Well, tell me what he said. Go on, get it out. I'm not gonna eat ye.'

'Or shoot me?' Seamus winced – he could hardly believe he'd said that.

Dan McGeady laughed quickly. 'It seems more like I'm gonna be the one to help ye out of this mess, Seamus, although ye probably won't like that. So tell me what he said.'

'It was you who squealed, he sais. You're the reason me da died the way he did. Then he sais ye shot Billy Flannagan to shut him up.'

Dan McGeady shook his head in disbelief. 'Fuck, he was good, all right, wasn't he, Seamus? I think I underestimated the deviousness of the bastard. Christ, could he weave a tangled web, or what?'

'Ye reckon?' Dry, eyes becoming slits.

'Oh, he was good, all right.' McGeady shook his head again. 'Ye deserve an explanation, kid, you and your ma both. Though she didn't really want to know before. She doesn't like me – never has. Bit of a personality difference, or somethin' . . . '

'Aye, she fuckin' has one.'

'Whatever ye think yourself, kid,' the older man said, sighing. 'Anyway, your da was no tout – she was always right enough on that score. None of us ever thought he was, but the Boys up the country said someone had said somethin', all right. Names were handed over, weapons that should never have been found in a million years were uncovered. Too easy. The Brits just walkin' into certain back gardens and diggin' them up, knowin' exactly where to go. Safe houses in Protestant areas of the city raided, and the Boys carted off. Sure what were the chances of somethin' like that happenin', eh?' Dan shrugged dismissively. 'So your da seemed to be the obvious choice, despite his record. Brave man, he was . . . though I'm sure your ma told ye as much.'

Seamus didn't reply, ever-conscious of the others in the room. Eddie McGeady, aged about nineteen or so, was eyeing him up indifferently. Seamus was nearly sure now that it was he who had killed the Special Branch man, though he was less certain if he had also tried to kill Seamus on a whim or of his own accord. Dan could have ordered him to do it, he knew that too. Paddy Monaghan, sitting there tight-lipped, a youth who had spent his life being able to erect a shield whenever necessary, though who had failed to do so when it came to the crunch. His silence, his dropping of the eyes, betraying the fact that he had told Seamus something he shouldn't have – something he had perhaps overheard from someone else's loose lips in another unguarded moment. Dan McGeady was an intelligent man, even the Special Branch man had acknowledged that. He could judge people accurately. More importantly, he could judge slivers of moments, expressions, body language. Paddy Monaghan hadn't been quick enough to erect his shield, and they all knew it.

'Aye, I'm sure she did,' Dan continued, apparently not in the least disconcerted by the silence. 'I don't have to tell ye how brave. The drink was his weakness, but sure we all have them, and it didn't affect him half the way some thought it did. He wasn't drinkin' hard up to Motorman.' The older man was lost in thought for a few moments, frowning darkly. 'One night I think he was on it – after Stevie's funeral, that was – but then we'd all been through a lot in the precedin' days. We'd all drank to forget, to ease the pain.' Dan sighed, tongue on his upper lip, eyes reflective. 'Billy Flannagan was another brave man as well, whether fightin' the Brits hand-to-hand in William Street or on the quiet end of an Armalite emptyin' a few mags at the army or the RUC. He had the balls needed for the job. But he too – like every one of us – had his weakness.'

'Are ye gonna tell me he squealed?'

'I'm gonna tell ye my version of the truth as I know it,' Dan McGeady said, shrugging. 'You can decide for yourself. The truth's a chameleon, after all, and perceptions differ from man to man, but the facts usually go unchallenged the more time passes.'

'And what were the facts?' Seamus asked, thickly. He found his eyes wandering to the picture of the Sacred Heart on the wall above the fireplace, then quickly passing over it, to drop and regard his slightly trembling hands. It was perhaps a time for prayers, but he hadn't either the energy or the inclination to invoke the questionable help the spirits were supposed to grant the faithful.

'They got to Billy in Castlereagh and told him their plans concernin' the invasion they'd named Motorman, a few things that MI5 had forgotten to filter down through their system to the Boys in Dublin. In exchange for that very important information, he told them a few things too, thinkin' that he was gonna save lives. He did, in the end-up,' Dan Mc Geady said, seriously. 'He saved one hell of a lot of lives, and not too many people know it.' Dan raised a palm and sat forward, eyes firmly upon Seamus. 'Why the fuck do ye think they let us out of Castlereagh with that invasion just under a week away? Goodwill? Because they liked us?' Dan McGeady shook his head. 'Nah, they let us out because they thought Billy was in their pocket after that – thought he was the latest and highest-placed recruit in their little army of moles. He was to be their last chance at convincin' us to make a run for it before the big guns were thrown in. But, havin' got a little from him, they thought they'd eventually get him to tell the whole lot. So they let us all out, coverin' their tracks.

'Billy Flannagan had influence as well, y'see. If he'd lived, I daresay he would have made it to the top of the movement. Up until the last few days before the Brits came in, there was a lot of debatin', and nobody seemed all that sure what we should do. After we got out of Castlereagh, he was able to convince a few hard-heads in the movement not to take a stand. Behind-the-scenes stuff, of course, top-secret, him workin' on all of the personalities one by one until he got them to agree to ship out. He was a great man, I always thought, because he achieved more than I ever did.

'His only weakness, in my eyes, was that he was a people person. Always thinkin' of the individual, the innocents. I used to be like that meself until I found out that it's a weakness we can ill-afford. I've tried it, and it doesn't work. I agreed back then that we did the right thing, but now, if I could go back, I'd argue against surrenderin' so easily. I think if we'd fought it out then to the last, we – those few of us who might have survived – wouldn't be fightin' now. Aye, we'd have lost one hell of a lot of casualties that mornin', all right, but that would have been the end of it all, in my books. The Irish government and the UN would have made a stand – they would have had to, due to international pressure, and this war would probably be long over by now. Aye, my attitudes have changed. They changed a long time back, and it was seein' what those bastards were prepared to do that changed them. Now I think like a different animal altogether. Utilitarian, that's me now, ye know what that means?'

'I'm not a simple bastard, and this isn't school!' Out of the corner of his eye, Seamus caught Paddy Monaghan sniggering slightly.

Dan smiled thinly. 'Aye, it's gettin' a load of the big picture, Seamus. The greatest good for the greatest number. Ye have to make sacrifices at times, if ye want to get what ye really want. Sometimes ye have to ignore the bleedin' hearts around ye who think that no war is worth a life, but sometimes you're equally as guilty if ye stand back and watch. Sometimes you're worse for watchin' your people gettin' trodden on when ye can stop it. All that is needed for evil to prevail is that good men stand back and do nothin' – that's the philosophy there, and it's as true as any other.'

Dan McGeady spread his hands. 'I'm sure that's why your ma hates me. I'm sure that's why a lot of people hate me, but – and I seem to remember tellin' ye this before somewhere – that's the cloak I've chosen to wear. The one that many leaders choose to wear, thinkin' as they do about the future and not the immediate present, thinkin' about the young to come, instead of the people of this generation. Thinkin' of the long war – the war that ye have to take to them through the ballot box and the Armalite both. And that's what we're preparin' for now. Because it's not just the wee eighteen-year-old squaddies that we're fightin', it's them and the fuckin' establishment.

'The wee Brits are just like the grunts who went into 'Nam. Gormless, brainless, out to earn a few bob, but, nah, that's not the fuckin' way to do it. Christ, I remember seein' one of those grunts on the TV with 'Charlie Go Home' written on the side of his helmet as he trekked through the hills of Vietnam, killin' the very people who lived there! There's a fuckin' perverse irony in that fuckin' statement somewhere,' the older man said, through tight lips.

'So we'll fight those ignorant wee tossers and their lords and masters. We'll fight the same kind of war that took them out of Palestine, out of Aden, the Persian Gulf, Malaysia, Borneo and a dozen other fuckin' colonies that they thought they'd rule for fuckin' ever, because violence is all they fuckin' understand, when it boils down to it. And they'll always talk to us, no matter how much they condemn us in public, no matter how much of a show they make of subjugatin' us for the loyalists. No matter how much they pretend to be drivin' us off into the back hills of stony Connemara and the like, just as they did with Irishmen of old. They'll talk to us, and they always will, because they always have done, even when they said they didn't, and sometimes we actually bomb the talks to life.

'The IRA have prevailed for over half a century, Seamus, and they aren't goin' to go away now. The Brits had us on our knees in '74 and '75, though they didn't fully know it, but they'll never have us there again. Long gone are the days when IRA stood for

'I Ran Away', because now we're runnin' nowhere. Aye, twenty, thirty years down the line – Jesus, hopefully far sooner! – this land will be free from everythin' British. And ye may think that's a very long-term view, but we've waited hundreds of years, so another hundred isn't really all that long. I dare say that most of us won't be here to see it, right enough,' Dan added, wryly, 'but our descendants will remember that we played our part. We didn't face a firin' squad in Kilmainham Jail, but our martyrdom will shine equally as bright, and they'll talk of us in the same breath as Connolly and Pearse. Maybe not me. Maybe others here in Derry, or Belfast, in Armagh or Fermanagh, anywhere. But then I'm only one of many, and if my name is lost in the grind of history, then so what? That's a small price to pay, isn't it?'

'Ye were talkin' about Billy Flannagan before ye started lecturin',' Seamus said, thickly.

'Aye, I was.' Easygoing, that smile, the eyes of flint nowhere to be seen, though expected. 'They'd sent word through Dublin that the invasion was comin'. The queen wanted her fuckin' land back and, so long as the barricades were up, she had no sovereignty in Free Derry. So the word came in via the messengers of MI5 – get your men out into Buncrana or further south, and we'll just roll the tanks in, take over, no trouble, no trouble at all. Ye can all come back and fight us later, some time when it all blows over. Funny, the way politics works, isn't it, Seamus? Us agreein' to run away and come back to fight another day. But that's what happened, behind the scenes, though we didn't actually let on that that was what we were gonna do. We weren't gonna give the bastards the satisfaction. Of course, it had to be done. It was equally as important to everyone that there'd be no innocents killed, no great loss of life. It was a compromise that was meant to leave everyone as happy as a pig in shit. At least, that's what I thought, until Billy told me the score, though by then near everyone of relevance had shipped out to the South.

'Thing was, they didn't say what they were goin' to do if we didn't comply,' Dan said, bitterly. 'Aye, it was Billy told us that eventually. They didn't tell us that Ted Heath had the navy offshore and the RAF just below the horizon ready to bomb and strafe the fuck out of the no-go areas, did they, though? They didn't say that they'd committed thirty-eight battalions of troops to the relief of those areas – the biggest single commitment of troops to any British operation since 1945. Bigger even than their commitment to Suez in 1956. Heath, he thought we were the fuckin' Vietcong or the Japanese, with thousands of kamikaze types ready to die for the cause and thousands of guns and rifles at our disposal all stored up there in St Mary's School.' Dan McGeady's eyes widened.

'Ye know what I'm sayin', Seamus? We had a few housin' estates under our control and they were goin' to strafe the fuckin' place, just like they'd done in Dresden durin' the war, just like the Germans had done to Coventry, like the Americans had done in Vietnam. Bomb us from the air and the fuckin' sea with a couple of two-thousand-pound bombs, just to placate the loyalists, as if we were a load of gooks hidin' out in the tunnels somewhere. Shoot up our housin' estates and kill anything and anyone who got in the way: men, women, children – it didn't matter who. Ye imagine the damage that would have done, Seamus? Can ye imagine how many lives would have been fuckin' lost in that vain bid at ethnic cleansin'? It would have made Bloody Sunday look like Jack the Ripper's day off.'

Dan McGeady paused for breath. He shook his head once more. 'They told this to Billy because he was the one who listened. He was the one who cared for people, and it showed in his face.

Your da, he was sayin' fuck all to anyone. Christ, he wouldn't open his cheeper, and I could hear them in the next cell, roarin' their fuckin' heads off at him, tellin' him to say somethin' – anythin' – goadin' him with every sick, vile taunt they could think of, the whole works. With me, it was different. I was quotin' various chapters of *Paradise Lost* and *Paradise Regained* to them, and those uneducated bastards thought I'd cracked and was ready for the funny farm, big time. "Give me the liberty to know, to utter, and to argue freely, accordin' to conscience, above all other liberties", I was sayin'. And they'd chop me on the back of the neck or whack me in the nuts, thinkin' to quieten me, so they could talk themselves.' Dan's eyes glistened.

'They never did quieten me that week, Seamus, and I ended up talkin' me fuckin' self hoarse. They never will. I've been a thrand bastard for a long time now – probably will be until the day I die. Same as your da was, same as ye are yourself. The childhood shows the man, as mornin' shows the day – there's a grain of truth in that, all right. But it wasn't so with Billy Flannagan.

'He wasn't a weak man but he'd never been hoisted before. I'd been hoisted twice before, me and your da both. But Billy, he didn't know what to expect, so he listened to what they were sayin'. And they told him it was a certainty that it was all gonna happen – and sooner rather than later, with him inside unable to tell anyone what he knew – if he didn't at least offer them somethin', anythin'. So he confirmed to them that most of the Boys were thinkin' of goin' over the border until things died down – said he'd try and convince the others to do the same, though he offered them a little more than he should have, he knew that much himself. He told them where a few hard-heads were stayin', where a few weapons had been dumped.' Dan frowned, then shrugged a shoulder. 'Ye see, they're crafty cunts that way. They get one bit, they bleed another bit, holdin' that first bit over your head, sayin' they'll tell your mates, your kin, shit like that. Crafty bastards, but that's how they operate. And of course, the rest, ye know. Two young fellas were killed in the invasion. Only two, but two is more than enough if they're your own. Two unarmed innocents who had just stepped out of their houses to watch the mighty British war machine making its way into the estates. And that wasn't easy to watch.' Dan sighed. 'It never is.'

Seamus dropped his head, aware of the lull. He wished the older man would finish talking, though he hadn't a clue as to what he would do when he did so. His head was pounding, the veins in his temples pulsating in an angry rhythm.

'But, like I sais, Billy was a people person,' Dan continued, wearily. 'He did what he did for his people. It was the lesser of two evils, as he saw it. Or so he believed. But his words had cost the life of his best friend, and he couldn't live with the guilt. He told me all about it one night as we were drinkin' – said I should have him shot, said he couldn't live no more with the guilt of your da's death hangin' over him. I told him that one death was enough, that ultimately he'd maybe saved thousands of lives by doin' what he did. But he was a people person, Seamus,' Dan repeated, softly, sadly. 'He believed that one life gone was one life too many. There was only one way to pay for that, accordin' to him. A few weeks later, he took his own with a handgun, no explanation, no nothin'. The reasons too were left out, so that no more would suffer than was necessary. Always thinkin' of others, Billy, that was the kind of him to the last. Me, I was in Galway at the time, seven or eight people with me when the news came down. Aye, a people person, thinkin' of everyone but himself to the last.'

Seamus looked at him, then looked away. Everything Dan McGeady was saying could have been just as true as everything the Special Branch man had told him. Shades of grey upon shades of grey. He didn't know what to believe any more. 'Aye, well even if that's the case,' he said, acidly, 'ye let me ma believe that me da was a tout. What kind of a thing was that to do? Ye must have seen what it did to her life – what it did to her personally. What it fuckin' did to me! What sort of a fuckin' thing was that to do to anyone?' Seamus snarled, bitterly.

Dan McGeady shrugged lamely. 'Ye can imagine the way she would have taken it from me. My explanation would have been looked upon as the savin' of me own skin, nothin' more. One more name tainted, one more controversy stirred up several months after your da's death, just when things were settlin' into place. Just when I believed – and I was obviously wrong, so ye have me heartfelt apology there – that your ma was makin' her way back up off the floor. Ye could never tell with her, y'see. She looked like she took it on the chin, and I knew no better – didn't want to cause her any further grief. So sometimes less is more. And – ye can believe it or not if ye want – I was tryin' to take a leaf out of Billy's book on that one. The lesser of two evils. Tell her, or leave it to die its own death. Still, it's up to you what you believe. I've done all that I can do to make it as plain and credible as I can. So . . . '

'So I'm in the shit because of you, then?'

Dan McGeady looked at him hard. 'I didn't live your life, Seamus. We're each the sum total of what has happened – or what we let happen to us – in our own lives. And we each make our own decisions. If she had known, your ma might have ended up a bitter wee woman, cursin' Billy Flannagan to death, hatin' me – that would never have changed, I'm certain of that. Hatin' the world and God forever, perhaps, because she'd have been sure in her heart of your da's innocence. Maybe she'd never have recovered. The only reason she did recover was because she had her beliefs. Strong-hearted, courageous, and only her beliefs brought her back from the edge. Though she had her doubts too as to your da's innocence, and they – as small as they undoubtedly were – held her in check, stopped her goin' off at a tangent to seek vengeance. Beliefs tainted with doubts, they keep ye sane and normal. Too much of one, you're a zealot. Too much of the other, you're liable to lie down forever. Your ma had the right mixture. She got up, eventually. She got on with it, I can say no more than that.

'You, on the other hand – you're a strong-minded wee lad. Maybe a bit too strong-minded for your own good at the moment, but that's neither here nor there. You've gathered that strength, I'm sure, because you've had to face the world the fuckin' hard way. But you've come through too, somethin' ye might never have done if your da had lived on and become merely a number, a statistic, a man with a past and future no different than many others. As it was, he was a hero, of sorts. Maybe not to the Brits or the loyalists, but then they have their own heroes, don't they?' Dan smiled.

'Created by war, created by lesser men, our heroes shine because we need them, because our own lives would be nothin' without them. And as much as we claim to despise them, to scold their actions, we often secretly admire such people. Not many people know about your da, of course, because he's just another man among many who shaped history, who shaped the world – our own small world – by doin' what he thought best. But those relevant in his life do now, and that should be enough. Still, when it all boils down to it, ye can't hold me responsible for things I had no control over, can ye?'

'It seems to me as if ye have no control over anythin' at all.'
He looked at Eddie McGeady through hate-filled eyes. The boy
merely smiled.

'I'm not runnin' the world,' Dan McGeady said, evenly. 'I'm
doin' me best, but I'm not fuckin' God. Causes can't always take
care of the myriad personalities that fight for them. Still, I'll help
ye out now, if I can.'

Seamus got up suddenly. Eddie McGeady went to rise, but
Seamus pulled the gun out from his waistband. The youth sat
back down again quickly, pale. 'Nah, you've helped me enough
already,' Seamus said, 'and I'm deep enough in the shite without
you throwin' me both ends of a rope. I'll help me fuckin' self
from now on, the way every other fucker in the world does.'

'Jesus, Seamy,' Paddy Monaghan gasped, his arms on the side
of the armchair, uncertain as to whether he should rise or not.
'Christ, what the fuck are ye doin'? Ye can't do that.'

Seamus snorted in disgust. 'Why not, Paddy? Everyone else
does. It seems to be the only thing that anyone in this fuckin'
country understands. Violence, or the threat of it. It's the only
thing that quietens people down for a while and makes them
listen to others. I'm beginnin' to think it's the only fuckin' way
forward.'

Dan shook his head sadly. 'Have I got me own James Earl
Ray, me own Lee fuckin' Harvey Oswald here? Get to ye that
much, did he, Seamus? Christ Almighty, I didn't give that fucker
Connors way enough credit, really, I never!'

'I'm shootin' no one. I just want to get the fuck out of here,
nothin' more. I've just listened to enough fuckin' crap from
everyone the last few hours and I've heard enough. I'm goin'. I
just don't want anyone tryin' to stop me, nothin' else.'

Dan raised the palms of his hands. 'Fair enough, Seamus.

Can't argue with that. You've said your bit, now you're headin' off. Though fuck knows where ye think you're goin'.' He looked at Seamus evenly for a moment, seemingly not too alarmed. 'I take it that's Dave's gun,' he said, eventually. 'You're not gonna look too good to the police now, are ye, Seamus? They likely know he was away meetin' someone tonight. Likely know exactly who it is, as well. So when they get there and find a stiff, and you and the man's gun both missin', shit, that's not gonna look too good at all. They're gettin' fucked off losin' their men that way – probably want to shoot ye on sight. Armed and dangerous and on the run, believed to be involved in a murder set-up, maybe in the murder itself. You could have shot Connors with his own gun – the forensics are goin' to take a while with that one.

'And in the meantime, do ye think that, when they see ye out and about, they're just gonna call ye over and ask ye a few questions to help eliminate ye from their enquiries? Or do ye think maybe they're gonna follow their shoot-to-kill policy, same way they always fuckin' do? And if they do let ye live,' Dan McGeady continued, airily, 'do ye think they're gonna let ye out of the slammer before you're seventy-five and pissin' into a nappy, 'cause ye can't make it to the bogs in time? Not unless ye have somethin' for them, of course,' Dan said, evenly. 'Then it'd be a different matter.' He looked between Paddy and Seamus once more, his expression blank. 'Then you'll get a bit of sympathy, a cup of tea, a wee safe house in England along with that wee girl of yours. Sure were ye not goin' across there anyway?'

Seamus looked hard at Paddy. The older youth obviously couldn't keep his mouth shut, either under the influence or not. Paddy sighed loudly and looked away. 'C'mon, Paddy,' Seamus said, suddenly. 'We're goin', gettin' the fuck out of here. The smell of bullshit in here is somethin' awful.'

Paddy Monaghan looked between Dan McGeady and Seamus.

'Aye, Paddy,' Dan said, smiling. 'You take care of him. Take him wherever it is he's goin'. But don't forget, I offered to help ye if the worst comes to the worst, Seamus Doherty. And make sure you're watchin' your back.' He paused a moment, his eyes neutral. 'Because the cops, they'll be lookin' for ye.'

Seamus nodded grimly and backed out of the room, Paddy Monaghan following him. Seamus maintained his distance all the way out to the car, watching as the slats of the blinds were separated, Dan McGeady's eyes never leaving him. Paddy Monaghan too was staring at Seamus, his face as white as a ghost, the older boy's eyes wide in disbelief at all that had occurred. He got into the car and hurriedly urged Seamus to do the same.

'We're fucked now,' Paddy Monaghan said, in muted disbelief. 'Jesus, I can't believe what ye just did there now, Seamus Doherty. Are ye some sort of a stumer, or somethin'? I mean, are ye really some sort of a simple bastard?'

Seamus rounded on him. 'What fuckin' choice did I have? What fuckin' choice have I ever had?'

Paddy rammed the car into first gear, chewing at his top lip and sitting there in silence until they were on the Strand Road, turning onto the Buncrana Road to avoid the town – to avoid what he knew would be a heavy police presence further down the road, an effective cordon, cars pulled in at the roadside, searches, harassment. As he gazed into the sky, shivering, he became aware of the helicopter in the distance. It was a while before he spoke.

'If ye think ye had no choice before,' he said ominously, with a shake of his head, 'then let me tell ye, Seamus, you've even less fuckin' choice now.'

FOURTEEN

Paddy pulled the car in hard halfway up the Duncreggan Road. Seamus frowned, perplexed as to why his friend would stop here. 'What are ye doin', Paddy?' he asked. 'Don't ye think we'd be as well gettin' in somewhere off the road?' Edgy, awaiting a rotating blue neon to turn down from the Northland, aware that the helicopter would be watching the roads for irrational vehicle movement. 'You're in as much danger as I am out here.'

Paddy didn't seem to be concerned with the danger that could come flying up or down the street at any moment. He was looking at the gun in Seamus's lap and brooding darkly. 'You've been fidgetin' with that fuckin' thing ever since we left Dan's house, Seamy!' he said, angrily. 'And I don't know whether ye realise it or not, but you're pointin' the fuckin' thing in my direction.' His eyes were accusing. 'Ye plannin' on pullin' the fuckin' trigger on me, is that it?'

Seamus looked down at his hand. It was no longer trembling, but Paddy was right. The gun was facing in the older boy's direction. He didn't think he had positioned it that way intentionally, though he knew he might have done so subconsciously. Then he realised he wasn't sure what he knew for certain any more. 'No, of course not,' he replied.

'Well, give it to me then. I know a hell of a lot more about guns than you do.' Seamus looked at him blankly, indecisive. Paddy shook his head, biting his lip. He slammed his palms on the steering wheel, making Seamus jump. 'Right, then, if you don't trust me enough to give me the gun, then stick it in your fuckin' trousers, out of the way. If a patrol stops us and you have that thing . . . ' He keyed the ignition. 'Just stick it out of the fuckin' way, that's all. And thanks, Seamy,' he added, bitterly. 'I'm tryin' to get ye the fuck out of the hole you've dug yourself, and ye think I'm gonna shoot ye. Christ!' he muttered, releasing the handbrake and moving off towards the Northland. 'Thanks very fuckin' much!'

Seamus stuck the gun in his belt and zipped his coat up a little. 'Well, what way would you be thinkin' if everythin' that had happened to me happened to you,' Seamus asked, frowning heavily because of his guilt. 'I've got the UVF after me one minute, lookin' to blow me away because of me love life. I've got the RUC and the SAS lookin' to stiff me because they think I'm a killer. And the fuckin' 'RA think I'm a tout, so they're probably lookin' to empty me too, big time. Jesus, Paddy, what the fuck would you think? Who the fuck would you trust?'

Paddy looked at him moodily, then looked away. He pulled the car in at the traffic lights at the top of the hill. Seamus glanced a little to his left along the Northland. The flow of traffic coming from the direction of the Rock Road had reduced to a trickle, slowed by the swirl of blue neon atop chunks of heavy grey armour plating, which indicated the presence of police jeeps. He put a hand up against his face, wishing the traffic lights green. Seconds later, Paddy took a right and went over the Northland, indicated left at the bottom of the dip and turned onto the Glen Road.

'I'm gonna sort things out for ye, Seamy,' Paddy said, with a sigh, a few moments later. 'But we have to remain calm about the whole thing. I'll sort it out but ye have to trust me.'

'Aye, well Dan McGeady sais you'll take care of me, all right.

But everyone's lookin' to do that, like I say. Why should I trust ye?'

Paddy laughed wryly. 'Because I'm your friend, Seamy, that's why.' He pulled the car to a halt outside a telephone box and sat for a second, thinking. 'You're plannin' on goin' away anyhow, aren't ye?'

Seamus nodded warily.

Paddy drummed his fingers on the wheel. 'Where's the girl at now?'

'She's in my house, waitin' for me. Ye gonna take me there?'

'You're not on the phone, are ye?'

Seamus shook his head.

'It's just that we can't go near the house. We can phone her, tell her to meet up with us later.'

Seamus sat there silently, trying to think of a way of his own – a way to gain some control over the situation. His mind, however, was a blank.

'Seamy, you're gonna have to start trustin' me here,' Paddy said, thickly. 'I'm goin' against everythin' in the Green Book here, puttin' my fuckin' life on the line for ye. You're gonna have to start helpin' me out a little, if we're to get away with this.'

Seamus nodded grimly, then gave him Sadie's number. Paddy got out of the car, went into the phone booth and rang the number. Seamus looked at him as he stood there making the call, Paddy's face lined, serious. He wondered whether the world was ever going to stop turning at such a dizzying speed and allow him some respite. Paddy was speaking, heavily involved in conversation, though Seamus couldn't pick out anything from the muffle of words. It was two minutes before the older youth returned to the car. He sparked the engine into life, drove off up the Glen Road, turned and drove off along the back road above Glenowen.

'Well?' Seamus let the question hang.

'She'll meet up with us in the mornin'.'

'Where?' Alarmed, but not wanting to show it.

'Donegal.'

Seamus sat there. County Donegal was immediately over the border. In southern Ireland, if you were a Protestant. In the Republic, Éire or the Free State, if you were a Catholic. Still, it wouldn't have mattered what you were if you had to traverse the checkpoints that dotted the three hundred and twenty miles or so of border territory. You still had to pass through them and you still had to give your name and address, provide identification. And by now – if what Dan McGeady had said was true – the Brits and the police would have had a very accurate description of Seamus. He felt his stomach somersault, remembering Dan McGeady's words. They wouldn't be looking to stop him, to make him surrender. On a dark night such as this, they wouldn't be hanging around to see whether Seamus and his driver were going to come quietly or try and race away into the Republic.

'And how do ye reckon we get over there? Half the fuckin' country lookin' for me, and you think we're just gonna sail over the fuckin' border?' Seamus shook his head, wondering if he shouldn't just climb out of the car, race off into the night, go and sit somewhere in silence and try to figure it all out for himself.

Paddy looked at him – the sort of look you'd reserve for someone you hated. Then he turned the car up a dark country road that led off up onto Sheriff's Mountain. The area was owned mostly by farmers; some of the land was reportedly going to be used in the future for new housing estates. There was no proper lighting on these back roads, their routes narrowly circuitous, and treacherous if driven on at speed. Paddy dimmed the headlights and drove at a moderate speed along the roads, cutting off every now and then at an unmarked fork, until Seamus lost track of the convoluted route. All the time, he was wondering whether Paddy Monaghan was putting his own life at risk or whether this was just another scheme to ensnare Seamus even further. After all, they were now in the middle of nowhere. Paddy claimed to have rung Elaine but he could equally have rung Dan McGeady and got new orders. A pig-farm, a pit of lime. He shivered, those thoughts making him edgy.

'Why'd she not meet us now?' The doubts were threatening to rip his mind apart.

'She'll meet us in the mornin',' Paddy replied, as if speaking to a petulant child.

'Then what did she say? What did you say to her. Did she ask why we were . . . ?'

'I got talkin' to Sadie, your neighbour,' Paddy said, evenly. He raised a stalling hand as Seamus was about to bluster out more enquiries. Seamus took a deep breath, fighting back the panic. 'The Brits and cops raided your house half an hour back,' Paddy continued. 'They're lookin' for ye, and they're still hoverin' about the street. But your ma's all right, Sadie sais. A wee bit upset, because they said ye set the cop up, and they gave her a wee bit of abuse about your da and stuff. But otherwise she's grand. She's in Sadie's now, along with Elaine . . . '

Seamus pictured his ma standing there in Dunree Gardens with a rolling pin in her hand, hoped Michael Stewart had stopped her going off the rails, hoped she wasn't thinking that he'd gone and done what they said he'd done, wondered if he could get talking to her soon, so that he could put her mind at rest. She wouldn't believe it, of course. She knew her son, always had done, though she might have her doubts. Doubts and beliefs, a little of each. They would keep her sane. He'd phone her first thing in the morning, he told himself. Phone her and let her know that he'd be going away for a while, until things blew over.

If they ever did. 'And Elaine? What . . . ?'

A deep breath. 'I didn't get talkin' to Elaine . . . '

'Right.' Trying to remain calm, but feeling as if he'd take a lunge at Paddy in a second if the older youth didn't come up with something better than that.

'But . . . '

'Aye, Christ, will ye get to the fuckin' point!'

Paddy swerved the car to avoid a jutting hedgerow, focusing into the blackness of the night, no more than ten to fifteen feet of road at a stretch visible to him. Not looking at Seamus, he said, 'I told Sadie to tell Elaine that she's to drive to Donegal in the mornin'. I left a number that she's to phone from a call box any time after seven, firstly to let us know that she's arrived, secondly to get directions on where to meet us. They might follow her, y'see – see if she'll lead them to us. If they hold her at the checkpoint, it won't for long. She hasn't done anythin', and it's you they're lookin' for, so everythin' should be all right.'

'Who might follow her?'

Paddy shrugged, his face serious. 'There's that fuckin' many, Seamy boy, that it's a question I may well be askin' you meself.'

*

Paddy suddenly turned the car into a dark laneway, stepping on the brakes as a four-barred steel gate loomed out of the blackness, the crunch of gravel beneath the car wheels indecently loud. A dog barked somewhere in the night as the older youth got out of the car, released a latch on the gate and peered furtively back down the road they had travelled for several moments, head raised, watching, listening. The older youth then got back in the car and drove into what seemed to be a farmyard. Seamus held his breath as the overpowering smells of manure and silage came wafting in through the air vents. He noticed a dull light going on in the small farmhouse up ahead, thin shafts of pale light spilling out from the door, which was slightly ajar. He thought he heard the click of something metallic and baulked at the sound, ready to turn and run, his insides stirring, memories resurfacing.

'It's me, Albert – Paddy Monaghan,' Paddy declared loudly, his hands held well away from his sides. A second, subdued click, torchlight directed across the yard in their direction, the beam rising up, to shine momentarily into both their faces.

'Paddy Monaghan,' the voice on the other end of the light said, in a bright whisper. 'Another midnight run, is it?' The light ran quickly over Seamus from head to foot, his torso of prime concern. 'Injured, is he? Shot? I heard on the news there that there was a shootin' incident somewhere down the road, but the reports were sketchy. Is the lad for the hospital in Letterkenny, then?'

Paddy laughed and went up to the man. 'Nah, this'll be an early-mornin' run, if that's all right. Might need to kip on your sofa for a few hours as well, if that's all right too.'

The older man nodded, turned and walked slowly back towards the house. Paddy summoned Seamus forward with his hand, and they followed the old man towards the slightly open door of the farmhouse.

The man was carrying a shotgun, which he broke, emptied of shells and then deposited in the corner of the first room, a pine-furnished kitchen complete with range. He didn't look back at the two youths as he did so, his eyes low, focusing on everything but those two. 'Not a problem. Ye want tea, then?'

Paddy shook his head. 'Nah, you get on back to your bed. I'll sort the sleepin' arrangements out. I'll be away before you're up, anyhow.'

'Ye know me,' the old man said, smiling, and moved into the second room. 'I'm an early riser. Up at six and never later. Habit of a lifetime. Might catch ye on the hop.'

'Well, I'll be away and back before that,' Paddy said, returning the smile. He followed the man through, beckoning Seamus to do the same. 'It'll take a good man to catch this boyo out.'

The older man shrugged as they entered the sitting room, with its comfortable and utilitarian furniture, dying peat fire, low beams and uneven floors. He moved towards another door at the furthest end, his gaze still elsewhere. 'Night then, lads. And good luck.'

Seamus and Paddy followed the sounds of his low footfalls moving slowly up creaking stairs. Seamus realised that the old man had hardly looked at him, hadn't even asked a name. When Seamus mentioned this to him, Paddy said that the old man was used to doing this – that if he was ever questioned he could honestly say that he hadn't really seen anyone or anything.

Paddy went over and crouched low beside the fire, then stuck some peat on the red-orange embers. 'Have a seat, Seamy boy, get yourself a few hours' kip.' He indicated that Seamus was getting the armchair nearest the fire. He moved away from the fire, lay down on the settee and propped pillows behind his head, not even removing his coat or shoes. 'I'll have ye over the border in a few hours.'

'What am I gonna do then?' Seamus asked, with a sigh, sitting down heavily on the chair in front of the fire. The exhaustion got him then. His legs felt heavy, sore, his arms tired. His eyelids were stinging too, tiredness finding him there in the renewed heat, though he doubted if he'd get to sleep.

'I'll sort it all out,' Paddy told him, with a wink. The older boy closed his eyes, arms behind his head. 'Have you across the shuck in England in a few days' time – a week or two at the latest. It might take a bit of plannin', but not that much. Send ye to the Isle of Man for a few days and then across to the mainland in a fishin' boat. Give ye the name of a friend who'll sort ye with a new social security and medical card, under the name of some guy who died around about the same time ye were born, give or take a year. Sure that's a voter's trick, that one – the reason why sometimes ye get a hundred and ten per cent votin' to each area of the North.' Seamy looked at him doubtfully.

Paddy laughed and opened one eye, mischievousness sparkling there. 'Nah, that's an exaggeration there, Seamy, but it happens, all right. Ye can take the rest from there yourself. The girl's family will get ye a job. Ye keep your head low, it'll all blow over. We do this stuff all the time.'

'Ye make it sound so fuckin' easy. It's not as simple as that – it can't be.'

'There are ways round everythin', Seamy boy. Ways round everythin'.'

'And how are ye plannin' on gettin' me across the border, come to that?' Seamus asked. Paddy hadn't removed the heavily ingrained doubt, no matter his efforts, and Seamus still expected answers.

Paddy smiled again. 'Like I say, Seamy, there are ways around everythin'.'

*

They were in an old Hillman Hunter that had long since seen better days, the engine grumbling beneath the bonnet, trundling along a thin, bumpy, earthen track, high hedgerows and barbed fencing to either side. Shallow ruts had been cut in the deeply compressed soil through time, the path rising and falling like a mini roller coaster that played heavily on the suspension. Seamus was sure another few hundred yards of this would shake the car to pieces. High gorse and bramble scraped the sides of the car now and then, and Paddy shifted gears clumsily to combat the vehicle's reluctance to make headway.

He had roused Seamus from a fitful sleep shortly after five by abruptly opening the living-room curtains, thin wisps of daylight breaking broadly across the horizon. Seamus had woken shivering, not believing that he had had the nerve to fall asleep in the first place.

'I've checked the area,' Paddy had told him, straightening the cushions on the sofa. 'Time to go. We can eat on the other side. Ye all right with that?'

Seamus had nodded pensively and Paddy had led him out into the muck-strewn concrete farmyard, past uninterested cows locked behind steel gates, further down past a placid black-and-white-patched collie dog which was lying, one eye opened, on a bed of straw in the furthest corner of the yard. The air had been chilly, the ground wet in places, dry in others, a faint mizzle having fallen in the earlier hours of that morning. Paddy had led him towards the car and told him to get in the back – to lie down low against the seat. Then they had set off. Now Seamus felt his stomach rumbling, nauseous with all the jolting.

'H-how . . . ?' He steadied himself, head lifting a little to regain some sort of equilibrium. 'How can ye just drive across?' Another deep breath. 'They have bollards across all the roads that don't have checkpoints on them.'

'"Roads", Seamus, that's the key word there. The Brits have

all the main roads blocked off, but these dirt tracks and laneways are roads too, are they not? Unapproved they might be, but roads they are, nonetheless. Not very comfortable, mind ye, but if ye criss-cross through enough of them, take a turn through the odd field, back-track this way and that . . . ' Paddy swiftly turned the wheel, a growling thunderstorm of gorse lashing the car, the hulk rising, to drop on the jarred suspension. Seamus swallowed hard. 'Then Bob's your uncle. And slow as ye like, that's the reason for the battered-out car. Belongs to a farmer, the Brits'll be thinkin'. Albert, they see him goin' to his work all the time, and his land skirts the border. After months of watchin', they see him and his routine, and they usually don't see anythin' else.' Another bump, a hard turn left, reversing to gain momentum as the ground rose abruptly, then quickly forward as it fell away again, the gears meshing in an angry growl.

Seamus was lost, and felt the hair standing on the back of his neck. He could have been going anywhere: he'd never felt as vulnerable in his life. It would only take a matter of split seconds for an SAS patrol to throw spiked caltrops across the dirt road, a thin second more for the tyres to give out, another for the shooting to begin. He shivered briskly, knowing that his life was completely in someone else's hands, and hating that thought.

The gun was all that made him feel safe, even though he'd never fired one before. That and thoughts that he'd soon meet up with Elaine. Elaine, who could change entire situations with one or two calming words – who could stand within a yard of him and make him ready to take on the world. He felt sick then, though it wasn't only the car grinding and bumping against the road that made him feel that way. The claustrophobia of the whole terrifying situation was killing him. Elaine wasn't here and, even though he was with Paddy Monaghan, he was more alone than he had ever been. He fought the tide of nausea by concentrating on the brambles lashing the windscreen, by watching the sky turn faintly pink and birds fly from the bushes as the car approached, their squawks signifying their anger at this disturbance.

It was with immense relief that, some thirty minutes later, he heard Paddy Monaghan say, 'There we are, Seamy, me boy. You're in Free Ireland, as near home in a boat as can be.'

Seamus dared to peek up from behind the front seat. When he did so, all he could see were cows, fields, hedgerows, stone walls and more fields. He didn't see anything that could have marked the beginning of the Southern state. A cottage in the distance, a further line of terraced houses high on a sharp rise, small and lost in the encircling ring of hills. 'Are ye sure?' he asked uncertainly.

'Aye, as sure as I'll ever be. Now get back down, Seamy, me boy,' Paddy called back. 'We've still a little ways to go yet.'

Seamus sighed and lowered his head. Brooding thoughts of the gun attack on the Special Branch man filled his mind once more, threatening to chase his sanity away. Hurriedly, he brushed those brutal memories away, replacing them once more with thoughts of Elaine.

*

The small chapel was high on a hill overlooking a great spread of farms – sprawling green and brown pastures for miles around – and was surrounded by an uneven stone wall broken by tall gates which were black and rusted, fixed firmly and immovably at an angle into thick seams of briar and wild grass. Seamus spied the weathered-green copper-clad steeple first, daring to stick his head up a little to peer out the front window as the day brightened perceptibly and the main roads eased the wear and tear on the car's suspension. A small graveyard with tumbled headstones and short stone obelisks spread up and behind the chapel, crabgrass and wild flowers growing over and around the graves. Paddy drove the car along the drive that led up to the chapel and around the back, secreting it behind a small outhouse. There he and Seamus got out of the car and the older youth urged Seamus to help him pull a tarpaulin across its rusted metal body. They walked around the front of the stone chapel, Seamus stretching, easing the coldness out of his bones, Paddy once more taking care to scan the thin, winding approach road below.

The thick oak doors were shut firmly together. Paddy searched around on the high ledge above the doorway, fumbling for a key he said he knew was there. Seamus surveyed the countryside, looking for familiar landmarks on the periphery, but finding none. He didn't know where it was exactly – though he knew it was somewhere in Donegal – and Paddy wouldn't say, telling him that it was better for them both if, from now on, he knew only what he had to know. The older youth would only repeat that they were now both as safe as houses; he would say nothing more on the subject. The view of rolling hills and deep green vales didn't settle Seamus any, however, the feeling of alarm that he had felt ever since last night never having left him completely. A wind stirred as they entered the cold interior of the run-down chapel, and Seamus shivered, surprised to see no one about the place.

'Deserted,' Paddy told him, brightly. 'Though there's food and tea out in the vestry, an old gas stove too and a little cutlery. At least there was the last time I was here, and the lads always take care to keep it replenished. Should be more than enough for two hungry men who might need breakfast. I hope you've a good hand for cookin'. Me, I'm the lousiest chef in the land.'

Seamus nodded and surveyed the dusty pews, the abandoned altar and the webs hanging across the arched roof of the chapel, slits of mosaic light shining wide through the remaining cobwebs of stained-glass windows, to spread colourfully across broad sections of the interior. Seamus shivered, ill at ease in the surroundings, wishing that Elaine would hurry up, and wondering if she'd left Derry yet – if she'd even made the first of the phone calls that Paddy had said she would have to make. He looked at his watch: ten past seven. 'Aye, ye want it now?' he asked, dully.

'A few minutes is time enough. Settle yourself down there for a minute, get yourself together. Have a fag.' Paddy offered him a cigarette and lit one for himself. 'Ye feelin' all right now? Or at least a wee bit better?' His eyes searched Seamus's, seeing the dismay there. 'You're in the South. Everythin's gonna be grand.'

Seamus took a seat on the nearest pew and nodded, thinking. He knew he was supposed to feel the same relief he felt every time he crossed the border, now that he was in the South of Ireland, away from the troubles of the North. But this time he felt no safer. Everyone knew that, although they were definitely off-limits in terms of being a part of the war zone, Donegal, Leitrim, Monaghan, Louth and Cavan – the five counties in the Republic directly across the border – had been a springboard for the IRA throughout its entire Northern campaign. Donegal, especially – despite its graceful religious tolerance on all sides, despite the fact that the Orange marches held there annually were regarded almost like carnivals by every section of the community – had often been used as a sanctuary by republicans, the lonely border farmhouses and mainly deserted strands and coves used as somewhere to store arms safely, and somewhere to launch attacks on the armed forces of the North and retreat to safely afterwards.

Also, the SAS response units hadn't been exactly truthful at times in declaring that they acknowledged that the border was sacrosanct, chasing into the South as they did at times after IRA operatives fleeing the aftermath of an operation. And the loyalists had struck here in the South too over the last few years, bombing Monaghan and Dublin in response to Willie Whitelaw's power-sharing executive and the Sunningdale Council of Ireland. If anything, Seamus mused sourly, the place was even more dangerous than the North at times: there was probably as much – or more – to worry about on this side of the border as on the other.

Paddy stubbed out his cigarette and waited for Seamus to do the same. Then the older youth led the way out to the sacristy. Seamus entered the room. It was sparsely furnished, with six wooden seats, a fridge, a gas stove and an old table, above which were two cupboards. Paddy rummaged around in the cupboards amongst an assortment of tins and pulled out tea bags. 'Anythin' there ye want, Seamy?'

Seamus looked in the cupboard. 'Not really,' he said. 'I'll eat later.'

Paddy shrugged. 'Aye, I can wait meself.' In the fridge he found half a carton of milk and a packet of biscuits. 'Not exactly hardy fare,' he said, with a sigh. 'I thought there was more but, fuck it, it'll do for now.' He put a kettle full of water on the gas stove, struck a match to it and then offered Seamus another cigarette. The air in the small room was cold and chill, a downdraft blowing in through a broken pane of glass in the window above. Seamus shivered and accepted the cigarette, sucking the comforting nicotine deep into his lungs. Paddy pulled his coat closer to his body and moved back into the main body of the deserted chapel.

'Keep an eye on the kettle, Seamus,' he said. 'I'm goin' to make a phone call.'

'Where?' Seamus said. He followed Paddy to the door, fighting to contain the panic in his voice.

Paddy smiled and pointed to another, smaller room at the far side of the altar. 'Calm it down a little, Seamy, for Christ's sakes! The hard work's over. I'm gonna phone, see if your girl has contacted that number yet. Then we're gonna meet up with her.' He looked at Seamus and broke into a grin. 'The hard work's over,' he repeated, with a wink. 'C'mon, chill out a little.'

Seamus drew his coat about him and shivered. 'Wouldn't be hard to do that in this place.'

'That's more like it. Develop a sense of humour – it works wonders for a man.' Paddy walked into the smaller room and closed the door behind him. Seamus placed tea bags in the pot when the water had reached the boil, turned down the gas and put two cups on the table. He was about to add the milk but then got a whiff of it – sour, curdled, maybe a week or more old. He threw the carton into a nearby waste bin. He searched the cupboards but there was no sugar to be found. Paddy came back into the sacristy a minute later, his grin still there.

'Elaine phoned the number and she was given directions about where to find us. She left your ma's after seven. The cops had hung around the Creggan for a while, then they'd left. She'll be here in another hour or so.' Paddy rubbed his hands together and blew into them. 'Now where's that tea? I'm bloody freezin'. Be glad to get back to the North, get into me bed.'

'It's black.'

'Aye, whatever. The hardships one has to endure, eh?'

Seamus sat down on the edge of the table, the cup warming his hands. He was thinking of his mother, how she'd do the same when she wasn't slightly interested in drinking tea. 'Me ma must be goin' out of her mind with worry', was all he could think of saying.

Paddy shrugged and sipped at his own drink. 'Things happen, Seamy, and I can't say I'm happy with the way this one went down. Really, I'm not. If I'd had my way . . . ' He left the thought unfinished. 'She'll be all right. She has Michael to look after her, sure doesn't she?'

Seamus nodded despondently, his eyes moist.

'Hey, I'll get a chat with her when I get back. Cheer yourself up a bit. This thing will blow over. You'll see her again. Just look on this as a break, or somethin'. You were thinkin' of headin' off soon anyhow, right?' Seamus dropped his head and nodded. 'Aye,' Paddy said, smiling. 'Well, it looks like you might have to go a bit earlier, that's all.'

'I can never go back.' That stark fact cut him like a knife and he clenched his jaw tight together, fighting back the tears. Paddy came over and put an arm on his shoulder, vainly trying to shake the sorrow from him.

'Ye can sometime. Sure what's to stop ye after the end of the month? When the op's over, the 'RA won't have a word to say against ye. They've fuck all on ye anyway. If Dan asks me, I'll just say he's bein' paranoid. If I say nothin', he can prove nothin' – end of story. The cops . . . well, ye can explain that ye panicked, ran off because ye thought the 'RA were tryin' to kill ye. They'll know ye never had a hand in it and they'll try to keep ye sweet, thinkin' you're gonna turn eventually. We'll organise somethin' to combat that at a later stage, eh? And Elaine's brother, sure he'll be curlin' up his toes soon enough, won't he? The way he's runnin' around with his head in the air thinkin' he fuckin' is someone, sure it comes to everyone who does that.' Paddy grinned, ducking his head to catch Seamus's eyes, playfully grabbing the back of his neck.

'Aye, maybe.' Despair finding him once more.

'Aye, *certainly*, ye mean. And until then, sure ye can head off to the Big Smoke. Get a job, relax, set yourself up for life. Sure maybe ye won't want to come back in time. Maybe your ma and Michael can visit ye over there. Maybe me and Eileen can too, dependin' on whether or not they allow me past the fuckin' docks, me a suspected terrorist and shit!'

Seamus caught the grin and started smiling. 'C'mon, lift the head,' Paddy said. 'Bring your tea and we'll go look out for the wee woman.'

Seamus nodded and got off the table, tea in hand. They walked down the aisle, towards the arched door. Paddy pulled it open a fraction, eyeing the winding thread of road below. 'We've seen a lot,' he said, suddenly. 'Been forced to grow up very quickly, the whole lot of us, haven't we?'

Seamus nodded thoughtfully, frowning. 'Aye, too fuckin' right we have. I feel like I've lived about twenty years or so in the last few days. The Branch man was tryin' to set me up to talk, ye know. He told me all that shit about McGeady and I nearly believed him.' Paddy nodded, sipped at his tea and produced another cigarette, chain-smoking them. 'Then Dan told me all that shit too and I haven't a notion as to whether I believe him or not either. I won't ever fuckin' know.'

Paddy had a fag in his mouth and, with his free hand, was searching for a match in his pocket. Seamus gave him a light. 'No one ever does, Seamy. Life never goes the way ye fuckin' plan it at all, it's never like ye see in the films at all. We find out very little – less than we ever should – in this world. Some things ye just have to make your own mind up about, because there are no real or concrete answers supplied. All ye have to know is what ye are, what ye believe in and what ye expect of yourself, nothin' else. Everythin' else just falls into place around it. It always does. Maybe not always as smooth or as quick as we'd like, but aye, it always does.' Paddy's eyes narrowed, catching sight of a glimpse of metallic white on the road, between the hedges. He stubbed his fresh cigarette out underfoot and moved behind Seamus, placing his cup on the pew. 'That looks like her now.'

Seamus peered through the crack in the door. 'Aye.' Turning. 'That's . . . ' He froze. Paddy was standing there, gun in hand. For a second the world ceased turning. His eyes found Paddy's, not knowing what he saw there. Paddy smiled and stuck the gun back in his waistband, grinning broadly.

'Ye still not trust me yet, Seamy? If I'd have wanted ye dead, I could have shot ye ages ago. Sure ye know that.'

Seamus breathed out, turning back to stare out at the vehicle flitting abruptly white every now and then between the hedgerows, following the scar of the road. His chest had constricted and he fought to regain his breathing. 'Aye, I guess so, all right.'

The hand on his shoulder again. Pushing past him, eyes narrowing. 'That her then?'

'That looks like her car, aye.'

'Good, I can hear me bed callin' out for me.' Paddy's eyes swept the countryside below, then narrowed again.

Seamus caught the serious gaze. 'What is it?'

'Another car some ways behind her, seen a flash of the windows in the sunlight. Two or three minutes behind. Might be nothin'. That's why we chose this particular place. Ye can see the whole of fuckin' Donegal from here. Could be a local, though ye never know.' The gun was produced once more, the safety catch released. 'Still, it's better to be safe than sorry. I'm goin' down there.' Paddy pointed to the sorry tumble of gravestones to the left of the driveway, the high, unkempt grass. 'I'll keep an eye out when she drives in. Ye stay out of sight, leave the door slightly open, nothin' more. Just in case. All right?'

Seamus nodded reluctantly as Paddy ducked low and made ready to go out the door. He turned. 'Hey, that thing ye have in your belt, ye any idea how to use it?'

Seamus took the gun out, examining it. Paddy came back and released the safety on the Browning. 'You just point it forward, pull the trigger every time ye get an itch to do so. Ye reckon ye can do that?' Seamus nodded. 'Not at me and the girl, mind, but anyone else is fair game if they're carryin' a weapon.' He winked at Seamus and scuttled off amidst the gravestones, staying low until he reached a wide, grey obelisk. He secreted himself behind it and, his body out of sight, gave Seamus the thumbs up. Seamus moved inside the old deserted building, the increasingly distinct sound of the approaching car all he could concentrate on.

FIFTEEN

The Peugeot slowed as it reached the front of the chapel, and Seamus heard the engine being cut, the door opening, light footfalls sounding on the concrete surface of the driveway. He impulsively wanted to dive out of the door and grab Elaine, to take her hurriedly by the hand and pull her into the sanctuary of the church, to seek out some dark recess where he could conceal her from any danger. But he remembered Paddy's warning that he was to remain inside and held that almost overwhelming temptation at bay with thoughts that it would all be over in a second or so. The car most likely belonged to a local, he convinced himself – someone a hundred miles outside their immediate world, someone to whom these events were as foreign as they were perhaps to Seamus himself. Still, he felt a knot of tension in his stomach and wondered if it would all go as easily as Paddy had said it would. Drawn up against the wall, he waited in the long shadows down the left-hand side of the aisle, gun raised. Wondering still if he could shoot a real live flesh-and-blood person, if it came down to it.

'Seamus.' The familiar lilt of her voice outside in the grounds, enquiring softly, as beautiful and gentle as ever. 'Seamus, where are you?'

And then the hard revving of an engine as the second car hurtled up the driveway, impossibly fast. The screech of tyres skidding across the asphalt, a door thrown open, a gunshot.

Seamus couldn't believe what he was hearing, and at first he thought he must be imagining it – that the past was replaying itself demonically in his mind. But then another crack, the bullet ricocheting off stone, whining into the early-morning air. The sound of someone crying out, the door of the chapel being pushed quickly open, the faint patch of dappled light falling upon the aisle replaced by a long, sweeping shadow. Seamus raised his gun, ready to fire, adrenalin surging through his veins, those long moments seeming to last forever.

But the shadow materialised into Elaine, squinting nervously as her eyes adjusted to the darkness. Then she saw him and moved hurriedly towards him. Another shot rang out, cracking the air. Seamus grabbed her, his only thought to pull her inside, away from the door. She started to speak but he held her against him, hand across her mouth, moving them both into the cold safety of the shadows, fast against the cool stone wall. Stilling her with a gentle but firm hand, feeling her concern lessen a little – enough. As they stood there in the shadows another exchange of rapid, angry shots rent the air. Seamus thought of Paddy Monaghan out there in the graveyard all alone. Raising the gun, he pushed Elaine gently back into the shadows.

'Where are you goin'?' Elaine asked, eyes wet, terror clearly registering there. Oceanic blue, even here in the filtered shadows of the chapel, lost so badly that he wanted to hold her against him forever. Her hands clutching at his, fighting to pull him back, to hold him there. Gently he released them. 'You can't go out there, they'll kill you . . . ' she gasped.

'Paddy's out there. I have to help him. I have to.' Pulling away, slowly releasing himself from her clutches, his eyes begging trust. 'I'll be careful, promise.' Moving cautiously towards the door, pushing it open fractionally with his feet, alarmed by another gunshot, the

337

sounds of a sudden whimper of pain. He stood behind one oaken door and poked the gun out of the other as the shooting stopped. And then Elaine was standing there beside him, clinging onto him, at his front, with her own beseeching eyes locked firmly onto his.

'Don't go out there, Seamus. Please . . . '

Trying to pull him back away from the door, selfish fear strengthening her grip so much that he couldn't release her hands from the lapels of his coat. 'Elaine, go back inside. Quickly . . . ' He pulled away, frozen momentarily in the sunlit doorway, Elaine still clinging on to him.

He saw the black-clad figure out of the corner of his eye, the hand rising up like quicksilver, flashing as he tried to push her back inside the door. The door splintered beside him, and the fierce crack of the gunshot sounded out a fraction of a second later. Elaine released her grip on his hands and he was happy about that, thinking that, if he could just get her back inside, the danger would pass. There was only one gunman that he could see. If only he and Paddy Monaghan could both . . .

And then Elaine's movements caught his eye. She'd been moving backwards of her own volition, he thought. But then she held one hand against the door and he saw the thin beam of light splashing in through a rent the width of a pencil in the door beside her. Created by the bullet, at about the height of her chest, a strange spray of red there upon her dress. Her face registering disbelief, her breathing stalled. He reached for her as she fell forward, slumping awkwardly against him. He caught her, despite the fact that he could hardly move himself, the corners of his world blurring as the horror of that immortal second registered with him, fighting for recognition with his mind, which refused to recognise that something so terrible had dared to occur beside him once again.

Her oceanic eyes were moist still, asking, searching, saying. Disbelieving. Though suddenly a fierce pain registered there and she became weighted, her hands clutching at his shoulders, the fingers clawing with no power. He caught her up tightly by the waist, thrown into the sunlight against the opened door by the momentum of her lifeless torso. Unable to speak, wishing his life and every breath into her body and denying to himself that such a thing could ever happen to him again. Holding her silently, in disbelief, as the entire mind-numbing scene registered terrifyingly with him.

He caught sight of a surreal film of movement out of the corner of his eye. From beside a second car that had drawn hurriedly up behind the Peugeot. A four-door Cortina, drawn up at an angle on the tarmacadamed drive, passenger door lying open, one black-clad gunman lying lifelessly upon the ground beside the car, blood seeping from a large exit wound in his back. Another gunman to his front, handgun raised to his front, pointed at Seamus now. Silent, unblinking, one hand outstretched, holding the other one firm. Paddy Monaghan beside the obelisk, raising his own gun quickly in response to that movement, firing once more. The second gunman crying out as the shot hit him high in the upper arm, reeling, the fixed posture lost forever, a low, guttural curse escaping the gunman's lips. Paddy Monaghan rising awkwardly and forcing himself slowly across the graveyard through the weave of stones, one hand held tightly to his left side, the other on the gun, pointing it directly at the gunman, concentrating intently on his now impotent target. Trickles of blood flowing over that hand, his own posture inept, sagging. Righting himself against an obelisk, moving slowly forward.

Seamus raised his own gun as the second gunman regained his senses and moved fractionally towards this weapon. He fired a shot into the earth, several feet away from the man. The figure recoiled quickly and clutched fast at his arm once more, then regarded Seamus warily, silent, unblinking. He looked between the two youths, seeming to weigh up his chances, but didn't move a muscle. Seamus glanced at Elaine ever so briefly once more, not knowing if he was more angered or pained by that despairing moment of acceptance. Her eyes had closed half over, the frightened stare replaced by an unseeing, deathly glaze. Seamus lowered her gently down onto the step outside the door and sat their with her for long moments, her head resting on his lap. His eyes lifting upwards after a time, filled with hate and trained on the hooded figure.

'Down on your knees! Hands behind your head! C'mon, you fuckin' wanker, do it now!' Paddy Monaghan's voice behind that order.

Seamus turned to him. The older youth was clearly in pain. Resting wearily against another tombstone, his gun carefully following the actions of the darkly clad figure as he slowly carried out the orders. The other man's eyes cold and deliberate, firmly fixed on Paddy.

Seamus looked down at Elaine, his tears falling on her cheek, unable to stop them. He closed her eyes with a gently trembling hand, holding her tighter than he ever thought he could, her torso lying across his knees, still warm. But she was dead, he knew that then, his whole world dying along with her. He saw Paddy Monaghan stumbling across the grass, moving in the direction of the chapel doorway, gun arcing, though always firmly directed at the other assassin.

Paddy leaned against the warm chapel wall, labouring for breath, face drawn, sweat on his brow, clearly in great pain. He took a glance down at Elaine and shook his head sorrowfully. 'I'm sorry, Seamy. Jesus, it wasn't . . . supposed to end up this way. I had this . . . this sort of feelin' that things might go all right, that if we . . . ' He wiped his bloodied hand against his trousers, shivering, blinking slowly, as if it took the greatest effort. Seamus looked up at him sadly and noticed Paddy's paling skin, his gasps for breath, the sweat along his forehead. Gently he slipped out from beneath Elaine, easing her down onto the sun-washed step, as if she were made of the most delicate porcelain. Still heavily in shock, his eyes blurring with tears. He lifted his own gun and took Paddy by the elbow, allowing the older youth to use him as a crutch.

'Sit down, Paddy. I'll get ye an ambulance, right and soon. Aye, right and soon.'

'Ah, there's no need, Seamy . . . Really . . . no need.' Paddy forced a laboured smile and sat down on the step, clearly in agony, his eyes closing briefly, then opening alertly.

Seamus found himself looking at the dark-clad figure, a terrible hate building within him. Wondering how one man could find such hatred within him to perform such deeds and then just stand there remorselessly, watching the terrible unravelling of lives. His thoughts were interrupted as Paddy nearly fell off the step of the chapel, blood thick on his hands, face down against the door, gun in his lap. Seamus righted him as best he could with one hand, cautiously watching the hooded figure all the while.

'Take your mask off,' Seamus called out, angrily. He felt a weak tug on his sleeve. Paddy opened his eyes, smiling thinly, ghostly white, sweating profusely. The tug became more insistent. 'C'mon, hurry up. I want to see your fuckin' face, you bastard!'

'Let him . . . keep his mask on, Seamy.'

Seamus looked at Paddy, wondering if he was delirious. But Paddy's eyes contained that same malicious glint as always, the sanity obviously there, despite his pain. 'Maybe we're better off not knowin', y'know,' he whispered, smiling thinly. 'Sometimes we're better off not . . . knowin' the answers. And it doesn't matter . . . who pulls the trigger . . . on ye, anyhow . . . does it, Seamy?' He winced sharply, pushing his hand tighter against his ribs, the blood saturating his shirt. He fixed Seamus with a strained, painful grin. 'I'd . . . rather die . . . knowin' what I know. Knowin' . . . what I believed in has . . . ended me life. I don't want . . . to have to go thinkin' about any other stuff at this stage of the game, eh?' The smile waning.

Seamus propped him up against the door. 'You're not dyin' on me,' he said, gruffly. His voice an order. 'No one else is dyin' on me, ever. You fuckin' hear me, Paddy Monaghan?'

Paddy nodded wearily. 'Aye, oh aye, I hear ye,' he replied, softly. 'But you're wrong there, Seamy. There's one more . . . for the dyin' here today. One more and then the game's over, eh?' He turned to look at Elaine, then shook his head sadly. Wincing with the effort, he turned back to Seamus. 'I didn't do all that much for anyone in me life, Seamy. I tried, y'know, but it didn't . . . always go the best at times. But I did me best most times, eh? Did the best I could do for me . . . mates and for you too, eh?' The agonised smile thinned. 'Now you . . . you do yours.'

Seamus nodded sadly, turning his gaze directly to the hooded figure to his front. He couldn't bear to watch Paddy Monaghan's eyes close over. He just kept staring at the hooded figure, the feel of the gun heavy in his own hand, wondering at what precise moment in his own life everything had started to go wrong.

*

The hooded figure had his hands high upon his head. Seamus was urging him into a field behind the chapel at gunpoint, unable to remain there in front of the violated building any longer. Feeling that even the dead shouldn't see the evils that he had planned, feeling that this chapel and the graves surrounding it had seen more than their fair share of death that day. Wanting to forget the scene for a few moments and concentrate fully on what he had to do, while the hatred was still fresh in his mind, his sanity still intact. Walking slowly, six to seven feet behind the figure, still numb with disbelief at what had occurred only minutes before. Wanting that hatred he had felt for a brief moment to build within him, to engorge his veins and flood his mind, so that he might at least plead insanity after pulling the trigger.

If only to himself and God. If God existed, which He didn't. Which He couldn't do, Seamus thought bitterly, if He valued life and everything He had ever created, only to watch it all destroyed in such reckless abandon by those who clearly had no love for Him. Seamus pushed that dismal theological conclusion from his mind and urged the hooded figure onwards. It might have been the correct place for philosophical meditation, he decided despondently, but it definitely wasn't the time. The grim starkness of death had distorted his thinking and all he could think of was Elaine and Paddy, both lying at the front of the chapel, their eyes closed over, their life's breath having left them.

He looked down and noticed that the field they were walking through was marshy, brown puddles hidden amidst the confluence of reeds and swamp grass, the water squelching up, around and into his shoes, saturating his socks. Cold, chilling his feet, so that they were nearly as numb as his mind. Still, he didn't care. He didn't care about anything any more, and knew he never would again.

Thoughts of his da came to him then, though he didn't know

why. He concluded that it must have been because this whole situation had evolved because of his da – because of his own fixation that his da had been a tout, when he had been nothing more than an ordinary man. No more, but certainly no less. No better than most of the people Seamus had known in his life, but certainly no worse than many. And because of that primary – and, as a result, distorted – belief, four people were now dead. Four people now added to the requiem of people he had been fortunate – or unfortunate – enough to have known in his thus far relatively short life.

The Special Branch man, Dave Connors. His life extinguished because, like the rest, he believed that his aims were worth dying for; that his flag, because it was the one flying from the ramparts, was the best. And one of his best friends, Paddy Monaghan, whom he had never completely trusted, because of one event that had occurred when they were younger – an event that, while utterly inexcusable, had been more the product of the stupidity of youthful misbehaviour than of outright malice – though who had in the end laid down his own life for Seamus. And in the last few minutes of Paddy's life, Seamus had seen him as he really was. Seamus felt intensely guilty about that. Paddy Monaghan had been a friend – as true a friend, Seamus guessed, as any man could ever be. The undercurrents had disappeared in his last few minutes of life and he too had died fighting his own personal cause. One gunman now lay dead also – Seamus hadn't even bothered to check who, because, as Paddy had rightly noted before dying, in the end it didn't really matter who he was. Death refused to acknowledge identity, the workings of a lifetime, fairness. He was another faceless casualty caught up in another aimless war, another invisible statistic that would never change his country one iota until people agreed to talk and, more importantly, to listen to each other. Still, their deaths paled in comparison to one other: it was Elaine whom he thought about more than the rest.

His girlfriend. She had given her life to save his, as if his had mattered more than hers. Which it never had, he knew – which it never could. An innocent, who believed that there was no cause worth fighting for, that there was more to life than killing and dying. Who had nearly convinced him, until the last two days of her life, that she was correct. Now she too was a casualty, the same as the rest of them. She hadn't been spared because of her beliefs, and Seamus felt that there was something very unjust about that. But then he recalled Dan McGeady's words, about how he had said that everyone needed their beliefs, that men were equally guilty if they just sat back and watched, if they did nothing when evil prevailed all around. And he wondered if that too was true – if Elaine had been punished for not doing enough, for not committing to either one cause or another instead of sitting on the fence. If fence-squatting too was equally as heinous a crime as every other one here in the world. And if it was, then Seamus knew that he too was perhaps guilty of that outrage.

He shrugged inwardly. There were no answers and perhaps, like Paddy, he felt he would be better off not knowing them even if there were. All he knew for certain was what he had seen, what he had been involved in. And all he had to know, according to Paddy, was what he was, what be believed in, and what he expected of himself. Each of the four people he had seen dying over the last twenty-four hours had been enacting a scene – perhaps taking part in a game in which they themselves had once made the rules, his mother would have said – living out their parts fully, in the belief that they could change a small piece of the world for the better. Believing that their contributions would slow the world down and everyone would see that their own personal demons had been the ones that were right and true of thought.

The part of the world that now spun around Seamus Doherty like a wayward top was on a downward gradient, careering out of control at a moment of its own choosing. Way out of control. Its axis tumbled, its path no longer its own decision.

'Stop.'

The hooded figure came to a halt near the top of the field, water up to the middle of his calves, black trousers curling in tight against his legs. He turned slowly to face Seamus. Silent, a dark sentinel, to which Seamus could not affix a scrap of humanity. He would need to do so, he knew, if he were to kill him. He would need to do so if he were to draw enough of that dark hatred up from his soul, to vent it fully against the man who now stood before him, eyes fixed coldly upon his. The balaclava fixed firmly in place, the eyes unblinking, staring, remorseless. Not a word had crossed his lips, and Seamus had wondered if he were indeed human, or if he were some black and evil god from the depths of Hades itself.

'You've taken my whole life away in the last few minutes,' Seamus said, softly, the utterance foreign even to him, a blow as physical as a slap. 'My whole fuckin' world, and you're standin' there without a fuckin' sound escapin' your fuckin' lips!'

The man merely stared at him. Seamus nodded grimly.

'Me girl used to tell me that it's a spiral,' he said, evenly, more to himself than anyone. 'This violence. It's one man hurtin' another. An endless, futile cycle that boils down to fear in the end. You afraid of me, me afraid of you. I never used to believe that.' He frowned deeply. 'I still don't know if I do. And me ma, she used to say that me da was chasin' shadows. I think we all are. What do ye think yourself?'

The hooded figure didn't reply but stood there silently, hands on his head. Seamus smiled thinly, though there was no mirth there. He sighed deeply, thinking about how ludicrous the situation was, about the power he held in his hand, about what he could possibly do to right the mess he was now in.

'Aye, chasin' shadows. Maybe they're right, I dunno,' Seamus said, eventually. He heard the bitterness in his voice and found himself looking up at the sky, which was slate-grey, clouds moving across a faint sun. 'I remember an old teacher of mine tellin' me that I had a hunger for learnin' once, y'know. By fuck, was he ever wrong there! I don't know all that much, though I do know one thing – it won't ever fuckin' end if we keep doin' this sort of stuff. It won't ever end.' He sighed deeply and raised the gun. 'One man dyin', another avengin' him, what's it all fuckin' about?' Silence. 'Dave Connors – cynical bastard that he was – he reckoned that the cycle's only ever broken when one man relents. Ye know what that means?'

The figure didn't reply. Seamus raised the gun, finger tense against the trigger. Tears in his eyes, falling down to stain his white shirt. He turned the gun into his own stomach and fired.

One shot. He gasped for breath, though he wouldn't cry out. Dignity, it was all he had left. If he could retain it, a voice roared out in his mind, if he had the nerve to see this agony through to the end.

One shot, because there was no way back and no way forward. One shot to the stomach, because he didn't want to die the way his father had died. A shot to the head – the death of an informer, a tout. And because he so wanted to watch the man's eyes in his final moments, to see if anything registered there. Because you could tell someone from their eyes, he'd been told that once, though now his thoughts were blurring and he couldn't remember who had told him. His mother, maybe. It didn't matter. You could see everything in the eyes. Someone had said it in passing, in the midst of some other conversation, in the midst of the longest and shortest of all times that had passed as his life, and that much had remained with him. It was all there in the eyes, and you didn't need to remove a balaclava to look into the heart.

The sky fell around him and for a moment he stumbled backwards, catching sight of the gunman to his front, confusion registering in the hooded figure's eyes. Seamus sank to his knees, eyes blurring for an instant, shaking himself fully to consciousness as a flash of searing, angry pain speared through his gut, up into his chest, ragged lightning coursing through his body. Strangely happy with what he had seen in the other man's eyes in that briefest of moments, despite the intense pain racking his body. The gun fell from his hand, splashing amongst the waterlogged reeds. He pushed one hand out to stop himself falling after it, though fell anyway, the water cold around his knees, soaking up the front of his trousers. Spreading across his stomach, mixing with the blood there, pooling as an indecent grey-red colour.

Seamus saw a spider to his front, moving across docken leaves, seeking the safety of the dark, cavernous hedgerow beyond. He caught sight of the gunman once more, stepping up beside him, lifting the gun out of the reeds, sticking it into his belt. Then moving directly to his front to watch him. The eyes confused now, pondering the inexplicable complexity of that final, wordless statement. Seamus smiled thinly again, took a deep breath to cease the pain flooding his belly, but couldn't hold it. Wondering as he breathed out if he had changed the world even a little.

It was growing colder. And he remembered that this morning had been lovely. Scarlet and pink pastel hues spreading soft across the horizon as Paddy Monaghan had pulled back the curtains in the farmhouse, correct in telling Albert that he'd be away before the old farmer rose from his bed. Colder, and then suddenly warmer. And Seamus breathed out softly again.

As the world righted itself on its axis and turned ever so slowly once more.